"Machine-gun-paced entertainment . . . A high-voltage thriller with the kick of a third rail . . . You can't put it down."
—*The Washington Post*

"A wild ride that keeps the suspense boiling to the end of the line."
—*Pittsburgh Press*

"A spellbinder that hurtles along like a runaway express train . . . harrowing, terrifying, and so, so good!"
—*Business Week*

"Diverting . . . entertaining . . . clever in its details, frequently quite funny and witty in its comments on how New York City functions."
—*The New York Times*

"By far the best thriller to surface in quite a while . . . [an]

THE TAKING
OF PELHAM
1 2 3

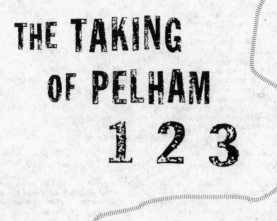

JOHN GODEY

BERKLEY BOULEVARD BOOKS, NEW YORK

THE BERKLEY PUBLISHING GROUP
Published by the Penguin Group
Penguin Group (USA) Inc.,
375 Hudson Street, New York, New York 10014, USA
Penguin Group (Canada), 90 Eglinton Avenue East, Suite 700, Toronto, Ontario M4P 2Y3, Canada
(a division of Pearson Penguin Canada Inc.)
Penguin Books Ltd., 80 Strand, London WC2R 0RL, England
Penguin Group Ireland, 25 St. Stephen's Green, Dublin 2, Ireland (a division of Penguin Books Ltd.)
Penguin Group (Australia), 250 Camberwell Road, Camberwell, Victoria 3124, Australia
(a division of Pearson Australia Group Pty. Ltd.)
Penguin Books India Pvt. Ltd., 11 Community Centre, Panchsheel Park, New Delhi—110 017, India
Penguin Group (NZ), 67 Apollo Drive, Rosedale, North Shore 0632, New Zealand
(a division of Pearson New Zealand Ltd.)
Penguin Books (South Africa) (Pty.) Ltd., 24 Sturdee Avenue, Rosebank, Johannesburg 2196,
South Africa

Penguin Books Ltd., Registered Offices: 80 Strand, London WC2R 0RL, England

This is a work of fiction. Names, characters, places, and incidents either are the product of the author's imagination or are used fictitiously, and any resemblance to actual persons, living or dead, business establishments, events, or locales is entirely coincidental. The publisher does not have any control over and does not assume any responsibility for author or third-party websites or their content.

THE TAKING OF PELHAM ONE TWO THREE

A Berkley Boulevard Book / published by arrangement with Laura Freedgood

PRINTING HISTORY
G. P. Putnam's Sons hardcover edition / 1973
Dell mass-market edition / October 1974
Berkley Boulevard movie tie-in premium edition / May 2009

Copyright © 1973 by John Godey.
Motion Picture Artwork © 2009 Columbia Pictures Industries, Inc. All rights reserved. Motion Picture
Photography © 2009 Columbia Pictures Industries, Inc. and Beverly Blvd LLC. All rights reserved.
Interior text design by Laura K. Corless.

ISBN: 978-0-425-22879-1

BERKLEY®
Berkley Boulevard Books are published by The Berkley Publishing Group,
a division of Penguin Group (USA) Inc.,
375 Hudson Street, New York, New York 10014.
BERKLEY BOULEVARD and its logo are registered trademarks of Penguin Group (USA) Inc.

PRINTED IN THE UNITED STATES OF AMERICA

10 9 8 7 6 5 4 3 2 1

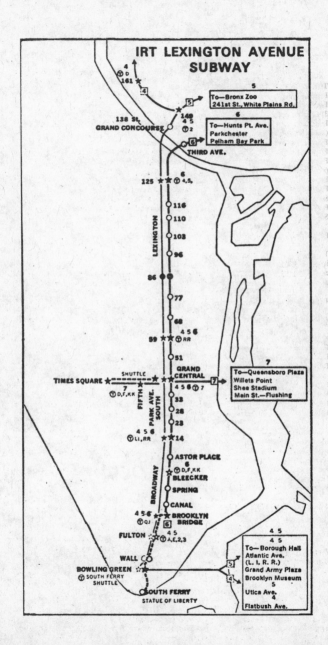

ONE

STEEVER

Steever stood on the southbound local platform of the Lexington Avenue line at Fifty-ninth Street and chewed his gum with a gentle motion of his heavy jaws, like a soft-mouthed retriever schooled to hold game firmly but without bruising it.

His posture was relaxed and at the same time emphatic, as if a low center of gravity and some inner certitude combined to make him casually immovable. He wore a navy blue raincoat, neatly buttoned, and a dark gray hat tilted forward, not rakishly but squarely, the brim bent at a sharp angle over his forehead, throwing a rhomboid of shadow over his eyes. His sideburns and the hair at the back of his head were white, dramatic against the darkness of his complexion, unexpected in a man who appeared to be in his early thirties.

The florist's box was outsize, suggesting an opulent, even overwhelming burst of blooms inside, designed for some once-in-a-lifetime anniversary or to make amends for an enormous sin or betrayal. If any of the passengers on the platform were inclined to smile at that joke of a florist's box, in respect of the unlikely man who held it so negligently under his arm, aimed upward at a forty-five-degree angle toward the grimy station ceiling, they managed to suppress it. He wasn't a man to smile at, however sympathetically.

Steever did not stir, or show any sign of anticipation or even awareness, when the approaching train gave off its first distant vibrations, gradually increasing through various levels and quantities of sound. Four-eyed—amber and white marker lights over white sealed-beam headlights—Pelham One Two Three lumbered into the station. Brakes sighed; the train settled; the doors rattled open. Steever was positioned precisely so that he faced the center door of the fifth car of the ten-car train. He entered the car, turned left, and walked to the isolated double seat directly facing the conductor's cab. It was unoccupied. He sat down, standing the florist's box between his knees, and glancing incuriously at the back of the conductor, who was leaning well forward out of his window, inspecting the platform.

Steever clasped his hands on the top of the florist's box. They were very broad hands, with short, thick fingers. The doors closed, and the train started with a lurch that tilted the passengers first backward, then forward. Steever, without seeming to brace himself, barely moved.

RYDER

Ryder withheld the token for a part of a second—a pause that was imperceptible to an eye but that his consciousness registered—before dropping it into the slot and pushing through the turnstile. Walking toward the platform, he examined his hesitancy with the token. Nerves? Nonsense. A concession, maybe even a form of consecration, on the eve of battle, but nothing else. You lived or you died.

Holding the brown valise in his left hand, the heavily weighted Valpac in his right, he stepped onto the Twenty-eighth Street station platform and walked toward the south end. He stopped on a line with the placard that hung over the edge of the platform, bearing the number 10, black on a white ground, indicating the point where the front of a ten-car train stopped. As usual, there were a few front-end haunters—as he had taken to thinking of them—including the inevitable overachiever who stood well beyond the 10 placard, and would have to scurry back when the train came in. The front-enders, he had long ago determined, expressed a dominant facet of the human condition: the mindless need to be first, to run ahead of the pack for the simple sake of being ahead.

He eased back against the wall and set his suitcases down, one on each side of him, just touching the edge of his shoes. His navy blue raincoat touched the wall only lightly, but any contact would ensure picking up grime, grit, dust particles, even, possibly, some graffito freshly applied in hot red lipstick and even hotter bitterness or irony. Shrugging, he pulled the brim of his dark-gray hat decisively lower over his eyes, which were gray and still and set deeply in bony sockets, promising a more ascetic face than the rounded cheeks and the puffy area around his lips justified. He leaned more of his weight against the wall and slid his hands into the deep slashed pockets of the coat. A fingernail caught on a fluff of nylon. Gently, using his free hand outside the pocket to anchor the nylon, he disengaged his finger and withdrew his hand.

A rumbling sound heightened to a clatter, and an express train whipped through on the northbound track, its lights flickering between the pillars like a defective movie film. At the edge of the platform, a man glared at the disappearing express, then turned to Ryder, appealing for communion, for sympathy. Ryder looked at him with the absolute neutrality that was the authentic mask of the subway rider, of any New Yorker, or perhaps the actual face New Yorkers were born with, or issued, or, *wherever* they were born, assumed once they won their spurs as bona fide residents. The man, indifferent to the rebuff, paced the platform, muttering indignantly. Beyond him, across the four sets of tracks, the northbound platform provided a dreary mirror image of the southbound: the tiled rectangle reading "28th Street," the dirty walls, the gray floor, the resigned or impatient passengers, the rear-end haunters (and what was *their* hangup?). . . .

The pacing man turned abruptly to the edge of the platform, planted his feet on the yellow line, bent at the waist, and peered back down the track. Down-platform, there were three more leaners, supplicants praying to the dark tunnel beyond the station. Ryder heard the sound of an approaching train and saw the leaners retreat, but only a few inches, giving ground grudgingly, cautiously challenging the train to kill them if it dared. It swept into the station, and its front end stopped in precise alignment with the overhanging placard. Ryder looked at his watch. Two to go. Ten minutes. He came away from the wall, turned, and studied the nearby poster.

It was the Levy's Bread ad, an old friend. He had first seen it when it was newly installed, pristine and unmarked. But it had begun accumulating graffiti (or defacements, in the official language) almost at once. It pictured a black child eating Levy's bread, and the caption read YOU DON'T HAVE TO BE JEWISH TO LOVE LEVY'S. This was followed by an angry scrawl in red ballpoint ink: BUT YOU DO HAVE TO BE A NIGGER TO CHEAT ON WELFARE AND SUPPORT YOUR LITTLE BLACK BASTARDS. Beneath that, in block letters, as if to cancel out bitterness with the simple antidote of piety, were the words JESUS SAVES. But still another hand, neither raging nor sweet, perhaps above the battle, had added PLAID STAMPS.

Three separate entries followed, whose message Ryder had never been able to fathom:

VOICE IDENTIFICATION DOES NOT PROVE SPEECH CONTENT. PSYCHIATRY IS BASED ON FICTION NOVELS. SCREWWORMS CAUSE SPITTING. After that, the ideologue took over again, riposte following riposte: MARX STINX. SO DOES JESUS CHRIST. SO DOES PANTHER. SO DOES EVERYBODY. SO DOES I.

Such as it was, Ryder thought, it was the true voice of the people, squeezing out their anxieties into the public view, never questioning that they deserved a hearing. He turned away from the poster and watched the tail of the train whip out of the station. He put his back against the wall again, between his suitcases, and looked casually down-platform. A figure in blue was walking toward him. Ryder picked out his insignia—a Transit Authority cop. He noted details: one shoulder lower than the other so that he seemed to be listing, bushy carrot-colored sideburns curling down to a point an inch below the earlobes. . . . A car length away the TA cop stopped, glanced at him, then faced squarely outward. He folded his arms across his chest, unfolded them, took his hat off. The hair on top of his head was reddish brown, several shades darker than his sideburns, and it was matted from the pressure of the hat. He looked into his hat, then put it back on his head and folded his arms again.

Across the tracks a northbound local arrived, paused, and moved on. The TA cop turned his head and found Ryder looking at him. He faced front immediately and straightened his back. It brought his low shoulder up and improved his posture.

BUD CARMODY

As soon as a train cleared a station, the conductor was expected to step out of the shelter of his cab and provide information and other assistance as requested by the riding public. Bud Carmody was well aware that too few conductors followed this regulation. More often than not they just hung around in the cab staring at the colorless walls racing by. But that wasn't the way *he* ran the job. He did it by the book, and more: He *liked* maintaining a neat appearance; he *liked* presenting a smiling countenance and answering dumb questions. He enjoyed his work.

Bud Carmody regarded his affection for the railroad as a matter of inheritance. One of his uncles had been a motorman (recently retired after thirty years on the road), and as a boy Bud had admired him extravagantly. On a few occasions—on calm, lazy Sunday runs—his uncle had smuggled him into the cab and even let him touch the controls. So, from boyhood on, Bud set his sights on becoming a motorman. Right after graduating high school, he took the Civil Service test, which offered the option of being a conductor or a bus driver. Although driving a bus paid better, he wasn't tempted; his interest lay in the railroad. Now, when he became eligible by serving six months as a conductor—only forty days more to go—he would take the motorman test.

Meanwhile, he was having a good time. He had taken to the job right from the start and had even enjoyed the training period—twenty-eight days of school, followed by a week on actual runs under the tutelage of an experienced man. Matson, who had broken him in on the runs, was an old-timer with a year to go to retirement. He was a good teacher, but he had soured on the job and was direly pessimistic about the future of the railroad. He predicted that five years hence it would be patronized exclusively by niggers and spies and maybe *run* by them, too. Matson was a walking encyclopedia of atrocity stories, and if you took him seriously, working a subway train was just a trifle less hazardous than frontline duty in Vietnam. Hour by hour, according to Matson, a conductor risked serious bodily injury or even death, and you could consider yourself blessed if you survived the day.

A lot of the older conductors—and even some of the

younger ones—peddled tales of horror, and while Bud
didn't exactly disbelieve them, he certainly hadn't had any
trouble himself. Oh, sure, a few times passengers had
cussed him out, but that was to be expected. The conductor was *visible*, so, naturally, he was blamed for everything
that went wrong. But outside of dirty looks and some
verbal abuse, he had had absolutely none of the bad expe-
riences the old-timers kept dwelling on, such as being spat
at, beaten up, robbed, stabbed, vomited on by drunks,
mobbed by school kids, or hit in the face by someone on
the platform as you leaned out of your window when the
train pulled out of a station. The last of these worried conductors the most, and there were a million horror stories:
about the conductor who had taken a finger in the eyeball
and eventually lost the eye; about another who had his
nose broken by a fist; about still another who was grabbed
by the hair and nearly pulled out the window. . . .

"Fifty-first Street, this station is Fifty-first Street."

He delivered his announcement into the mike in a
clear, cheerful voice, and it pleased him to know that it
was heard simultaneously in all ten cars. As the train
moved into the station, he inserted his skate key (it was
properly known as a drumstick key, but everyone called it
skate key) into the receptacle in the bottom of the panel
and turned it to the right. Then he inserted the door key
and, as soon as the train stopped, pressed the buttons to
open the doors.

He leaned far out of his window to check the passengers getting on and off, then shut the doors, rear section
first, then front section. He checked his indication box,
which was lit up to show that the doors were all closed

and locked. The train started, and he hung out the window for the regulation three car lengths, to make sure that nobody was being dragged. This was where a lot of the old-timers cheated, with their morbid fear of being assaulted.

"Grand Central station, next stop. The next stop is Grand Central."

He stepped out of the cab and took up a position against the storm door. He folded his arms across his chest, and studied the passengers. It was his favorite pastime. He played at trying to figure out, from the passengers' appearance and attitudes, what their lives were like: what kind of work they did, how much money they made, where and how they lived, even what place they were headed for. In some cases it was easy—delivery boys, women who looked like housewives, domestics or secretaries, old retired people. But with others, especially the better class, it posed a real challenge. Was a well-dressed man a teacher, a lawyer, a salesman, a business executive? Actually, except for rush hours, there weren't too many of the better class riding the IRT; it ran a poor third to the BMT and the IND. He couldn't explain why. Maybe it was a matter of routes, of better neighborhoods, but it was hard to prove that. It might be due to the fact that the IRT was the oldest of the three divisions, with fewer routes and less equipment (which was why its training period was only twenty-eight days compared to thirty-two on the other divisions), but you couldn't really prove that either.

He braced himself against the roll of the train (actually, he liked the motion and his ability to adapt to it the way a sailor developed sea legs) and focused his attention on

the man sitting facing the cab. He was striking for his
size—breadth, really, he wasn't all that tall—and his white
hair. He was well dressed in a dark raincoat and new hat,
and his shoes were highly polished, so he was certainly no
messenger, in spite of the large, fat florist's box between
his knees. That meant he had bought the flowers for someone and would be delivering them in person. Looking at
him, the kind of tough face he had, you wouldn't have
thought of him as somebody who bought flowers. But you
couldn't tell a book by its cover, which was what made life
interesting. He could be anything—a college professor,
a poet. . . .

The decelerating train dragged under Bud's feet. He
set the pleasant puzzle to one side and went into the cab.

"Grand Central station. Change for the express. This is
Grand Central. . . ."

RYDER

Over the years, Ryder had developed some theories about
fear—two, to be exact. The first was that it had to be handled the way a good infielder played a ground ball; he didn't
wait for it to come to him, he went to meet it, he forced
the issue. Ryder coped with fear by confronting it. So
that, instead of looking elsewhere, he stared directly at
the transit cop. The cop became aware of his scrutiny and
turned to him, then quickly averted his gaze. After that he
kept his eyes to the front, self-consciously rigid. His face
was slightly reddened, and Ryder knew that he would be
sweating, too.

Ryder's second theory—which the cop, helpfully, was illustrating—was that people in tight situations showed stress because they wanted to. They were appealing for mercy for their harmlessness, as a dog did who rolled on his back for a fiercer or larger dog. They were making a public display of their symptoms, rather than controlling them. He was convinced that, short of pissing your pants, which was involuntary, you only showed fear to the degree that you wanted or allowed yourself to show.

Ryder's theories were offshoots of the very simple philosophy that ruled his life and that he rarely talked about. Not even under friendly pressure. *Especially* not under pressure, friendly or otherwise. He remembered a conversation with a doctor in the Congo. He had walked bloody-legged to a forward aid station to have a bullet removed from his thigh. The doctor was an Indian, with an elegant, amused air, who plucked a spent rifle round out of his flesh with a flourish of his forceps, a man who was as interested in form as substance, a man with style, which didn't at all explain what he was doing serving in a crazy little African war between two highly disorganized factions of wild-eyed niggers. Except money. Except? It was a good enough reason.

The doctor held the bloody metal up for him to view before flipping if into a basin, then cocked his head and said, "Are you not the officer they call Captain Ironass?"

The doctor wore major's pips, not that rank meant all that much in this funny army, except as an insigne of a man's salary. The doctor dragged down a hundred or two more a month than he did.

"Excuse me," Ryder said. "You're looking at it. Is it iron?"

"No need to get shirty," the doctor said. He framed a packing against the wound and discarded it for a smaller one. "Just curiosity. You've developed a bit of a reputation."

"For what?"

"Fearlessness." He held the packing in place deftly with slender brown fingers. "Or recklessness. Opinion is divided."

Ryder shrugged. In a corner of the medical tent a black soldier, half-naked, lay doubled up on a stretcher, crying softly but persistently. The doctor found him with a long look, and the man became silent.

"I'd be interested in hearing your own judgment of the matter," the doctor said.

Ryder shrugged again and watched the brown fingers applying tape to the dressing. Wait until the tape had to be pulled away from the hair. *That* would be a test of courage. The doctor paused, his dark face turned upward humorously.

Ryder said, "You've probably seen more than I have, Major. I defer to you."

The doctor spoke confidently. "No such characteristic as fearlessness. Recklessness, yes. Not caring, yes. Some people wish to die."

"Meaning me?"

"Can't really say, not knowing you. All I know is rumor. You can put your trousers on now."

Ryder examined the bloody tear in his pants before pulling them up. "Too bad," he said. "I was counting on you for a conclusion."

"I am not a psychiatrist," the doctor said in half apology. "Merely curious."

"Not me." Ryder picked up his steel helmet—it was remaindered World War II Wehrmacht goods—and put it on, tapping it down firmly so that the short brim shadowed his eyes. "I'm not the least bit curious."

The major flushed, then gave a sporting smile. "Well, I do think I've gained an insight to why they call you Captain Ironass. Take care of yourself."

Watching the unhappy profile of the transit' cop, Ryder thought: I could have given the Indian doctor an answer, but he would probably have misinterpreted it and concluded that I was talking about reincarnation. You live or you die, Major, that's my simple philosophy. You lived or you died. Which didn't translate as either recklessness or fearlessness. It didn't mean you courted death or saw no mystery or loss in death. It just canceled out most of the complications of existing, just reduced the principal uncertainty of life to a workable formula. No excruciating exploration of possibilities, just the stark profundity of yes or no: You lived or you died.

A train was coming into the station. Near the transit cop, directly under the number 8 marker, a leaner was bent so far forward that he appeared to have overcommitted himself. Ryder tensed and almost made a first step toward the man, to pull him back to safety, thinking: No, not today, not now. But the man drew back at the last moment, his hands thrown out wardingly in a belated reflex of fright. The train stopped, and the doors opened.

The transit cop stepped in.

Ryder looked at the motorman. He was sitting on his metal stool, his arm resting on his half-open window. He was a black man—no, black was a misnomer, Ryder thought, a political color; actually, he was a light tan— and he was indifferently covering a stretching yawn with his hand. He glanced out of his window without interest, then checked his indication box, which, like the conductor's, lit up when the doors were closed and locked.

The train started. Its designation (since headway between local trains was five minutes at this time of day) would be Pelham One One Eight, according to the simple, effective system that identified a train by the prefix of its terminus and the suffix of its time of departure from that terminus. Thus, having left Pelham Bay Park station at 1:18 P.M., its designation was Pelham One One Eight. On the return trip from its southern terminus, Brooklyn Bridge station, its new designation would be something on the order of Brooklyn Bridge Two One Four. At least, Ryder thought, that would be the case on a normal day. But today was not a normal day; today there would be some considerable disruption of the schedule.

As the third car of the train went by, Ryder spotted the transit cop. He was leaning against a pole, and his right shoulder was low, so low that he looked as if he were standing on an incline. Suppose he hadn't got on the train? They had prearranged a signal for aborting if some unforeseen danger arose. Would he have used it? Would he have withdrawn from the engagement to fight another day? He gave a minimal shake of his head. No need to answer. What you might have done didn't count, only what you did.

The last car of the train sped past the platform and into

the tunnel toward Twenty-third Street. New passengers were appearing. A young black man—this one was the color of bitter chocolate—was first, splendid in a sky-blue cloak, red and blue checkerboard pants, tan shoes with a three-inch heel, a black leather beret. He came on in a loose-jointed swagger, strutted by, and took up his position a car length beyond the 10 marker. Almost immediately, he leaned over the platform and stared northward with affront.

Peace, brother, Ryder thought, Pelham One Two Three will be pulling in in less than five minutes, and being hostile toward the track won't bring it along any sooner. The young black turned suddenly, as if aware that he was being watched. He faced Ryder squarely, his eyes defiant, glaring out of clear, hard whites. Ryder met the challenge without interest, his own eyes mild, and thought: Relax, brother, conserve your energy, you might need it.

WELCOME

At Grand Central, responding to the hold signal, three horizontal yellow lights, Pelham One Two Three kept its doors open, waiting for the next express train to pull in.

Joe Welcome had been on the platform for fifteen minutes, restless and edgy, checking the arrival and departure of local trains against his watch, glaring at the express trains for their irrelevance. Fidgeting, he had walked an erratic sentry post of thirty or forty feet, alternately eyeing the women on the platform and himself in the mirrors of the vending machines. The women were all crummy and made his lip curl. An ugly broad was a curse. He derived more satisfaction from his own image—the handsome, reckless face, olive skin a shade paler than usual, the dark eyes glowing with a strange fire. Now that he had got used to the mustache and the sideburns that curved inward toward his lips in a pointed flourish, he kind of liked them. They were a hell of a good match with the soft glossy black of his hair.

When he heard Pelham One Two Three come in, Joe Welcome walked back to the last car. He was sharp and jaunty in his navy blue raincoat, slightly suppressed at the waist, ending an inch or two above the knees. His hat was dark gray, with a narrow curled brim and a bright yellow cockade flowering out of the band. When the train stopped, he went in through the last door, pushing against the flow of three or four people seeking to get out. His valise, brown and tan in wide alternate stripes, banged against the knee of a young Puerto Rican girl. She gave him a sidelong resentful look and muttered something.

"You talk to me, spic?"

"Why'n you watch where you go?"

"Up you brown ass, righ'?"

She started to say something but, assessing the malice of his smile, changed her mind. She stepped out of the train, looking back over her shoulder indignantly. Across the platform, the express train came in, and a few passengers trickled into the local. Welcome glanced into the rear half of the car, then began to walk toward the front, looking at the passengers on both sides of the aisle. He passed into the next car, and as the door slid shut behind him, the train started with a sudden jerk, throwing him off balance. Recovering awkwardly, he glared forward at the motorman eight cars ahead.

"Mother," he said aloud, "where you learn to drive a fucking train?"

Still glaring, he walked on, his eyes sweeping the passengers. People. Meat. No cops, nothing that looked like a hero. He walked with confidence, and the sharp sound of his footfall compelled attention. It pleased him to see so many eyes turn up to him, and it pleased him even more to stare them down, mowing a whole row of eyes down like ducks in a shooting gallery. He never missed. Bang, bang, down they went. It was his eyes. *Occhi violenti*, his uncle had called them. Violent eyes, and he knew how to use them, he knew how to scare the piss out of people.

In the fifth car, he located Steever at the far end. He flicked a look at him, but Steever ignored him, his face stolid and vacant. On his way to the next car he brushed by the conductor, a young stud neatly dressed in pressed blue, the golden Transit Authority badge on his billed hat brightly polished. He hurried on and reached the first car as the train decelerated. He put his back against the door and placed his valise on the floor between the points of his Spanish shoes.

"Thirty-third Street, station stop is Thirty-third Street."

The conductor's voice was high-pitched but strong, and the amplification made it sound like the voice of a big man. But he was a pale redheaded string bean, Welcome thought, and if you hit him right you would probably break his jaw like a piece of china. The image of a jaw fragmenting like a fragile teacup struck him as funny. Then he

frowned, remembering Steever sitting there like a chunk
of wood with that flower box between his legs. That was
Steever, a dumb ape. Plenty of muscle, but *just* muscle; upstairs was an empty room. Steever. With the flower box,
yet.

A few passengers got off; a few entered. Welcome
picked out Longman, sitting opposite the motorman's cab.
He was quite a distance away. The car was seventy-two
feet long, right? Seventy-two feet, and it had forty-four
seats. The BMT and the IND, what they called the B-1
and B-2 divisions (IRT was the A Division, right?), were
seventy-five feet long, and they had up to sixty-five seats.
Big deal, making him learn that shit. Nothing.

As the doors started to shut, a chick bumped it back
with her shoulder and slipped in. He looked at her with
interest. Short-short miniskirt, long legs in white boots,
a little round ass. So far so good, Welcome thought, now
let's see the front view. He smiled as she turned, and
checked off great boobs stretching away at some kind of a
light-pink sweater under a short green jacket that matched
the little skirt. Big eyes, heavy fake lashes, wide gorgeous
mouth with lots of bright-red lipstick, long black hair falling straight down out of one of those sexy soldier hats with
the brim curved up on one side, flat against the crown.
Australian? Anzac. An Anzac hat.

She took a seat in the front half of the car, and when
she crossed her legs, the little skirt climbed halfway up
to her neck. Nice. He concentrated on the long expanse
of thigh and leg and visualized them wrapped around his
neck. For starters.

"Twenty-eighth Street." The conductor's voice, singing out like an angel. "Next stop is Twenty-eighth Street."

Welcome wedged his hip securely against the brass handle of the door. Twenty-eighth Street. Okay. He made a rough count of the seated passengers. About thirty or so, plus a couple of kids standing up, looking out of the front storm door. About half of them would have to get the boot. But not the chick in the funny hat. She was staying, no matter what Ryder or *anybody* said. Crazy, thinking about pussy at a time like this? So he was crazy. But she was staying. She would provide, like they say, the love interest.

LONGMAN

In the first car of the train, Longman sat in the seat that corresponded to Steever's, five cars back. It was directly opposite the shut steel door of the motorman's cab, decorated with an elaborately scripted signature in hot pink: PANCHO 777. His package, covered in heavy wrapping paper and bound with coarse yellow twine, was marked in black crayon: "Everest Printing Corp., 826 Lafayette Street." He held it between his knees, with his forearms resting on its top, and his fingers loosely burrowed beneath the intersection where the strands of twine were knotted.

He had boarded Pelham One Two Three at Eighty-sixth Street, to make certain that, at some point before Twenty-eighth Street, he would find the seat opposite the cab unoccupied. Not that that particular seat was essential, but he had been stubborn about it. He had won his point, but only because nobody cared about it one way or another. He realized now that he had pressed for it because he knew there would be no opposition. Otherwise, Ryder would have made the decision. Wasn't it actually because of Ryder that he was here at all, about to plunge into a nightmare wide awake?

He watched the two boys at the window of the storm door. They were about eight and ten, identically plump and round-faced, both healthfully flushed and intent on their game of driving the train through the tunnel, to an orchestrated accompaniment of appropriate clicks and hisses of voice and tongue. He wished that they weren't there, but it was inevitable. On any given train, at any given time, there was sure to be a kid or two—sometimes, an adult!—romantically playing motorman. Some romance!

When the train reached Thirty-third Street, he began to sweat. Not gradually, but all at once, as if a heat wave had suddenly swept through the car. It broke out all over his body and face, an oily slick that fogged the dark shades over his eyes and spilled down his chest, his legs, his crotch. . . . For an instant, as the train entered the tunnel, it bucked, and he felt a heart-stopping surge of hope. His mind leaped to round out the picture: Something wrong with the motor, the motorman hits the brake and lays dead. The shop sends a car knocker; he looks it over, scratches his head. So they have to cut the power, dump their load, lead their passengers to an emergency exit, and haul the train away to the yard. . . .

But the buck disappeared, and Longman knew—as he

had all along—that the train was okay. Either the motorman had made a clumsy start, or it was just a train that
bucked, one of those dogs that motormen hated to get
stuck with.

Not because he believed in them, but out of desperation, his mind sought out other possibilities. Suppose one
of the others had suddenly taken sick or been in an accident? No. Steever wouldn't have the brains to *know* he
was sick, and Ryder . . . Ryder would get off his deathbed
if he had to. Maybe Welcome, feisty and crazy as he was,
had gotten into a fight over some fancied insult—

He looked back to the rear of the car and saw Welcome
there.

I'm going to die today.

The thought came unbidden to his mind, accompanied
by a sudden gust of heat, as though a flash fire had been
touched off inside his body. He felt suffocated and wanted
to tear his clothing off and give his burning body air. He
fumbled at the button at the neck of his raincoat and
worked it half free before stopping. Ryder had said they
weren't to open any part of the coat. His fingers forced
the button back through the buttonhole.

His legs began to tremble, shivering down their length
to his shoes. He placed his hands on his knees, palms flat,
and pressed downward to nail his feet to the dirty composition floor, to stop their involuntary little jig of fear. Was
he being conspicuous? Were people staring at him? But he
didn't dare look up to see. Like an ostrich. He looked at
his hands and saw them crawl under the knotted twine on
the package, twist into it until they began to hurt. He
pulled his fingers away, examined them, and then blew

cooling breath on his reddened index finger and forefin-
ger. Through the window opposite his seat the gray rushing wall of the tunnel blinked out and widened into the
tile of the station wall.

"Twenty-eighth Street. Station is Twenty-eighth Street."

He was up on his feet. His legs were trembling, but he
was moving well enough, dragging his package after him.
He stood facing the cab door, bracing against the train's
rapid deceleration. Outside, the platform was becoming
less of a blur, slowing down. The two boys at the storm
door were making hissing noises as they put the brakes
on. He glanced at the rear of the car. Welcome had not
moved. Through the storm door he watched the platform
jerk to a stop. People were moving forward, waiting for
the doors to open. He saw Ryder.

Ryder was leaning against the wall, very relaxed.

TWO

DENNY DOYLE

Somewhere on the run, Denny Doyle had spotted a face on a platform that reminded him of someone. It kept tantalizing him until, just as he was pulling out of Thirty-third, it popped into his head like a light snapping on in a dark room. It was a black Irish face, one of those bony ones you always saw in pictures of dead members of the IRA. The person it reminded him of was that *Daily News* reporter, a year or so back, who had come snooping around to write an article on the subways. The TA Public Relations Department had made Denny available to him, as a typical veteran motorman—as they put it—and the reporter, a sharp enough young donkey, had asked a lot of questions, some of which seemed ridiculous at first, but were pretty smart when you thought about it.

"What do you fellows think about when you're driving the train?"

For a wild second, Denny thought that the question was a trap, that the reporter had somehow latched on to his secret, but that was impossible. He had never breathed a word of it to a living soul. Not that it was so criminal, just that a grown man wasn't supposed to play silly games. Not to mention that the TA sure wouldn't be delighted to hear about it.

So he had handed the reporter a deadpan answer. "A motorman don't have time to think about anything else except his job. There's a lot to it."

"Come on," the reporter said. "Day in and day out you're going down the same set of tracks. How can there be a lot to it?"

"How can there *be*—" Denny put on a look of indignation. "It's one of the busiest railroads in the world. You know how many daily trains we run, how many miles of track—"

"They gave me a handout," the reporter said. "Over four hundred miles of track, seven thousand cars, eight or nine hundred trains an hour in rush hour. I'm impressed. But you really ducked my question."

"I'll answer your question," Denny said righteously. "What I think about is driving the train. Meeting the schedule and observing the safety rules. I watch the signals, the switches, the doors, I try to give the passengers a smooth ride, I keep an eagle eye on the rail. We have a saying, 'Know your rail—'"

"Okay. But still. Don't you ever think of, oh, let's say, what you're going to eat for lunch?"

"I *know* what I'm going to eat for lunch. I fix it myself in the morning."

The reporter had laughed, and the line about the lunch actually turned up in the story the *News* printed a few days later. His name was mentioned in the story, and he was famous for a few days, though Peg had been a little annoyed. "What do you mean *you* fix? Who hauls herself out of bed every morning to put up your lunch?" He explained that he wasn't trying to rob her of any glory, that it had just come out that way. Then, to his surprise, she said, "What in hell *do* you think of?"

"I think about God, Peg," he had said solemnly, and she had told him to save that bullcrap for Father Morrissey and then reversed her field again and started crabbing about not getting any credit for making his lunch, and all their friends would be thinking she stayed in bed until noon. . . .

But what could he do—tell her that he added up weight? A steady, sober (most of the time) pillar (like they say) of the church? Yet, dear Jesus, you had to do *something* or flip your lid. The truth of it was that driving a subway train did get to be automatic after almost twenty years—you developed a connection between your eyes and the signals, between your hands and the controller and brake handle, and everything seemed to work all by itself. He hadn't made a serious mistake in almost twenty years.

In fact, in his whole time in, he had made only one real mistake, and that shortly after he finished his training and mandatory six months' yard duty. He had jumped a ball, dear God. Not because he was adding up weight; he wasn't even doing it back then. But it had happened—moving along at forty miles an hour, he had breezed right through a red signal. To his credit, he realized it right away, but by the time he hit his brake the trippers had worked and emergency braking stopped the train. That was the whole thing. No accident. A sudden stop that jolted the passengers a little, but nobody hurt and no complaints. He had climbed down to the track and reset the tripper by hand, and that was that. Later he got a real reaming out, but old man Meara, the supervisor, had taken into account that he was a green hand and didn't write him up. In fact, he had *never* been written up, which proved something.

The reason was that he did know his rail, and knew it so damn well that he didn't *have* to think about it. He knew more than his rail; he understood how the trains worked. Once he learned something he didn't forget it. Not that it mattered so far as being a safe, on-time motorman was concerned, but he did know that each car was driven by four 100-horsepower traction motors, one for each axle, and that the third rail fed in 600-volt direct current through the contact shoes, and that moving his controller into power position sent a signal to each car's motor control unit. . . . He even knew that the sonofabitches cost almost a quarter of a million dollars apiece, which meant that when you were operating a ten-car train, you were in charge of two and a half million dollars' worth of equipment!

The truth was that you did almost the whole job automatically, *without* thinking about it. Take the holding lights back at Grand Central. He had known they were up without really seeing them and known when they went off.

Now, heading for Twenty-eighth, he was doing it all automatically, the controller pegging up at exactly the right interval from switching to series to multiple, his eye or instinct, whatever you called it, taking in the signals, green, green, easing through the amber toward the red, knowing he was at the exact right speed for the red to turn amber ahead of him, knowing that if he did have to hit the brake, he could do it without shaking up the passengers. You didn't *think* about all that; you just *did* it.

So if you didn't have to think about driving the train, you could afford to think about something else to keep your mind occupied and kill the monotony. He was willing to take a bet that plenty of other motormen played games. Vincent Scarpelli, for instance, from something he had once let drop, Vincent added up the number of tits he carried. Tits! At least his own pastime was not sinful.

He added up weight. At Thirty-third, he had dropped about twenty riders and picked up maybe a dozen. A loss of about eight. At 150 pounds per passenger (if the people who made elevators figured capacity on that basis, it was good enough for him), the net loss was 1,200 pounds, giving him a current total of 793,790 pounds. Naturally, that was a rough approximation. He could never tell *exactly* how many people got on or off, considering the length of the train and how little time he had to count them, so it was really just an educated guess. But he was pretty good at it, even in the rush-hour mob scene.

He realized it was kind of foolish to keep adding in the weight of the cars, since that never changed (approximately 75,000 pounds per car on A Division, with B-1 and B-2 running a little higher) except for the amount of cars. But it made the numbers more impressive. Right now, for instance, although he was only carrying 290 passengers (43,500 pounds) plus a 1-pound allowance each for books, newspapers, packages, ladies' handbags (290 pounds), you added in ten cars at 75,000 pounds each for the grand total of 793,790.

Where the game got to be fun was in rush hour, when the platform pushers jammed people in so that you could hardly believe it. Actually, the real action was on an express, and that was where he had established his all-time record. According to the Transit Authority, the top limit you could squeeze into a car was 180 (220 in a BMT car), but that was 'way too low. At times, especially when there were delays, you got at least another 20 per car—all 44 seats filled and a good 155 to 160 standing. So that you could really believe the old story about the man who died of a heart attack at Union Square and had to travel into Brooklyn before enough passengers got out to give him room to fall down.

Denny Doyle smiled. He had told the story himself, claiming that it had happened on his train. If such a thing could have happened, it would probably have occurred one rush hour a few years ago. A main had burst and flooded the tracks, and by the time they got moving again there was a sea of humanity on the platforms, and stops at each station ran to three or four minutes, with people committing murder to board the trains. That night, at one point, he had been hauling over 200 passengers per car, *plus* packages—well over a million pounds!

He smiled again and jockeyed the brake handle as he swept into the Twenty-eighth Street station.

TOM BERRY

Eyes shut, sprawled in his seat in the front section of the first car, Tom Berry gave himself in trust to the train, soothed by its predictable rocking and yawing, lulled by the dissonant medley of its noises. The stations had slipped by in a pleasant blur, and he made no effort to keep a tally on them. He knew he would rise at Astor Place, prompted by habit and that sixth sense, somehow allied to the instinct for survival, that New Yorkers developed in all the compartmented phases of their embattled coexistence with the city. Like animals in a jungle, like plants, they adapted, they mutated toward specific defenses and suspicions created to cope with specific threats. Cut a New Yorker open and you would discover convolutions in his brain, tracks in his nervous system, that were not present in any other urban citizenry anywhere.

He smiled at his conceit and lingered over it, refining it, even working up the casual phrasing he would use in telling it to Deedee. It occurred to him, not quite for the first time, that he was *zeroed in* on Deedee. Like the falling tree in the forest that made no sound unless somebody was there to hear it, nothing counted unless he shared it with Deedee.

It might be love. At least, that was one possible label to put to the complexity of crazy and contradictory emotions they were tangled up in: sexual frenzy, hostility, wonderment, tenderness, and a state of almost permanent confrontation. *That* was *love*? If so, it damn well wasn't the way poets defined it.

The smile on his lips flattened out, his brows formed a frown as he considered yesterday afternoon. He had taken the subway steps three at a time and half run to her freaky pad with his heart beating high in the excitement of seeing her. She opened the door to his knock (the doorbell had been out of order for three years) and immediately about-faced and walked away with the precision of a soldier in close-order drill.

He remained near the door, his mouth unhinged on an aborted smile. Even in this moment of dismay and approaching anger she knocked him out, and never mind the uniform that worked overtime at disguising her beauty: the denims raggedly cut just above the knees, the steel-rimmed glasses, the shiny brown hair dragged back at the sides of her head and then allowed to fend for itself.

He regarded the brooding eyes and the jutted lip. "You're regressing. I recognize that pout. You discovered it when you were three years old."

"Your college education is showing," she said.

"Night school."

"Night school. Yawning students and an instructor in a rumpled suit sweating out the hour in excruciating boredom."

He edged toward her, careful not to catch his foot in the shabby torn rug that provided bare cover for the floorboards that slanted upward, then dipped again, like something that had been deranged by an earth tremor and never properly subsided again. He was smiling, but without humor.

"Bourgeois contempt for the lower orders," he said. "Some people can't afford to go to college by day."

"People. You're not people, you're the enemy of the people."

The dark anger in her face stirred him perversely (or maybe not so perversely, given the narrow band that separated love from hate, that conjoined passion and rage), and he responded with an erection. Because he felt that it would give her an advantage to know it, he turned his back and walked away to the opposite side of the room. The orange-crate bookshelves leaned drunkenly. The paint-thickened mantelpiece was piled with more books, and below it the nonworking fireplace held books, too. Abbie Hoffman, Jerry Rubin, Marcuse, Fanon, Cohn-Bendit, Cleaver—the standard prophets and philosophers of the Movement.

Her voice floated across the room. "I'm not going to see you anymore."

He had expected it and had gauged the exact tone, down to the last nuance. Without turning, he said, "I think you ought to change your name."

He meant to throw her off-balance with an irrelevancy. But as soon as he spoke, he recognized the ambiguity of his words and knew she would misinterpret them.

"I don't believe in marriage," she said. "And even if I did, I would sooner shack up with a . . . well, with an anything . . . than marry a pig."

He faced her, his back against the mantelpiece. "I wasn't proposing marriage. I meant your name. Deedee.

It's too cute and frivolous for a revolutionary. Revolution-
aries should have no-nonsense names. Stalin, steel. Lenin,
Mao, Che—hard, dialectical names."

"Like Tito?"

He laughed. "Score one. Actually, I don't even know
what your right name is, was."

"What's the difference?" Then, shrugging, she said,
"Doris. I detest it."

She detested a number of things besides her name: the
Establishment, the political system, male dominance, wars,
poverty, cops, and, especially, her father, that eminently successful accountant who had provided her with silks, satins,
love, capped teeth, and an education at an Ivy League college, and who almost—but not quite—understood her and
her present needs, and from whom, to his extreme distress,
she would now accept money only in the direst straits.
Well, she wasn't so terribly wrong about most of what
she thought and felt, but her lack of consistency about
some of it bugged him. If she hated her father, she shouldn't
take money from him at any cost, and if she hated cops, she
damn well shouldn't be sleeping with one.

She was flushed, and very pretty, and somehow defense-
less. He said gently, "Well, all right, what have I done?"

"Don't try to bluff me out with that fake innocence.
Two friends of mine were in the crowd, and they saw the
whole thing. You *brutalized* an innocent black man."

"Oh. Oh, yes. Is that what I did?"

"My friends were there, on St. Marks Place, and they
told me exactly what happened. Not a half hour after you
left here—left my *bed*, you bastard—you reverted to type;

you beat the life out of a black man who was doing absolutely nothing wrong."

"He wasn't exactly doing nothing wrong."

"He was urinating in the street. Is that a serious crime?"

"It was more specific than urinating in the street. He was urinating on a woman."

"A white woman?"

"What's the difference what color she was? She objected to being pissed on. And don't tell me that it was an act of political symbolism. He was a stupid mean bastard, and he was maliciously pissing on a woman."

"So you beat him to a pulp."

"Did I?"

"Don't try to deny it. My friends saw the whole thing, and they recognize police brutality when they see it."

"How did they describe what happened?"

"Don't you think I understand that nothing is better calculated to stir up savagery in a white racist than the sight of a black penis, that universal threat, that threat of superior potency?"

"It didn't look all that potent. In fact, it was shriveled from the cold."

"That's not the point."

"Look," Berry said patiently. "You weren't there. You didn't see what happened."

"My friends saw it."

"Okay. Did your friends see him pull a knife on me?"

She looked at him scornfully. "Exactly the kind of thing I *expected* you to say."

"Your friends didn't see that part of it? And they were right there—right? Well, I was right there, too. I saw what was happening, and I intervened—"

"By what right?"

"I'm a cop," he said in exasperation. "I'm being paid to maintain order. Okay, so I represent the forces of repression. But is it repressive to prevent people from pissing on other people? That punk's rights weren't being infringed upon; the woman's were. The Constitution gives everybody the right to freedom from being pissed on. So I stepped into the situation. I intervened on behalf of the Constitution."

"Above all, don't try to be funny about it."

"I pushed him away from the woman, and I told him to button up and get the hell off the street. He buttoned up, all right, but he didn't get off the street. He pulled a knife, and he went for me."

"You didn't hit him or anything?"

"I gave him a shove. Not even a shove. A nudge, to get him moving."

"Ah. Excessive force."

"*He* used excessive force. He came at me with a knife. I took it away from him, and in the process I broke his wrist."

"Breaking a man's wrist isn't using excessive force? Couldn't you have taken the knife away without breaking his wrist?"

"He wouldn't let go of it, and he kept trying to stab me. So I broke his wrist. The only alternative was to let him stick the knife in me, and I'm not ready to go that far yet for the sake of good community relations."

She was silent, frowning.

"Or," he said deliberately, "to please my girl and her half-baked radical ideas."

"Damn you!" She moved with astonishing speed, hurling herself across the room. "Get out of here! Get lost, you pig! Pig!"

He underestimated the force of her rush. It slammed him back against the quivering mantelpiece. Laughing, protesting, he tried to catch her busy hands, but she surprised him again. She doubled up her fist and hit him in the stomach. It didn't hurt him, but it doubled him over in a violent protective reflex. When he straightened up, he grabbed her shoulders and began to shake her. Her teeth rattled. He saw a look of pure rage come into her eyes, and she tried to knee him in the groin. He twisted away, then caught her knee and imprisoned it between his thighs. Once again, he erected. She felt him against her, and stopped struggling, and looked at him in astonishment.

And so to bed.

At climax, straining beneath him, her cheeks wet with tears, she whispered, "Pig. Piggie. Oh, my pig. . . ."

As usual, she would not let him kiss her good-bye or even touch her once he had strapped the .38 back on. But neither did she make her customary impassioned plea that he dispose of his gun or, even better, turn it on his masters.

He smiled and reflexively touched the bulge of the gun against his bare skin. The train stopped, and he opened his eyes a slit to check the station. Twenty-eighth. Three more stops, a four-block walk, five wind-sucking flights of steps. . . . Was it the perversity of their relationship that attracted him? He shook his head. No. He ached to see her. He ached for her touch, even her anger. He smiled again, in memory and anticipation, as the train doors rattled open.

RYDER

Waiting for Pelham One Two Three to arrive, Ryder looked at the front-enders, studying them incuriously. Four of them, four overachievers. The young black with the fancy threads and the death-dealing eye. A Puerto Rican, thin, undersized, wearing a soiled green battle jacket. A lawyer—anyway, he looked like a lawyer, taking into account the attaché case, the sharp eyes, the brooding stance of a schemer. A boy of about seventeen, carrying schoolbooks, his head down, his face a flame of active acne. Four. Not four people, Ryder thought, four units. Maybe what was going to happen would cure them of being front-enders.

Pelham One Two Three came down the track. The amber and white marker lights at the top were like a pair of mismatched eyes. Beneath them, the sealed beams, which were the real eyes of the train, seemed by some optical trick to waver, to flicker like a candle in a wind. The train came on, as always with the appearance of going too fast to be able to stop. But it came to a smooth halt. Ryder watched the front-enders converge on the door and enter. The dressed-up black turned into the front half of the car, the others to the rear. He picked up his bags, holding them both somewhat awkwardly in his left hand, his shoulder dragged down with their weight. He walked toward the platform without haste, his right hand in the pocket of his raincoat on the grip of the automatic.

The motorman was leaning far out of his window, looking back down the platform, watching the passengers board the train. He was middle-aged, with a ruddy face and silvery gray hair. Ryder rested his shoulder against the side of the train and, in the same moment that the motorman became aware that his view of the platform was blocked off, placed the muzzle of the gun against his head.

Whether it was the sight of the gun, or the impact of it on his flesh, or even the unexpectedness of Ryder's looming presence, the motorman jerked his head back in a violent reflex and struck it jarringly against the window frame. Ryder crooked his hand inside the window and this time carefully placed the gun against the motorman's cheek, directly under his right eye.

"Unlock your cab door," Ryder said. His voice was flat, uninflected. The motorman's small blue eyes were tearing, and he seemed dazed. Ryder leaned on the gun, feeling the softness of the cheek give to the pressure. "Pay attention to me. Open your cab door or I'll kill you."

The motorman nodded his head but didn't otherwise move. He looked stricken, paralyzed; his high-colored skin had turned gray.

Ryder spoke more slowly. "I'm going to tell you this just once more, and then I'm going to shoot your face off. Open up the cab door. Don't do anything else. Don't make a sound. Just unlock your cab door, and do it now. *Now*."

The motorman's left hand moved, touching the steel door, sliding along it blindly until it felt the latch. His fingers were trembling, but they turned the latch, and Ryder heard the tiny click as the lock disengaged. The door was pulled open, and Longman, who had been waiting inside the car, edged into the cab, pulling his package after him. Ryder withdrew his gun from the motorman's face and tucked it back in his coat pocket. He carried his bags into the train. The moment he was inside, the doors shut. He felt them slide against his back.

THREE

BUD CARMODY

A voice said, "Turn around, I got something to show you."

With the car doors open, Bud Carmody was hanging out the window, observing the Twenty-eighth Street platform. The voice came from directly behind him. An instant later something hard jarred the base of his spine.

The voice said, "This is a gun. Come in and turn around slow."

Bud pulled his head in. As he turned, the gun remained in contact with his body and ended up nested weightily in his ribs. He was nose to nose with the white-haired, heavyset man with the florist's box. He had brought the box into the cab with him.

Bud said in a pinched voice, "What's the matter?"

"Do exactly like I tell you," the man said. "If you

don't, I'm going to hurt you. Don't make no trouble." He twisted the gun slightly. The front sight pinched the thin skin over Bud's ribs, and he almost cried out with the pain. "You going to do exactly what I tell you to do?"

"Yes," Bud said. "But I haven't got any money. Don't hurt me."

Bud tried not to look at the man, but they were so close together he couldn't avoid it. The man's face was large, dark-complected, with the kind of blue beard he would have to shave twice a day if he wanted to stay neat. His eyes were light in color, hazel, halfway hidden by thick lids. The eyes seemed to have no expression in them and no depth. There was no entrance in them—as he had heard eyes spoken of—no entrance to the soul. He couldn't imagine those eyes showing any feeling, especially not pity.

"Go back out the window," the man said. "Check your rear section cars, and if the platform is clear, shut them up. Just the rear section. Keep the front cars open. You got that?"

Bud nodded. His mouth had gone so dry that he wasn't sure he could speak if he tried. So he nodded, vigorously, three or four times.

"Then do it," the man said.

The gun shifted back to his spine as Bud turned and put his head out of the window.

"Clear?" the man said. Bud nodded. "Then close them up."

Bud pressed the button, and the rear half doors shut and locked.

"Stay right where you are," the man said, and then put his head out of the window beside Bud's.

It was a tight squeeze, but the man didn't seem to notice it or care. He was looking toward the front, and Bud felt the man's breath on his cheek. Beside the first car someone was talking into the window of the motorman's cab. It looked natural enough, but Bud knew that there was a connection with the man in his own cab. He saw the man at the front straighten up.

"The second you see him go in the train, shut the rest of the doors," the man beside him said. Up front, Bud watched the man enter the car. "Okay, close them up."

Bud's fingers, which were already in position on the panel, pressed hard. The doors slid shut. The indication box lit up.

"Get back inside," the man said. They stood facing each other again. The man nudged him with the gun. "Announce the next station."

Bud pressed the transmitter button and spoke into the mike. "Twenty-third Street, Twenty . . ." His throat was tight, it pinched his voice off, and he couldn't finish.

"Do it again," the man said. "Do it better this time."

Bud cleared his throat and wet his lips with his tongue. "Twenty-third Street next."

"Good enough," the man said. "Here's what you got to do next. Walk through the train to the first car."

"Walk up front to the first car?"

"Right. Walk, and keep walking until you get to the first car. I'll be following behind you with the gun in my pocket. If you try to pull something, I'll shoot you in the back. In the spine."

The spine. Bud shivered. The steel bullet smashing into his spine, pulverizing it, taking the support away so that his whole body would collapse. And the pain: the bone of the spine fragmenting, shooting razor-sharp slivers through his flesh, his organs. . . .

"Get started," the man said.

As Bud edged out of the cab, his hip brushed against the florist's box, and he reached out instinctively to steady it. But it was surprisingly stable and hardly moved. He turned to his right and opened the storm door, and the man followed. He hesitated for an instant on the threshold plates, then opened the second door and went into the next car. He didn't hear any footsteps behind him as he went forward through the train, but he knew the man was behind him, his hand on the gun in his pocket, as he had promised, ready to crack his spine like a dry twig. He kept his eyes straight ahead as he walked from car to car.

The train began to move.

LONGMAN

Longman felt lightheaded, almost dizzy, as he waited for the cab door to open. *If* it opened. He grasped at the possibility in desperation. Maybe Ryder, whom he could no longer see, would have a change of heart; maybe something unforeseen would happen and stop everything cold.

But he knew, as certainly as he knew the depths of his own fear, that Ryder would have no change of heart, that he would be able to handle something unforeseen.

The two boys were looking at him, smiling shyly, seeking at the same time his approval and indulgence for their game. Their innocence and trust touched him, and he found himself smiling at them, although a moment ago he would not have thought himself capable of it. For an instant, matching warmth with warmth, Longman was at ease, but then he heard a soft rubbing against the cab door, as if, inside, a hand were moving over it.

He heard the click of the lock being sprung. He wavered for a fraction of a second, fighting down a panicky impulse to drop everything and just run. Then he picked up his package by the string, opened the door, and went into the cab. As he pulled the door shut behind him, he saw Ryder's arm and gun disappear back through the window. Moving awkwardly, he reached for his own gun—remembering guiltily that it should have been in his hand when he entered the cab—and pressed it into the motorman's side. The motorman was pouring sweat, and Longman thought: Between the two of us, the cab will begin to stink like a locker room.

He said, "Get rid of your seat," and the motorman obeyed with almost comical speed, jumping up and folding the seat back with a clatter. "Now move over to the window."

He heard a light tap at the door and, as he slipped the latch, noticed that the indication box was lit up. Ryder opened the door and, after placing his Valpac and valise on top of Longman's package, squeezed inside. The cab was crowded now, with barely enough room left to move around in.

"Go ahead," Ryder said.

Longman crowded against the motorman so that he

could square off comfortably in front of the panel. His hands went toward the controls, then stopped. "Don't forget what I told you," he said to the motorman. "You try touching that mike pedal with your foot and I'll shoot it off."

All the motorman was trying to do was stay alive so he could collect his pension, but Longman had spoken for Ryder's ears. He was supposed to have warned the motorman about the foot pedal that activated the radio microphone earlier, but had forgotten it. He glanced toward Ryder for approval, but Ryder's face was impassive.

"Get started," Ryder said.

Like bike riding or swimming, Longman thought, it was one of those things you never forgot how to do. In the most natural way his left hand found the controller, his right the brake handle. But to his surprise, touching the brake handle made him feel a little guilty. A brake handle was a very personal thing. Every motorman was issued one his first day on the job, and he kept it, the same one, from then on, carrying it to work, removing it at quitting time. In a way, it was like his badge of office.

The motorman, sounding scared, said, "You don't know how to drive it."

"Don't worry," Longman said, "I won't wreck you."

Pressing down firmly to nullify the deadman's feature, the safety device that automatically stopped a train if the motorman were suddenly stricken, Longman nudged the controller to the left, into switching position, and the train began to edge out of the station. He entered the tunnel at a crawling five-mile-an-hour speed and immediately began to check out the signals without even having to think about it. Green, green, green, amber, red. His hand caressed the smooth metal of the controller, and with a sudden sense of exhilaration he thought of how exciting it would be to ram the controller up through series position and into multiple, right up against the post, rocketing through the tunnel at fifty, with the walls zipping by, the lights flashing like blurred stars, the signals obliging him so that he wouldn't even have to touch the brake until he slammed into the next station. . . .

But they were only going for a short ride, and he kept the controller in switching. He estimated three train lengths out of the station, then knocked the controller off and eased the brake to the right. The train rocked to a halt. The motorman looked at him.

"Smooth stop—right?" Longman said. He had stopped sweating, and he felt fine. "No jerk, no snap, no pull."

The motorman, responding eagerly to the tone of his voice, smiled broadly. But he was still sweating heavily, and his pinstripe overalls had stained to a darker color. Out of old habit, Longman checked out the signals: green, green, green, amber. The open window beside the motorman let in the familiar stink of grease and dampness.

Ryder's voice brought him down to earth. "Tell him what you want," Ryder said.

Longman said to the motorman, "I'm taking the brake handle and the reverse key, and I want your cutting key." He pulled the reverse key out of its receptacle. He held his hand out. The motorman looked uneasy but without a word fished the cutting key out of the bulging pockets of his overalls. "I'm leaving the cab now," Longman said, and was pleased at how calm he sounded. "Don't try anything."

"I won't," the motorman said. "I really won't."

"Better not," Longman said. He felt a sense of superiority over the motorman. An Irishman, but the soft kind, not the fighting kind. He was scared enough to piss. "And remember what I said about the radio."

"All right," Ryder said.

Longman put the brake handle and the bulky keys in his raincoat pockets. He squeezed by Ryder and the stacked bags and left the cab. The two boys stared at him in awe. He gave them a smile and a wink and walked back through the car. One or two of the passengers glanced at him as he passed up the aisle, but without interest.

RYDER

"Turn your back," Ryder said. "Face the window."

The motorman looked back at him apprehensively. "Please . . ."

"Do as I say."

The motorman slowly faced about to the side window. Ryder removed his right glove, hooked an index finger into his mouth, and withdrew the pads of medical gauze first from beneath his upper and lower lips and then from the inside of each cheek. He bunched the sopping pads of gauze into a single ball and dropped it into the left pocket of his raincoat. From his right pocket he took out a cut-down length of nylon stocking. He removed his hat, pulled the stocking over his head, and, after adjusting the eye slits properly, put his hat on again.

The disguises had been a concession to Longman. For

his own part, Ryder had argued that, with the exception of the motorman and conductor, nobody on the train would be likely to notice them before they put on their masks. And even if they did, it was a fact—the police themselves were the first to admit it—that untrained citizens were notoriously unreliable in their descriptions of people. And even if the motorman and conductor were a little more accurate, an Identikit portrait was nothing to worry about. Nevertheless, he had not disputed the point with Longman, except to reject anything elaborate. What the disguises boiled down to eventually were Longman's eyeglasses, Steever's white wig, Welcome's false moustache and sideburns, and filling up the hollows and slendernesses of his own face with gauze.

He touched the motorman lightly on the shoulder. "You can turn around now."

The motorman glanced at the mask, then averted his eyes in a pointed but somewhat tardy demonstration of his lack of interest in what Ryder looked like. It was, Ryder thought dryly, a friendly gesture.

He said, "You'll be getting a radio call from Command Center before long. Ignore it. Don't answer. Do you understand?"

"Yes, sir," the motorman said earnestly. "I promised the other man I wouldn't touch the radio. I'm going to cooperate with you." He paused. "I want to stay alive."

Ryder didn't answer. Through the front window the tunnel ran off into the distance, dimly lit except for the sharpness of the signal lights. He noted that Longman had stopped the train less than ten paces from the light indicating an emergency power box.

"They can call all they want to," the motorman said. "I'm deaf."

"Keep quiet," Ryder said.

It would be another minute or two before the Grand Central Tower, becoming restive, would contact Command Center with the advice: "All signals clear in area, train laying down." For himself, Ryder thought, it was a dead interlude with nothing for him to do but see that the motorman behaved himself. Welcome was at his post, guarding the rear storm door; Longman was on his way to the cab of the second car; it was a safe assumption that Steever and the conductor were moving forward through the train. He trusted Steever implicitly, although he had less brains than either of the others. Longman was intelligent but a coward, and Welcome was dangerously erratic. They would all be fine if everything went smoothly. If not, their weaknesses would begin to show.

"Command Center calling Pelham One Two Three. Command Center calling Pelham One Two Three. Come in, please."

The motorman's foot moved involuntarily toward the foot pedal that could be used alternatively with the button on the microphone itself, to transmit. Ryder kicked him in the ankle.

"I'm sorry. It was automatic. My foot just moved. . . ." The motorman's voice petered out, his face remained screwed up in an apology so profound it was almost a form of remorse.

"Pelham One Two Three, do you read me?" The radio voice paused. "Pelham One Two Three, come in. Speak up, Pelham One Two Three."

Ryder tuned the voice out of his consciousness. By now Longman would be in the cab of the second car, with the door locked, and the brake handle, the reverse key, and the cutting key emplaced. Severing the cars, even allowing for a degree of rustiness, would take less than a minute. . . .

"Dispatcher calling Pelham One Two Three. Do you read me? Please report, Pelham One Two Three. . . . Come in, Pelham One Two Three!"

The motorman looked at Ryder with open appeal. For the moment his sense of duty, and perhaps, fear of disciplinary action, overrode his fear for his life. Ryder shook his head sternly.

"Pelham One Two Three. Pelham One Two Three, where the fuck are you?"

LONGMAN

The passengers blurred into a faceless mass as Longman went to the rear of the car. He didn't dare look at them for fear of calling attention to himself, despite Ryder's assurance that he would have to fall flat on his face to be noticed ("And even then," Ryder had said, "most of them would pretend nothing had happened"). Welcome was watching his approach with a crooked smile, and as usual the mere sight of Welcome made him nervous. He was a weirdo, a maniac. A man who had been fired by the *Mafia* because he misbehaved?

Welcome's smile vanished as Longman came up, and he remained squarely in front of the door. For an instant

Longman was convinced that Welcome wouldn't budge, and panic began to rise in him like the mercury column in a thermometer. But then he stepped aside and, with a mocking smile, slid the door open. Longman took a deep breath and went through.

Between the cars he paused, visualizing, beneath the steel threshold plates, the thick electric cables that transmitted power from car to car, and the neat grasp of the couplings. The door to the second car opened, and he saw that it was being held by Steever. The conductor stood beside him, young and frightened. Steever handed over the door key, which he had taken from the conductor. Longman unlocked the cab door and went inside. He locked the door and proceeded to arm the panel. He fitted the brake handle into place, then fished the reverse key out of his pocket. About five inches long with a shiny surface, it was a wrench-type handle that fitted into a receptacle on the flat portion of the controller, which would now move the train either forward or backward, depending on the position of the reverse key. Finally, he emplaced the cutting key—similar to the reverse key in appearance, but with a slightly smaller head.

Except in the yard, a motorman rarely had occasion to cut or reverse a train, but it was a simple enough process. Longman turned the cutting key, and the coupling between the first and second cars unlocked. He set the reverse key in reverse position. Then, pressing down on the deadman's feature, he edged the controller into switching position. The open couples disengaged smoothly, and the nine cars of the train moved backward. He estimated a distance of about 150 feet and gently applied the brake.

The train stopped. He removed the brake handle and the two keys, stuffed them into his pockets, and stepped out of the cab.

Here and there in the car a passenger was squirming with impatience at the delay, which had now stretched into several minutes, but no one seemed alarmed. Nor did it seem to bother them that their car had moved backward. But it would bother the Tower, all right. He could just imagine what must be going on in the Tower.

Steever held the storm door for him. He stepped out onto the flange of the threshold plate, crouched low to ease the impact, and jumped down to the concrete roadbed. The conductor followed, and then Steever. They walked quickly through the tunnel to the first car. Welcome opened the door, stepped out on the threshold plate, and, crouching, extended a hand to help them up.

Longman was relieved that he didn't try to fool around.

FOUR

CAZ DOLOWICZ

Fleshy, edematous, his belly straining the buttons of his jacket, Caz Dolowicz moved with deliberate speed through the crowds entering and leaving the Grand Central terminus of the shuttle. He belched in a series of light, purse-lipped expulsions at almost every step, bringing a measure of relief from the painful accumulation of gas that pressed upward against his heart. As usual, he had eaten too much lunch and, as usual, had admonished himself that he would live to regret his appetite, by which he meant that he would one day die of it. Death as a phenomenon held no particular terrors for him, other than that it would screw him out of collecting his pension. But that was a big exception.

A few steps past the Nedick's stand—whose effluvium of roasting frankfurters, enticing an hour ago, now made him gag—he pushed through the inconspicuous gate with its sign reading TO SUPER'S OFFICE and hurried past the ramp with the nine-foot Dempster cans holding refuse from the Grand Central concessions. Eventually, the garbage train would come and the Dempsters would be rolled on, but meanwhile they stank and encouraged the rats. Dolowicz was amazed, as always, that the unlocked gate didn't tempt the curiosity of passersby, except for the occasional drunk who stumbled through it in search of the john or God knew what. Just as well—they could live without civilians wandering into the Tower and asking stupid questions.

As he entered the tunnel, he wondered how many people—even employees—knew that it was the old right-of-way; although the tracks had been removed, the original roadbed remained. As he walked on at his heavy, steady pace, Dolowicz caught here and there the glint of an eye. Not a rat, but one of the army of cats that lived in the tunnel, never seeing the light of day and preying on the rats, which infested the passage by the thousands. "The rats are big enough to pick you up and carry you away," they had told him solemnly on his first day as a towerman. But not as big, although he had never seen them, as the rats which were supposed to inhabit the heating section of the Penn-Central. According to the famous story, a man trying to duck the cops had found his way into the heating system and, bewildered by the maze of passages, had got lost and, eventually, had been completely devoured by the rats, down to the marrow of his bones.

Directly ahead of him, a train charged down at him head-on. Smiling, he walked straight toward it. It was the northbound express, and in another moment it turned away. On that first day, twelve years ago, nobody had bothered to warn him about the northbound, and when it came thundering toward him, he had flung himself into the trough in terror. It was still one of the simple pleasures of his life to escort a new man down the tunnel and watch what happened when the northbound came hurtling down the track.

The week before, he had escorted some subway brass from Tokyo through the tunnel, and it was a great opportunity to check out the Oriental so-called impassivity. Some impassivity—when the northbound roared down at them, they turned chicken like everybody else and screamed and scrambled. But they recovered fast and thirty seconds later were bitching about the stink. "Well," he had told them, "it's an underground tunnel, not a botanical garden." They also had some complaints about the Tower itself—too drab, too shabby, too gloomy. Dolowicz thought they were silly. Okay, it was just a long, narrow, unadorned room with a few desks, a few phones, a toilet. But, as they say, beauty is in the eye of the beholder, and what made the Tower beautiful was the Model Board, stretched high across one wall, recording in colored slashes of light the routes and movements of every train that passed through the sector, all of it superimposed on a map showing the tracks and the stations.

He climbed the steps and entered the Tower Room, the control center he ran for eight hours a day. Tower Room. Actually, the technical name for it was Interlocking Plant, but nobody ever called it that. It was Tower Room, or simply the Tower, named after the old-time towers raised above the railroad tracks at key points, as the subway towers were located underground at key points on the system.

Dolowicz took in the scene. His towermen were all busy at their flashing consoles, watching the action on the Model Board as they spoke to desk trainmasters, dispatchers, and towermen at adjoining key points. His eye went to Jenkins. A woman. A woman towerman. And a black woman, yet. He couldn't get used to the idea, even after a month. Well, he had better get used to it; the talk was that a lot more women were taking the towerman test! What next—motormen? Motorwomen? Not that he had any complaints about Mrs. Jenkins. She was a quiet person, clean, soft-spoken, competent. But still . . .

On the left side of the room, Marino was beckoning to him. Dolowicz, his eye on the Model Board, walked over to Marino's chair and stood behind him. On the board, a southbound local was standing between Twenty-eighth and Twenty-third.

"He's laying dead," Marino said.

"I see that," Dolowicz said. "How long?"

"Couple, three minutes."

"Well, get onto the squawk box to Command Center so they can contact the motorman."

"I did," Marino said, aggrieved. "They're trying to raise him. He don't answer the radio."

Dolowicz could think of a number of reasons why the motorman wouldn't answer the radio, the chief being that he wasn't in the cab, that he had climbed out to reset a tripper that had accidentally cut him dead or maybe to fix a hung door. Anything more serious, he would have radioed in for a car knocker. But whatever, he was required to report to Command Center by radio.

Still looking at the Model Board, he said to Marino, "Unless he's a jerk, the reason he didn't call Command Center is because his radio is probably busted. And the lazy bum won't exert himself to pick up a telephone. They got it too good these days."

When he had first joined the system, there was no such luxury as two-way radios. If a motorman got into trouble, he would climb down out of the cab, walk the track to one of the telephones placed at 500-foot intervals in the tunnel, and report in. The telephones were still there to be used if necessary.

"The sonofabitch is going to get written up for this," Dolowicz said. The gas pocket stabbed his heart. He tried to force a belch and failed. "What train is it?"

"Pelham One Two Three," Marino said. "Hey, he's starting to move." Then Marino's voice rose in astonishment. "For Jesus Christ sake, he's moving *backwards!*"

RYDER

When Longman rapped his knuckles against the metal of the cab door, Ryder held him up for a moment while he undid the lock of the brown valise and took out the submachine gun. The motorman gasped. Ryder unlocked the cab door, and Longman stepped in.

"Put your mask on," Ryder said. He kicked Longman's package. "And get your weapon out."

He squeezed out of the door and shut it behind him,

the tommy gun held vertically along his pants leg. In the center of the car, making no effort to be inconspicuous now, Steever was pulling his gun from the florist's box, which was now neatly split down the center, where it had been prescored and joined by scotch tape. At the rear of the car, Welcome straightened up from his valise. He was grinning, and his tommy gun was trained down the length of the car.

"Attention," Ryder said in a loud voice, and watched the passengers turn toward him, not in unison but raggedly, varying with their reaction time. He held the gun in the crook of his arm, the barrel resting on his right hand, the fingers of his left curved around the trigger behind the magazine. "You will all remain seated. Nobody will move. Anyone who tries to get up, or even moves, will be shot. There will be no further warning. If you move, you'll be killed."

He braced himself as the car began to move slowly forward.

CAZ DOLOWICZ

The red slashes on the Model Board in the Grand Central Tower began to wink.

"He's moving," Marino said. "Forwards."

"I can see that with my own eyes," Dolowicz said. He was bent forward, his hands braced on Marino's seatback, looking up at the board.

"Now he stopped," Marino said in a hushed voice. "He stopped again. About halfway between the stations."

"A pure mental case," Dolowicz said. "I'm going to have that motorman's ass."

"Still stopped," Marino said.

"I'm going down there and see what the hell's going on," Dolowicz said. "And I don't care *what* his excuse is, I'm going to have his ass."

He remembered Mrs. Jenkins. Her face was impassive. Christ, Dolowicz thought, if I have to watch my language, I'm going to pack it in. Did they think of *that* when they opened up towerman classification to women? How the hell could you run a railroad without swearing?

As he opened the door, a raging voice blasted through the speaker: "What the fuck is going on with that crazy train? Will you for Christ sake get some goddamn supervision down there?"

It was the desk trainmaster's voice, screaming into his microphone from Command Center. Dolowicz grinned at Mrs. Jenkins' stiff back.

"Tell his nibs supervision is on the way," he said to Marino, and hurried out of the Tower and down the steps into the tunnel.

RYDER

The submachine guns represented a substantial outlay of money—sawed-off shotguns, which were terrible weapons in their own right, were much cheaper—but Ryder considered them a sound investment. He didn't particularly care for them as weapons (granted, they were murderous at short range, but they were inaccurate, with a tendency to pull high and to the right, and at a distance of 100 yards they were almost useless) but valued them for their psychological effect. Joe Welcome called the tommy gun the weapon of respect, and, his nostalgia for the traditional weapon of the gangster era to one side, he was right. Even the police, who were aware of its limitations, would show some deference for a weapon that could spew out 450 lethal .45 caliber rounds per minute. Most of all, it would impress the passengers, with their standard movie-inspired image of tommy guns cutting people down in rows.

The car was hushed, except for the squealing wheels and the creak of metallic joints, as Longman eased the train slowly through the tunnel. Steever, in the exact middle of the car, faced Welcome at the far end. Both were masked. For the first time, Ryder took account of the passengers in the front half of the car. Sixteen of them. A dozen and a third, the way you reckoned a commodity. But, however dispassionately he viewed them, individuals forced their way into focus:

The two small boys, saucer-eyed, probably more fascinated than frightened to find themselves actors in a real-life TV drama. Their plump mother, hung up between two conventions: fainting or protecting her cubs. A hippie type with shoulder-length blond Jesus Christ hair and beard to match, wearing a Navajo-patterned woolen poncho, a headband, and leather-thonged sandals. Comatose. Either bombed out or sleeping off a high. A flashy dark-haired girl in an Anzac hat. A high-class hustler? Five blacks: two almost identical boys carrying packages—long, bony, sad faces, with huge eyes showing disproportionate amounts of white; the dashing militant type of the plat-form, with his Che beret and Haile Selassie cape; a middle-aged man, smooth-skinned, handsome, well turned-out, holding an attaché case on his lap; a stout placid woman, probably a domestic, wearing a coat with a patchy silver fox collar, legacy from some beneficent Mrs. An old white man, tiny and alert, rosy-cheeked, duded up in a cashmere coat, a pearly Borsalino hat, a foulard silk tie. A female derelict, color indeterminate, a wino, layered in coats and sweaters, unimaginably scabbed and grimy, snuffling in a semiconscious daze . . .

And others. Figures in a city landscape. Except for the black militant, who was staring at him in direct challenge, the other passengers were doing their best to be inoffen-sive, self-effacing. Good enough, Ryder thought, they were simply cargo. Cargo with a fixed value.

The car dragged under his feet, bucked, and came to a stop. Steever turned inquiringly. Ryder nodded, and Steever cleared his throat and spoke. His voice was heavy, monotone, muffled, the voice of a man who spoke little.

"Everybody in the back half of the car," Steever said. "Up on your feet. Everybody. Be quick about it."

Ryder, anticipating the stirring in his half of the car, said, "Not you people. Stay where you are. Sit fast. Don't even move. Anybody who moves will be shot."

The black militant moved in his seat. Deliberately, with carefully measured defiance. Ryder trained the muzzle of the gun on his chest. He moved again, wriggling his hips, and then subsided, content with his demonstration of intransigence. Ryder, too, was content; the challenge was ceremonial, it could be ignored.

"Everybody up. Move ass. You understand English? On your frigging feet!"

Welcome, from the rear of the car, ad libbing, getting into the act. It was wrong. The passengers were docile enough; it was pointless to risk scaring them into a stampede. Well, he had anticipated that Welcome would improvise, and it was too late for regrets.

The cab door opened, and Longman came out, prodding the motorman ahead of him with the tip of his gun. Longman spoke softly to the motorman, who nodded and looked for a seat. He wavered before an empty place beside the hippie, then moved on and fell heavily into a seat alongside the stout black woman. She accepted his presence tranquilly and without surprise.

Ryder nodded to Longman. Longman, with the motorman's door key in his hand, bent to the keyhole above the handle on the front storm door. The two boys, backed against the door, were in his way. Longman put his hand between them, not roughly, and separated them.

The plump woman cried out. "Brandon. Robert. Please don't hurt them." She jumped to her feet and took a step toward the boys.

"Sit down," Ryder said. The woman stopped and turned to him, her mouth shaping a protest. "Don't argue. Sit down." Ryder waited until she returned to her seat, then motioned to the boys. "Get away from the door. Sit down."

The woman reached out for the boys and drew them to her convulsively, planting them between her spread legs, their original and ultimate safe harbor.

Longman opened the door, stepped out onto the

threshold plate and, as the door slid shut, dropped to the
tracks. Ryder checked off his passengers, shifting the
muzzle of his gun from one to the other, its movement
deliberate, intimidating. The girl in the Anzac hat tapped
her foot restlessly on the filthy white and black squares of
the floor. The hippie was nodding, smiling, his eyes still
closed. The militant black, with his arms folded across his
chest was staring with accusatory stoniness at the Uncle
Tom across the aisle, the well-dressed black with the attaché case. The boys were squirming with embarrassment
in their mother's scissors hold. . . . At the rear of the car
the passengers were now facing the door three abreast,
with Welcome worrying at them like a sheep dog.

Without warning, the lights in the car went out, and
the emergency lights blinked on. The passengers looked
alarmed, their faces hollower in the diminished light cast
by the incandescent bulbs, less numerous and intense than
the fluorescent tubes that ran the length of the car on each
sidewall and along the center of the ceiling. The power
was now out in the sector between Fourteenth and Thirty-
third streets on all four tracks, local and express, northbound and southbound.

Ryder said, "Conductor. Come here." The conductor
came to the center of the car and stopped. He was very
pale. Ryder said, "I want you to walk all of those passengers back down the track."

The conductor said, "Yes sir."

"Collect all the passengers in the other nine cars of the
train, too, and lead them all back to the Twenty-eighth
Street station."

The conductor looked worried. "They might not want to leave the train."

Ryder shrugged. "Tell them their train isn't going any-place."

"I will, but—" The conductor's voice became confidential. "Passengers hate to get off a train, even when they *know* it's not going to move. It's funny—"

"Just do as you're told," Ryder said.

"Can I go, please?" The girl in the Anzac hat, making a production of crossing her legs, then leaning forward earnestly. "I've got this terribly important appointment."

"No," Ryder said. "No one in this half of the car will leave."

"A very important audition. I'm in the theater—"

"Sir?" The young mother, craning over the heads of her boys. "Please, sir. Please? My two children are very high-strung—"

"Nobody leaves," Ryder said.

The old man in the cashmere coat said, "I'm not asking to leave, but. But shouldn't we at least be fully informed what's going on, at least?"

"Yes," Ryder said. "What's going on is that you're being held by four desperate men with machine guns."

The old man smiled. "I guess if you ask a foolish question . . ."

"Could you give us some idea of how long we'll be detained?" the girl in the Anzac hat said. "I'd hate to miss this audition."

"That's enough," Ryder said. "No more answers. And no more questions." If the girl's effort to hustle him and the old man's aplomb were equally transparent, he was satisfied; neither of them was likely to turn panicky.

Longman came in through the storm door. His gun was tucked under one arm, and he was brushing his hands against each other to rid them of dust and grime. It was probably months, or even years, since the emergency power box had last been used. Ryder gestured, and Longman trained his gun on the passengers. Ryder went back to the rear of the car. The conductor was assuring the passengers that there was no danger from the third rail.

"The power is off, ma'am. One of those gentlemen was kind enough to cut the power."

Welcome guffawed, and there was even a timid ripple of laughter from the passengers. The conductor blushed, then went through the door and jumped down to the roadbed. The passengers began to follow, more awkwardly. Those who hesitated, intimidated by the drop, were sped along by Welcome, using his gun as a prod.

Steever came back to Ryder and said in a whisper, "Five of them up front are spades. Who's going to shell out for spades?"

"They've got the same value as anybody else. Maybe more."

"Politics, right?" Steever shrugged.

When all but three or four passengers had disappeared through the rear door, Ryder walked back to the front of the car and went into the cab. It stank of sweat. Ahead, through the front window, the tunnel lights, on DC, had gone off. But the signals and emergency lights, which were on AC, remained on. Close by, there was a single blue light indicating an emergency telephone and, ahead, an unbroken procession of green signal lights.

Ryder lifted the microphone from its peg near the front window and felt for the black button which would activate the transmitter. But before he could press it, a voice filled the cab.

"Command Center to Pelham One Two Three. What the *fuck* is on? You cut the power? Without phoning Power Central to explain? Are you reading me? Are you *reading* me? This is the desk trainmaster. Come in, goddamn it, come in, Pelham One Two Three, you crazy sonofabitch!"

Ryder flicked the button. "Pelham One Two Three to Command Center. Do you read me?"

"Where the hell have you been? What's *with* you? What are you trying to do to the railroad? Why didn't you answer your radio? Come in. Come in, Pelham One Two Three, and start talking."

"Pelham One Two Three to Command Center," Ryder said. "Command Center, your train has been taken. Do you read me? Your train has been taken. Come in, Command Center."

FIVE

TOM BERRY

Tom Berry told himself—had been telling himself—that there was absolutely no point when he could have taken suitable action. Maybe if he hadn't been daydreaming, thinking of Deedee instead of duty, maybe if he had been reasonably alert, he might have sensed that something suspicious was going on. But by the time he opened his eyes he could count four submachine guns, any one of which would have turned him into a side of bloody meat before his hand even touched his gun.

Not that there weren't plenty of cops who would have made a move anyway, committed willful suicide, responding by reflex to the hard indoctrination that started on their first day at the Police Academy: a compound consisting of a sense of mission, *machismo*, and contempt for the criminal. Brainwashing, Deedee would have called it. Yes, he knew cops like that, and not all of them were stupid, and not all of them were decent people. Brainwashed, or just men who took their mandate seriously? Himself, with a .38 in his belt, he had simply sat on his reflexes. If it was any consolation, he was alive and well, and probably at the end of his career as a cop.

He had been trained and sworn to uphold the law, to enforce order, not just stand by like the public he was pledged to protect. Cops were not expected to snooze through the commission of a crime or reckon the odds against them too finely. Not even cops in plain clothes or cops off duty. They were expected to meet force with force, and if they got killed for their pains, it was in the highest tradition of police work. Line of duty.

Well, if he had drawn his gun, he would certainly have upheld the highest tradition of the force, for both bravery and dying. As a reward, he would have been given an inspector's funeral, with the commissioner and the mayor present and the rest of the brass turned out in pressed uniforms and white gloves and, when it appeared on the eleven o'clock television news, not a dry eye among the watchers. A high-class way to go, even if you were in no position to appreciate its grandeur and solemnity. Who would have mourned for him—mourned him truly, not institutionally? Deedee? Would Deedee mourn him or remember him beyond tomorrow except in terms of a missing person between her legs? Or would she wake up to the realization of what "off the pig" meant in terms of spouting lifeblood and shattered bone and ruptured organs?

He opened his eyes a slit and saw that the scene had changed somewhat. The one who had climbed out of the car, presumably to cut the power, had returned, and the tall one, the leader, was just entering the motorman's cab. The heavy one was in the center of the car, facing front, and the fourth man was overseeing the herding of the rear-section passengers out of the car. So, Berry thought, the odds were no longer a prohibitive four to one, but a mere prohibitive two to one. It was a golden opportunity. To get slaughtered. "You see, sir"—he was explaining himself to a grim captain—"I didn't care about myself, I just didn't want any passengers to get hurt, so I refrained from drawing my gun and instead continued to plan how the public interest could be served to the best advantage of all and in the highest tradition of the department."

He grinned slackly and shut his eyes. Decision confirmed. Sorry, Mr. Mayor and Mr. Commissioner, don't feel bad; somebody will blow a cop's head off before the month is out, so you won't really be deprived of your solemn processional. Sorry, Deedee. Deedee, would you have worn a black love bead to celebrate your dead pig lover?

The heavy presence of the .38 against his stomach gave him no comfort. He would have made it disappear if he could; it kept reminding him that he had neglected to become a brave corpse. Deedee. Deedee would understand. She would congratulate him on having raised his consciousness, at his liberation from being a witless instrument of the repressive society. But his superiors would take a different view. There would be an investigation, a departmental trial, dismissal from the force. All cops would despise him, even those who were blatantly on the take. No matter how corrupt they were, they were not so corrupt that they would fail to get themselves killed uselessly.

One ray of sunshine: You could always get a new job. Getting a new life was tougher.

CAZ DOLOWICZ

As Dolowicz began to walk back through the old tunnel, his indigestion, which had vanished, or at least been submerged by his anger at the inexplicable behavior of Pelham One Two Three, came out of hiding. He hurried past the stink and sizzle of the orange juice stand, and puffed his way up the steps to the terminal. He went through the concourse to the street, and waved down a cab.

"Park Avenue South and Twenty-eighth."

"You're from out of town," the driver said. "How I know, the natives still call it Fourth Avenue. Like Sixth Avenue. Only the shitkickers call it Avenue of the Americas. Where you from?"

"The South Bronx."

His belly bounced on the fulcrum of his low-slung belt as he ran down the steps at the Twenty-eighth Street station. He flashed his identification card at the change booth clerk and charged through the gate. A train was standing in the station with its doors open. If Pelham One Two Three was still lying dead in the tunnel, the signal blocks would hold up this train, Pelham One Two Eight. As he started toward the south end of the platform he realized that the train was lit only by the dim battery-operated emergency lights. He hurried on to the front car. The motorman was leaning out of the window.

"When did the power go?"

The motorman was an old-timer, and he needed a shave. "Who wants to know?"

"Caz Dolowicz, the Grand Central Tower trainmaster, wants to know."

"Oh." The motorman straightened up. "It went out a couple of minutes ago."

"You radio Command Center?"

The motorman nodded. "Dispatcher said to sit here and wait. What's up—man under?"

"I'm going to goddamn well find *out* what's up," Dolowicz said.

He went on to the end of the platform and descended to the roadbed. As he started through the darkened tunnel, it occurred to him that he could have used the motorman's radio to find out about the power, but it was just as well. He was always in favor of seeing things for himself.

Spurred by anger and anxiety, he began to trot along the roadbed. But his gas pains forced him to slow down again. He kept trying vainly to belch, massaging his chest in an attempt to dislodge the gassy pocket. Pain or no pain, he trudged on steadily, until he heard voices in the tunnel. He stopped and, with narrowed eyes, peered through the dimness at a bulky wavering shape coming down the track. It looked, ferchrisesake, like a crowd of people.

LONGMAN

Longman had been cool enough in the tunnel, pulling the emergency switch to knock out the power, as he had been earlier—and even enjoyed himself, in a way—cutting the cars and driving the train. He felt fine when he was doing the technical things. Actually, he was still okay when he came back to the car, but the moment Ryder went into the cab he had begun to sweat again. It brought home to him how secure he felt with Ryder, even though the man's attitude scared him stiff half the time. He had never really established *any* kind of relationship with the other two. Steever was efficient but inaccessible, a closed system, and Welcome was not only cruel and kinky, but probably a certifiable maniac.

The submachine gun seemed to be vibrating in his hands, as though it were picking up the agitated beat of his own blood. He braced the butt more firmly under his elbow and eased up the tightness of his grip, and the gun became steadier. He shifted his eyes anxiously to the cab door, but jerked them to the front again at the sound of a low warning whistle from Steever. He focused on the passengers in the row of seats to his right. They were his responsibility, and the left row was Steever's. Ryder had arranged it that way so that they wouldn't be in each other's line of fire. The passengers were silent, hardly stirring.

All the passengers were now out of the rear section of the car. It looked empty and abandoned. Welcome was profiled toward the storm door, his feet braced wide apart, his machine gun pointed down the track. He looked to be spoiling for action, and Longman was convinced that he was praying for something to go wrong so that he could kill somebody.

His face was so sweaty now that he worried about the

nylon clinging to it and giving its conformations away. He started to glance at the cab door again, but a sudden sound to his right brought his head around sharply. It was the hippie, his eyes shut, stretching his leg out into the aisle. Steever was calm, watchful, motionless. Welcome was peering out at the tracks through the rear window.

Longman strained for some sound from behind the cab door but could hear nothing. So far the operation had gone without a hitch. But it would all go down the drain if they balked at paying. Ryder had assured him that they had no reasonable alternative. But suppose they decided not to be reasonable? You couldn't predict the behavior of people that certainly. What if the cops made the decision, and got hard-nosed about it? Well, in that case a lot of people would die. Including themselves.

Ryder's credo: You live or you die. It was an abhorrent thought to Longman, whose own credo, if he had ever verbalized it, would have been *survive at any cost*. Yet, of his own free will, he had signed on at Ryder's terms. Free will? No. He had drifted into it helplessly, in a sort of dream state. He had been fascinated by Ryder, but that didn't explain everything. Wasn't it he himself who was responsible for their getting to know each other at all? Wasn't it his own idea? Hadn't he brought it out into the open himself and then refined it from a game, a playfully vengeful fantasy, into something criminal and profitable?

He had long ago stopped thinking of their first meeting as accidental. The more accurate, more awesome word was "fate." From time to time he had mentioned the idea of fate, but Ryder had been indifferent to it. Not that he didn't see the point, just that he didn't care, it didn't signify. Something happened, it led to something else—beyond that Ryder didn't look into causes, didn't get excited by coincidences. Something happened, it led to something else.

They had met at the state unemployment office on Sixth Avenue and Twentieth Street, on one of the straggling, dispiritedly patient lines of unemployed inching forward to where a civil servant made a cabalistic entry in their blue-covered "books" and gave them a voucher to sign for their weekly checks. He had first noticed Ryder on an adjoining line—a tall, slender man with black hair and fine, intense features. Not what you would call a man's man, yet somehow suggesting depths of hidden strength and a quality of controlled confidence. Actually, that assessment had come later. What caught Longman's eye at first was a good deal simpler: The man stuck out in that crowd of spades and spies, long-haired boys and girls, and nondescript beaten-down middle-aged people (the last of which, Longman reluctantly admitted, was his own category). Actually, Ryder wasn't extraordinary, and in any other place he wouldn't have stood out.

Sometimes people struck up conversations on the lines to help pass the time. Others brought along something to read. Longman usually picked up a *Post* on his way to the unemployment office and never talked to anybody. But when, a few weeks after he had first seen him, he found himself directly behind Ryder on a line, he had begun a conversation with him. He had been hesitant at first, because Ryder was obviously someone who kept his own counsel and might freeze a man out if he didn't want to talk. But finally, half turning, he had shown him the headline on his *Post*.

ANOTHER 747
OFF TO CUBA

"It must be catching, like a disease," Longman said.

Ryder nodded politely but said nothing.

"I don't understand what they get out of it," Longman said. "Once they get to Cuba they're either thrown in the clink or they have to go out in the sun and cut sugarcane for ten hours a day."

"I couldn't say," Ryder's voice was unexpectedly deep and authoritative. A boss' voice, Longman had thought uneasily, and yet not quite, something else to it he couldn't quite put his finger on.

"To take all that risk for a coolie's job, it don't make sense," Longman said.

Ryder didn't exactly shrug, but Longman realized that he had lost interest in the subject, if in fact he had ever had any. Ordinarily, Longman would have pulled back at that point; he didn't usually force himself on people. But Ryder had piqued his interest, and in some way he didn't quite understand, he wanted to win his approval. And so he went on and uttered the words which, in the long run, were to prove prophetic.

"When there's something in it for them—a lot of money, say—then I can understand it. But to take all that risk for nothing . . ."

Ryder smiled. "Everything is risk. Taking the next

breath is a risk; you might inhale something poisonous. If you won't take a risk, you have to give up breathing, too."

"You can't," Longman said. "I read someplace that it's impossible to stop breathing voluntarily, even if you try."

Ryder smiled again. "Oh, I think you can manage it if you go about it the right way."

After that, there didn't seem anything more to say, and the conversation lapsed. Longman went back to his *Post*, feeling that he had somehow made a fool of himself. When Ryder finally had his book stamped and had signed his voucher, he nodded pleasantly to Longman before leaving. Longman, at the counter, turned to watch Ryder go out through the glass doors.

A week or two later Longman was as much surprised as flattered when Ryder came over to join him at the counter of a coffee shop, where he had stopped for a sandwich. Ryder seemed easier to talk to this time—not exactly friendly, but a little more responsive in his reserved way. The conversation was casual and impersonal, and afterward they walked to the unemployment office together and joined the same line.

Longman felt more at ease with Ryder now, less like an intruder. He said, "I noticed there was still another one of those plane hijacks this week. Read about it?"

Ryder shook his head. "I'm not much of a newspaper reader."

"This one wasn't so lucky," Longman said. "He never made Cuba. When they came down for refueling, he showed himself, and an FBI sharpshooter shot him dead."

"It beats chopping sugarcane."

"Being dead?"

"Being dead is an improvement on a lot of things I can think of. Trying to sell mutual funds, for example."

"Is that your line of work?"

"I tried to make it my line of work for a few months." He shrugged. "I turned out to be a lousy salesman. I guess I don't like asking people for things." He was silent for a moment. "I prefer telling them what to do."

"You mean being a boss?"

"In a way."

"Salesman wasn't your regular line of work?"

"No."

He offered no further explanation, and even though his curiosity was aroused, Longman didn't pursue it. Instead he talked about himself.

"I was working on a construction project, small houses out on the Island. But the builder ran out of money, and I was laid off."

Ryder's nod was noncommittal.

"I'm not a construction worker by trade," Longman said. "I was a subway motorman."

"Retired?"

"I'm only forty-one."

Ryder said politely, "That's just about what I figured your age to be. That's why I was surprised at the idea that you might be retired."

It was a gracious apology, but Longman wasn't fooled. He had a worn look, a grayness, and people usually overstated his age. He said, "I had about eight years in as motorman. But I quit the system. That was a few years ago."

Whether or not he was convinced, Ryder wasn't going to make any more of it. He merely nodded. Ninety-nine out of a hundred men would have followed up by asking why he had quit. True, Ryder simply might not give a damn, but even so, it would have been normal curiosity to ask. Annoyed, Longman asked a counterquestion which, in deference to Ryder's reticence, he would otherwise have avoided.

"What was your line? I mean your regular line?"

"The military. I was a soldier."

"Twenty-year man? That's a pretty good deal, I guess, if you can stick it out. What was your rank?"

"My last grade was full colonel."

Longman was disappointed. He knew from his own year in the service that men of thirty—which was what he reckoned Ryder's age to be—did not become full colonels. He hadn't figured Ryder to be a bullshitter. He nodded, and was silent.

Ryder said, "Not the American army."

The explanation didn't entirely allay Longman's suspicion; it simply deepened the mystery. What army *had* Ryder served with? He had no trace of a foreign accent; he certainly sounded American enough. The Canadian army? But a thirty-year-old wouldn't become a colonel in that army, either.

He stepped up to the counter to have his book processed, then waited for Ryder to complete his turn. Outside, they fell in step, and began to walk uptown on Sixth Avenue.

"Going anywhere in particular?" Longman said.

"Thought I'd take a walk."

"Mind if I tag along?' I haven't got anything to do."

They walked to the mid-Thirties, impersonal again—

commenting occasionally on something in a shop window, on the women barging in and out of the department stores at Thirty-fourth, on the noise and smell of the traffic. But the puzzle bothered Longman, and finally, while they waited at the curb for the cross-town traffic to go by, he blurted it out.

"What army *were* you in?"

Ryder paused for so long a time that Longman was on the verge of apologizing. But then Ryder said, "The last one? Biafra."

"Oh," Longman said. "Oh, I see."

"And before that the Congo. Also, Bolivia."

"You're a soldier of fortune?" Longman read a great deal, adventure novels, and so the concept was not entirely alien to him.

"That's a fancy name for it. Mercenary is more accurate."

"Meaning someone who fights for money?"

"Yes."

"Well," Longman said, thinking not so much in terms of fighting for money as killing for money, and somewhat aghast at the idea, "I'm sure the money was secondary to the adventure."

"The Biafrans were paying me twenty-five hundred a month to lead a battalion. I wouldn't have touched it for a penny less."

"Biafra, the Congo, Bolivia," Longman said wonderingly. "Bolivia. Isn't that where that Che Guevara was? You weren't on his—"

"No. I was with the other people—the side that killed him."

"I didn't exactly think you were a Commie," Longman said with a nervous laugh.

"I'm whatever I'm paid to be."

"It sure as hell sounds like an exciting and glamorous life," Longman said. "What made you quit it?"

"The market dried up. No job opportunities. And no unemployment insurance."

"How does a guy get into work like that?"

"How did you get into driving a subway train?"

"That's different. I got into it because I had to make a living."

"That's how I got into soldiering. Would you like a beer?"

After that, the walk and the beer became a weekly custom. At first, Longman had been puzzled that someone of Ryder's class bothered with him, but he was shrewd enough to guess the answer. Like himself, like so many people in the city, Ryder was lonely. And so they became companions of a sort, for an hour or two a week. But, after those first revelations, they returned to an impersonal relationship.

Then, one day, it changed.

Once again it started, innocently enough, with a newspaper headline. They read it in a paper lying on the bar when they stopped for their beer.

TWO DIE IN
SUBWAY SHOOTOUT

Two men had tried to stick up a change booth at a subway station in the Bronx. A transit cop who had been on the station had drawn his gun and shot both robbers dead. A picture showed the two dead men sprawled on the station floor and, behind them, the change clerk peering out between the bars of his booth.

"Addicts," Longman said knowledgeably. "Nobody else would go for the money in a change booth. There's not that much involved to warrant the risk."

Ryder nodded, without interest, and there the matter would have ended—as Longman had so often reminded himself—if he had not gone on, if he had not, bartering for Ryder's esteem, taken his fantasy out of its hiding place.

"If I wanted to perpetrate a crime in the subway system," he said, "I sure as hell wouldn't hold up a change booth."

"What would you do?"

"Something sensational, something where there would be a big payoff."

"Like what?" Ryder's interest was nothing more than courteous.

"Like hijack a train," Longman said.

"A *subway* train? What could anyone *do* with a subway train?"

"Hold it for ransom."

"If it was *my* subway train, I would tell you to keep it before I paid to get it back." Ryder was amused.

"Not the train itself," Longman said. "Ransom for the passengers. Hostages."

"Sounds too complicated," Ryder said. "I don't see how it could work."

"Oh, it might work. I've thought about it, from time to time. For laughs—you know?"

It was true, in a way, that he had thought it out for laughs, but the bitter kind. It was his revenge against the system. But it was only a shadow revenge, a game that he played, and it never once entered his mind to be serious about it.

Ryder set his beer glass down and turned on his stool to face Longman squarely. In a firm, level voice, the voice of command, as Longman now understood it to be, he said, "Why did you leave the subway system?"

It wasn't the question Longman expected—if he had expected anything at all except mild interest. It took him unawares, and he found himself blurting out the truth. "I didn't quit. I got the boot."

Ryder kept looking at him, waiting.

"I was innocent," Longman said. "I should have fought it, but—"

"Innocent of what?"

"Of wrongdoing, naturally."

"What kind of wrongdoing? What were you charged with?"

"I wasn't *charged* with *anything*. It was only insinuations, but still they forced me out. You sound like a district attorney."

"Sorry," Ryder said.

"Hell, I don't mind talking about it. They framed me. The beakies had to find a victim—"

"Beakies?"

"Special inspectors. Undercover men. They go around in plain clothes, checking up on trainmen. Sometimes they even dress up like kids, you know, long hair. Spies is what they are."

"They're called beakies because they're nosy?" Ryder smiled.

"That's what everyone thinks. Actually, they got their name—like the bobbies in London—from the first chief of Security Services on the old IRT, way back. His name was H. F. Beakie."

Ryder nodded. "What did they accuse you of doing?"

"Some gang was supposed to be passing dope," Longman said defiantly. "You know, transporting it from downtown to uptown, giving it to a motorman, and then someone picking it up in Harlem, supposed to pick it up, uptown. The beakies tried to pin it on me. But they never had any evidence; they never caught me with any. How could they, if I didn't do it?"

"They tried to frame you?"

"They did frame me, the bastards."

"But you were innocent."

"Sure I was innocent. Do you think I would do something like that? You know me."

"Yes," Ryder said. "I know you."

KOMO MOBUTU

Up to the point where he became enraged by the two black boys, Komo Mobutu had kept his cool. The event was no place, not his business *at*-tall. Somebody could rip off the subway twice a day, and he wouldn't blink an eye. If it didn't have nothing to do with the revolutionary aspirations of the oppressed black people, it didn't exist, it wasn't *here*.

It gave him a sense of perverse pleasure to be involved—not that he was really *in*volved, more like *ex*volved—because he rode the subways. He wasn't no taxi-limousine-penthouse-attaché-case-747-first-class-ticket-free-cocktails-from-ofay-stewardesses type like that international clique of so-called Brothers on the coast and in Paris and Algeria. He was a righteous *working* revolutionary, and even if he had the bread, he would still ride the people's *con*veyance, and, for long-distance, he would still fly Greyhound.

Ordinarily—when some big gray mothers weren't ripping it off with armament that made his mouth water—he almost enjoyed the subway because he had a way of passing the time. A pastime, you could say, not a wastetime but a powertime. He would pick out a gray peeg, fix his righteous eye on the sumbitch and just stare him out of sight. More often than not, the sumbitch got so uptight that he changed his seat or went into another car. Some of them even got so nervous and sweaty that they got off the train before their station. All he did was stare, but they read in his eyeballs the tre-*menjous* anger of a people at long last raising up against 300 years of repression and genocide. There wasn't one single whitey who didn't dig that message in his unblinking maroon eyes and didn't fade out of the challenge. He had never lost one yet. He *hyp*matize the sumbitches! If *every* Brother did the eye thing, they could generate enough power to paralyze the whole peeg population.

Mobutu sat with a very erect back in his seat, facing a fancy white fox in an Anzac hat, looking straight through the whore. When the old dude sitting next to him had spoken up he didn't even turn his head. Screw it all, it wasn't *ger*mane. But now, from the corner of his eye, he dug the two black boys sitting across the aisle. They were both very dark, good African types, maybe seventeen or eighteen. Delivery boys, serving the master, carrying the white man's packages for him. What burned his ass most was what they were doing with their eyes. Big soft brown eyes, and they were rolling them around like marbles in the whites, making them a kind of a grin, wagging their goddamn tail so the man wouldn't get mad and shoot a bullet up their ass.

Almost before he knew that he was doing it, he was shouting across the aisle in a fury. "Goddamn you, you two niggers, get your goddamn eyes straight, you hear?" He glared at them, and they looked back at him, startled. "You stupid niggers, you too *young* to be Tomming. Get your eyes straight and look the man in the fucking eye!"

Every eye in the car was on him, and as he stared at one after the other of them, he lingered on the well-dressed *Nee-gro* with the attaché case. His face was expressionless, detached. A white nigger, long lost to the cause, and not worth the bother. But the two boys. . . . It might be worth putting on a little demonstration for them.

Turning to face the man with the gun but addressing the boys, he said, "You don't have no cause to be scared of *no* white motherfucker, Brothers. Someday soon we are going to take that gun away and ram it down his peeg throat!"

The man with the gun, stolid, even bored, said, "Shut up your goddamn mouth."

"I don't take orders from no white motherfucker peeg!"

The man made a gesture with his gun. "Come over here to me, loudmouth."

"You think I'm afraid of you, peeg?" Mobutu got to his feet. His legs were shaky, not with fear but in anger.

"I just want you over here," the man said. "Come on over."

He walked to the center of the car and stood before the man, his back very straight, his hands clenched into fists at his sides.

"Go do it," he said. "Go shoot me. But I warn you, there are many more like me, thousands and thousands, and we promise to cut your peeg throat—"

Effortlessly, without passion, the man brought the gun across his body, and smashed it on a diagonal across Mobutu's left temple. Mobutu felt the impact—a stunning pain, a red rain in his eyes—and he reeled backward, thumping to the floor in a sitting position.

"Go sit down, and never open your mouth no more."

Mobutu heard the man's voice dimly. He touched his face and realized that blood was dripping down into his eye socket from a mashed eyebrow. He stood up, then fell back into his seat beside the old man. The old man put out a hand to steady him. He shook it off. The car was hushed.

"He asked for it," the man who had hit him said. "Don't nobody else ask for it."

Mobutu took out his handkerchief and pressed it to his forehead. Through his right eye he focused on the black messenger boys. Their eyes were still bugged, their lips pendulous. Sheet, Mobutu thought, I took a blow for nothing. They will never be nothing but fucking field hands.

Everyone in the car was studiously avoiding looking at him, even those who might ordinarily be fascinated by the sight of blood.

SIX

FRANK CORRELL

The headquarters of the Metropolitan Transportation Authority, commonly called the Transit Authority, is located in a large granite-faced building at 370 Jay Street in what is known as "downtown Brooklyn." 370 Jay is a comparatively new and modern structure surrounded by many older, darker-toned, more graceful and architecturally complicated buildings that constitute the heart of Kings County's official center: Borough Hall, courthouses, administrative bureaus. Although this area of Brooklyn is not just another Brooklyn joke, nevertheless it is classed as a province of the island across the nearby river, and suffers loss of stature thereby.

The administrative functions of the Transit Authority are spread throughout 370 Jay in offices ranging in style from styleless, to Civil-Service-utilitarian, to the dignified thirteenth-floor suite of the top executives of the authority, which is approached through a large, discreetly lighted anteroom guarded casually by a transit patrolman.

If space is at a premium in many of the offices in the building—notably, just below, on the second floor, in the cramped quarters of the TA Police Nerve Center—it is prodigally cheap in the third-floor area occupied by the Trainmasters' Office, better known as the Command Center. Three divisional units are scattered widely, even wastefully, through an enormous, block-long, high-ceilinged area with so much space that the arrangement seems provisional. Each of the three divisions—A Division, or IRT; B Division, or BMT; and B-1 Division, or IND—occupies its own enclave at widely separated intervals. The most active and visible members of a divisional group are the desk trainmaster and his dispatchers.

IRT, the oldest but smallest division, has four dispatchers assisting the desk trainmaster. They sit at steel desks with electric consoles through which they can speak to every motorman in their section by two-way radio. Each division is split into sections along geographical lines; on the IRT, for example, into East Side, West Side, aboveground tracks in the Bronx, and so forth. The consoles on the dispatchers' desks are similar to those in the Tower Rooms, with the major exception that the Tower consoles are unable to communicate directly with the motorman's cab.

Each call the dispatchers receive from a train, or initiate themselves, is recorded in a log: identification number of the train, nature of the call; action taken. A typical call to Command Center might involve a motorman reporting a fire under a platform at a given station. After ascertaining the extent and seriousness of the fire, the dispatcher proceeds to advise the motorman on whether or not to proceed, to stand by or to empty his train of passengers ("dump his load"). He then gets in touch with the appropriate department: Maintenance (known as car knockers), Tower, Power Central (cut or restore power, as the case might be), the Transit Police—whichever one or combination of these is indicated.

The dispatchers report to the desk trainmaster, who in turn is subordinate to a supervisor, who does not concern himself with the minute-to-minute operation of the division. The desk trainmaster's console allows him to reach the motormen in all sections, which is to say, every motorman in the division. The desk trainmaster is the boss; he is responsible for keeping the trains running smoothly and on time. He earns his pay on any day, but particularly when there is an emergency that threatens the functioning of the division. Then his job is to work out a flex, an emergency schedule which will keep the trains running: switching locals to express tracks and vice versa, moving trains from the East Side line to the West, ordering motormen to dump their load or travel light—any of a variety of intricate improvisations designed to make a schedule flexible, to maintain service in the face even of major catastrophes like a derailed train or a collision. Such things have been known to happen on the best run of railroads.

An adjunct of the Command Center is the Communications Desk, which announces schedule changes and emergencies through the station PA systems, to keep passengers advised. The messages are recorded by the Communications Desk on tape and cassette and relayed to the stations. When there are major delays or emergencies, the desk gets in touch with the media—newspapers, radio, and television—and keeps them abreast of developments.

Frank Correll knew all of this, as well as he knew himself, though he couldn't have described it, or thought it necessary to, any more than he could have described his body. If you asked him how he lifted his arm, he would scowl and say, "You just lift it," meaning there are some things you don't have to think about. That was precisely how he regarded the Command Center and his vital role in the operation of A Division as one of three desk trainmasters who functioned in three shifts around the clock.

Although a desk trainmaster doesn't monitor every call that comes in to his dispatchers, nevertheless he must possess a sort of psychic divining rod that helps him smell out serious trouble before the dispatcher apprizes him of it. Frank Correll's sixth sense had cued him in to awareness that there was a bad problem with Pelham One Two Three. After telling Grand Central Tower to get the lead out, he took over from the dispatcher, trying to raise the train from his own console, riding the edge of his chair, his head forward of his body, like a snake in striking position, aimed at the boom mike that curled out of the console.

But even he was not prepared for the nature of the problem when Pelham One Two Three at last came through, and he lapsed into a short but uncharacteristic silence. Then he let out a roar, and all over the vast area of the Command Center men broke into grins. Even among desk trainmasters—who are traditionally the glamorous, hard-bitten, mercurial stars of the Transit Authority and who act their role to the hilt—Frank Correll was famous. Thin, wiry, impatient, loudmouthed, charged with a superfluity of energy, he was perfectly cast for the part. And so nobody, hearing his outburst, had reason to suspect anything out of the ordinary.

Correll calmed down or, at least, banked the fires of his temper and said quietly, or what passed for quietly with him, "I heard what you said. What do you mean *taken the train*? Explain. No. Wait a second. Also, you cut the power. Why did you cut the power, and why haven't you reported the reason to Power Central? Come in, and you better make it good."

"Do you have a pencil, Desk Trainmaster?"

"What kind of shithead question is that? Is this the motorman?"

"It's not the motorman. Listen to me carefully. Pay attention. Do you have a pencil?"

"Who the hell *is* this? Are you authorized to be in the motorman's cab? Identify yourself."

"Listen to me, Desk Trainmaster, I don't want to repeat myself. Listen. Your train has been taken by a group of heavily armed men. The power has been cut, as you know. So has the train. We are in the first car of the train, and we are holding sixteen passengers and the motorman hostage. We will not hesitate to kill all of them if it becomes necessary. We're desperate men, Desk Trainmaster. Over."

Correll cut out and hit his six button, which, among other things, automatically cut him in to the Transit Police. His hands were shaking with anger.

CLIVE PRESCOTT

One of the MTA chairman's secretaries phoned downstairs to Lieutenant Clive Prescott to inform him that the distinguished visitors from Boston, back from their lunch with the chairman, were at this moment on the elevator, descending from the thirteenth floor to the second, and please to remember that they were *personal* friends of the chairman and therefore were to receive the highest order of preferential treatment.

"I'll have the red carpet out as soon as I finish vacuuming it," Lieutenant Prescott said. He hung up and went out to the information desk guarding the approaches to Transit Police Headquarters—or the Nerve Center, as the cops themselves liked to call it—and waited for the elevator to discharge its precious cargo.

It pleased him perversely, watching their reaction as he stepped forward to greet them, that they were not quite able to conceal their surprise at his being something different from what they had expected—a *shade* different, he thought with delicate irony. But they recovered smoothly (he was forced to admit) and shook his hand without any sign of distaste or restraint. After all, they overlooked no bets, and—who could tell?—someday he might move to Boston, where a black man's vote, however regretful the fact, counted exactly as much in the ballot box as anyone else's.

They were politicians, and Irish—and what else was new?—one guarded, one hearty. Their names were Maloney (hearty) and Casey (guarded). Their almost identical sharp blue eyes took in, not entirely without prejudice, Lieutenant Prescott's handsome sharkskin suit (slight suppression, high center vent), boldly striped red-white-black shirt, Countess Mara tie, tapered Italian shoes (fifty-five dollars—on sale); and their little snub noses inhaled the fragrance of Canöe. Their handshake was at the same time crisp and warm—the grip of men who shook hands as a way of life.

"We're a bit crowded here, you'll find. . . ." But Prescott let the complaint drop. They would be as bored hearing it as he would be making it. More briskly, he said, "The brass has its offices through there. . . ." A vague gesture. "That one is Chief Costello's. . . ." The visitors exchanged a swift glance that Prescott read as: Well, praise God for Costello, an honest Irish name; it would be too much if the top man also turned out to be colored. "This way, please, gentlemen."

It was protocol to go first to Operations, where visitors signed the logbook, but Prescott decided to reverse the order. With a little luck, what had been a quiet morning in Operations might turn exciting. Yesterday there had been a bomb scare on an IND station (it had turned out to be a false alarm), and Operations had been steaming with calls to and from patrolmen searching the station and tracks. It would have made a good show for the visitors. He steered them away from Operations toward Teletype and the Roll Call Unit.

Relaxed, a casual lecturer to an elite class of two, Prescott stood in the teletype area and explained the clattering machines. "We're wired up with the New York Police Department going and coming. We get all their calls on teletype, and they get ours. Two separate machines handle MABSTOA—the city-owned bus lines—and the Service Division."

The visitors looked sleepy. Prescott didn't blame them. An uninterested speaker makes for an uninterested listener. He had done this bit so many times that it sickened him. Being a desk cop, with too many public relations functions, was like being no cop at all. But he was being paid for it. And so, he thought with an inward sigh, let's trot out the gee whiz facts.

"Perhaps you'd like to have some background on the department." He paused, and in the silence the NYPD teletype clicked steadily and placidly. "As you may know, the strength of the TA police force is approximately thirty-two hundred men, or slightly more than ten percent of the strength of the NYPD. That may seem small, but actually we rank among the first twenty-five police forces in the entire country. Our beat is a vast one—two hundred and thirty-seven miles of track, four hundred and seventy-six stations, about sixty percent of it underground. You look surprised?"

Neither man had looked the least bit surprised, but now, to oblige, they contrived to do so.

"Actually," Prescott said, "there are two hundred sixty-five underground stations and one hundred seventy-three elevated. . . ."

He paused, and Maloney came up with a surprise of his

own. In a sharp voice he said, "That only adds up to four hundred thirty-eight. You said there were four hundred seventy-six."

Prescott smiled indulgently, as at an apt pupil. "And, as I was about to say, there are thirty-eight stations that are open cut, embankment and surface. I don't want to inundate you with facts . . ." But that was exactly what he did want to do, stifle them with facts, bore them as much as he himself was bored. "You may be interested to know that the highest station on the railroad is Smith-Ninth Street in Brooklyn, eighty-seven and a half feet from the street to the base of the track. On the other hand, the deepest underground station is One Hundred and Ninety-first Street at St. Nicholas Avenue, one hundred eighty feet below the street surface at track level."

Maloney said, "You don't say." Casey covered a yawn.

"Grand Central," Prescott said blandly, "is the busiest station, passenger-wise, on the entire road, clocking over forty million fares a year. The busiest station train-wise is West Fourth Street on the IND Line—a hundred trains an hour in each direction during the peak load period."

Maloney said again, "You don't say." Casey was still yawning.

Prescott thought vindictively: If he doesn't shut his mouth, I'm going to tell them how many escalators there are. "There are seven thousand cars in service. Oh, yes, there are ninety-nine escalators. Well, all of that, including stairways, mezzanines, and so forth, all of that must be covered with thirty-two hundred cops, twenty-four hours a day. As you probably know, there's a cop on every station and train in the system between the hours of eight at night and four in the morning. Since we instituted this watch, we've cut crime about sixty percent."

Casey stopped yawning and said defensively, "We have our share of crime in the Boston subway, too."

"Not to compare with yours, though," Maloney said graciously.

"Thank you," Prescott said. "Like the city police, we deal with robbery, assault, many kinds of violence, drunkenness, accidents, illness, abusiveness, vandalism, purse snatching, pickpockets, molesters, rowdy youths—in fact, every conceivable kind of crime and disorder. And, if I may say so, we deal with it competently. We carry firearms, of course—off duty as well as on. . . ."

Casey was launching another yawn, and Maloney's gaze was wandering to the clacking NYPD teletype.

Prescott took his cue from Maloney. He herded his visitors over to the machine. "This gives us a complete record of every single call that goes through the NYPD."

Maloney scanned the moving sheet of paper. "There's nothing but stolen cars." He took another look. "Nineteen fifty Oldsmobile. Who would want to steal a nineteen fifty Oldsmobile?"

Prescott decided to skip Roll Call Unit. "And now," he said, "we'll go to Operations, which is really the heart of the Nerve Center."

The heart was beating very languidly, Prescott observed as they entered the large room, cut up by glass dividers into a maze of squares and rectangles. There was some activity, but it was routine. Prescott leaned against the glass wall that separated Operations from Records and allowed the visitors to take in the scene. Naturally enough, they zeroed in on the huge police map covering the far wall.

"We call that the Status Board," Prescott said. "It pinpoints the disposition of all the men in the field. The red lights represent the IRT cops, and the yellow are for the BMT and IND. Operations and the men patrolling are in constant contact with each other. A lot of the patrolmen are equipped with two-way radios, which cost eight hundred dollars each, and all the others report in by phone regularly once each hour. More often, if they have any problem."

"It's pretty," Maloney said. "All those colors."

Maloney had the eye of a poet. The long board was divided into pastel shadings of yellow, red, orange, blue, green, delineating the various areas in the system, and the lights, changing and flickering to show the shifting positions of the patrolmen, added their own touch of color. All in all, Prescott admitted it did make a pretty constellation.

Garber was the operations lieutenant and, being the key man in the setup, acted like the key man in the setup. Prescott introduced Maloney and Casey, and Garber, swarthy, dark-bearded, shook hands impatiently and brusquely ordered them to sign the register.

Prescott said, "These gentlemen are friends of the chairman. *Dear* friends."

Garber grunted. He wasn't giving an inch, Prescott thought. Busy, harried, important cop, the public safety rested squarely on his shoulders, and he didn't care if the visitors were friends of Jesus H. Christ himself. Oh, well.

Prescott said to the visitors, "Please step over here, gentlemen." They followed him obediently, but even Maloney was showing signs of wanting to yawn, and both pairs of guileful blue eyes looked fatigued. "These are the assignment desks, one for each of the three subway divisions. Each is in charge of a sergeant, assisted by a patrolman and a radio operator. You'll notice that their consoles are very similar to those you saw in the Command Center. When a call comes in, reporting an incident, the deskman scribbles a message on an electrowriter, which registers on the radio man's desk. He in turn calls the patrolman in the field and directs him to proceed to where the incident is taking place. This is a very busy section, ah, usually."

He had never seen it deader. Two of the sergeants were leaning on their elbows and smoking; a couple of the radio operators were chatting with each other.

"I wish you could have been here yesterday," Prescott said. "We had a bomb scare, and we were really humming."

The IND sergeant, who had been listening, said helpfully, "A week ago, in a single half hour, we had three unrelated knife fights."

"It usually hums," Prescott said.

"Two dead, three wounded, one critical. The critical is still on the danger list, so we may eventually have a third dead."

"Over there," Prescott said, "behind the glass partition, we have Records. Keeps a record of all the activities of the day—summonses, arrests, injuries, all incidents. They maintain an arrest book, which is similar to the police rap sheet—"

Behind him, he heard Garber let out a shout, slam his phone down, and yell, "Roberts, wake up. Some gang has hijacked a train on A Division. They say they're armed with automatic weapons. Bring in all units on Lexington Avenue line in vicinity of Twenty-eighth Street. . . ."

"Hijacked a subway train?" It was Casey's voice, suddenly awake, halfway between astonishment and laughter. "What the fuck would anybody want to hijack a subway train for?"

"Where'd the information come from?" Prescott said to Garber.

"Desk trainmaster. He's talking to the hijackers in the cab of the train."

"Gentlemen," Prescott said to the visitors, "I believe the chairman is expecting you."

He hustled them out of the anteroom and pressed the elevator button. As soon as the car arrived and he had put them in it and sent them on their way to the thirteenth floor, he ran for the exit and bounded up the steps to Command Center on the floor above.

RYDER

Waiting in the cab for the desk trainmaster to return to the radio, Ryder acknowledged that the greatest hazard of the whole operation—barring uncertainty about whether or not the other side would act rationally—lay in the fact that he would be spending a great deal of time in the cab, which meant that he would not be in personal command of his force for long periods at a stretch.

It was something less than an ideal army. Longman a coward, Welcome undisciplined, Steever steady but in need of guidance. Two whose courage he could count on (Steever and Welcome), one for intelligence (Longman), one for discipline (Steever, and add Longman unless he collapsed under pressure). It all left a good deal to be desired, but so had all his commands in the past. The strangest of all were a company of Congolese. Utterly without fear, more than willing to die. But they lacked a rationale. You lived or you died, yes, but you didn't commit suicide. The Congolese struck him as people who were willing to die for the sheer pleasure or excitement of it. Arabs were wild, too, but they had a degree of imagination, and they knew—or thought they did—the stakes they were dying for. The perfect soldier, it occurred to him, would be a combination of Longman's intelligence, Steever's discipline, and Welcome's dash.

So—depending on how you did your arithmetic—his force consisted either of three flawed soldiers or one complete one.

"Pelham One Two Three. Come in, Pelham One Two Three."

Ryder pressed the transmit button. "Are you ready with a pencil, Desk Trainmaster?"

"A nice sharp pencil. You going to dictate?"

"I want you to write down exactly what I tell you. *Exactly*. Do you read me?"

"I read you, you crazy bastard. You're off your goddamn rocker, pulling something like this."

Ryder said, "I'm about to give you seven items. The first three are informational; the remainder are specific instructions. They're quite brief. Take them down precisely as I give them to you. Point One: Pelham One Two Three is completely in our control. We own it. Have you got that?"

"What are you people, nig—colored guys? Panthers?"

"Point Two, Desk Trainmaster. We are heavily armed with fully automatic weapons. Check me."

"I check you, you madman. You can't get away with this shit."

"Save the extraneous comment. Point Three: We are serious, desperate men, and we have no scruples about killing. Don't take us lightly. Check me."

"Do you know you're screwing up the whole goddamn East Side line?"

"Check me."

"Go ahead. Let's hear the rest of this crap."

"Point Four: You will not attempt to restore power until we instruct you to."

"Oh, beautiful!"

"Check me, Desk Trainmaster."

"Up your black ass!"

"If you restore the power," Ryder said, "we'll shoot one of the passengers. And we'll continue to shoot one every minute until the power is pulled again."

"Shithead, the cops are going to be all over you."

"Point Five," Ryder said. "If anyone attempts to interfere—police, TA personnel, anyone—we'll kill the passengers. Do you read me?"

"You are something *else*."

"Point Six: You will contact the mayor at once. Inform him that we demand a million dollars for the release of the car and the passengers. Check me."

"Keep dreaming, criminal."

"Point Seven. The time is now two thirteen. The money must be in our hands in one hour. The clock is running as of now. The money will be in our hands no later than three thirteen. If it isn't, thereafter for every minute past the deadline we'll kill one hostage. Have you got that, Desk Trainmaster?"

"I got it all, gangster. But if you expect me to do anything about it, you're even crazier than I thought."

You devised a strategy based on the logical reaction of the other side, Ryder thought, or it was worthless. But rank stupidity could wreck you. "Listen to me, Desk Trainmaster. I want you to patch me in to the Transit Police. I repeat: Patch me in to the police."

"Here's one now, gangster. A cop. Have a good time."

Ryder waited, and a new voice came on, slightly out of breath. "What's this all about?"

"Identify yourself," Ryder said.

"Lieutenant Prescott, Transit Police. Identify *your*-self."

"I'm the man who stole your train, Lieutenant. Ask the desk trainmaster to let you see his notes. Don't be too long about it."

Waiting, Ryder could hear the lieutenant's breathing. Then: "Prescott to Pelham One Two Three. I read it. You're crazy."

"Very well, I'm crazy. Does that give you comfort? Is it a reason for not taking me seriously?"

"Look," Prescott said. "I take you seriously. But there's no way you can get away with it. You're underground; you're in a tunnel."

"Lieutenant, look at the seventh point. At precisely three thirteen we'll begin executing the passengers, one each minute. I suggest that you contact the mayor at once."

"I'm a Transit Police lieutenant. How do I go about getting to the mayor?"

"That's your problem, Lieutenant."

"Okay. I'll try. Don't hurt anybody."

"Report to me immediately for further instructions after you've contacted the mayor. Over and out."

SEVEN

240 CENTRE STREET

Although the Transit Police have a direct line to Police Headquarters, that old and forbidding building at 240 Centre Street, the call advising of the hijacking of Pelham One Two Three was fed into the 911 line, the emergency system designed to speed up police response to exigent calls. In doing this, the operator who took the call was not expressing disdain for a secondary police force or being evenhandedly democratic, but merely acting on procedure in the interest of efficiency and full employment of the headquarters computer.

The message containing such information as time of call, location of incident, nature of emergency, was typed into the computer, which performed some twenty-five to thirty operations in three seconds, and delivered a readout to the radio room.

Granted that stealing a subway train wasn't an everyday occurrence, nevertheless the dispatcher who handled the call didn't get overly excited about it. When you dealt with riots, mass murders, catastrophes of every conceivable nature, the alleged theft of a subway train, while it had an intriguingly kinky sound, was thus far nothing to write home about. The dispatcher followed routine procedure.

The readout informed him which of the dozen or so sector cars patrolling in each of the bordering precincts, the 13th and 14th, were available. He then radioed the designated cars, 13 Boy and 14 David, and instructed them to check out the incident and report back at once. Depending on the report and its judgment of the seriousness of the incident, Planning would order up an appropriate force to cope with the situation, through a rising scale of signals: for example, a Signal 1041 (a sergeant and ten men), 1042 (sergeant and twenty men), 1047 (eight sergeants and forty patrolmen), and including higher ranks as well.

In less than two minutes, one of the sector cars reported. "Fourteen David to Central. K."

"Go ahead," the dispatcher said. "K."

But while the dispatcher was receiving 14 David's report from the scene, another report was being transmitted on an elevated level. Lieutenant Prescott had contacted Chief Costello of the Transit Police, who had in turn phoned the chief inspector of the NYPD, with whom he was personally acquainted. The chief inspector, who was practically out of the door of his office on his way to catch a plane for a vital conference in Washington at the offices of the Justice Department, turned the matter over immediately to

Planning, ordering a major mobilization, which would involve manpower from other boroughs, mainly Brooklyn and the Bronx. Then, regretfully, he left for the airport.

Patrol cars from the 13th and 14th precincts converged on the affected area to control traffic and open up passage for all arriving police units, which would be rushing to the site by way of predetermined access routes. Such routes are available to expedite delivery of men and vehicles to every part of the city.

The Tactical Police Force was ordered out to handle the inevitable crowds.

A police helicopter was ordered into the air.

Special equipment was issued to members of the Special Operations Division: machine guns, submachine guns, shotguns, tear gas, rifles equipped with scopes for sniper use, bulletproof vests, searchlights, bullhorns. Much of the ammunition would be .22 caliber, to minimize the danger of ricochet casualties among police and bystanders.

A number of the division's "big trucks" (the size of a small truck) and "small cars" (the size of a large station wagon) sped to the scene. These vehicles are an awesome arsenal of weapons, rescue equipment, and specialized tools and instruments. Both carry keys for the opening of subway emergency exit grates, and the big trucks carry generators.

With the possible exception of a limited number of plainclothes detectives who would be scattered inconspicuously on the scene, all the forces would be uniformed. In large and necessarily confused operations, detectives are used sparsely and kept safely in the background, since in the heat of action, and especially if they draw a gun, they may be mistaken for criminals.

The designated officer in overall charge of the operation was the borough commander. His rank is assistant chief inspector, and his command, known as Manhattan South, encompasses the entire area south of Fifty-ninth Street to the Battery. His headquarters, the borough office, is located in the Police Academy on East Twenty-first Street, little more than a brisk ten-minute walk to the scene of the incident. However, he did not walk. He rode to the scene in an unmarked four-door chauffeur-driven car.

In all, at the height of the operation, more than 700 police personnel would be involved.

WELCOME

With the Thompson hanging down along his right leg, Joe Welcome looked out the window of the rear door. The tunnel was dark and shadowy, with an abandoned look. It was a little spooky, reminding him of a carnival he had been at once, late at night, after everything was shut down. The stillness bugged him. He would have appreciated seeing a piece of paper floating around or even one of those rats that Longman claimed lived in the tunnels. If he saw a rat, he might pop it. At least it would be action.

He was a sentry with nothing to watch, and he was getting itchy. When they were planning the trick and Ryder was spelling out the assignments, he made it sound important: "sole responsibility for securing our rear." But it turned out to be dullsville. Not that it was so glamorous up front, either—guarding a bunch of scared-shitless squares—but at least Steever had had a little fun beating on the smartass spade's head.

Since then, the passengers were little angels, hardly even moving. Longman and Steever didn't have anything to do except stand there. He would like it better if the passengers woke up and tried to pull something. Not that they had a chance. They would be chopped meat before they got their ass six inches off the seat, Steever would see to that. Maybe Longman would zap them, and maybe not. Longman was supposed to be a brain, but he was a creep, and he was yellow. Steever had guts, but he had shit where his brains belonged.

He turned his eyes to the chick in the boots and the funny hat. She looked like talent. Her legs were crossed, one white boot swinging. He followed the leg up to the exposed thigh, smooth and round, in pink panty hose which, if you squinted your eyes a little, looked like naked flesh. And maybe she didn't know it? He sent his mind traveling the rest of the way up the route, between the lines of the crossed legs, right home to where it all lived— a fine black bush, and a slit like a mouth standing up on one end. If there was an opening, before they got through the job, he would ball that juicy bitch. Joey, you're one crazy ginney!

Crazy. Well, he had heard it so many times, maybe it was true. But what was so wrong with crazy? He lived the way he wanted to, and he got his kicks. Crazy? Okay. Who else would be thinking about gash during a million-dollar heist? In the next hour they could all wind up dead. So what would a sane guy want his last thoughts to be about if not gash—getting ahead in the world?

He turned back to the tunnel. Nothing. A few green signals on the uptown side, some blue lights . . . dullsville. What was taking Ryder so long? Himself, he liked fast action; you go in and you get out, no waiting around and no complications.

Ryder. He wasn't wild about Ryder, but you had to give him two things: He was a good organizer, and he had guts, for sure. But he was a cold-ass stud. Even in the Organization, where they also had this thing about discipline, not to mention that old-country shit of *rispetto*, respect, at least they weren't cold-ass. They were wops, and you always knew what was on a wop's mind. When a wop was pissed off, he let you know it. You didn't have to have any kind of a dream book to interpret screaming Sicilian curses. Ryder never raided his voice.

Not that he liked wops that much either, or he wouldn't have changed his name. He remembered the judge asking him if he knew that Joseph Welcome was an exact translation of Giuseppe Benvenuto. He needed some big Yid to bring that up. People had been kidding him about it practically since the day he was born. The only one who had ever done it in a nice way was Miss Linscomb, back in high school, and then later the bitch had turned on him.

Miss Linscomb, Latin I, who had given him a zero on his report card. A real gasser—Giuseppe Benvenuto, with his Latin heritage, getting the all-time low grade for Latin in the school's history, a zero, a goose egg. But what nobody ever knew was why she did it. She had kept him after class one afternoon, and he began to get ideas. She let him put his hand on her tit and kissed him with her tongue out, but when he went ape and unzipped himself and tried to put his pecker in her hand, she had turned chicken. *Giuseppe! How dare you! Clothe yourself at once,* and she had turned her back to him. But he was wild. He locked his arms around her waist and rammed himself up against her ass. She started to struggle, but all that did, her tight little ass grinding against him, was to make him come in thirty seconds flat. All over the back of her dress!

She wasn't able to report him without a lot of explaining, so she took her revenge with the zero in Latin. He was surprised to see how well he could recall her: a plain pale Protestant broad with little peaky tits and terrific legs and that twitchy tail. It suddenly occurred to him, for the first time, that maybe she didn't *have* to rotate her ass like that, that she could have broken away from him without too much trouble. Maybe the only reason she got mad at him and pinned the zero on him was because he came all over her dress?

Well, it was too late to get smart. No instant replays.

The boys in the Organization picked up on his name, they had a weakness for those funny nicknames, and so, when he had made his one appearance in the public press— on an assault rap that was dropped for lack of evidence— the newspapers wrote him up as Giuseppe (Joey Welcome) Benvenuto. That was a few weeks before he pulled the stunt that got him fired. The Organization had ordered him to mess up a couple of guys, but instead he offed them. What the hell was the difference—he just wanted to make his bones in a hurry, was all. But they gave him a beautiful reaming out. Not that they gave a shit about the guys he killed, but he had disobeyed orders. Discipline. Instead of admitting he was wrong and promising to be a good boy, he gave them a lot of guff, and next thing he knew he was out on his ass. Fired by the Mafia!

They never laid a hand on him, so maybe everything you heard about nobody ever leaving the Organization unless it was feet first was a lot of crap. But he had been worried about it, and maybe if it wasn't for his uncle, his Zio Jimmy, who was a big *capo*, maybe something *would* have been done to him. Well, screw all the ginneys. He didn't need them. He had been making a living on his own without having to soil his hands with work, and if this deal came off he would have a hundred thousand out of it, and that was more money than a lot of ginzos in the Organization made in ten years, and forget the crap you read in the papers.

His eyes were tearing from all this staring into the tunnel. He dabbed at them with the nylon, then returned to his scrutiny of the deserted track. But it wasn't deserted. In the distance—he squinted his eyes to sharpen his vision—in the distance, someone was walking the roadbed, coming straight on.

ANITA LEMOYNE

The machine guns were freaky, but Anita Lemoyne wasn't frightened by them. Nobody was going to hurt her; the others, maybe, like the bigmouthed spade, but not her. Now and then she met a man she couldn't turn on, but not every day. Even if a man didn't like her particularly, he was sold out by that ounce or two of flesh he wore between his legs. Tough as these gunmen might be, they weren't about to destroy a commodity whose value they appreciated, if only objectively. So she wasn't scared, just annoyed, because if this crazy thing didn't wind itself up pretty soon, it was going to cost her money.

She sat calmly—she knew how to keep a poker face, just as she knew how not to—but she was beginning to fidget. She couldn't afford to be hung up in a goddamn subway train three lousy stops away from her destination, hijack or no hijack. The John she was on her way to see was a hundred-and-a-half trick, and he didn't like people being late. She had once heard him ream out a girl, his pursy little child's mouth twisting like a worm as he told her, "If we're able to split a second in our business, I see no reason why a whore should be fifteen minutes late." And he had turned the girl out and never used her again.

His business was television, and he was some kind of heavy hot dog in the news end of it. Producer or director or what-all. The indispensable man, to hear him tell it. Maybe he was. At least he lived like it—pad at Number One Fifth, summer house in Southampton, boat, cars and the rest of it. He had a few kinky ideas about sex, but who didn't? And who was she to question anybody's preferences? Short of being hurt, which she wouldn't stand for, there was no dopey turn she wouldn't try. The television character liked two girls at a time—which was pretty commonplace—and he had worked out a pretty weird series of combinations and permutations, as he called it. Fine with her, though she had been getting the feeling lately, from the things he liked best, that he was an unconscious homo and that if he ever got on to himself, he would make the girls disappear and buy himself a nice young boy.

But she wasn't about to tell him so, not as long as the yard-and-a-halves kept rolling in. Which they wouldn't be doing much longer if she wasn't to hell out of this mess and on her way to the Astor Place station before much more time went by. It wasn't only that she would blow a fee. Prissy mouth wouldn't take it into consideration that she was late because some goons were pointing tommy guns at her. He'd boot her out on her ass just the same and probably tell her that even if they were held up at howitzer point at the network, they would still have split-second timing.

Her foot, which up to now hadn't stopped kicking to the rhythm of her impatience, suddenly froze. Could she con one of those four bastards into letting her go? Crazy— but how could you tell if you didn't try? Hadn't the one at the rear been eyeballing her ever since she got on the train? And was still doing it, from fifty or sixty feet away? She could recall what he looked like before he put on the mask: a ginzo, a Latin lover, pretty in the face. She knew the type—a creep, but cunt crazy. Okay—but how was she supposed to operate when he was half a mile away. One of the other three? The tall one, the leader, was out of sight in the motorman's cab. The heavyset one or the nervous one? Maybe, though neither of them had given her a decent look so far. Still, she hadn't really been working at it; she hadn't turned it all on yet.

The creep suddenly began to shout. He had the rear door open, with the machine gun stuck through it, and he was beating his gums at a high-decibel level out into the tunnel.

LONGMAN

First blood.

That was the traditional railroad term describing the first time an engineer killed someone on the tracks, and Longman had applied it, somewhat erroneously, he realized, to Steever hitting the loudmouthed spade with his gun. He avoided looking at the victim, sitting there and dabbing at his face with a bloody handkerchief, but out of sight was not quite out of mind, and his legs were still a little shaky. Steever's blow, so calmly delivered, tuned up his sense of disbelief again. How, if he had been in his right mind, how could Ryder ever have talked him into it? How could he have let Ryder hypnotize him out of his living mind?

But was that what really happened? Had he meekly followed Ryder against his own will? Standing here now at the front of the car, with the submachine gun an alien weight in numb hands, sweating lightly but steadily under his mask, he admitted that he had not been so passive as he wanted to believe. In fact, he had cooperated eagerly. And he had been conning himself when he pretended that it was all fun and games, a running gag to divert them as they drank their weekly beer after the unemployment office. The truth was that Ryder had tacitly conceded that the hijack was conceivable; what remained was whether or not it was workable. Thus, Ryder's probings, his goadings, were entirely serious, leading up to a decision for or against commitment, and Longman knew it. Why, then, had he gone the route? Well, for one thing, Ryder had excited him and stimulated his imagination. But beyond that, he wanted to earn Ryder's regard, it was important to appear competent and intelligent and even courageous in Ryder's eyes. Finally, as he had once rationalized it, Ryder was a natural leader, and he himself was a natural follower, perhaps even a hero worshiper.

He recalled his surprise, the week following the first mention of the subject, when Ryder broached it directly.

"I've been thinking about the subway hijack. It seems preposterous."

"Not at all," Longman said, and didn't realize until much later that he had risen to Ryder's bait. "It could really be pulled off."

Ryder began to ask questions, and presently Longman began to see the vagueness of the plan he had worked out. Ryder put his finger on the imperfections with uncanny skill, and Longman, challenged and wanting to prove himself to Ryder, found himself sweating out the answers. For example, Ryder had pointed out that a force of approximately thirty men would be required to keep the passengers in all ten cars under control. Longman was stunned to realize how impractical he had been about such a basic point, but he had almost immediately come up with a solution—cut the first car out of the train. Ryder had nodded and said, "Yes, a dozen hostages give you as much leverage as a hundred." But he was not always so successful.

He spent the next week questioning details and working

out solutions, and at their next meeting he trotted out his homework without waiting to be asked. Ryder attacked again, probing for weaknesses, forcing him to defend himself. Ryder made no effort to help solve problems or add refinements; he simply played devil's advocate, a gadfly stinging Longman's invention into activity. It was only later, when the technical problems were out of the way, that Ryder began to contribute ideas of his own.

One day—it must have been their sixth or seventh meeting—Ryder said, "Determined people could probably succeed in taking the train, but I'm not satisfied they could get away."

"I admit it's tough," Longman said casually. "Very tough."

Ryder looked at him sharply, then came as close to a smile as he usually allowed himself. "You've been thinking about it."

Longman grinned, too, but suddenly thought: That's why he steered away from it before, he knew I would anticipate the question, and he was giving me lots of time to work on it.

"Well, yes," Longman said. "I gave it a few minutes of my spare time. I think I know how it can be done."

"Tell me," Ryder said.

It spilled out of him eagerly and proudly, and when he was finished, he looked at Ryder in triumph.

"Another round," Ryder called out to the waiter. Then he said to Longman, "Let's do it."

Attempting to match Ryder's nonchalance, Longman said, "Sure, why not?" But he felt suddenly dizzy, and later he was to recall that it was how he felt on the verge of going to bed with a woman.

Yet there was still time to back out. He needed only to have said no. True, he might have lost Ryder's esteem, but there would have been no reprisals. And there was something more than Ryder involved. It was as if his whole life reared up before him, a dreary, squalid grayness—loneliness, scrabbling for a living, the lack of a real friend, man or woman. At forty-one, if not exactly unemployable, he was at best doomed to a succession of inane, menial, or dead-end jobs. That was the story of his life since he had left the transit system, and it could only get worse. What probably convinced him finally to make this last desperate pitch for a better life was the bitter memory of a period when he had been an apartment-house doorman. Holding doors for people who never really acknowledged his existence, even those who condescended to greet him; dashing out into the rain to whistle up cabs; relieving strapping matrons of their bundles; walking dogs for residents who were away for the day or who simply didn't want to go out in inclement weather; arguing with snotty errand boys; turning away drunks who wanted to come inside to warm up; smiling and groveling and pulling at the bill of his cap. A flunky, a servant in a maroon monkey suit.

It was a powerful memory, and it sustained him throughout the months of preparation, although he never shook off the foreboding feeling of a man approaching a critical operation in which the chances of dying in the surgery were at least as good as those of survival. . . .

Joe Welcome's voice shattered the silence, as terrifying

as an act of sudden violence. Longman turned pale under his mask. A car's length away, Welcome was squared off in front of the door, screaming into the tunnel. Longman knew, was certain, that Welcome would fire and that someone, whoever was out there, would die. And so the actual firing was almost an anti-climax. Before the echo died, Longman was already pounding frantically on the cab door with his fist.

CAZ DOLOWICZ

Like a thin somber Pied Piper, the conductor stood at the head of a line of passengers that straggled far back on the roadbed into the darkness. It was cool in the tunnel, drafty and damp, but the conductor was sweating, his fair skin stained pink, worry lines embedded in the smoothness of his forehead.

Dolowicz shouted, "I don't give a damn if they were armed with cannons." His voice echoed off the walls. "You aren't supposed to leave your train without authorization."

"They *made* me. I didn't have any choice."

"Like the captain of a ship leaving his ship, it's the exact same thing."

Dolowicz heard out the conductor with a rapidly increasing pressure in his chest, and a new pain in his stomach and head, as if the growing list of disasters—cutting the train, moving the front car, intimidating the passengers and crew, cutting the power—as if each of these produced a corresponding reaction in a different organ.

"They said they would *kill* me. . . ." The conductor ran out of voice, and turned to the passengers, appealing for corroboration. "They had *machine* guns!"

Several of the passengers nodded their heads gloomily, and from back in the shivering line a voice called out, "Let's go, let's get outta this dump." Other voices picked up the refrain, and Dolowicz realized the danger of panic.

"Okay," he said to the conductor. "Okay, Carmody. Carmody? Okay, get these passengers back to the platform at once. There's a train in the station. Use its radio to tell Command Center what you just told me. Tell them I'm on my way to investigate."

"You're going *down* there?"

Dolowicz brushed by the conductor and started down the track. The line of passengers were strung out farther than he had expected, there must have been nearly two hundred of them. They called out to him as he went by, complaining about their interrupted trip, threatening to sue the city, demanding the return of their fare. A few warned him to be careful.

"Just keep moving along, folks," Dolowicz said. "It's not dangerous. The conductor will take you back to the station, it isn't far. Just keep moving, folks, step lively, nothing to worry about."

After clearing the last of the passengers, Dolowicz was able to cover ground more quickly. His anger renewed itself at the sight of the nine cars that had been cut away standing uselessly, hulkingly, their weak emergency lights giving them a pathetic half-life. A pocket of gas backed up against his heart and caused him a moment of intense pain. He concentrated on a belch and succeeded in bringing one halfway up his windpipe, giving him relief or the illusion of relief. He pursed his lips and strained his abdominal muscles, but it was useless. The pain returned.

He plodded on doggedly, head down, until, a hundred yards forward, he looked up to see the pale illumination in the first car of Pelham One Two Three. He fell into a half trot, but almost immediately slowed to a walk again. As he came closer, he saw that the rear storm door was open and that a man was standing in it, like a cut-out silhouette. It occurred to him to approach cautiously, but the warning flashed by, leaving cold rage in its place. Bastards! Daring to monkey with his railroad! He pressed on, massaging his left tit to cozen the pain or dislodge the gas pocket.

A voice traveled down the tunnel from the mouth of the car: "Stay where you are, Johnny."

It was a loud voice, echoing, distorted by the acoustics of the tunnel. Dolowicz stopped dead in his tracks, not in obedience but outrage. Gulping for breath, he shouted back, "Who the fuck are *you* to give orders?"

"I said to stay back."

"Bullshit," Dolowicz yelled. "I'm the trainmaster, and I'm coming on board." He started walking again.

"I warned you to stay back." The voice was a shout now, with an edge of violence to it.

Dolowicz waved a hand at him in dismissal.

"I warned you, stupid!" The voice was almost a scream.

Dolowicz looked up at him from a distance of a dozen feet, and in the same instant that he realized the man was pointing something at him, he saw the muzzle flash, bright as a sunburst, and felt a sharp intense pain stitch across his stomach. He had one more conscious thought, a surge of fury at this new indignity added to, laid on top of, the gas pain.

He never heard the stuttering burst of the gun, racketing off the walls in a prolonged echo. Dead, he staggered two paces backward before lurching to his left and collapsing across the polished rail.

EIGHT

ARTIS JAMES

Transit Patrolman Artis James was out on the street, or, more accurately, in the lobby of an office building on Park Avenue South, down the street from the Twenty-eighth Street station. He had come up ostensibly to buy a pack of cigarettes, but actually he was goofing off. He had felt in need of a relaxing interlude of chatter with Abe Rosen, who ran the cigar stand in the building.

Artis James and Abe Rosen had formed their friendship on a mutual attraction of opposites, and it throve on a diet of kidding based on watchfully modulated ethnic abuse which they managed to keep well this side of accidental (or unconscious) offense. This day they exchanged fifteen minutes of soft insults, as usual, and then Artis took his leave.

"See you tomorrow, gonif," Artis said.

"So long, schwartzer."

Artis went out into the sunlight. As he started down the station entrance steps, it didn't occur to him to bemoan the fact that he was leaving the outside for the duration of his tour of duty. The underground was his element, as the high air was the airman's, the sea the sailor's. He was almost through the gate, waving to the change booth clerk, before he remembered that he had turned his radio off. He switched on, and a call came through at once. He cleared his throat and acknowledged.

"Where the hell have you been?"

"Sorry, Sarge, I had to go outside, I had an 'Eighty—"

"That's no reason to go off your radio."

"I had to help this 'Eighty into a cab," James said glibly. "She was an elderly person and so weak I couldn't hear her voice. When I put her into a cab, I had to get her address, and in order to hear her, I turned down the radio."

"Some story. Never mind. Where are you now?"

"Twenty-eighth, southbound platform, just going in."

"Help maintain order there. Help is on the way. Platform very crowded?"

Artis noticed a train at the platform, its doors shut. Outside, some people were banging their fists against the doors and windows.

"I can handle it," Artis said. "What's the problem?"

After a pause, the sergeant said, "Look, don't react to this. Train has been hijacked. Don't react. Assistance on the way. Maintain order on the platform, and don't say very much. Over and out."

As soon as Artis appeared on the platform, he was

surrounded by passengers demanding that the train open its doors to them.

"Minor technical problem," Artis said. "Relax. We'll have it adjusted soon."

"What kind of a technical problem?"

"Anybody hurt?"

"Goddamn mayor oughta be impeached."

"Calm down, everybody," Artis said. "Just be patient, and—"

At the south end of the station he saw a boil of people climbing up from the roadbed onto the platform. He shook off the passengers and hurried quickly forward. Half a dozen people started babbling in high excitement. While he was trying to calm them down, he saw a young conductor at the end of the platform.

"The train is hijacked," the conductor said shrilly. "Get through to somebody. Armed men, with machine guns—"

Artis held up his hand to stem the flow of the conductor's hysteria. Shifting the radio on its shoulder strap and bringing it against his mouth, he said, "Patrolman Artis James calling Nerve Center. Patrolman James calling Nerve Center."

"Come in, Patrolman James."

"There's at least a hundred passengers coming up off the tracks." The passengers who had been waiting for the train to open its doors were crowding around him, and mingling with those who had been on the hijacked train. "No way to keep the secret. I'll get lynched if I continue to pass off that crap about technical difficulty. Can't you put it on the station speaker?"

"Communications Desk will have something coming

over in a couple of minutes. Just keep them quiet, and get everybody away from the south end of the platform."

The conductor was screaming at him. ". . . down the track. I warned him, but—"

"Hold on," Artis said into the radio, and then to the conductor: "Say that again."

"The Grand Central trainmaster went down the track. To the train."

"Sarge, the conductor says a man identified as the Grand Central trainmaster went down the track. Hold on. . . . How long ago was that, Conductor?"

"I'm not sure," the conductor said. "A few minutes?"

Passengers spoke up in a dissonant chorus, some disputing, others supporting the conductor's time estimate.

"Cool it," Artis said. "Cool the noise." He spoke into the radio. "A few minutes ago. Come in."

"Jesus. He's nuts. Look, James, you better go after him. See if you can catch him and turn him back. Move fast, but don't in any way get involved with the criminals, and exercise extreme caution. Repeat. Exercise extreme caution. Acknowledge."

"On my way. Over and out."

Artis James had been on the roadbed just once before in the line of duty. With another cop he had chased three kids who had snatched a purse and taken off down the track. The chase had been exhilarating, and there was a sense of community in working with a partner. The trains had been running, of course, which added a spice of danger. Eventually, they had picked the three kids up at gunpoint, trying to force an emergency exit, and led them back quaking to the station.

But this wasn't much fun. The darkened tunnel was haunted by shadows, and although the danger from running trains was eliminated, he was heading toward a band of heavily armed criminals. And no matter how much assistance was on the way, right now he was on his own. It occurred to him that if he had just spent a few extra minutes rapping with Abe Rosen, some other lucky cop might have drawn this assignment. But the thought shamed him, and mindful of the trainmaster plunging ahead into mortal danger, he picked up his pace. After skirting the ghostly cut cars of Pelham One Two Three lying dead on the track, he began to run, taking long, loping steps, coming down softly on his toes and the balls of his feet.

He was puffing by the time the lights of the front car of Pelham One Two Three came into view. A short while later he made out a wavering shape some distance in front of him on the roadbed. He started running again, bent over for concealment, and ahead of him the trainmaster took on bulky definition. Suddenly there were voices in the tunnel, angry and echoing. He kept on, but more prudently than before, advancing from pillar to pillar, taking momentary shelter before moving on.

He was sixty or seventy feet from the car, behind a pillar, when a staccato burst of gunfire reverberated through the tunnel, repeating itself like a funhouse echo. Blinded by the muzzle flash, his heart pounding, he pressed himself into the ungiving metal of the pillar.

It must have been a minute before he risked peering around the edge of the pillar. A haze hung in the air near the rear of the car. There were several figures looking out of the storm door. The trainmaster was sprawled on the track. He thought for just a moment of trying to work his way back to safer ground, but the danger of being seen was too great. Instead, first taking the precaution of turning the volume down, he unslung his radio and, in a whisper, called the Nerve Center.

"Speak up, ferchrisesake, can't hardly hear you."

Whispering, he explained why he had to whisper, and proceeded to describe the shooting of the trainmaster.

"So far as you can tell he's dead?"

He strained to hear the voice of the sergeant. It was dispassionate; it was collecting facts. "He's lying there," Artis said, "and they shot him with a machine gun, so he must be dead."

"You sure he's dead?"

"Must be," Artis said. "You expect me to go up there and feel his pulse?"

"Take it easy. Go back to the station and await further instructions."

"That's *it*," Artis whispered urgently. "If I move, they *see* me."

"Oh. Then stay where you are until assistance arrives. But take no action, *no action* without specific instructions. Check me."

"I check you. Stay put, and no action. Right?"

"Good enough. Over and out."

RYDER

A dead soldier, Ryder thought, peering through the rear door, the other side has suffered a casualty. The body might have been a fat doll, kewpie eyes squeezed shut, pudgy hands clasped to a stomach pouring out red sawdust. The head lay across a rail, the upturned cheek tinged green in the reflection of a signal light.

"I wasted him," Joe Welcome said. Through the slits in his mask his eyes were glowing. "The bastard kept on coming after I warned him. I stitched him right across the belly."

Ryder studied the body. Almost to himself he said, "He's dead," speaking out of long experience.

"Bet your ass," Welcome said. "Five, six slugs, right in the bull's-eye."

Ryder looked out past the body—it didn't count for anything; it was no longer a threat, if it had ever been—at the terrain: the roadbed, the burnished tracks, the grimy walls, the pillars that might conceal a man. There was no movement, only the becalmed darkness of the tunnel fitfully relieved by the bright signals, the lights marking the telephones, the power boxes, the emergency exits.

"I got the action started," Welcome said. He was taking short, shallow breaths, and the nylon sucked into and out of his mouth. "I got us on the scoreboard."

He was all revved up, Ryder thought, his blood mixture enriched by a killing. "Tell Steever to come back here. I want you and Steever to change places."

"How come?" Welcome said. "What are you changing the plan for?"

"The passengers know you shot somebody. They'll be easier to handle because they'll be intimidated by you."

Welcome's nylon stretched to a hidden smile. "You better know it."

"Don't go off the handle," Ryder said as Welcome started to move off. "Just play it cool; they'll behave themselves."

Ryder went back to his observation of the tunnel. Steever came up behind him and waited silently for him to speak.

"Take over back here," Ryder said. "I want Welcome up closer to me so I can keep an eye on him."

Steever nodded, and peered over his shoulder at the track. "Dead?"

"Maybe it was necessary. I didn't see it. But he's trigger-happy." Ryder jerked his head toward the front of the car. "The bleeding man. You hit him?"

"Had to," Steever said. "Won't he make the people nervous? Welcome?"

"I'm going to talk to them."

"It going okay?" Steever said.

"On schedule. I predicted it would be slow at the start. They're still stunned on the other side. But they'll get hold of themselves, and then they'll go our way."

Steever nodded, content. He was a simple man, Ryder thought, a good soldier. It was going okay or it wasn't, and he would do his job either way. He asked for no guarantees. He took a chance and would accept any outcome, not because he was a gambler but because his uncomplicated mind understood perfectly the terms of his employment. You lived or you died.

Ryder went forward. Against the center post Steever had vacated, Welcome had taken up a widespread stance, and the passengers were scrupulously looking in another direction. Longman, wedged in the angle formed by the storm door and the front edge of the cab door, seemed to have shrunk. The shooting had left him terrified. In fact, he must have been close to panic when he had been pounding the cab door during the shooting. Ryder had heard the shots himself, muffled by the isolation of the cab, but he had ignored them, as he had ignored Longman's pounding, until he was finished speaking to the Command Center. Coming out of the cab face to face with Longman, he had read his state of mind at once. It was astonishing how much expression you could intuit through the nylon mask.

He took up a position to the left of Welcome and spoke at once, without preamble. "Before, some of you asked for information." He paused and watched the passengers turn toward him, some alertly, some in surprise or apprehension. "The information most important to you is this— you are hostages."

There were one or two groans and a suppressed scream from the mother of the two boys, but for the most part the passengers accepted the news with composure, although a number of them exchanged questioning glances, as if, uncertain of how to react, they sought guidance. Only the black militant and the hippie seemed unaffected. The black's right eye, showing around the edge of his bloody handkerchief, was a hard, disciplined blank. The hippie was smiling beatifically down at his wriggling toes.

"A hostage," Ryder said, "is a form of temporary insurance. If we get what we want, you'll be released unharmed. Until then, you will do exactly what you're told."

The elegantly dressed old man said in a calm voice, "And if you don't get what you want?"

The other passengers avoided looking at the old man,

as though to disavow complicity; he had asked the question none of them wanted answered. Ryder said, "We expect to get it."

"What do you want?" the old man said. "Money?"

Welcome said, "That's enough out of you, Grandpa. Button up."

"What else is there?" Ryder said to the old man, and gave a twitch of a smile under his mask.

"So. Money." The old man nodded, as if in confirmation of a judgment. "And if you don't get the money?"

Welcome said, "I can stop you, old man, I can put a bullet right through your talker."

The old man took notice of him. "My friend, I'm only asking a few sensible questions. We're all reasonable people, right?" He returned to Ryder. "If you don't get the money, you'll kill us?"

"We'll get the money," Ryder said. "What should concern you, all of you, is that we won't hesitate to kill you if you get out of line. Keep that in mind."

"Okay," the old man said. "Listen—off the record, just a little curiosity—what's your asking price? Can't you give us a little sneak preview?" The old man looked around the car but found no takers; he laughed alone.

Ryder went down the aisle to the front of the car. Longman stepped out in front of him.

"Move back," Ryder said. "You're in the line of fire."

Longman edged to the side, then brought his head forward and whispered, "I think we got a cop sitting there."

"What makes you think so? Which one?"

"Take a look. You ever see anybody looked more like a cop?"

Ryder picked him out. He was sitting beside the hippie, a huge, bulky man with a heavy stolid face and that quality of beefiness that wasn't softness but power. He was dressed in a tweed jacket and loafers, a rumpled shirt, and a slightly soiled rep tie. Not exactly spit-and-polish, but that didn't mean anything; nobody cared how a detective dressed.

"Let's frisk him," Longman whispered. "If he's a cop, and carrying a gun . . ." His whisper got away from him, turned into a harsh, audible croak.

When the question of frisking the passengers had risen, weeks ago, they had decided against it. The chances that anybody would be carrying a gun were small, and only a fool would attempt to use one against such enormous odds. As for knives, a more likely weapon, they didn't constitute a threat.

The man unquestionably had the look of a veteran detective. "Okay," Ryder said to Longman. "Cover me."

The passengers drew their feet back overzealously, shrinking away from him as he walked through the aisle.

He stopped in front of the man. "On your feet."

Slowly, keeping his upturned eyes fixed watchfully on Ryder's face, the man stood up. Next to him, the hippie was industriously scratching himself under his poncho.

TOM BERRY

Tom Berry caught the whispered word "frisk," a professional word that registered where a more ordinary one might not have. The tall man, the leader, seemed to be studying him, briefly weighing some proposition advanced by the whisperer. A wave of heat swept over him. Somehow, they had made him. The heavy Smith and Wesson .38, with its graceless two-inch barrel, was snugged firmly in his belt, weighty against his bare skin beneath the concealing poncho. And what was he going to do about it?

The question was urgent, the alternatives easy to understand. By the terms of your training and conditioning and oath, your gun was a sacred object, and no man could be permitted to take it from you. You defended it as you would defend your life; it *was* your life, your transubstantial life. So you didn't give it up unless you were the kind of poltroon who wanted to live at any cost. Well, that was exactly the kind of poltroon he was. He would suffer them to discover his gun and his tin, and take them both away, without so much as flexing a muscle to protect his, ah, honor. They might belt him around some, but they weren't likely to go any further. There was no purpose to killing him once he was disarmed. A cop without a gun was no threat, just somebody to laugh at.

Let them laugh. Like the contempt of his colleagues, it would hurt some, but not fatally. Scorn and laughter were wounds that healed with time.

And so, once again, steadfast in principle, he had chosen dishonor over death. Not that Deedee would see it in that light. In fact, she might be pleased by it for a complexity of reasons, among which, he hoped, might be the apolitical one that she cared for him deeply. There would certainly be no complexities about the attitude of the department in general and his precinct captain in particular. Unequivocally, they would rather see him dead than disgraced.

But then the leader of the hijackers started toward him, and his synapses—training, conditioning, brainwashing, whatever you wanted to call it—spat squarely in the eye of his intellect, and he became a cop who believed all the shibboleths. He slid his hand under his poncho and began to scratch himself, moving his hand steadily across his stomach until the fingers brought up against the hard wooden butt of the .38.

The leader loomed above him, his voice at the same time impersonal and threatening. "On your feet."

Berry's fingers had already closed on the butt when the man at his left stood up. And so, easing his hold on the gun, Berry didn't really know, and was relieved of the burden of having to know, whether or not he would have drawn. His coppishness, he thought, blinked on and off like a sign on a Chinese restaurant.

For the first time, Berry saw how much like a cop the standing man looked. The leader, with the muzzle of the Thompson squarely on his belt buckle, was frisking him efficiently with one hand, pulling and tugging at his clothing, patting him thoroughly. When he was satisfied there was no weapon, he took the man's wallet, and after ordering him to sit down, went through it quickly. He threw it into the man's lap, and the flip of his wrist made him seem, for the first time, almost playful.

"Newspaperman," he said, "ever been told you look like a policeman?"

The man's face was red, and he was sweating, but his voice was steady. "Frequently."

"You're a reporter?"

The man shook his head, and said in an aggrieved tone, "When I walk through a slum neighborhood, they throw rocks at me. No. I'm a drama critic."

The leader appeared bemused. "Well, I hope you like our little show."

Berry suppressed a laugh. The leader walked away and went back inside the motorman's cab. Berry began to scratch himself again, his fingers retreating from the revolver, crawling like a crab across his damp skin until they emerged from beneath the poncho. He folded his hands across his chest, lowered his chin, and grinned vacuously at his toes.

RYDER

In the cab, Ryder was remembering a bright, sunny day that accented rather than softened the tawdriness of the city streets. He had been walking with Longman, who suddenly stopped short and, almost in a spasm of desperation, blurted out the question that must have been plaguing him for weeks.

"Why is a person like you doing this? I mean, you're smart, and a lot younger than me, you could make a living, have a life. . . ." Longman paused, to give his words emphasis, and said, "You're not really a criminal."

"I'm planning a criminal act. That makes me a criminal."

"Well, okay." Longman waved the point away. "But what I want to know is *why*."

There were several answers, each of which would have been partially true, which was to say, partially untrue as well. He might have said that he was doing it for money, or for excitement, or because of the way his parents had died, or because he didn't feel things quite the way other people did. . . . And perhaps any of those would have been enough for Longman. Not that Longman was stupid, simply that he would accept any reasonable solution to the mystery over none at all.

But instead he said, "If I knew why, I probably wouldn't be doing it."

The evasion seemed to satisfy Longman. They continued their walk, and the question never came up again. But Ryder was aware that he had plucked it out of the air because it had a solemn psychiatric ring to it, not because he believed it or, for that matter, had any interest in either the question or the answer—his own or *anybody's* answer. As he reminded himself now, standing in the motorman's cab (a sequestered place, like a confessional, figuratively halfway between the outer crust of the earth and hell), he was neither a psychiatrist nor a patient. He knew the facts of his life, and that was enough for him. He felt no need to interpret them, to fathom the meaning of his life. Life—anybody's life—struck him as a rather heavy-handed joke that death played on people, and it was as well that you understood it. "We owe God a death." He recalled reading that in Shakespeare. Well, he was a man who paid his bills when they came due and didn't have to be dunned.

A girl had once told him, in pity and anger, that something had been left out of him. He didn't doubt it and thought that she had actually understated the case. Some *things* would have been more accurate. He had tried to explore himself, probing for the missing ingredients, but in an hour had lost interest in the whole idea and dropped it. It occurred to him now that lack of exigent interest in himself was probably another one of those missing ingredients.

He knew the facts of his life, and he realized that they might have acted to incline him this way or that. But he had allowed them to. Whether you drifted with the current or tried to fight it, you reached the same destination—death. It was a matter of indifference to him what route he took, except that he preferred something scenic over something expedient. That made him a fatalist? Okay, he was a fatalist.

He had learned much about the value of life from the example of his parents, who had died of accidents within a year of each other. His father's accident consisted of a heavy glass ashtray that had come sailing out of a window, thrown by an irate woman at her husband, who had ducked. The ashtray whirled downward, struck his father in the head and smashed his skull. His mother's accident was cancer, a cluster of cells suddenly running rampant in the body of a robust woman and killing her after eight months of agony and appalling destructiveness.

If his parents' deaths—which he did not see as different or even discrete events—did not alone give birth to his philosophy, they certainly planted the seed. He was fourteen that year, and he had acknowledged the loss without actually mourning it, perhaps because he had already cultivated an unusual detachment derived from the sensed absence of love in his parents' marriage, which more or less included their feelings toward their only child. He recognized that some of the things that were "left out" were a heritage from his parents, but he had never held it against them. It wasn't only the love things that were missing, but the hate things as well.

He went to live with an aunt in New Jersey, a younger sister of his dead mother. The aunt taught school and was physically austere, an angular woman in her late thirties. She turned out to be a secret drinker and masturbator, but beyond those two humanizing flaws she remained formal and distant. According to some whimsical last wish of his mother he was enrolled at a military academy near Bordentown and rarely saw his aunt, except for the holidays and an occasional weekend. In the summers she placed him in a boys' camp in the Adirondacks while she went off on an annual European vacation. On the whole, since he had never known an affectionate family life anyway, it was an arrangement that suited him well enough.

He regarded his school as inane and its headmaster, a retired general, as an ass. He made few friends, and no close ones. He was neither big enough to be a bully nor small enough to be a victim. He was drawn into two fights in his first week and demolished his opponents with such cold and offhand viciousness that he never had to fight again for the remainder of his stay at the school. Although he had quick reflexes and was quite strong for his weight, sports bored him, and he participated only when they were compulsory. Academically he was in the top 10 percent of the class. Socially, by choice, he was a loner. He never joined group excursions to a local whorehouse or took part in the occasional gangbang of a willing town girl. Once he went off to a whorehouse on his own and failed to get an erection. Another time he was picked up by a girl who drove her car to a lakeside parking place and seduced him successfully—for her, that is. He erected satisfactorily, but was unable to ejaculate, which pleased the girl well enough. He had a single homosexual encounter, which he enjoyed no more than he had the heterosexual, and after that, he eliminated sex from his schoolboy curriculum.

Nothing in his military subjects at school or in two years of ROTC at college—or, for that matter, when he was drafted, in basic training or officers' training school—prepared him for his discovery of a métier once he went into combat. It was in Vietnam, in the halcyon days when Americans were "advisers," and a buildup to more than half a million men would have seemed an unlikely prospect. Holding the rank of second lieutenant, he had been assigned as adviser to an ARVN major leading a hundred men on some ill-defined mission to a hamlet a few miles northwest of Saigon. They were ambushed on a dusty, foliage-cramped road, and would have been wiped out to a man if the enemy—they were Vietcong, tiny men in sweaty jerseys and khaki shorts—had been better disciplined. But when the ARVN unit retreated (actually, turned their backs and ran in a panic), the ambushers broke their cover and chased them in the open.

The major and another officer had died in the first volley, and the remaining two officers were dazed and helpless. With the help of a sergeant who spoke some

English, Ryder rallied his troops and organized a resis-
tance. Eventually, and discovering in the process that he
was fearless—or, more accurately, that the thought of
death did not terrify him or in any way affect his
competence—Ryder mounted a counterattack. The enemy was routed, which is to say melted away, but left behind a sufficient number of dead and wounded so that the
episode was construed as a victory of sorts for the
ARVN.

He fought frequently after that, leading small detach-
ments on limited raids. If he didn't precisely take pleasure
in killing, certainly he found a measure of satisfaction in
discovering his competence. At the end of his tour he was
returned to the States and reassigned as an instructor at
an infantry camp in Georgia, where he remained until he
was mustered out.

He returned to his aunt's house, where some changes
had taken place—his aunt was drinking less and had given
up masturbation in favor of a lover of sorts, an elderly lawyer of goatish disposition and, apparently, prowess. For
lack of anything he really cared to do more, rather than
genuine interest or curiosity, Ryder used his accumulated
pay to make a tour of Europe. In Belgium, at an out-of-
the-way bar in Antwerp, he met a loud, cheerful, hard-
faced German who recruited him as a mercenary for the
fighting in the Congo.

With the exception of his brief service in Bolivia,
Africa—one part of it or another, one side or another, one
political persuasion or another—kept him gainfully em-
ployed, and he was reasonably content. He learned much
about fighting on various terrains and leading troops of

contrasting degrees of competence and bravery, and he was wounded three times all told, twice superficially and once seriously, a spear thrust that spitted him like a sheep and yet contrived to miss most of his vital organs. A month later he was back in combat.

When the market for mercenaries dried up, he knocked around in Tangier for a bit, drifting. There were opportunities to do some smuggling (hashish out, cigarettes in), but he turned them down; at that time he drew a sharp distinction between fighting for money and an illegal enterprise. He met a Jordanian, who promised him service with King Hussein, but it never panned out. Eventually he returned to the States to find that his aunt and the old lawyer had sanctified their arrangement with marriage. He packed up his few belongings and moved to Manhattan.

A few weeks after he began working as a salesman of mutual funds he drifted into an affair with a woman who declined to buy his shares but was eager to receive him into her bed. She was an avid, even rapacious, partner, but although he had learned some skills, he had no compelling sex drive. The woman professed to be in love with him, and perhaps she was, but his pleasure at poking inside a predictable variety of orifices was indifferent. The day he was fired from his job he stopped seeing the lady. Neither event stirred him.

He could not have said why he accepted Longman's friendship, except that it was offered, and it wasn't worth the bother to refuse it. Nor could he explain to himself why, having rejected a criminal venture in Tangier, he was willing to embrace one in Manhattan. Perhaps it was because the strategical and tactical problems appealed to him.

Perhaps because his boredom had reached a high point that it had not in Tangier. Almost certainly because the money meant the end of having to earn a living in uncongenial ways. Even more certainly because the high risk appealed to him. But, finally, motivation didn't matter, only the action leading therefrom.

NINE

CLIVE PRESCOTT

Lieutenant Prescott's boss, Captain Durgin, called Command Center to report the news about Dolowicz. Prescott reached over Correll's shoulder and took the phone. Correll clapped his hand over his eyes and slumped in his seat with a moan.

"I'm going across the river to Twenty-eighth Street," the captain said. "Not that they'll give us much of a play. The cops, I mean. The real cops. They'll hog the ball."

Correll suddenly sat upright and threw his arms out full length over his head in a gymnastic supplication to the heavens.

"Everything is climbing up the chain of command," the captain said. "Ours from Chief Costello to the chairman. Theirs to the commissioner, to the mayor . . . What's that racket?"

Correll was addressing the high ceiling in a hoarse, passionate voice, cursing the killers of Casimir Dolowicz, pledging God's vengeance and his own in the same breath.

"The trainmaster," Prescott said. "I guess Dolowicz was his buddy."

"Tell him to shut up, I can't hear anything."

From the farthest reaches of the Command Center, small groups of men were converging on Correll, who suddenly quieted and, collapsing in his chair again, began to sob.

"Stay put, Clive," the captain said. "Maintain contact with the train until we work out some other means of communication. Are they saying anything?"

"They've been silent for the last few minutes."

"Tell them we reached the mayor. Tell them we need more time. Jesus, what a city. Any questions?"

"Yes," Prescott said. "I'd like to get in on the action."

"That's not a question. Stay right where you are." The captain hung up.

The groups from the other parts of the Command Center—trainmasters and dispatchers of the other divisions—had arrived. Rolling cigars in their mouths, they surrounded the console and looked down dispassionately at Correll. Correll, whose moods—Prescott had determined—were intense but short-lived, abandoned tears in favor of pounding his desk in anger.

"Gentlemen," Prescott said. "Gentlemen." A dozen faces turned toward him, cigars twitching in thin-lipped mouths. "Gentlemen, this desk is now in effect a police post, and I'll have to ask you to clear out."

"Caz is dead," Correll said tragically. "Struck down in his prime."

"Gentlemen," Prescott said.

"Fat Caz has been taken away from us," Correll said.

Prescott stared sternly at the group around the console. The blank faces returned his gaze, cigars rotating, and then, still expressionless, they began to drift away.

Prescott said, "See if you can raise the train, Frank."

Correll's mood shifted again. His wiry body stiffened, and he shouted, "I refuse to dirty my hands speaking to those black bastards."

"How can you tell what color they are over the radio?"

"Color? I mean black-*hearted*," Correll said blandly.

"All right," Prescott said. "Now, let me sit down so I can work."

Correll jumped to his feet. "How do you expect me to keep the line running if you take my console away?"

"Use the dispatchers' consoles. I realize it's awkward, Frank, but it can be done." Prescott slipped into Correll's chair. Leaning forward, he activated the boom mike. "Command Center calling Pelham One Two Three. Command Center to Pelham One Two Three."

Correll clapped his hand to his forehead. "I never thought I'd live to see the day when talking to murderers got priority over running a railroad that the life of the city depends on. Where is the justice of it, for God's sake!"

"Come in, Pelham One Two Three, come in. . . ." Prescott deactivated the mike. "We're concerned about saving the lives of sixteen passengers. That's *our* priority, Frank."

"Screw the passengers! What the hell do they want for their lousy thirty-five cents—to live forever?"

He was role playing, Prescott thought, but only partially. He was a true believer, and all true believers had tunnel vision. Beyond Correll, he saw the A Division dispatchers at their consoles, frantically trying to cope with the calls pouring in from perplexed motormen all along the line, so swamped that they had given up any pretense of logging the calls.

"If I was handling it," Correll said, "I'd go storming in there with guns and tear gas and manpower—"

"You're not handling it, thank God," Prescott said. "Why don't you start working out a flex and leave the police work to the police?"

"That's another thing. I have to wait for word from the super. He's consulting. What the hell is there to consult about? I have to move my trains north and south of the dead sector. But that still leaves me with a mile-long gap, all four tracks out, right in the center of the city. If you just gave me power on two tracks, even *one* track—"

"We can't give you any power."

"You mean those murderers won't *let* you give me power. Don't it make you sick, taking your orders from a gang of frigging pirates? It's piracy on the high frigging seas!"

"Try relaxing," Prescott said. "You'll have your railroad back in an hour or so, give or take a few minutes—or lives."

"An *hour*," Correll screamed. "You realize we're creeping up on rush hour? Rush hour with a whole section out of use? Pandemonium!"

"Pelham One Two Three," Prescott said into the mike. "Calling Pelham One Two Three."

"How do you know those bastards aren't bluffing? How do you know they're not *counting* on our being soft on lives?"

"Soft on lives," Prescott said. "You're something, Correll, you're a bunch of *something*."

"They *say* they're going to hurt the passengers, but they might be bluffing you out."

"Like they bluffed us out with Dolowicz?"

"Oh, God." In another emotional quick change, Correll's eyes filled with tears. "Fat Caz. A beautiful man. A white man."

"You've got a great touch with the language, Correll."

"Old Caz. A railroad man in the old tradition. Pat Burdick would have been proud of him."

"If he walked into those guns, he was stupid," Prescott said. "Who is Pat Burdick?"

"Pat Burdick? A legend. The greatest of the old trainmasters. The stories about him? I could tell you a dozen."

"Some other time, maybe."

"One day," Correll said, "a train was laying dead at ten minutes to five. Ten minutes to five! Right before rush hour?"

"I'm going to try raising them again," Prescott said.

"The motorman called on the telephone—this was well before the time of two-way radios—and said there was a dead man lying on the track right in front of his train. Pat says, 'Are you sure he's dead?' 'Sure I'm sure he's dead,' the motorman says. 'In fact, he's stiff as a board.' So Pat screams, 'Then, goddamn it, prop him up against a pillar and get your train moving. We'll pick him up after rush hour!'"

"Command Center to Pelham One Two Three. . . ."

"That's the kind of a railroad man Caz Dolowicz was. You know what Caz would be saying to me right now? He'd be saying, 'Never mind me, Frank old buddy, just keep the railroad running.' Caz would *want* it that way."

"Pelham One Two Three to Command Center. Pelham One Two Three to Lieutenant Prescott at Command Center."

Prescott's finger shot out to the transmitter button. "This is Prescott. Come in, Pelham One Two Three."

"I'm looking at my watch, Lieutenant. It reads two thirty-seven. You're down to thirty-six minutes."

"The bastards," Correll said. "The murdering bastards."

"Shut up," Prescott said. He spoke into the mike. "Be reasonable. We're cooperating. You're not giving us enough time to work with."

"Thirty-six minutes. Check me."

"I check you, but the time is too short. You're dealing with a bureaucracy. It moves slowly."

"Time it learned how to move fast."

"It's involved. You know, we don't have a million dollars just lying around."

"You haven't agreed yet to pay it. The money isn't hard to raise—not if you're serious about it."

"I'm a simple cop, I don't know much about those things."

"Then find somebody who does. The clock is moving."

"I'll be in touch as soon as I have word," Prescott said. "Be patient. Just don't hurt anybody else."

"Else? What do you mean by *else*?"

A blunder, Prescott thought, they didn't know somebody on the track witnessed Dolowicz's death. "People back on the station heard gunfire. We assumed that you might have hurt somebody. One of the passengers?"

"We killed somebody out on the track. We'll kill anyone else we see on the track. *And* a passenger. Keep that in mind. Any infraction and we'll kill one hostage."

"The passengers are innocent people," Prescott said. "Don't hurt them."

"Thirty-five minutes left. Contact me when you have word on the money. Check?"

"Check. I ask you again—don't hurt those people."

"We'll hurt as many as we have to."

"Back to you soon," Prescott said. "Over and out." He slumped back in the chair, wrung out with suppressed anger.

"Christ!" Correll said. "To listen to you pleading with that bastard—it makes me ashamed to be an American."

"Go away," Prescott said. "Go play with your trains."

HIS HONOR, THE MAYOR

His Honor, the mayor, lay abed in his private living quarters on the second floor of Gracie Mansion with a running nose, a stupefying headache, aching bones, and a temperature of 103.5—plagues enough to insinuate the

possibility that he was the victim of a plot by his numerous enemies in and out of the city. But he recognized that
it would be paranoid to suspect the Other Side of, say,
having introduced flu germs to the rim of his martini
glass, since they lacked the imagination to conceive of
such a trick.

The floor beside the bed was littered with official
business which he had discarded unread in a touch of
petulance he felt himself entitled to. He lay uncomfort-
ably on his back, unshaven, chilled, from time to time
groaning in self-pity. He gave no thought to the work of
the city going undone, because someone would do it. In
fact, he was aware that since early morning, in the two
large official rooms on the first floor, a group of his aides
were busy with matters of state, riding the phones to City
Hall, where their work was expedited (and in some cases
duplicated) by still other aides. The phone by the mayor's
bedside was connected, but he had issued orders that no
calls were to be put through barring a major disaster such
as Manhattan Island slipping off into the bay, a circumstance he sometimes prayed might come to pass.

It was the first morning since he had taken office—
barring an occasional vacation in a warm sunny place or
the odd time when a riot or a catastrophic labor dispute
had kept him up all night—that he had not left the mansion at seven sharp for City Hall, and he felt both truant
and disoriented. When he heard a boat whistle somewhere
on the river beyond his window, it suddenly struck him
that his predecessors—all good men and true—had been
hearing such whistles for thirty years. It was a highly no-

tional thought for His Honor to entertain. An intelligent and educated man (the Other Side disputed the first and denigrated the second), nevertheless he had no taste for the romance of history, nor did the house he lived in by the indulgence of the electorate exert any stranglehold on his interest. He knew, but only by rote, that the mansion had been built in 1897 as a private home by Archibald Gracie, that it was a creditable, if not magnificent, example of the Federalist style, and that its downstairs rooms contained a Trumbull, a Romney, and a Vanderlyn, none of them representative of the artists' best work, but name paintings, nevertheless. The expert on the building and its contents was his wife, who had once majored in art or architecture, he forgot which, and who had briefed him on what little he knew.

Presently, he dozed and dreamed apolitical sexual dreams. When the phone rang, he was in the shameful act of kissing (mouth open, tongue hotly probing) a monk in a Swiss Alpine monastery. He struggled out of the hot grasp of the monk (who was naked under his robe) and lunged for the phone. He picked it up and snarled a phlegmy and incoherent monosyllable. The voice on the phone, speaking from one of the downstairs rooms, was that of Murray Lasalle, one of his deputy mayors, the first among equals, the man referred to by the press most frequently as the "spark plug of the administration."

Lasalle said, "Sorry, Sam, it can't be helped."

"God's sake, Murray, I'm about to die."

"Postpone it. We have a bitch of a crisis on our hands."

"Can't you handle it? You handled the third Brownsville riot, didn't you? I feel genuinely awful, Murray. My head is throbbing, I can't breathe, every bone in my body hurts—"

"Sure I can handle it, like I handle every other nasty job in this stinking misbegotten city, but I won't."

"Don't ever let me hear you say won't. There's no such word in the lexicon of a deputy mayor."

Lasalle, who had a cold himself—of appropriately lesser grandeur than the boss'—said, "Don't give *me* lessons in politics. Don't do that, Sam, or, sick as you are, I'll remind you—"

"I'm kidding," the mayor said. "Sick as I am, I have more sense of humor than you have or will ever have. Well, what's the calamity? It better be good."

"Oh, it's good, all right," Lasalle said with relish. "It's a blue-ribbon ballbuster."

The mayor shut his eyes against the coming revelation as though against a blinding sun. "Well, tell me. Don't milk the suspense."

"Okay. A gang of men have seized a subway train." He overrode the mayor's voice. "Have seized a subway train. They're holding sixteen citizens and the motorman as hostages, and they won't release them unless the city pays a million dollars in ransom."

For a moment, in his fever, the mayor thought he was still dreaming, that his mind had fled the Alpine scene and landed in a more familiar native nightmare. He blinked his eyes and waited for the dream to dissolve. But Murray Lasalle's voice was gratingly real.

"Did you ever hear me, ferchrisesake? I said that some men had hijacked a subway train and were holding—"

"Shit," the mayor said. "Shit, goddammit, shit." He had led a sheltered childhood and never learned to swear convincingly. He had long ago learned that swearing, like foreign languages, is best learned at an early age, but because he regarded it as a social grace, he never gave up trying to master it. "Shit. Fuck. Why do people think up such things to torment me? Are the police on the scene?"

"Yes. Are you ready to discuss this thing sensibly?"

"Can't we let them *keep* the goddamn subway train? We've got plenty of others; we'll never miss it." He coughed and sneezed. "The city hasn't *got* a million dollars."

"No? Well, you'd better find it. Somewhere. Even if you have to liquidate your Christmas Club account. I'm coming right up."

"Shit," the mayor said. "Shit and damn."

"I want you to have your head clear by the time I get upstairs."

"I haven't decided to pay it yet. A million dollars. Let's discuss it." Murray was too quick off the mark; he was too fondly trustful of his instinct, which was exclusively political. "Maybe there's another way out."

"No way out."

"You know how much snow a million dollars will remove this winter? I want a fuller picture of the situation and other viewpoints—the police commissioner, that bastard who's supposed to be running the Transit Authority, the controller—"

"You think I've been sitting on my ass? They're all on their way over. But it's a waste of time. After all the bullshitting is over, we'll still do it my way."

"—and Susan."

"What the hell do we need Susan for?"

"For domestic tranquillity."

The phone slammed in the mayor's ear. Damn Murray Lasalle. Shit Murray Lasalle. He was brilliant and a bear for work and worth his weight in ruthlessness, but he had to learn to curb his arrogant impatience with slower-moving Christian minds. Well, maybe this was the time to teach him that other people could make decisions, too. And that's what he would do, sick as he was.

POLICE COMMISSIONER

From the rear seat of his limousine, speeding uptown on the FDR Drive, the police commissioner spoke to the borough commander at the scene of the crime.

"What's it like there?" the commissioner said.

"Murder," the borough commander said. "As usual, they came out of the woodwork. I estimate twenty thousand spectators, and more pouring in all the time. I'm praying for a hailstorm."

The commissioner leaned to his right for a glimpse of the clear blue sky over the East River. He straightened up at once. He was an incorruptible and intelligent man who had come all the way up from patrolman, and although he understood that the luxurious black limousine was a valid, even necessary, prerogative of his rank, he would not sit in it comfortably, as though in this way to dissociate himself from unseemly opulence.

"Got barriers up?" he said to the borough commander.

"Certainly. And muscle courtesy of the Tactical Police Force. We're holding our own and trying to push new arrivals off into the side streets. I mean *push*. We're not going to be winning any new friends."

"Traffic?"

"I've placed a patrolman at every intersection from Thirty-fourth to Fourteenth, and crosstown from Fifth to Second. I suppose the backwash is making trouble elsewhere, but the immediate area is under control."

"Your second in command?"

"DCI Daniels of Special Operations Division. He's breathing fire. He wants to go into the tunnel and clean those bastards out. So do I."

"Don't let me hear that kind of talk," the commissioner said sharply. "Stand by, take up tactical positions, and await further instructions. Nothing more."

"Yes, sir, that's exactly what we're doing. All I'm saying is that it goes against my grain."

"Never mind your grain. Do you have all the emergency exits manned up top?"

"Both sides of the street, as far south as Union Square. I've got about fifty men in the tunnel—north and south of the train, well concealed. All wearing vests and armed with machine guns, riot guns, tear gas, Mace, the whole goddamn arsenal. And a half-dozen snipers with night scopes. We could fight the Vietnam War down there."

"Just make sure it's understood that nobody is to move. Those people will kill. They proved it by killing that trainman. We're taking all their threats seriously."

"Those are my orders, sir." The borough commander paused. "You know, sir, some of the snipers report that they can see people moving around in the car fairly freely. A couple south of the train say that the hijacker in the motorman's cab is exposed and an easy shot."

"No, damn it. You want to get all those passengers massacred? I repeat—we take their threats seriously."

"Yes, sir."

"See you remember it." The commissioner checked the progress of his car against the landmarks in the river. The driver, with his siren screaming, was weaving through the traffic on the drive like a broken field runner. "Did you interrogate the passengers they turned loose?"

"Yes, sir, as many as we could latch onto. Most of them melted away or simply got swallowed up in the crowd. The others are contradictory witnesses. But the conductor, a nice young Irish kid, is helpful. We know how many took the train, and how—"

"A dozen?"

"Four. Just four of them, wearing stocking masks, armed with what would appear to be Thompson submachine guns. Dressed in black raincoats and black hats. According to the conductor, they're well organized and familiar with the methods of subway operation."

"Yes. You might put somebody on the files of discharged transit employees. Not that it will help at the moment."

"I'll ask the transit police to take it on. There are a few hundred of *them* here, too. Including their chief. In person."

"I want him treated with the utmost respect."

"Communications are awkward. TA Command Center is the only direct contact with the hijacked car. The DCI has set up his command post in the motorman's cab of a train standing in the Twenty-eighth Street station, and he can use its radio to talk to the Command Center, but not the hijacked car. Standard two-way radio—he can hear the Command Center's end of a conversation with the hijackers, but not the hijackers'. I asked the hijackers through Command Center if they would allow us to communicate with them directly by bullhorn in the tunnel, and they refused flatly. They *like* it complicated."

The commissioner braced himself as the limousine eased off the drive, its siren scattering cars like frightened birds. "We're leaving the drive. Anything further?"

"Another warning from the hijackers about the time limit. They remain firm on it. Three thirteen."

"Who is the person in direct contact with them?"

"A TA police lieutenant. Seems sharp, according to the DCI. What reason would those people have for not agreeing to bullhorns?"

"Psychological, I guess. Show us who's boss. I'm signing off now, Charlie. Keep everything cool, and I'll be in touch the moment we have a decision."

The limousine swung into the climbing driveway adjoining Carl Schurz Park. It barely slowed at the white guard house as the two patrolmen on duty snapped to attention and saluted. At the top of the incline the limousine entered a circular drive at the side of the mansion, with the river visible over a large expanse of lawn, and, beyond it in the near distance, Hellgate Bridge.

The driver came to a lurching stop behind three other black official limousines. The commissioner jumped out of the car and started on a trot for the verandaed front of the house.

TEN

THE CITY: MIXED MEDIA

Newspaper reporters and photographers arrived at Park Avenue South and Twenty-eighth Street a few minutes after the police themselves; in fact, many police units were still en route. With their special brand of self-assurance they contrived to penetrate the police lines, an agglomeration of wooden barriers, cars, mounted police and the sinewy bodies of patrolmen, most of whom wore the distinctive sky-blue helmets of the Tactical Police Force. The newsmen flowed toward the downtown subway entrances on the southwest and northwest corners. They attempted to enter but were beaten back by the police. Working their way through the lines at the curb, they streamed across Park Avenue South to the uptown entrances. Repulsed again, they recrossed the avenue and began to collar brass.

"What's the situation to this moment, Inspector?"

"I'm not an inspector; I'm a captain. I don't know anything."

"Has the city decided to pay the ransom?"

"Is the trainman's body still lying in there?"

"How can you tell he's dead?"

"Who's in charge of the operation?"

"I'm not answering any questions," the captain said. "I don't know any answers."

"Are you under orders not to say anything?"

"Yes."

"Who issued them?"

"They weren't meant to apply to the press. What's your name, Captain?"

"Who issued those orders?"

"I did. Now get lost."

"Look, this isn't Germany, Captain."

"Right this minute, it is. It's Germany."

"What's your name, Captain?"

"Captain Midnight."

"Joe, take a picture of Captain Midnight."

Radio reporters, packing tape recorders on their backs and carrying their microphones overhead for protection as they pushed through the crowds, concentrated their fire on "the little man."

"Officer, how do you estimate the size of this crowd?"

"Very large."

"The largest you've ever seen gathered at the scene of a crime?"

The TPF man, his back and shoulder muscles straining as he fought to contain a bulge in the line of spectators, grunted his reply. "Looks like it. But you can't tell about crowds. Might not be."

"Would you describe it as an unruly crowd?"

"Compared to some, I'd have to say it was ruly."

"I appreciate that while what you're doing might not be as dramatic as catching crooks, it's a very arduous and important part of police work. Congratulations on a good job well done. And what is your name, sir?"

"Melton."

"You've just been listening to Officer Milton of the TFP—that's Tactical Police Force—TFP, here on the scene of the subway hijack at the intersection of Twenty-eighth and Park Avenue South. Thank you, Officer Milton, holding back the crowds. Here's another gentleman, standing by my side is another gentleman, I believe a plainclothes detective, also helping crowd control. Sir, am I correct in assuming you are a plainclothes detective?"

"Well, I don't guess so."

"You are *not* a detective?"

"I am not."

"But, nevertheless, you are helping the police hold back this huge crowd."

"I'm not holding nobody back; they're holding *me* back. I'd like to get out of here and get to hell home."

"I see, sir. My error. Thank you very much. You look like a plainclothes detective. Do you want to tell us your actual line of work?"

"On welfare."

"I mistook you for a detective, as you know. Good luck to you, sir, in your efforts to find your way out of here and reach your home."

With a single exception, the television stations put the news of the hijacking on the air within seconds of receiving the story on their news tickers. Most of them broke into the ongoing soap opera, movie or housewife-giveaway show to make the announcement, then went back to their program. Several, less willing to offend their faithful midday audiences, ran a slow-moving strip across the bottom of the screen, thus making it possible to enjoy fact and fiction at the same time. The delinquent channel lagged behind the others by forty-five seconds, unhappily trapped in the middle of a commercial when the flash came through.

The news departments of the stations—networks and locals—sent crews with mobile equipment winging off downtown. Universal Broadcasting System, the largest of the networks, sent the largest and most plushly equipped crew of any and, in addition, dispatched Stafford Bedrick, their news superstar, in person. Ordinarily, Bedrick covered only the most dignified news events—Presidential inaugurations, assassinations on the ambassadorial level or better—but he had volunteered for this assignment, sensing its vast potential in human interest.

Some camera crews commandeered offices in buildings overlooking the scene and through their windows shot panoramic views of the crowd; of the surrounding cityscape, with its brick and mortar gleaming frostily in the bright sunlight; of the hundreds of police cars; and, with zoom lenses, of various interesting faces and well-stacked girls. Meanwhile, other crews and reporters circulated at the street level. Most of them, frustrated in their efforts to reach the police command post which had been set up in a parking lot on the southwest corner next to the subway entrance, kept themselves occupied with "man-in-the-street" interviews.

"And you, sir—" The well-known reporter of city news on a six o'clock telecast thrust his microphone into the face of a man with three chins, a cigar in the mouth, and a sheaf of racing forms bunched in the right, or gesturing, hand. "Do you have some comment on the drama taking place under these very sidewalks?"

The man stroked his chins and faced head-on to the camera. "What particular part you want me to commentate on?"

"Suppose we tackle the subject of safety in the subways. Some people feel that our subways are jungles. Any comment?"

"Jungles?" The man with the cigar spoke in a voice rich in the rhythms of the sidewalk. "In my opinion, however, they're jungles. Jungles!"

"In what way are they jungles?"

"They're full of wild animals."

"Are you a regular user of the subway, sir?"

"Every single day, if you call that regular. What am I supposed to do—walk from Brooklyn?"

"Are you apprehensive on these daily rides?"

"What else?"

"Would you feel more secure if, instead of eight hours a day, the trains and platforms were manned by the transit police a full twenty-four hours a day?"

"Twenty-four hours a day *minimum*."

Turning for his laugh to a matrix of thrusting faces be-hind him, the man dropped his racing charts. The camera followed him meticulously as he scrambled for them in a thicket of legs; the microphone was held low to pick up his effortful grunt. But, by the time he straightened up, he had lost his place to a thin, huge-eyed black boy who had been forced to the front randomly by the pressing crowd.

"And you, sir, may we have your thoughts about the subway?"

The boy, eyes cast down, mumbled, "It do the job."

"Your opinion is that it do . . . does the job. I take it, then, that you would disagree with the previous gentle-man, who feels that the subway is dangerous?"

"Oh, it plenty dangerous."

"Dirty, gloomy, inadequately cooled or heated?"

"Yes, sir."

"Crowded?"

The boy rolled his great eyes. "Man, you know it."

"Well, then, summing up—"

"It do the job."

"Thank you, sir. Yes, young lady?"

"I met you before. A three-alarm fire in Crown Heights, last year?" The young lady was a middle-aged woman with a towering blond beehive coif. "My opinion is it's a scandal."

"What are you referring to specifically?"

"Everything."

"Can you be more specific?"

"What's more specific than everything?"

"Okay. Thank you." The reporter was bored. He knew

that most of his interviews would be thrown out in favor of more pertinent coverage, although the editors might salvage a brief clip or two for laughs to leaven the grimness of the story. "You, sir, would you stand right here?"

"Hello, Wendell. Okay if I call you Wendell?"

"Sir, the hijackers are demanding one million dollars for the release of the hostages. What position do you think the city should take?"

"I'm not the mayor. But if I *was* the mayor—God forbid—if I *was* the mayor, I would run this city better than the mayor runs it." He frowned at a chorus of cheers and catcalls. "The first thing I would do, if I was mayor, I would get rid of welfare. Next, I would make the streets safe. Next, I would reduce the fares. Next . . ."

Wendell converted a yawn into a somewhat strained smile.

Stafford Bedrick knew how to use his famous face and voice as instruments of his will. He dispatched them as outriders, as laser beams of personality, and they cut a path to the very center of things, the police command post in the parking lot. His entourage followed, beasts of burden laden with cameras, cables and sound equipment.

"Inspector? Stafford Bedrick. How are you?"

The borough commander whirled, but outrage was nipped in the bud by instant recognition of a face that was more familiar to him than his own. Almost by reflex, he checked the position of the camera and smiled.

"You won't remember it," Bedrick said with transparent modesty, "but we've met a number of times before. When those hoodlums tried to set fire to that Russian outside their consulate? And I believe when the President addressed the UN?"

"Sure," the borough commander said, and prudently turned his smile off; the PC frowned on intimacy with the media, regarding it as a subtle form of corruption. "I'm afraid I'm pretty busy here at the moment, Mr. Bedrick."

"Stafford."

"Stafford."

"I realize that this is not the ideal time for an interview, Inspector—I hope to have that pleasure some time in the future on *Summit Talks*, my regular show—but perhaps a few words of reassurance that the police are exerting every precaution to protect the lives of the unlucky hostages."

"Exerting every precaution."

"The burning question of the moment, of course, is being settled a few miles upriver from here at Gracie Mansion. Is it your opinion, Inspector, that the ultimate decision will be to pay the ransom?"

"Up to them."

"As a police officer, if the decision were yours to make, would you pay the ransom?"

"I do what I'm told."

"Discipline is, of course, the handmaiden of duty. Sir, would you care to comment on the rising rumor that this crime is the work of a political group—a revolutionary rip-off, as it were?"

"I haven't heard any such rising rumor."

"Inspector—" The borough commander's uniformed driver called to him from the open door of the car. "Radio, sir, the commissioner."

The borough commander turned abruptly and made for the car, followed closely by Bedrick and his crew. He entered the car, slammed the door, and rolled up the windows. Reaching for the hand mike, he saw a camera lens pressed against the window. Turning his broad back, he faced the opposite window. Another camera appeared.

Within five minutes of the announcement of the hijacking on television and radio, the news desk of *The New York Times* accepted a telephone call from a man who identified himself as Brother Williamus, Minister of Sabotage of BRAM, an acronym for Black Revolutionists of America Movement. In a rich, fruity and rather jovially menacing voice, the Minister of Sabotage said:

"I desire to inform you that hijacking that underground flier, you know, is a revolutionary sabotage action of BRAM. You know? Striking swiftly, you know, and ferocious, a storm-unit task force of BRAM have use this means to convey upon the white downtrodders the determination, you know, and aim of the Movement to hit Charlie where he live, namely, the pocketbook. The money obtain through this revolutionary expropriation act will be used to further the revolutionary aspirations of BRAM toward the Black Brother, wherever he may be, you know, and further liberation for the Black Man. And Woman. Right on?"

The subeditor who was taking the call asked Brother Williamus to supply some details, as yet unknown to the general public, to prove that his organization was indeed responsible for the hijacking.

"Sheet, man, I tell you *detail*, then you know as much as I know."

Without such details as evidence, the subeditor said, it would be possible for *anybody* to claim credit for the crime.

"Anybody else claim credit is a motherfucking liar. And don't you come on with that *crime* jive. It an act of, you know, purely political revolutionism."

"Okay, Minister," the subeditor said. "Do you have anything to add?"

"Just this one thing: BRAM urge black brothers all over the country to emulate this political act and hijack they *own* subway train, you know, to put down white capitalism. Provided they *is* a subway in they *town*."

A second caller came on the line at once, speaking in an accent that in some eerie but compellingly authentic fashion combined the modulations of Brooklyn and Harvard Yard.

"Powuh to the pee-a-pul! On behalf of the Central Committee of the revolutionary students' and workers' mobilization, SWAM, Students and Workers of America Mobilization, I inform you that the rip-off of the subway train is the work of SWAM. Further, it is merely the opening gambit, or skirmish, if you will, of a blueprint for revolutionary terror drawn up by the Central Committee of SWAM to terrorize the running dogs of the repressive and exploitative pig ruling class of America and bring it to its knees."

"Are you familiar with BRAM?" the subeditor said.

"Bram? There's Bram *Stoker*. Who wrote the film *Dracula*?"

"This BRAM is a black revolutionary movement. One of their officials phoned a moment ago, claiming credit for the subway hijacking."

"With all fraternal respect and deference to the black brother, his claim is a fucking lie. I repeat categorically— it is a revolutionary rip-off of SWAM, the first act of a terrorist anti-pig program—"

"Yes. I will ask you, as I did the previous caller, to authenticate your claim by citing details of the holdup not yet revealed—"

"Entrapment!"

"Do I take your answer to be no?"

"You're insidiously clever, you pig jackals of the running dog press. Will you use the story?"

"Maybe. My boss will eventually make that decision."

"Your boss! Man, can't you see you're as much exploited as the worker and peasant? Except that the mailed fist is concealed in a silk glove. Get your head together, man, recognize that you're just in a slightly more privileged boat than your brothers in the factory and the field."

"Thank you for your call, sir."

"You don't have to call me *sir*, man. You don't have to call *anybody* sir! Get your head together. . . ."

In all, the *Times* received over a dozen calls from such claimants, the *News* an equal number, the *Post* a few less. In addition, each paper was besieged by people offering pejorative characterizations of the hijackers, clues to their identity and plans for overcoming them; people requesting information concerning relatives and loved ones who might conceivably be passengers on the affected train; and people tendering their opinion on the question of whether or not the city should pay the ransom, on the philosophical, psychological and sociological motivations of the hijackers, and, above all, on the wickedness of the mayor.

The switchboard at City Hall was inundated. Public relations men, clerks and even secretaries were detailed to handle these calls, with instructions to make no commitments and, above all, to avoid irritating the callers to the detriment (the qualifying word "further" was tactfully omitted) of the mayor.

"If the city pays these bandits off, it will be an open invitation to every crook and crackpot in the city to hijack something. I'm a homeowning taxpayer, and I don't want my money used to coddle criminals. Not one penny for tribute! If the mayor knuckles under, he has lost my vote and the vote of my family in perpetuity."

"I understand that the mayor is weighing the question of paying the ransom. Weighing? What's more important, human lives or a few paltry dollars? If one of those passengers suffers death or injury, you can tell that fine mayor of ours that I will not only not vote for him, but I will dedicate the rest of my life to exposing him for the monster he is!"

"Call out the National Guard. Send them in there with fixed bayonets, and wipe out those crooks! I volunteer my help even though I will be eighty-four next month. Things like this didn't go on when I was a boy. I never go in the subway, anyway. I'm a fresh-air fiend."

"Can you please find out if my brother is on the train? He said he might come over today. He usually leaves the house around one thirty; I feel it in my bones that he's on that train. His kind of luck, all his life he's had it. If you can find out if he's on the train, not that I'll worry less, he could also be under a truck. . . ."

"God bless the mayor. Whatever he decides, I want him to know that he's a wonderful man. Tell him I'm praying for him."

"I am a Young Duke, you know? If there are any Puerto Rican brothers on that train, we demand the city to pay recompense for any injuries or agonies that they suffer. The Puerto Rican people are oppressed bad enough without they have to put up with lack of dignity when they go for a ride on the overpriced subway trains. And if it turns out some of the hijackers are Puerto Rican brothers, the Young Dukes demand full amnesty for them. These demands are nonnegotiable!"

"I'm not *saying* that the hijackers are colored, but if ninety-nine percent of the crimes in this city are committed by the colored, it stands to reason that the odds are ninety-nine to one that the hijackers are colored."

"Pass this on to the police. All they have to do is flood the subway tunnel. . . ."

ELEVEN

HIS HONOR, THE MAYOR

In ordinary circumstances His Honor, the mayor, might have enjoyed sitting above the battle while his subordinates debated the merits of a given subject, each astride his own hobbyhorse of bias and self-interest. But now, drowning in his runaway fluids, lightheaded with fever, he feared that his judgment would be impaired and that he might make a faulty decision, which is to say one that would be politically unprofitable. Not that he was so unprincipled as this might suggest, because he undoubtedly would—as he always did—temper expediency with decency, a fatal human failing he was helpless to rectify.

Present at his bedside, in addition to the police commissioner, the controller, the chairman of the Transit Commission, the president of the City Council and Murray Lasalle, were his wife and his physician.

Propped up on a pillow, snorting and snuffling, struggling to keep his rheumy eyes open and his wavering interest glued to the subject, His Honor, the mayor, permitted Murray Lasalle to moderate the conference with his usual mixture of sharp intelligence, impatience, and gutter toughness.

"The issue," Lasalle said, "and we have no time to waste, the issue is whether to pay the ransom or not. Everything else—whether we have the money or not, whether or not we can legally offer it, where we're going to get the cash, whether or not we can catch the hijackers and recover the money—everything else is secondary. And we can't discuss it at length, or we'll have seventeen more corpses on our hands. I'm going to allow one fast round of argument, five minutes' worth all told, and then we're going to take a decision. Ready?"

The mayor listened to the debate with only half an ear. He knew that Lasalle had already arrived at a decision and expected him to support it. For a rarity, political advantage and his best instincts coincided. The balance of praise against censure would be favorable. The *Times* would gravely support him on humanitarian grounds. The *News* would grudgingly approve, yet contrive to blame him for having allowed the incident to occur at all. Along traditional lines, Manhattan would be for him, Queens against. The well-to-do would say aye, the taxi driver nay, the black community would be indifferent. Nothing ever changed. He knew for a fact that the city had already chosen up sides on the propriety of his having the flu.

He blew his nose bubblingly in a wad of cleansing

tissues, which he tossed on the floor. The doctor eyed him professionally, his wife with disgust.

"Keep it short," Murray Lasalle said. "One minute per man, and then we turn it over to Hizzoner for a decision."

"You can't limit a critical discussion like this to a matter of thus-and-so-many seconds," the controller said.

"Second the motion," the president of the council said. Like the controller, he was regarded as being "no friend of the mayor," a designation that cut cleanly across party lines.

"Look," Lasalle said, "while we're futzing around, those killers down in that drab, dirty hole are ticking off the minutes until they start shooting hostages."

"Drab, dirty hole, is it?" the TA chairman said. "You're talking about the longest, busiest, and safest subway system in the entire world."

The Transit Authority was a complicated state-and-city combined operation, and the chairman was unequivocally the governor's man. He was not a popular figure in the city, and the mayor knew that he could pin at least part of the blame on him if anything went wrong.

"Let's get started," Lasalle said, and nodded to the police commissioner.

"Well, we're mobilized to the fullest extent," the police commissioner said. "I can go down in there with enough firepower and chemical devices to wipe them out. But I couldn't guarantee the safety of the hostages."

"In other words," Lasalle said, "you're for paying the ransom."

"I hate to give in to criminals in a thing like this," the police commissioner said, "but so far as the innocent being slaughtered with the guilty, it would be Attica all over again."

"Vote," Lasalle said.

"I abstain."

"Shit." Lasalle turned to the TA chairman. "You're up."

"My entire concern," the chairman said, "is with the safety of my passengers."

"Vote."

"A refusal to pay up would cost us the faith and trust of our passengers. We'll lose some revenue anyway, for a while. We must pay the ransom."

"Pay with *what*?" the controller said. "Is this coming out of your budget?"

The chairman smiled bitterly. "I'm tapped out. I haven't got a penny."

"Neither have I," the controller said. "I advise Hizzoner not to make any commitments of a financial nature until we know where the money is coming from."

"I take it your vote is nay," Lasalle said.

"I haven't yet expressed my philosophy on this thing," the controller said.

"No time for philosophy," Lasalle said.

"But I don't doubt there's time for *her* philosophy?" The controller inclined his head stiffly toward the mayor's wife, who had once spoken of him as "a Scrooge without hope of redemption."

With a curling lip, the mayor's wife responded in the argot she had learned in her days as a Wellesley undergraduate and, unlike her husband, became proficient in. "He fucking-aye-right *better* be."

"Thank you, Madam Mayor," Lasalle said. He nodded to the president of the council. "Your turn."

"I vote nay for the following reasons—"

"Okay," Lasalle said. "One abstention, one aye and two nays. I vote aye, and that makes it two-two. Sam?"

"Wait a minute," the president of the council said. "I want to explain my decision."

"No time," Lasalle said. "People's lives are at stake."

"I'm going to explain my reasons," the president of the Council said. "First and foremost, I'm for law and order. I'm for waging warfare against criminals, not coddling them with large sums of money."

"Thank you, Mr. President," Lasalle said.

"I have one more thing to say."

"Goddammit," Lasalle said. "Don't you people know we're up against a lethal deadline?"

"The second thing I have to say is this," the president of the Council said. "If we pay these criminals off, we'll be setting up a situation like the airlines. Knuckle under to these gangsters, and everybody and his brother will be hijacking subway trains. How many million dollars can we afford?"

"Which we haven't got," the controller said.

"And so, Mr. Mayor," the president of the council said, "I urge you to vote in the negative as far as paying ransom is concerned."

"As before," Lasalle said, "two yesses, two noes, and one abstention. That leaves the deciding vote up to Hizzoner."

"And if it had turned out three to one against?" the controller said.

"It would leave the deciding vote to Hizzoner," Lasalle said flatly. "Sam. Will you wrap it up, please?"

The mayor sneezed suddenly and forcefully, floating a fine spray into the air. It amused him to see everyone flinch. "I thought *you* had it wrapped up, Murray."

"Don't play games," Lasalle said, his eyes narrowing. "If you care a damn about those poor captive citizens—"

"Coming from you, that's a laugh," the mayor's wife said. "You spell citizen V-O-T-E."

The mayor was taken by a strangulated fit of coughing. The doctor, observing him critically, said, "This man is in no condition to be pressured. I won't permit it."

"Christ," Lasalle said. "Wives and pill pushers. Sam, don't you realize we haven't got an alternative? We have to get those hostages out of there safe and sound. Do I have to remind you—"

"I know all about the election," the mayor said. "I just don't like the way you're hectoring everybody. I'd like to see a little democracy around here."

"Wise up," Lasalle said. "We're trying to run a city, not any goddamn democracy." He looked pointedly at his watch. "Sam, you better get off your ass."

The mayor turned to his wife. "Darling?"

"Humanity, Sam, everything for humanity."

"Go ahead, Murray," the mayor said. "Arrange for the payoff."

"I said that ten minutes ago." Lasalle pointed his finger at the police commissioner. "Pass the word to the bad guys that we're paying." To the controller: "What bank do we do the most business with?"

"Gotham National Trust. I hate to do it, but I'll phone—"

"*I'll* phone. Everybody downstairs. Let's move it."

"Humanity," the mayor's wife said to her husband. "You're full of the stuff of humanity, darling."

"He's full of it, all right," Lasalle said.

RYDER

Even with the light in the cab turned off, Ryder knew he presented an easy target. He didn't doubt there were police in the tunnel, hidden and watchful, and that several of them, lined up on the broad front window, would have him squarely centered in their sights. But unless the police decided to fight it out instead of paying the ransom—in which case he would simply be the first of many to die—or one of the snipers gave in to an irrational impulse, he was running no greater risk than the other three in their more sheltered positions. His cover was circumstance, and it gave him reasonable protection. As in war, he asked no more and would accept no less.

He had little patience with romantic or idealistic concepts of war. Such descriptions as "held out to the last man," "fought with utter disregard for their safety," "against overwhelming odds" struck him as being the pathetic rallying cries of losers. He knew the classic examples, most of them from wars of antiquity, most of them monuments to inept planning, idiot pride or miscalculation: the Light Brigade, the Alamo, Pickett's Charge, Thermopylae. All these were military mistakes. Holding out to the last man meant that you were wiped out; utter disregard for safety needlessly multiplied your casualties; fighting against overwhelming odds implied being outmaneuvered (true, the Israelis had won the Six-Day War, but they had nullified the other side's numerical advantage by being there fustest with the mostest). He accepted the idea of sacrifice for his little command, but only for tactical advantage, never for glory.

His "command"—an ironically fancy name for the little band of misfits he had recruited so casually. Except for Longman, he hardly knew them; they were bodies chosen to fill the ranks. Actually, it was an open question whether he had recruited Longman or Longman had recruited him. A little of both, perhaps, the distinction being that he had volunteered and Longman had been a reluctant draftee. If Longman's fear was stronger than his fascination, it was nevertheless unequal to the combination of fascination and greed, and this had brought him in—and kept him in.

In a way, Ryder realized, he had enlisted Welcome and Steever to balance Longman, who was intelligent, imaginative, and a coward. He had found them through the man who had sold him his armament, like himself a former mercenary, who had been forced to retire after he had been badly shot up. Now he was a dealer in weapons, with a warehouse in a run-down area of Newark and a hole-in-the-wall office on Pearl Street. His blind was a business as a factor of hides and skins, and his office, in addition to a hundred-year-old desk, contained a phone, some stationery, and floor-to-ceiling bins of leathery skins that he dusted once a month for appearance's sake.

Submachine guns were no great deal for him to supply. If you wanted them badly enough, he could get you tanks, armored cars, howitzers, land mines, even a two-man submarine complete with torpedoes. When the arrangement was completed for the sale and delivery of four Thompson submachine guns and some sundries, the dealer fished up a bottle of whiskey, and the two refought some old battles (including a number in which they had been on opposite sides). At one point the phone had rung, and after a brief but argumentative conversation, the dealer had hung up and said in exasperation, "One of my boys. Crazy as a coot."

Ryder had merely nodded incuriously, but the dealer had gone on.

"I wish somebody would take him off my hands and save me the trouble of killing him," the dealer said with morose humor. Then, looking at Ryder thoughtfully: "Maybe you'll do it?"

"Do what?"

"I don't know what. It just occurred to me—you're buying four tommy guns. You got all your personnel picked out?"

Ryder said that he hadn't and that he was open to suggestion. It was typical of him, he thought now, that he had given armament priority over people.

"So maybe you'd be interested in this maniac?"

"You're not exactly making him sound like attractive merchandise."

"I'm a sincere man. Right?" The dealer paused and, when Ryder stared at him unresponsively, shrugged and went on. "This boy happens to be a square peg in a round hole. I've got him out in Jersey running my warehouse, but he's bored. He's an action character, a swinging dick. If I was ripping something off, if I needed a gun, a soldier, I would hire him right away. If I had a submachine gun, for instance, that needed a shooter, I wouldn't hesitate to put him behind it. Guts to burn."

"But crazy."

"Only a *little*. Crazy is a way of speaking. I don't mean psychotic. Wild. Uninhibited, say. But gutty and tough and . . ." He cast about for a word, and brought it out with a look of surprise. "And honest. *Honest.*"

Ryder smiled. "You think I'm going to do honest work with those tommies?"

"What you're going to do with them is not my business. But if you're in the market for a shooter, this boy could fill the specifications. By honest, I mean that he is not a double crosser, that he won't sell somebody out. That's not so easy to find these days. Does that part hit you?"

"It's a consideration, unless he's *too* honest."

"Nobody is *too* honest," the dealer said flatly. "Look, can it hurt to take a look at him?"

Ryder had taken his look the following week. The boy was cocky and tough and too intense for comfort, but Ryder didn't regard these qualities as serious drawbacks. The main question was whether or not he could take orders, and on this point Ryder had never been completely satisfied.

Eventually, he brought up the Organization. "I understand you left them to go into business for yourself. But you're working for somebody."

"He told you that, the boss?" The boy looked contemptuous. "That's a bunch of crap. I quit them because they're a bunch of old fuckers, and they got old-fashioned ways. I hope what you got in mind ain't old-fashioned."

"I wouldn't say so. In fact, I don't think it's ever been done before."

"What they call unprecedented?"

"It's dangerous," Ryder said, watching the boy closely. "You could get killed."

Welcome shrugged. "I didn't expect you were offering a hundred gees for something where you couldn't get hurt." He fastened his brightly glowing eyes on Ryder and said aggressively, "I don't scare. Even the Organization didn't scare me."

Ryder nodded. "I believe you. Can you take orders?"

"Depends on who's giving them."

Ryder curled his index finger in and touched it to his chest.

"I'll be honest with you," Welcome said. "Right now I can't promise. I don't know you, you know?"

"Fair enough," Ryder said. "Let's talk about it again in a few days."

"You're a quiet stud," Welcome said. "And I'm a loudmouth. But quiet don't have to be bad. The boss told me a few things about you. You had a career. I respect that."

The following week, after another talk, and not entirely without misgivings, Ryder signed Welcome on. Meanwhile, he had met Steever, and about Steever he had had few reservations. He, too, had come recommended by the weapons dealer.

"Fellow came looking for work. Business is slow, so I couldn't put him on. Have a talk with him. Looks like a good soldier."

In the caste system of the underworld, Steever was a heavy, as opposed to someone like Longman, who would be classified as a brain. Ryder probed his background thoroughly. He had come originally from the Midwest, had graduated from petty theft and strong-arm work to armed robbery, and had served time once, appropriately enough, when he had stepped out of his class and attempted a confidence hustle. Since then he had been arrested seven or eight times and been brought to trial twice, but had no additional convictions. About Steever, Ryder had no doubt that he would take orders.

"If it works," Ryder said, "you'll make a hundred thousand dollars."

"That's a big score."

"You'll earn it. It's a high-risk job."

"It figures," Steever said, meaning, Fair enough, I don't expect something for nothing.

And so, for better or worse, he had his army.

MURRAY LASALLE

Murray Lasalle allowed his secretary to look up the number of the bank for him but warned her that he wanted to initiate the call himself; it was no time for protocol, although, in normal circumstances, he knew its value and exploited it. The secretary, an old Civil Service war-horse, was miffed at this expropriation of her rights and became even more so when Lasalle, sitting on the edge of a desk in the historic downstairs room that had once been Archibald Grade's salon, urged her to "move her ass." Since she had begun working for Murray Lasalle, her anti-Semitism, nurtured in her girlhood in the rich culture of an Irish neighborhood in Brooklyn, but tempered by her years of service with a spectrum of people she thought of as "all kinds," had undergone a virulent rebirth.

Lasalle dialed the number with impatient flicks of his finger and told the switchboard operator that the mayor's office was calling, that it was an emergency, and that he must be put through to the chairman of the board immediately. He was connected with the chairman's secretary.

"The chairman is on another phone," the secretary said. "He'll be happy to speak to you as soon as—"

"I don't care whether he's happy about it or not. I want to speak to him right this very instant."

The secretary fielded his rudeness smoothly. "He is engaged in an overseas call, sir. I'm sure you understand."

"Don't back talk me, sister. This is life or death, seventeen lives, *minimum*. So you better break in, and no more back talk."

"I'm not permitted to do that, sir."

"Look, if you don't get your ass inside his office and get his attention, you're going to be prosecuted to the full extent of the law for criminal obstruction of the law."

"Hold on, sir." For the first time, the secretary's voice faltered. "I'll see what I can do."

He waited, drumming his fingers on the desk, and then a plummy voice filled his ear, "Murray! How are you, old man? Rich Tompkins here. What's the flap, Murray?"

"How the hell did I get *you*? I asked for the boss, goddammit, not his lousy press agent."

"Murray!"

Protest, terror, a prayer for mercy were contained in

those two syllables, as Lasalle had known there would be; he had struck at the soft underbelly. Rich Tompkins was vice-president in charge of public relations for Gotham National Trust, a position of importance and dignity, the chief purpose of which consisted in suppressing matter adulterous to the bank's image of purity from becoming public knowledge. He was a well-thought-of conservative pillar of the banking community, but he had a disreputable skeleton hidden in the closet of his past—for five mad months, after graduating from Princeton and before finding his true métier, he had worked as a movie press agent. It was the equivalent, in his world, of having been Jew or a priest, and he lived in a permanent state of fear that his incriminatory secret would be revealed and destroy everything: hundred thou salary, Greenwich estate, a forty-foot yacht, lunches with the governor of the Stock Exchange. . . . He had been a scholarship student at Princeton and had no ancestral fundament of family or finances. Stripped of his position and perks, he was wiped off the face of the earth.

Coldly, Murray Lasalle said, "What are you doing on this phone?"

"Oh, that's easily explained," Tompkins said eagerly.

"Explain it."

"You see, I was already in the chairman's office when Miss Selwyn came in, she told me about . . . Can I help, Murray? In any way that I can possibly help—"

In three sentences, Lasalle informed Tompkins of the situation. "Now, unless you can personally authorize the transfer of a million dollars, I want you to break into that old windbag's conversation. Immediately. Do you read me?"

"Murray . . ." Tompkins' voice was almost a wail. "I can't. He's talking to Burundi."

"Who the hell is Burundi?"

"It's a country. In Africa? One of the newly formed underdeveloped African republics?"

"I'm not impressed. Get him off and onto my phone."

"Murray, you don't understand. Burundi. We *finance* them."

"Who is *them*?"

"I told you. Burundi. The whole *country*. So you see why I can't—"

"I see only a former movie flack obstructing the function of the city government. I'll blow your secret, Rich, don't make any mistake about it. Get him for me in thirty seconds, or I'll blow the whole thing sky high."

"Murray!"

"The countdown has begun."

"What can I tell him?"

"Tell him to tell Burundi that he's got a most urgent local call waiting, and he'll phone them back."

"My God, Murray, it takes four days to get a call through; their telephone system is very underdeveloped."

"Fifteen seconds left, and then I start tipping the media. Republic Pictures, Vera Hruba Ralston, pimping studs for hard-up actresses visiting New York—"

"I'll get him. I don't know how, but I'll get him. Hold!"

The wait was so brief that Lasalle envisioned Tompkins leaping across the room, and cutting off the call to Burundi in mid-syllable.

"Good afternoon, Mr. Lasalle." The chairman's voice

was grave and measured. "I understand the city has an emergency?"

"A subway train has been hijacked. Seventeen people are being held hostage—sixteen passengers and the motorman. Unless we deliver a million dollars in less than a half hour, all seventeen will be killed."

"A subway train," the chairman said. "What a novel idea."

"Yes, sir. You understand about the haste, sir? Is there any problem about that much cash being available?"

"Through the Federal Reserve Bank, none whatsoever. We are members, of course."

"Good. Will you arrange at once for us to be given the money with all possible haste?"

"Given? How do I take *given*, Mr. Lasalle?"

"Lent," Lasalle said, his voice rising. "We want to borrow a million. The sovereign City of New York."

"Borrow. Well, you see, Mr. Lasalle, there are certain technicalities involved. Such as authorization, signatures, terms, duration of loan, and perhaps some other details."

"We haven't got time for all that, with all due respect, Mr. Chairman."

"But *all that*, as you put it, is of importance. I too have a constituency, you know. The directors and officers and stockholders of the bank, and they will ask—"

"Look, you stupid cocksucker," Murray screamed, and then paused, awed by his own audacity. But it was too late for apology or retreat, and in any case they were not his style. He plunged on, his voice an open threat. "You want to keep our business? I can take it around the corner to another bank, you know. And that's only the beginning.

I'll find violations on every one of your goddamn stand-pipes!"

"No one," the chairman said in slow wonderment, "no one has ever called me by *that* epithet before."

It was an opportunity to make generous amends, but Lasalle pushed on recklessly. "Well, I'll tell you something, Mr. Chairman. If you don't get started on that money this instant, it's going to be on *everybody's* lips."

PRESCOTT

The decision at Gracie Mansion had been relayed from the PC to the borough commander, from the borough commander to Deputy Chief Inspector Daniels in the cab of Pelham One Two Eight at the Twenty-eighth Street platform, and from the DCI to Prescott at Command Center. Prescott called Pelham One Two Three. "We agree to pay the ransom," he said. "Repeat, we'll pay the ransom. Acknowledge."

"I read you. I will now give you further instructions. You will obey them to the letter. Confirm."

"Okay," Prescott said.

"Three points. First: The money is to be paid in fifties and hundreds, as follows: five hundred thousand dollars in hundreds and five hundred thousand dollars in fifties. Check me."

Prescott repeated the message slowly and clearly, for the benefit of the DCI, who would be monitoring the call and would hear his end of the conversation.

"That works out to five thousand hundred-dollar bills,

and ten thousand fifty-dollar bills. A total of fifteen thousand bills. Point Two: These bills are to be put up in stacks of two hundred bills each, bound with a thick rubber band lengthwise and another widthwise. Confirm."

"Five thousand hundreds, ten thousand fifties, in packs of two hundred bills, bound fore and aft with rubber bands."

"Point Three: All the bills will be old bills, and the serial numbers will be random. Check me."

"All old bills," Prescott said, "and no serial number sequences."

"That's all. When the money arrives, you will contact me again for additional instructions."

Prescott signaled Pelham One Two Eight.

"I picked it up from your repeats," the DCI said, "and the message is already on its way to the mansion."

But Prescott repeated it again, in the event that the hijack leader was monitoring. He probably wouldn't care that the police were listening in, but there was no point in taking a chance that he might object.

The DCI said, "Get back to them and try to get us more time."

Prescott called Pelham One Two Three and, when the leader answered, said, "I passed on your instructions, but we have to have more time."

"It's two forty-nine. You have twenty-four minutes."

"Be reasonable," Prescott said. "The money has to be counted, put up in stacks, brought all the way uptown. . . . It just isn't physically possible."

"No."

The flat, unyielding voice left Prescott momentarily

stunned with a sense of helplessness. Across the room, Correll was in full cry, apparently in the process of working out a flex. The same kind of bastard as the hijackers, Prescott thought, concerned with *his* thing, and screw the passengers. He calmed himself and returned to the console.

"Look," he said, "give us another fifteen minutes. Is there any point to killing innocent people if it's not necessary?"

"Nobody is innocent."

Oh, Jesus, Prescott thought, he's some kind of a lunatic. "Fifteen minutes," he said. "Is it worth slaughtering all those people just for fifteen minutes?"

"All?" The voice sounded surprised. "Unless you force our hand, we have no intention of killing them all."

"Of course you don't," Prescott said, and thought: It's the first human or near-human emotion that cold voice has expressed. "So give us the extra time."

"Because if we killed them all," the voice said calmly, "then we would surrender our leverage. But if we kill one or two or even five, there are still enough left for leverage. You will lose one passenger for each minute over the deadline. I won't discuss it any further."

Prescott wavered on the edge of rage, hopelessness, a willingness to demean himself in any way that was necessary, but he knew that all of it, any of it, would come up against an implacable will. And so, fighting to control his voice, he shifted his ground. "Will you let us pick up the trainmaster?"

"Who?"

"The man you shot. We'd like to send a stretcher down to take him away."

"No. We can't allow that."

"He may still be alive. He may be suffering."

"He's dead."

"But you can't be sure."

"He's dead. But if you insist, well put a half dozen rounds into him to put him out of his misery, if any."

Prescott folded his arms on the console and slowly lowered his head. When he looked up again, his eyes were streaming with tears, and he could not tell whether they were caused by rage or pity or some soul-destroying combination of both. He balled up a handkerchief and pressed it deeply into each of his eyes in turn, then signaled the DCI. He said in a disciplined voice, "No time extension. Flat refusal. He'll kill a passenger for every minute we're late. He means it."

The DCI, in a voice as inflectionless as his own, said, "I just don't think it's physically possible."

"Three thirteen," Prescott said. "After that we can start scratching passengers, one per minute."

FRANK CORRELL

Hyped up, noisy, leaping athletically from console to console, Frank Correll devised a flex to keep the entire line from being paralyzed.

Lexington Avenue line trains departing from Dyre Avenue and East 180th Street in the Bronx were diverted to the West Side tracks at 149th Street and Grand Concourse.

Trains which had already proceeded south of 149th were switched over to the West Side line at Grand Central.

South of Fourteenth Street, some trains were run off into Brooklyn; others were sent around the loop at City Hall or South Ferry, which brought them back northward to the Bowling Green station, where they began to pile up.

MABSTOA buses were commandeered to portage riders to other lines in the midtown area.

The shifting of trains to the West Side required elaborate precautions to keep those tracks from being swamped.

It was a messy improvisation, but at least it avoided a catastrophic standstill. "Like the mail has to move," Frank Correll shouted, "like the show must go on, the railroad gotta keep running."

MURRAY LASALLE

Murray Lasalle assaulted the handsome staircase two steps at a time and entered the mayor's room. His Honor was lying on his face, his pajamas pulled down and his bare rump waving in the air as the doctor profiled toward it with a hypodermic syringe. It was a shapely and practically hairless butt, and Lasalle thought: If mayors were elected on the beauty of their asses, His Honor could reign forever. The doctor plunged with his needle. The mayor groaned, flipped over, and pulled up his pajama bottoms.

. Lasalle said, "Get out of bed and put your clothes on, Sam, we're going downtown."

"You're out of your mind," the mayor said.

"Utterly out of the question," the doctor said. "Ridiculous."

"Nobody asked you," Lasalle said. "I make the political decisions around here."

"His Honor is my patient, and I will not permit him out of bed."

"Well, I'll get a doctor who will permit it. You're fired. Sam, what's the name of that spade intern at Flower Hospital? The one you used your influence to get into med school?"

"This is a very sick man," the doctor said. "His very life might be endangered—"

"Didn't I tell you to get lost?" Lasalle glared at the doctor. "Sam—that intern, Revillion, I'm going to get on the blower to him—"

"Keep him the hell away from here. I've had it with doctors."

"He won't have to come near the place. He can diagnose you over the phone."

"Murray, ferchrisesake," the mayor said, "I'm sick as a dog. What's the sense of it?"

"What's the sense of it? Seventeen citizens in jeopardy of their lives and the mayor cares so little about them that he won't even put in an appearance?"

"What good is putting in an appearance? So I can get booed?"

The doctor moved around the bed and picked up the

mayor's hand by the wrist. "Let go of that," Lasalle said sharply. "You've been replaced by Dr. Revillion."

"He isn't even a doctor yet," the mayor said. "I think he's a fourth-year student."

"Look, Sam, all you have to do is go down there, say a few words to the hijackers on a bullhorn, and then you can come right back and get into bed again."

"Will they listen to me?"

"I doubt it. But it has to be done. The Other Side will be there. You want *them* to get on the bullhorn and plead for the citizens' lives?"

"They're not sick," the mayor said, coughing.

"Remember Attica," Lasalle said. "You'll be compared to the governor."

The mayor sat up abruptly, swung his feet over the edge of the bed, and pitched forward. Lasalle caught him while the doctor, after a first instinctive move, stood his ground stonily.

The mayor, with effort, raised his head. "This is crazy, Murray. I can't even stand up. If I go downtown, I'll get even sicker." His eyes widened. "I might even die."

"Worse things can happen to a politician than just death," Lasalle said. "I'll help you on with your pants."

TWELVE

RYDER

Ryder opened the cab door, and Longman, stepping back to give him room, touched his arm with trembling fingers. Ryder walked out from under his hand and went to the center of the car. At the rear, Steever sat against the steel outside wall of the car, his gun pointing at an angle toward the track. In the center, Welcome stood with his legs astride, holding his gun with one hand. A man who swaggered even when he was standing still, Ryder thought.

He took up a position slightly in front of Welcome but off to one side to keep a clear field of fire.

"Your attention, please."

He watched the faces turn toward him, slowly and reluctantly or in a sudden almost spastic reaction to his voice. Only two of the passengers met his eyes—the old man with grave but lively interest, the militant black defiantly over the pink-dyed curtain of his handkerchief. The motorman was white-faced, his lips moving silently. The hippie wore his dreamy zonked-out smile. The mother of the two boys kept touching them compulsively, as if to commit them to memory. The girl in the Anzac hat was sitting erect, a calculated pose to bring her breasts forward, to accentuate the curve of her thighs. The wino woman was drooling, her spittle discolored. . . .

"I have further information for you," Ryder said. "The city has agreed to pay for your release."

The mother drew her children close to her and kissed them compulsively. The militant's expression remained unchanged. The old man clapped his small, well-cared-for hands together in a soundless applause that had, or seemed to have, no trace of irony.

"If everything proceeds according to schedule, you will be released unharmed to go about your business."

The old man said, "By according to schedule, you mean what?"

"Just that the city keeps its word."

"Okay," the old man said. "I would still like to know, just from curiosity, how much money?"

"A million dollars."

"Each?" Ryder shook his head. The old man looked disappointed. "That figures to about sixty thousand apiece. That's all we're worth?"

"Shut your mouth, old man."

Welcome's voice, but it was mechanical, uninterested. Ryder saw why: He was playing games with the girl. Her glamor pose was strictly for Welcome's benefit.

"Sir." The mother was leaning toward him, crushing

her boys together. They squirmed with embarrassment. "Sir, the instant you get the money, you'll let us go?"

"No, but soon afterwards."

"Why not *then*?"

"No more questions," Ryder said. He took a backward step toward Welcome and said in an undertone, "Stop your fooling around with that girl."

Only barely lowering his voice, Welcome said, "Stop worrying. I could handle this crowd of slobs and hump that broad at the same time without missing a stroke."

Ryder frowned but said nothing. He went back to the cab, ignoring Longman's anxious look, and went inside. There was nothing to do now but wait. He wasted no effort in speculation on whether or not the money would be delivered within the deadline. It was out of his hands. He didn't even bother to look at his watch.

TOM BERRY

As soon as the leader returned to the motorman's cab, Tom Berry put him out of mind and resumed thinking about Deedee—specifically about the first time he had met her, and generally about the way she had affected his head. Not that he hadn't been entertaining some vaguely uncoplike thoughts on his own, but they weren't pressing. What Deedee accomplished was to make him examine his assumptions seriously.

He had been on plainclothes patrol in the East Village now for three months. It was a volunteer detail, and God knew why he had stuck his neck out, except that he had been bored witless by duty in an area car with his partner, a fat-necked unreconstructed Nazi type who hated Jews, Negroes, Poles, Italians, Puerto Ricans, and almost everyone else, and was violently in favor of war—the one in Vietnam, as well as all past and future wars. So he had let his hair grow down to his shoulders, raised a beard, put in a supply of ponchos, headbands, and beads, and gone down among the Ukrainians, the motorcycle freaks, street people, addicts, weirdos, students, radicals, acidheads, teen-age runaways, and dwindling hippie population of the East Village.

The experience had turned out to be kooky and kinky, but not boring. He had gotten to know and like some of the hippies, some of the hustlers in hippie clothing (in a way he was one himself), and some of the sharp black men leading a joyous and charismatic existence on the strength of a skin color that was high fashion in those purlieus, and, eventually, through Deedee, some of the highly motivated revolutionary kids who were refugees from middle-class comforts and the elite campuses of Harvard, Vassar, Yale, and Swarthmore. Not that he would want to run a revolution with them in the ranks, or that Mao would be particularly crazy about them, either.

He had met Deedee during his first week on duty, when his instructions had been to acclimate himself and pick up the mores of the community. He had been studying the titles in the window of the bookstore on St. Marks Place—a mélange of Third World, Maoist, and American Movement pundits from Marcuse to Jerry Rubin—when she came out of the shop and stopped to look at the window display. She was dressed in denims and a T-shirt, and was standardly nonconformist: long hair streaming over her shoulders, no bra, no makeup. But the hair was lustrous and clean, the denims and T-shirt laundered (back then, he was still making such distinctions as his first judgments), the figure willowy, the features open and just missing beauty by a shade.

She became aware of his scrutiny. "The books are in the window, baby." It failed of toughness because her voice was not a street voice but soft, well modulated.

He smiled. "I was digging the books pretty good until you came along. You're prettier."

She frowned. "You're pretty, too, but I didn't try to demean you by saying so, did I?"

He recognized the polemics of Women's Lib. "I'm not into the male chauvinist bit. Honest."

"You may *think* you're not, but you gave yourself away."

She walked off, in the direction of Second Avenue. For no particular reason he trailed after her. She frowned for the third time as he ranged alongside her.

He said, "Buy me a cup of coffee, will you?"

"Fuck off."

"I'm tapped out."

"Go uptown and panhandle." She looked at him sharply. "Are you hungry?"

He said that he was. She took him to a coffee shop and bought him a sandwich. She took it for granted that he was a member of the Movement—that amorphous search-for-a-better-world flux of young people that was sometimes political, sometimes social, sometimes sexual, sometimes a form of mimicry, and often a combination of all of those—and as they chatted, she became increasingly exasperated at his ignorance of various aspects of it.

He found her charming and irritating at the same time and didn't want to arouse her suspicion, although she seemed to have none, only a kind of indignation that he could be so poorly informed. So he said, "Look, I only copped out recently, I'm just beginning to learn what the Movement is all about."

"You had a straight job?"

"In a bank, would you believe it," he said glibly. "I hated it, and finally I got around to chucking it, to doing my thing."

"Well, you don't quite know what your thing is all about yet, do you?"

"But I want to learn," he said, and looked away from her in a situation that called for a long, meaningful glance into a girl's eyes. He was, at least, learning about *her* pretty fast. "I really want to get into it."

"Well, I can help you."

"I appreciate it," he said gravely. "Do you like me a little better now?"

"Better than what?"

"Than before."

"Oh," she said in surprise, "I liked you well enough."

They met the next day, and she began his ideological education. The following week she took him to her pad, and they shared a stick of grass and went to bed, already half in love. He had to do some sleight of hand with his gun to keep her from seeing it. But a few days later he was careless, and she spotted him slipping it into the waistband of his pants when he was getting dressed.

"This? Maybe it's crazy, but I was mugged once, and hurt very badly. . . ."

Her eyes were huge with shock as she pointed to the short barrel of the .38 and said, "What are you doing with a pig gun?"

He might have tried to improvise further, but he found that he didn't have the stomach to lie to her. "I'm . . . well, Deedee, I happen to *be* a pig."

She surprised him by hitting him on the jaw—a closed-fist punch that staggered him, and then she sank to the floor and, with her head down in her arms, cried heart-breakingly, like any ordinary bourgeois chick. Later, after recrimination, vituperation, accusation, confession, and protestations of love, they decided not to break off, and Deedee vowed secretly—though she didn't keep it a secret for very long—to dedicate herself to the liberation of a pig.

LONGMAN

Longman had never been convinced of the necessity of imposing a stringent time limit on the delivery of the ransom money, and he had argued vehemently against the forfeiture of the passengers' lives as a penalty.

"We have to intimidate," Ryder had said, "and we have to be convincing. The moment they stop believing that we mean what we say we're through. We intimidate by setting a tough deadline, and we convince by killing when we threaten to kill."

In the crazy framework of this undertaking, Ryder was always right. His arguments went directly to the success of the operation, and on those terms you couldn't question their logic, bloodcurdling as it might be. Nor did he always argue on what Longman considered to be the "radical" side of an issue. On money, for example, he had taken a more conservative view than Longman himself, who had been for demanding five million dollars.

"Too much," Ryder had said. "They might balk at it. A million is the kind of sum people can understand, tolerate. It has a standard ring to it."

"That's just guesswork. You don't *know* they won't pay five million. If you're wrong, it's a lot of money out of our pocket."

Ryder had given one of his rare smiles at Longman's phrase. But he had been firm. "It's not worth the risk. You stand to end up with four hundred thousand, tax free. It's all the money you'll ever need. It's a big improvement on unemployment benefits."

The matter was settled, but the conversation left Longman wondering just how important the money was to Ryder; whether, in fact, it wasn't secondary to the adventure itself, the excitement, the challenge of leadership. The same question might apply to Ryder's past as a mercenary. Would anybody risk his life in battle if he wasn't driven by some other—more compelling—impulse than just money?

Ryder had certainly not counted pennies buying what he called "matériel." He had financed everything himself, without even asking Longman if he could share costs or so much as mentioning reimbursement when they scored. Longman knew that the four submachine guns had come high, not to mention the ammunition, the handguns, the grenades, the money belts, the specially tailored raincoats, the metal construction that he had designed under Ryder's prodding and that they referred to as the Gimmick. . . .

Longman became aware of Welcome and the girl in the Anzac hat. In spite of Ryder's rebuke, nothing had changed. If two people, separated by ten or fifteen feet, could be said to be screwing, that was what Welcome and the girl were doing. It was queer, kinky. Not that he was a prude. He had done it all, everything in and out of the book, first with that bitchy ex-wife of his and more recently with accommodating whores when he had the money. He had done it all, simple and fancy, and enjoyed it, but, chrisesakes, not in public!

ANITA LEMOYNE

Anita Lemoyne gave the creep a long passionate look to keep his fires burning, before she glanced down at the tiny gold watch on her wrist. Even if she could get out of the lousy train right this minute and start running like hell, stripping as she went, she still couldn't reach the television freak's pad in time to become a deck in what the bastard called his whore sammawich.

It was a rotten life and a rotten city. If she reckoned what she had to put out just to make the rent in that fancy high-rise she lived in (not to mention greasing up doormen and superintendents and renting agents and cops), it added up to a hell of a lot of tricks with no return. If there was some way to do it, she would blow the city and find a little house with a yard in the suburbs or even the real deep country. Sure—and live how? Put out a shingle to catch the rube

johns? Fuck in a flowery bower with the whisper of trees
mingling with the grunts of the johns and her own calculated screams of ecstasy? Some dream. There *were* no johns.
In the suburbs they fucked each other's wives, and in the
deep country they fucked sheeps in the summertime and
played poker all winter until the snow melted and they
could start chasing sheeps again.

The creep was still zeroed in on her, his eyeballs practically popping out through the holes in the mask. He was
preening himself, God's gift to women, shooting out
sparks of—what did they call it?—maximo. One thing
for sure—it took a wacked-out character to think about
pussy when he was right in the middle of ripping off a
subway train. And what about herself—did it make any
sense to be sitting there opening and closing her legs as if
she was creaming at the very sight of him?

Well, she was a pro, and she could no more not react in
a professional way than she could grow a mickey between
her legs. Besides, it was a scary situation, and it wouldn't
hurt to make a friend out of the horny creep. Even though
she didn't think they would deliberately harm her, accidents could happen with so many guns around. Sure, she
was an innocent bystander, but she had seen too many
pictures on the front page of the *News* of innocent bystanders lying around in their blood while some cop bent
over them feeling sorry and scratching his dumb ass. I
don't want to be no innocent bystander, she thought, I got
to get out of here! If it did me any good, I would blow the
creep. Right this minute, with an audience, I would kneel
down on the floor in front of him. . . .

Looking at him in panic, she formed a red suggestive

circle with her mouth. The creep got the message. In front, right below the belt, his raincoat began to form a tent.

WELCOME

Joe Welcome remembered a girl who once said to him, "I never met any cat who was more ready to do it than you." And this was a real mink, this girl, all you had to do was throw a dirty thought at her and she was down on her back and spread out. One time, he remembered, they fell out of the sack and went into the kitchen, and by the time the mink finished putting the coffee up and came to the table he was sitting in her chair, and she sat down on a big surprise. That was the time, bouncing up and down on his pole, when she gave him her testimonial.

Any time, Welcome thought, and any *place* too. Floor, bed, ceiling, vestibule, dark alley, sitting, standing, or riding a bicycle. Or in the middle of heisting a subway train!

Right this second, with a machine gun in his hand, about a million cops in the tunnel, and a tough getaway coming up, he was ready. The chick in the funny hat could *see* he was ready, and that mouth of hers was saying, Put something in it, baby. It was crazy to even be thinking the way he was at a time like this, but didn't everybody say he was crazy? Sure he was—cunt crazy. And what was wrong with a healthy stud being cunt crazy? It was nature!

Right now, with his joint aching and the chick practically begging for it, he was going to blow his stack if he couldn't get it off. How? Where? Christ, any place. He could take her down to the other end of the car and lay her right out on the seat. Let the passengers watch. He'd show them some first-class action. Ryder would go wild. But Ryder was in the cab, so screw Ryder. Screw Ryder anyway. He had handled Ryder before, when he came out, and he could do it again, anytime. If Ryder wanted to try him, he was ready. Any time.

KOMO MOBUTU

Mobutu's wound had bled itself out, although it still seeped somewhat into his saturated handkerchief. I blew my cool, he thought, I took a hit upside my head for a couple of niggers who will suck white ass to they last day on earth, gnawed to death by the rats of exploitation. He looked at his red handkerchief and thought, I would not mind shedding my blood, every pure black drop of it, if it would help to set my people free. But face it—sometime it do not avail, it simply do not avail.

He felt a tap on his arm. The old dude beside him was offering a large folded handkerchief.

"Take it," the old man said.

Mobutu pushed the handkerchief away. "I got my own." He held the bloody rag up and the old man turned pale, but didn't give up.

"Go. Take my handkerchief. We're all in the same boat."

"Old man, you are in your boat, and I am in my boat. Don't sell me no same boat deals."

"Okay. So we're boats that pass in the night. But take the handkerchief anyway. Please be a good boy."

"I do not accept castoffs."

"Castoffs I cast *off*," the old man said. "This handkerchief I bought maybe a month ago."

"I will take nothing from a white peeg, so fuck off, old man."

"White, granted." The old man smiled. "Pig, you happen to have the wrong religion. Come on, young man, let's be friends."

"No way, old man. I am your enemy, and one day I will cut your throat."

"That day," the old man said, "*I'll* borrow *your* handkerchief."

Mobutu touched his handkerchief to his torn brow. It squeegeed, too wet to absorb any longer. He looked at the thick folds of the old man's handkerchief, which he had surely bought with profits wrung from the blood of black brothers and sisters. The handkerchief truly belonged to them, to him. It was a small enough reparation.

"Sheet," Mobutu said, and took the handkerchief.

"Not a sheet," the old man said, "just a little handkerchief."

Mobutu stared at the wrinkled, oversolemn face. Damn if the old dude wasn't putting him on.

THIRTEEN

THE CITY: UNDERGROUND SCENE

The Twenty-eighth Street southbound platform was the arena of what was to be described later as a "mini-riot." The borough commander, shortly after his arrival on the scene, had dispatched a squad of patrolmen down the stairs to clear the platform. They straggled back ten minutes later, sweating, disheveled, and angry, one of them limping badly, another streaming blood from a clawed face, a third nursing a bitten hand. Not only had the passengers—except for a docile few—refused to leave, but they had hurled invective, drowned out instructions with derisive shouts, resisted being herded toward the exit, and, finally, resorted to violence. The squad had arrested six citizens, four of whom had been lost on the way to the street as the result of harassment and obstruction by the crowd. One of the surviving arrestees was a black lady who had been punched in the eye by a patrolman after she kicked him in the ankle; the second, a young man with a scraggly beard and a mass of crinkly hair, had been clubbed, reason unstated, and was semiconscious, drooling, and probably concussed.

The crowd, the reporting sergeant continued, was unruly and violent. A number of windows had been broken in the train standing at the platform, and there were other instances of vandalism: Posters had been torn down, benches overturned, toilet paper taken from the lavatories and thrown around like confetti. The DCI, unable to hear the radio in the motorman's cab over the hubbub, was in a rage and had respectfully requested that the borough commander send down a force in sufficient numbers to clear the fucking platform of every last single fucking citizen.

The borough commander ordered a detail of fifty Tactical Patrol Force men and ten detectives to enter the station. With drawn nightsticks, the police charged into the tightly massed passengers on the platform and in five minutes had succeeded in moving the crowd toward the exit. However, a bottleneck developed; many of the passengers demanded that their fare be refunded. In the ensuing melee an undetermined number of passengers and at least six cops suffered injury. The captain in charge fought his way through to the change booth and ordered the clerk, a middle-aged man with wispy gray hair, to pass out a token to each passenger. The clerk refused, demanding authorization. The captain drew his service revolver, pointed it at the gray-haired clerk through the bars of his cage, and said, "Here's your authorization, and if you don't start handing out those tokens, I'll blow your goddamn mouth out of your goddamn ugly face!"

An additional number of citizens and police were injured in the crush to get on line for the return of the token (more than a dozen seriously enough to require medical attention, four to be hospitalized), but fifteen minutes from the time that the force had entered, the last of the passengers was pushed up the steps to the street. No unauthorized personnel remained on the station platform except (unknown to the police) three men, one black and two white, total strangers to each other, who were industriously raping a young black girl, age fourteen, in the women's lavatory.

COMMAND CENTER

The Communications Desk of the Command Center continued to cut cassettes containing bulletins directed toward clearing the station platforms in the area affected by the power cut. Played over the station PA systems, they urged passengers to leave the platforms for alternate routes—"a short walk to the BMT, IND, or West Side lines," "Your attention is called to the MABSTOA buses, no charge"—which would carry them north or south to their destination. Each message contained an adjuration to "clear the stations, please, by order of the New York City Police."

Although a number of people responded and sought the

open air, the majority refused to budge ("It's the way they are," the TA police chief said to the borough commander. "Don't ask me to explain it, it's just the way they are"). To avoid a repetition of the Battle of Twenty-eighth Street, the police made no effort to clear any other platforms by force. Instead, they mounted guards at the street entrances to keep newly arrived passengers from descending. This measure proved effective except at the Astor Place station, where a group of passengers, under inspired leadership, rushed the entrance, overwhelmed the guards, and stormed down the stairs to the platform.

THE CITY: OCEANIC WOOLENS BUILDING

In the lobby of the Oceanic Woolens Building (the eponymous company had long ago emigrated to the South and cheaper labor, but the name remained irrevocably engraved over the august doorway), Abe Rosen was enjoying the most fantastic business of his life. Spectators were streaming off the streets and into the lobby, gathering four deep in front of his little stand. As fast as his display stock of candy bars disappeared, he would open new supplies, which were bought right out of the cardboard boxes. He sold out his stock of cigarettes completely in a half hour, including the unpopular brands. Then his cigars began to go (cigarette smokers and even women took them as a substitute) and finally, for lack of anything else to buy, his newspapers and magazines.

The lobby had become all but impassable, since many of the spectators remained, smoking, eating candy, reading magazines and newspapers, and inventing and circulating dozens of rumors about the hijacking.

Sooner or later Abe Rosen heard them all.

"A dozen ambulances just took off screaming. Seems they turned the third rail on by mistake, and some passengers were on the tracks. When you get that juice in you, a million volts . . ."

"Castros. A bunch of Cuban Commies. The cops chased them into the tunnel and they commandeered a train. . . ."

"This cop outside told me they give them a ultimatum. If they don't surrender by three o'clock, the cops are going in and blasting them out. . . ."

"They're talking about cutting off the air in the tunnel, the compressors, you know, and when they start gasping, they'll come crawling out. . . ."

"You know how they're going to get away? The sewers. They got a map of the sewers, and they know exactly where the big mains connect with the subway. . . ."

"They're asking a million for each passenger. They got twenty, which is a cool twenty million dollars! The city is trying to jew them down to half a million each. . . ."

"The mayor? Forget it. The only direction he ever goes is uptown. If this train had got heisted at, say, a Hundred Twenty-fifth and Lenox Avenue . . ."

"Dogs. All they got to do is loose a pack of Dobermans, and sic them into that train. So they might shoot half the dogs, but the other half will tear their throats out. And the beauty part is that all you're losing the lives of are dogs!"

"They're bringing in the National Guard. The only question is how can they get a tank down there. . . ."

Abe Rosen kept saying, "Yeah, yeah, yeah." He believed nothing and doubted nothing. Near three o'clock he was completely sold out—every pack of cigarettes, every cigar, bar of candy, newspaper, magazine, even his last pack of flints. He sat on his scarred wooden stool with nothing to do and a sense of bewilderment and loss. Three o'clock and nothing to do but shake his head sadly at the people who still came up to the counter hoping to buy something, anything at all. Through the lobby doors he could see part of the huge crowd, standing patiently, waiting for God knew what—a body being carried out on a stretcher, a sheet over its face and helpless feet sticking up; the sound of gunfire; somebody with blood on him. . . .

Suddenly, he remembered Artis James. The schwartzer had gone back to duty right about the time it all started. Could Artis be involved? Nah, he answered himself, with thousands of cops, did they need a subway shamus? Most likely, they would have Artis guarding the chewing gum machines.

Idly, Abe watched a man come out of the elevator, stop in his tracks, and stare in surprise at the boiling activity in the lobby. The man came over to the stand.

"What's up, Mac?" he said.

Abe shook his head in wonderment. What's up, Mac? A half a block away the crime of the century, and this dumb goy didn't know what was up.

"What could be up?" Abe said, shrugging. "A parade or something."

CLIVE PRESCOTT

Lieutenant Prescott, who had been the best basketball player in the history of his little college in southern Illinois, had not been quite good enough for the pros. He had been chosen late in the draft and worked hard during his tryout, but been dropped before the season opened.

He was essentially a doer, what he would have called, if he didn't think it pretentious, a man of action. His desk job at headquarters did not suit him, although he recognized that it was highly privileged and, for a black man, a distinguished one. Lately he had been thinking of looking around for something else, even if it meant taking less money, but he knew it was hopeless because of his four hostages to fortune—his wife, his two kids, and his pension.

He sat at the desk trainmaster's console and stared at the constellation of flickering lights, feeling sorry for himself and for the captives on Pelham One Two Three. He held himself in some measure responsible for both. He should, for example, have been three inches taller and had a more reliable outside shot; he should, for another, have been able to persuade the leader of the hijack gang to extend his deadline. With about twelve minutes remaining and the money not yet on its way, there wasn't a chance of making it. And he had no doubt that the hijackers would keep their word and kill some passengers as penalty.

Across the room, Correll was all bombast and motion, shunting trains here and there, haranguing motormen and towermen, screaming at a MABSTOA dispatcher, hysterical and happy. A contented man, Prescott thought sourly, a man who adored his work, who throve on the ultimately solvable adversity. "Prop him up against a pillar until after rush hour. . . ." The true believers were truly blessed of the Lord. And so were the active, he thought. He jumped to his feet and made three mindless circuits of the console, then sat down suddenly and signaled Pelham One Two Eight at the Twenty-eighth Street platform.

DCI Daniels said briskly, "Yeah, what is it?"

"Sir, I'm checking to see if the money is on its way yet."

"Not yet. I'll let you know."

"Good," Prescott said. "It's on its way. I'll pass the word to Pelham One Two Three. Over."

"I said *not yet*, ferchrisesake."

"Yes, sir," Prescott said. "And it's just a question of how long it takes to run it uptown?"

"Look," the DCI said irascibly, "I'm telling you the money isn't—" He stopped abruptly, and Prescott thought: The old bastard has finally remembered that Pelham One Two Three could monitor the dispatcher's end of the call but not the respondent's. "Okay," the DCI said. "I think I know what you've got on your mind. Go ahead."

Prescott called Pelham One Two Three. "Lieutenant Prescott. The money is on its way."

"Yes."

The leader's voice was uninflected, the meaning of his affirmative ambiguous, so that Prescott couldn't tell whether he had monitored the call or not. But it didn't matter.

"We're cooperating," Prescott said. "You can see that.

But it's physically impossible to get through city traffic in eleven minutes. Do you read me?"

"Ten. Ten minutes."

"It can't be done. It's not for lack of trying, it's just the condition of city traffic. Will you give us a ten-minute extension?"

"No."

"We're moving as quickly as we can," Prescott said. He heard the pleading in his voice and knew that just beneath it lay rage. "All we need is a little more time. Give us a break."

"No. The deadline is three thirteen."

The flat inflexibility of the voice was deadly. But Prescott kept trying. "All right. It's out of the question for us to get the money to you by three thirteen. But suppose we can get it to the station entrance by then. Will you change the deadline from delivery to you to arrival at the station? Will you do that for us, at least? Come in. Come in, please."

After an interval that was so protracted that Prescott had decided to call again, the leader's voice suddenly came back. "All right. I agree. But no more concessions. Do you understand?"

Prescott's breath, expelled in a rush, tasted sour. "Okay. If there's nothing else, I'd like to pass the word on."

"Nothing else. Call me as soon as the money arrives for further instructions. Over and out."

So I took action, Prescott thought, and bought a few minutes of time. The only trouble is, it won't do any good. Even with the revised timetable, the money couldn't possibly reach the station by three thirteen.

ARTIS JAMES

TA Patrolman Artis James was uncomfortable, not only physically but mentally. At a distance of about sixty feet from the rear of the hijacked car, scrunched behind a pillar, he was adequately covered, but there was no leeway at all for movement, and his muscles were stiff and aching. But aside from that, he was beginning to feel spooked. The tunnel was gloomy, and the wind that blew through it carried all sorts of imaginary whispers.

Not that *all* of them were imaginary. He knew that there were police in the tunnel behind him—maybe twenty, thirty, fifty, armed with riot guns, sniper's rifles, machine guns, and all those weapons trained on the car or, to put it another way, aiming in his general direction. Furthermore, he couldn't be sure they had been advised of his presence; it was the kind of detail the brass overlooked in their concern with the big picture. So he pressed hard into the begrimed unyielding steel of the pillar and tried not to move. A crappy situation. Not only did he have to avoid being spotted by the hijackers, but he had to worry about arousing the suspicions of the cops behind him. For all he knew, some goddamn commando type might sneak up behind him and cut his throat to—as they said on the TV movies—prevent an outcry.

His right wrist, pressed to his side, felt the oblong shape of the cigarettes he had bought from Abe Rosen, and he had a sudden unbearable craving for smoke in his lungs. Then it occurred to him that if things went badly, he might never smoke again, and the meaning of death took shape: not being able to eat again, or sleep with a woman,

or take a satisfying crap. . . . The whole idea was so painful
that he waved it away with a sharp dismissive gesture, then
froze as he realized that he had exposed his hand. Nothing
happened, but he was shaken. Why didn't somebody help
him, out here in no-man's-land? He was the forgotten
man. Nobody gave a shit about a black man.

On the other hand, if he was a white man, his face and
hands would shine out in the darkness. So maybe there was
some virtue in being a nigger, after all. The thought made
him smile, but not for long. He snapped his mouth shut,
thinking: But my teeth, goddamn, my teeth are lily white!

HIS HONOR, THE MAYOR

Tires squealing, the commissioner's car swung down the
incline from the mansion, and one of the cops on guard at
the sentry house fell back into a bed of rhododendrons
to escape being run down. The commissioner sat directly
behind the driver, with Murray Lasalle in the middle and
the mayor, huddled under a plaid blanket, at the other
window. As the car straightened into East End Avenue,
the mayor produced an explosive sneeze, and the motes
danced in the sunlit interior of the car.

"Use a tissue," Lasalle said. "You want to make us all
sick?"

The mayor wiped his nose on the blanket. "This is
crazy, Murray."

"I don't do crazy things," Lasalle said coldly. "I have a
good reason for everything I do."

"Going down into that damp, windy tunnel—that isn't crazy?"

"Bundle up nice and warm," Lasalle said.

The commissioner was speaking on his confidential radio line. The mayor said to Lasalle, "What's he doing?"

"Telling them you're coming. Look, all you have to do—and it's the least you *can* do—is get on a bullhorn and make a dignified plea for mercy."

"Suppose they shoot at me?"

"Stand behind a post. Anyway, they have no reason to shoot at you."

Sick as he was, the mayor got off a joke. "You mean they're out-of-towners?"

"Relax," Lasalle said. "Just do your turn, and then we'll drive you home and you can get back into bed. Think of it as a benefit appearance."

"If I thought it would actually help—"

"It will."

"The hostages?"

"No," Lasalle said, "you."

BOROUGH COMMANDER

From the borough commander's command post in the parking lot near the southwest entrance to the Twenty-eighth Street station, the crowd resembled a gigantic un-coordinated cellular organism whose protoplasm was highly agitated but not quite suicidally so. For all its flux it remained a massive entity. The borough commander kept

looking at his watch, sometimes openly, sometimes surreptitiously. The minutes were ticking off anarchically, like
unmanageable cancer cells. "Three oh three," the borough commander said. "Ten minutes, and they haven't
even started yet."

"If they kill somebody," the TA police chief said, "I'm
for going down there in force and wiping them out."

"I'm for doing what I'm told to do," the borough
commander said, "whether I like it or not. If they kill one,
there's still sixteen left. If we go in shooting, they'll likely
all get killed. You want to take a decision like that on your
head?"

"So far," the TA police chief said, "nobody has asked
me to make *any* kind of decision."

The police captain who had given his name to a newspaper reporter as Captain Midnight placed himself squarely
in front of the borough commander and saluted. His face
was tomato red. "Sir," he said angrily, "what are we doing?"

The borough commander said, "We're standing around
and waiting. You have any ideas?"

"Sir, I don't like feeling so goddamn helpless. Also,
it's rotten for the men's morale to see bums getting away
with—"

"Oh, go away, Captain," the borough commander said
wearily.

The flush spread on the captain's face, reaching his
eyes. He stared murderously at the borough commander,
then wheeled abruptly and pushed his way out of the
command post circle.

"I don't blame him," the borough commander said.

"He may not be smart, but he's a man. But it's not a time for men; it's a time for negotiators."

"Sir—" A sergeant, sitting in the rear of the borough commander's car, with his legs braced on the pavement, held out the hand set. "It's the PC, sir."

The borough commander took the hand set, and the commissioner's voice said, "Fill me in."

"We're waiting for the money to get here. It isn't started yet, and I can't see how it can get here on time. The next move is theirs." He paused. "Unless my orders are changed."

"They're not," the commissioner said flatly. "I'm calling from the drive. We're on our way down. The mayor is with me."

"Wonderful," the borough commander said. "I'll hold the crowd for him."

The commissioner's breathing was labored for a moment. "When he arrives, His Honor will make a personal appeal to the hijackers."

Speaking with control, the borough commander said, "Anything else, Commissioner?"

"That's all," the commissioner said heavily. "That's all there is, Charlie."

THE FED

Although minutes are not kept of such trivial matters, there is little doubt that never before in the sixty-year history of the Federal Reserve Bank had the chairman of a great member bank of the stature of the Gotham National

Trust phoned the president of a Federal Reserve Bank about so undignified an amount as a million dollars. In the normal course of events, requests for cash deliveries, many far in excess of that amount, are made through regular channels, much as the ordinary depositor in a bank makes a withdrawal. The member bank sends along an authorization—not much more complicated than the average withdrawal slip at a neighborhood bank, although the figures are astronomically larger—signed by a bank officer, the Fed counts out the money, dumps it into a canvas sack, and signs it out to the armored car service dispatched by the member bank.

That's really all there is to it, and that's why the Fed, in its homespun way, refers to itself as a bank for banks. On a more sophisticated level, of course, the Fed functions as an extragovernmental agency in controlling the flow of money in order to keep the national economy in equilibrium. That is to say, roughly, it increases the supply of money in periods of recession and unemployment and decreases it in periods of prosperity and inflation.

The Fed does not ruffle easily; in fact, it is virtually unflappable. Yet it underwent a mild case of nerves in the wake of the call from the chairman of the Gotham National Trust to its president. Not because of the call, however unique it might have been, but because of the tradition-flouting instructions concerning the handling and packaging of the money. The Fed ordinarily has one way, and one way only, of making up the huge levies of cash it services to its member banks: all money is put up in packets of one hundred bills each, which are bound by a strip of paper width-wise; these are then collected into packs of ten, which are tied with white string and known as bundles. New, mint-fresh bills come wrapped in wrapping paper, are known as a brick, and resemble a ream of inexpensive bond paper.

The Fed *does not* put bills up in packets of two hundred; it *does not* bind them in rubber bands; and it *does not* select used bills to order. Normally, it makes up its packages randomly from whatever bills are available at the moment, usually a mixture of both new *and* used.

But of course, when the order comes from its own president, the Fed *does* do what it normally does *not*.

All incoming and outgoing cash is handled on the third floor of the Federal Reserve Building at 33 Liberty Street in the center of New York's great financial district. The building is an impregnable fortress, a square block of monolithic stone, with barred windows on its lower floors. The visitor to the third floor—there are not many—enters through a massive gate watched over by an armed guard and, as long as he remains, is scrutinized by closed-circuit television cameras. After passing through another gate, he finds himself in a corridor, long, rather ordinary, containing a few wooden trunks on wheels; these are used to transport sums of money throughout the building, to and from the vault. Armed guards stand about. On the visitor's left, behind gates, are the security elevators in which money is taken down to the loading platforms on the Maiden Lane side of the building. Farther along the corridor, behind grilled windows, is Paying/Receiving; behind panes of glass, Sorting/Counting.

Paying/Receiving is the depot for a constantly flowing two-way traffic in cash. Receiving clerks accept and sign for incoming sacks of bills sent to the Fed by member banks, and then pass them along to Sorting/Counting across the aisle. Paying clerks make up outgoing packages for withdrawal by member banks, sack them, and turn them over to the bank's armed guards for delivery.

Sorting/Counting processes the money sent to the Fed by its member banks. The counters, mostly men and immured in individual cages, break open the seals on the canvas money bags (when new the bags are white, but they quickly turn a dirty gray to match the color of the New York air) and count the number of packets in each, but not the number of bills in a packet.

The sorters, most of whom are women, occupy a large office of the bullpen type. The sorters' technique consists of taking a batch of bills, creasing it lengthwise, and then, almost faster than the eye can see, distributing it according to denomination into various slots in a machine; a tachometer automatically counts the bills as they are fed in. Despite their dazzling speed, the sorters spot worn and damaged bills and mark them for destruction and even pick out counterfeits, which the tellers at the banks are supposed to spot but frequently overlook.

The bad bills, with a tinge of humor, or perhaps merely distaste, are known as mutts.

The special order for a million dollars requested by the chairman of the Gotham National Trust was filled by a Paying clerk in just a few minutes. Suppressing his annoyance at the unorthodox departure from procedure, he selected ten bundles of fifties, each bundle consisting of ten packets of one hundred fifties; and five bundles of hundreds, each bundle consisting of ten packets of one hundred hundreds. He then systematically cut the strings of the bundles, and proceeded to pair packets and tie them with a thick rubber band. Each new packet of two hundred bills was approximately an inch thick. When piled neatly together, the total of fifteen thousand bills made a block approximately twenty inches high and twelve inches deep.

When he was finished, the clerk put the block of bills into a canvas bag, which he then pushed through his raised window to two guards waiting in an adjoining room. The guards hurried out of the room with the money, which weighed about twenty-five pounds, and bustled down the corridor to their right. Another guard opened a gate leading to the security elevators, and they rode down to the street-level loading platform.

PATROLMAN WENTWORTH

Cops in the Special Operations Division were not unaccustomed to improvisation, even on a grand scale, but Patrolman Wentworth, sitting behind the wheel of a "small truck" parked on the sidewalk in front of the loading bays of the Federal Reserve on Maiden Lane, was nevertheless impressed by the lavishness of the occasion. His partner, Patrolman Albert Ricci, was practically shocked into silence by it, which Wentworth accounted a blessing. Ricci was a nonstop talker with a single theme: his large and volatile Sicilian family.

Wentworth looked with pleasure at the eight men of the motorcycle detachment sitting astride their bikes, booted, goggled, and leathered, occasionally goosing their engines with a little touch of the accelerator. His own engine was running, too, and from time to time he raced it. It was smooth and powerful, but nothing to compare with the deep stutter of the cycles.

A voice came over the radio, important and impatient, demanding to know whether they had the money yet. It was the fifth such call in the last five minutes. "No, sir, not yet, sir," Ricci said. "Still waiting, sir." The voice cut out, and Ricci, shaking his head, said to Wentworth, "Something. Really something."

Pedestrians negotiating the narrow old street kept glancing at the truck, especially at the motorcycle escort. Most of them moved on without stopping, but one little group had formed across the street. They carried cases chained to their wrists, and Wentworth figured them to be runners with, probably, hundreds of thousands, maybe millions, in securities in their cases. He saw a couple of kids stop and talk to the motorcycle cops, eyeing their bikes with awe. But they moved on when they were met with cold stony silence from the cops.

"You feel honored having the Gestapo for an escort?" Wentworth said to Ricci.

"Something," Ricci said. "Really something."

"Not only that," Wentworth said, "but a cop at every intersection all the way uptown. Don't say, 'Something, really something.'"

"You think we got a chance of making it?" Ricci looked at his watch. "What's taking them so long in there?"

"Counting," Wentworth said. "You realize how many times you have to wet your thumb when you're counting out a million?"

Ricci gave him a suspicious look. "You're shitting me. They must have a machine or something."

"Right. A machine that wets their thumbs."

Ricci said, "We can't make it. It's a physical impossibility. Even if they was to come out with the money right this minute—"

Two guards came running out of the bay, each holding an end of a canvas bag, each with a drawn gun. They ran to Wentworth's window.

"Other side," Wentworth said, and gunned his motor. Ricci opened his door. The guards tossed the bag into his lap and slammed the door shut. The motorcycle cops were starting to move, shoving off with their right foot, their sirens already building volume. "And away we go," Wentworth said. He heard Ricci reporting on the radio.

At the corner a cop waved to them and they turned right into Nassau Street, one of the narrowest thoroughfares in the city. But cars were pulled up on the sidewalks, and they sailed uphill past John Street, leveled off and roared by Fulton, Ann and Beekman. At Spruce, where Nassau Street ended, they circled to the right, and entered Park Row, on the wrong side of the street, with City Hall just to their left.

It was beautiful, Wentworth thought, roaring against the stopped traffic, the bike cops opening everything up with their sirens and the roar of their motors.

"Don't spill the money, Al," Wentworth said, laughing with exhilaration.

"Them bastards tossed it right square on my balls," Ricci said. "It aches like a bastard."

Wentworth laughed again. "If they have to cut it off,

the mayor will pay a sympathy call at the hospital. You're a lucky cop."

"We can't make it," Ricci said. "No way."

At the Municipal Building, Wentworth swung over to the right side of the street. Traffic coming off Brooklyn Bridge was being held up on the ramp. Beyond Chambers Street, he whipped into Centre Street in the wake of the motorcycles and raced past the white-pillared Federal Court Building, the old City Courthouse, filthy with city grime but still handsome, and the huge pile of the Criminal Courts Building. At Canal they turned left, whipping between pulled-over cars and trucks, and zigzagged to Lafayette, where they turned north again.

Wentworth had only half believed that there would be a cop at every intersection, but it was true. The number of cops tied up in the operation was staggering. The streets must have been empty of police elsewhere, and burglars and muggers were probably having a field day. The brake lights of the motorcycles twinkled red, and he saw up ahead of them a car blocking an intersection. He tapped his brake, but the bikes drew away from him, and he realized that they had no intention of stopping, that their braking had been instinctive. He shifted his foot back to the accelerator. A cop was holding the side of the stalled car, seemed to be pushing it, but the car didn't budge. Then, just as the cycles seemed about to smash into it, the car started up with a roar and pulled away. Wentworth cleared the corner in the wake of the motorcycles.

"One more like that," he said, "and we'll *all* have crushed balls." He was shouting to make himself heard over the medley of sirens, motors and echoing windslip.

"We can't make it," Ricci shouted back.

"I'm not even gonna try. Next corner, as soon as the bikes clear it, I'm turning left, and keep on going, and you and me, we got ourselves a million dollars."

Ricci shot a look at him, combining uncertainty, fear, and—Wentworth was certain of it—wistfulness.

"Think of it as a gratuity," Wentworth said. "Your share is a half a million. You realize how many tons of pasta that would buy? It could feed that fucking dago family of yours for the rest of their miserable lives."

"Look," Ricci said, "my sense of humor is as good as your sense of humor, but I don't like racial slurs."

Wentworth grinned as another corner and another guardian cop went by in a blur. The broad avenue ahead was Houston Street.

BOROUGH COMMANDER

At 3:09 the small truck containing the ransom money reported an accident crossing Houston Street. To avoid hitting a pedestrian who was defiantly crossing in front of them—possibly because he viewed the shrieking sirens as an infringement of his constitutional guarantees as a New Yorker—the two lead motorcyclists had swerved sharply and sideswiped each other. Both riders were thrown. Before they had stopped rolling, Ricci was on the radio. Central signaled the borough commander. Instructions? The borough commander ordered two cyclists to drop off to help the injured policemen. Everyone else to keep going. *Keep going.* Elapsed time, ninety seconds.

The group surrounding the command post in the parking lot shook their heads helplessly. Captain Midnight was pounding the fender of a car with his fist. He was crying.

A roar from the crowd half a block away caught the borough commander's attention. The helmets of the TPF cops began to bob antically, and he could see them straining to contain sudden bulges in the crowd front. Rising on his toes, he caught a glimpse of the mayor, bareheaded but wrapped in a blanket. He was smiling and nodding his head, and the crowd was booing him. The commissioner was by his side, and they were heading toward the command post with the help of a half dozen TPF cops.

The borough commander looked at his watch: 3:10. He looked at it again almost immediately. Still 3:10, but the sweep second hand was racing at high speed. He looked southward down the avenue and then at his watch again.

"They can't make it," he muttered.

A hand tapped him on the back. It belonged to Murray Lasalle. Beside him, the mayor was smiling, but he was pale and drawn, and his eyes were tearing and half-shut. He was leaning wearily against the commissioner.

Lasalle said, "The mayor is going down into the tunnel with a bullhorn to make a personal appeal to the hijackers."

The borough commander shook his head. "No can do."

Lasalle said, "I wasn't asking for your permission. All I want you to do is to make the arrangements."

The borough commander looked at the commissioner, whose features were absolutely blank. He read the commissioner's expression as a hands-off policy, and that suited him well enough.

"Sir," he said to the mayor, "I appreciate your concern in this matter." He paused, marveling at the diplomacy of his language. "But it's out of the question. Not only for your own safety, but for the safety of the hostages."

He saw the commissioner nod his head minimally. The mayor, too, was nodding, but whether in agreement or from sheer physical weakness, he couldn't tell.

Lasalle eyed him briefly, then turned to the commissioner. "Mr. Commissioner, order this man to comply."

"No." It was the mayor, his voice firm. "The officer is right. It would only louse things up and maybe get me shot in the bargain."

Lasalle said ominously, "Sam, I warn you—"

"I'm going home, Murray," the mayor said. He reached into his pocket, took out a scarlet woolen stocking cap, and pulled it down over his ears.

"Jesus," Lasalle said, "have you flipped?" The mayor started to walk off. Lasalle chased after him. "Sam, for God's sake, since when does a politician wear a hat with a hundred thousand people watching him?"

The commissioner said, "Carry on, Charlie. I'll see them off and be right back. You're running the show."

The borough commander nodded, remembering that it was the mayor, not the commissioner, who had scotched Lasalle. Maybe the commissioner would have spoken up if the mayor hadn't jumped in, but still, he would have felt better if the commissioner had been faster on the draw.

A siren screamed on the avenue. The borough commander whirled around, but the siren suddenly died.

Someone said, "Burglar warning on a parked car."

The borough commander looked at his watch: 3:12. "That TA lieutenant had the right idea." He turned to the walkie-talkie man. "Signal the DCI. Tell him to get word to the hijackers that the money has arrived."

FOURTEEN

RYDER

Ryder switched on the overhead light in the cab and looked at his watch: 3:12. In sixty seconds he would kill a hostage.

TOM BERRY

Tom Berry felt rage erupt unbidden from some deep volcanic core inside him. He recognized it as *macho*, atavistic maleness, a primitive anger at being humiliated and its concomitant urge to strike back, to prove his masculinity.

For a dizzy moment he was tensed to spring, his vocal cords vibrating to a wild, unreleased scream. But nothing happened. The even stronger atavism of survival held him back, and he subsided. Trembling, he began to comb his fingers nervously through his long blond hair. Instinct had elected against self-slaughter. He couldn't go it alone.

But, he thought slyly, in union there was strength. The other passengers. Swiftly, he formulated a plan for concerted action and passed it along by telepathy. He warned them to wait for his signal. One by one, expressionless, they acknowledged by thought wave. Ready?

He brought his hand away from his hair in a sharp downward slash, and the plan went into action. The diversion unit acted first: The wino lady tumbled off her seat into the aisle; the old man feigned a heart attack; the hustler stripped off her pantyhose. The mother and her boys went to the aid of the wino lady, who produced a switchblade from the infinite layers of her clothing and passed it to the mother. The stout black lady got up and chafed the old man's wrists, her bulk effectively blocking out the line of sight between the hijackers at the front and center of the car. Her hair pie exposed, the hustler undulated toward the Latin lover boy.

At the precise instant when she threw her pantyhose into his face and disarmed him with a vicious judo chop, the assault force, led by the militant spade, joined the action. Separating into two groups, one squad of three knocked down the hijacker at the front of the car and then made way for the theater critic, who fell on him and knocked the breath out of him. The main force stormed down the aisle toward the heavyset hijacker at the rear. His finger tightened on the trigger of his submachine gun, but before he could fire the mother of the boys, throwing from behind her ear, sent the switchblade whizzing the length of the car. With dazzling accuracy, the blade pinned the heavyset man's hand to the butt of the gun. An instant later he disappeared under a half dozen eager bodies.

Berry himself was waiting for the leader to appear. When he rushed out of the cab, he simply put out a deft foot, and the leader went crashing to the floor, the gun jarring loose from his grip. He snaked out a hand for it, but the old man was too fast for him. Scooping it up, he trained it on the leader's chest.

"Don't shoot," Berry said quietly. "This one is mine."

The leader got up and came on in a maddened rush, his fists swinging. Berry measured him coolly and threw a perfect overhand right. The leader went down with a crash, twitched once, and then lay still. The cheering passengers lifted Berry to their shoulders and began a triumphal processional through the aisle of the car. . . .

Breathless from the whirlwind action, Berry inhaled deeply and thought: In fantasy there is self-preservation. A man's a man for all that, isn't he, without having to get himself killed to prove it?

CLIVE PRESCOTT

"Pelham One Two Three. Come in, Pelham One Two Three." Prescott's voice was vibrant with emotion.

"Pelham One Two Three to Command Center. I read you." The leader's voice, as always, was calm and unhurried.

"The money has arrived," Prescott said. "Repeat: The money has arrived."

"Yes. All right." A pause. "You made it just on the tick."

A flat statement of fact. No emotion. Prescott was outraged, remembering the quaver in the DCI's voice when he relayed the information, remembering how his own feeling of relief had left him trembling. But the leader was impervious to feelings. Ice water for blood. Or psycho. He had to be psycho.

"And if we went a tick further," Prescott said, "you'd have knocked off an innocent person?"

"Yes."

"For a tick. Is that all a life is worth?"

"I will now give you instructions for delivery of the money. You will follow them to the letter. Acknowledge."

"Go ahead."

"I want two policemen to walk down the track. One to carry the bag with the money, the other to carry a lit flashlight. Acknowledge."

"Two cops, one with the money, one with a flashlight. What kind of cops—Transit or NYPD?"

"No difference. The one with the light will flash it continuously from side to side. When they reach the car, the rear door will open. The one with the money will toss the bag onto the floor of the car. Then both of them will turn around and walk back to the station. Acknowledge."

"Check. That's it?"

"That's it. But keep in mind that the ground rules remain in full effect. Any action on the part of the police, any wrong move, and we'll kill a hostage."

"Yeah," Prescott said. "I could have guessed that part of it."

"You have ten minutes to deliver the money. If it isn't here by then—"

"Yeah," Prescott said. "You'll kill a hostage. It's getting monotonous. We need more than ten minutes. They can't walk it that fast."

"Ten minutes."

"Give us fifteen," Prescott said. "It's a hard walk on the roadbed, and one of them will be carrying a heavy package. Make it fifteen."

"Ten minutes. No further discussion. When we have the money in hand, I'll call you back with final instructions."

"Final instructions for what? Oh, the getaway. You'll never be able to pull it off."

"Check your watch, Lieutenant. I've got three fourteen. That gives you until three twenty-four to deliver. Over."

"Over," Prescott said. "Over, you bastard!"

PATROLMAN WENTWORTH

Patrolman Wentworth, pushing the accelerator to the floor in the wake of the roaring motorcycle escort, reached Union Square at 3:15:30, whipped through the rightward dogleg bounded by Klein's to the east and Union Square park to the west, and sailed through an open route up the Avenue to 28th Street in forty seconds. A lieutenant, no less, signaled a U-turn. He cornered sharply, jolted the center ramp with his left rear tire, and pulled up in a rubber-burning stop in the parking lot as the motorcycle escort tailed away.

Wentworth recognized the borough commander,

coming toward them in a lumbering heavyweight trot. From the side of his mouth, Wentworth said, "We're in fast company, Al. I figure for our fine work he hands us a two-grade promotion on the spot."

The borough commander, breathing hard, yanked Ricci's door open and shouted, "Throw that goddamn bag out!"

Ricci, flustered, gave the bag a heave. It struck the borough commander and buckled his knees. He picked it up and tossed it to two cops who were standing by—a TPF patrolman in blue helmet and a TA sergeant.

"Move it," the borough commander shouted. "You got about eight and a half minutes. Never mind the fucking salutes. Take off!"

The TPF cop hiked the bag over his shoulder and, with the TA sergeant beside him, ran to the subway entrance. The borough commander watched the sky-blue helmet and the serge cap disappear down the stairs, then turned briefly to Wentworth and Ricci.

"Don't hang around here," he said. "We got too many cops as it is. Report in to your dispatcher and go back to work."

Wentworth put the car in gear and drew out of the crowded command post sector. "Inspector Gracious," Wentworth said to Ricci, "he sure has a heartwarming way of saying thanks."

"Jumped two grades," Ricci said. "It's a wonder he didn't bust us back down to probationary."

Wentworth swung southward onto Park Avenue South. "Now you wish I made that turn, like I said, and run away with all the money?"

"I wish," Ricci said gloomily, and reached for his microphone.

"Bust your ass, and not so much as a well done or thank you. So it wasn't practical to run away with the money, but would anybody know if we dipped in for a thousand or two?"

"The hijackers would have reported the missing money," Ricci said, "and we'd be up the creek."

Ricci spoke to the dispatcher. Wentworth waited until he signed off. "I'm sorry we didn't boost a few packages, I honestly mean it. But the hijackers would holler police corruption, and you think anybody would take our word against the word of those bums? Never! That's how much they trust New York's Finest. I wish I was a criminal, so I could win a little respect from somebody."

SERGEANT MISKOWSKY

The only previous time TA Sergeant Miskowsky had been on the track in his eleven years on the force had been when, as a patrolman, he had chased a couple of drunks who had taken it into their dumb heads to jump off the platform and gallivant down the tunnel. He remembered being scared stiff about stumbling and falling into the power rail as he ran down the track after the drunks, who were whooping it up as they staggered along the roadbed. Eventually, he had chased them up onto the next platform, where they ran into the arms of another TA patrolman.

He felt spooked now, and the hairs on the back of his neck were prickling. The tunnel was dark, except for the signal lights, bright and green as emeralds. It should have been very quiet, but it wasn't—the wind made a soft noise, and there were odd rustlings that he couldn't identify. After they passed the nine empty cars of Pelham One Two Three, he knew that the tunnel was crawling with cops. Every once in a while you could make one out in the shadows, and a couple of times he could have sworn he heard several of them inhale at the same time. Spooky as hell. Not that the TPF cop seemed to be affected by it. He loped along easily, as if the money slung over his shoulder was weightless.

He held his five-cell flashlight tightly in his hand—they would be in one beautiful jam if he dropped it—swinging it slowly from side to side, touching the rails, the rust-and-dirt colored roadbed, the streaked walls. They were making good time, but Miskowsky was beginning to suck wind. The TPF cop, even with his burden, was breathing like a baby.

"There she is," the TPF cop said.

Miskowsky saw the pale emanation of light down the tunnel and began to sweat. "You realize we're walking right straight into four submachine guns?"

"Hell, yes," the TPF cop said. "It's got me pissing." He winked cheerfully.

"Not that there's any real danger. We're just the messenger boys."

"I guess," the TPF cop said indifferently. He hiked the canvas bag to a new position on his shoulder. "At that, you know, twenty-five or so pounds, it's not so much weight for a million bucks."

Miskowsky laughed nervously. "I just thought of a hell

of a note—suppose we got mugged. You know what I mean? Suppose a couple of muggers . . ." But the thought was too frivolous to pursue; it would put him in a bad light.

"That's not so funny," the TPF cop said. "A police officer I know, he did get mugged last week, when he was off duty. Slipped up on him from behind, and coldcocked him with a steel rod wrapped in a newspaper. Took his wallet, his credit cards, his gun. The gun, that's serious."

"Well, we're in uniform. They don't go around mugging cops in uniform."

"Not yet. That day will come."

"Somebody in the rear door of the car," the TPF cop said. "See him?"

"Jesus," Miskowsky said. "I hope he knows it's us. I hope he don't get confused and start shooting."

"Not yet," the TPF cop said.

"What do you mean, not *yet*?"

"Not till he can see the whites of our eyes." The TPF cop glanced sidelong at Miskowsky and laughed softly.

ARTIS JAMES

Artis James was numb. He felt as if he had been in the tunnel forever and would remain forever. It had become his element. Like the fish's element was the water, his element was the tunnel—an underground ocean, dark, damp, whispering.

He did not dare look behind him for fear of what the shadows might contain. Even the car ahead was more reassuring, because it was a known quantity. He turned the peak of his cap to the rear and put his eye to the edge of the pillar as if it were a vertical keyhole and saw part of a figure come into view, half of the head, the right shoulder. It remained for about ten seconds, then withdrew. It kept returning at intervals of a minute or so, and Artis knew it was the rear lookout checking the track, his submachine gun muzzle pointed forward like an exploring antenna. The second time the figure appeared it occurred to Artis that against the light in the car it made a good target for somebody. Granted, the revolver was inaccurate at that distance, except for an exceptionally good shot. Like himself, for instance. Given time to aim carefully, bracing his gun and wrist against the edge of the pillar, he knew he could pick it off.

He tried to remember the exact orders he had been given by the Operations sergeant. Stay put? Something like that: Stay put and no action. Still, if he could offer a dead criminal as an apology, could they penalize him for not obeying his orders to the letter? When the blocky figure next showed itself in the door Artis' revolver was in his hand, the barrel resting on the wrist of his left hand. He lined it up in the sight, watched it withdraw, and returned the revolver to his holster. But he drew it again at once and took up his firing position. When the figure next came into alignment, he squeezed the trigger.

With the safety off he would have had himself one dead criminal. After the figure withdrew, he flicked the safety on and off a few times, for no good reason, and reholstered the revolver. But he couldn't be sure the last flick hadn't left the safety on fire, so he drew again and checked. It had been on safety; he was too careful with a gun to make that kind of mistake. He held onto the gun, and it was hanging by his side the next time the figure showed. After it disappeared, he lined up on the doorway, and this time, for kicks, he flipped the safety to fire.

When the figure reappeared, it lined up in his sight as if by appointment. Artis drew a deep breath and squeezed off. The shot echoed through the tunnel like a bomb explosion, and he heard, or thought he did, the tinkle of glass as the bullet drilled through the window. He saw the figure pull back sharply, and he knew he had scored a hit. Then the tunnel became a madhouse of racketing gunfire and muzzle flash bouncing spitefully off the walls. He dug in behind his pillar as bullets spanged toward him, and he was sure that if he wasn't killed by the hijacker he would catch it from behind if the cops in the tunnel returned the fire.

FIFTEEN

SERGEANT MISKOWSKY

When the shot rang out, Sergeant Miskowsky screamed, "They're shooting at us," and dropped to the roadbed, pulling the TPF cop down with him. There was a burst of machine-gun fire. Miskowsky buried his head in his arms, and there was a second burst.

The TPF cop pushed the canvas sack in front of them. "Not that it would stop anything," he whispered. "A million bucks, and a bullet would go through it like shit through an open window."

The firing stopped, but Miskowsky waited for a full minute before raising his head. The TPF cop was peering curiously over the sack at the rear of the car.

"What do we do now?" Miskowsky whispered. "You feel like getting up and walking into that firepower?"

"Hell, no," the TPF cop said. "We don't move until we find out what's going on. Christ, lying in all this shit, I'll never get my uniform clean."

With the shooting stopped, the tunnel seemed twice as dark as before, the silence more profound. Miskowsky, keeping low behind the soft bulwark of the bag, was grateful for both.

RYDER

As Ryder started down the aisle, the passengers, following him with glazed eyes, seemed stunned by the violence of the gunfire. At the rear, the window of the storm door had collapsed. Welcome stood facing it, half exposed to the tunnel, his feet braced on the floor in a litter of shattered glass. The muzzle of his gun, poking through the empty window, moved in a slow circle, probing the tunnel like the feeler of some malevolent insect. Steever, sitting on the isolated seat, looked relaxed, but Ryder could see that he had been hit. There was a dark wet patch on his right sleeve, just below the shoulder.

He paused in front of Steever and looked down at him inquiringly.

"Not too bad," Steever said. "I think it went right through and came out."

"How many shots?"

"Just one. I let go a few rounds." He tapped the gun lying across his lap. "Couldn't see nothing out there, so there wasn't no sense to shooting. I guess I got mad. Then this one"—he nodded minimally toward Welcome—"he come running down and ripped off a burst."

Ryder nodded and edged up beside Welcome. Through the glassless door the tunnel was still and shadowy, an underground forest of dun-colored pillars. There were men out there, but they were perfectly concealed.

He eased back from the opening. Welcome was quivering with tension, and his breathing was shallow and rapid.

"You left your post without orders," Ryder said. "Get back to the center of the car."

Welcome said, "Fuck yourself."

"Go back to your post."

Welcome whirled suddenly, and whether by intention or not, the muzzle of his gun touched Ryder's chest. Then the pressure increased, and through the material of his raincoat he could feel the hollow ring of the bore, but he didn't shift his eyes. He kept them level, focused on Welcome's, glowing darkly in the slits of his mask.

"Go back to your post," Ryder said again.

"Shit on your orders," Welcome said, but Ryder knew, whether by the intonation of his voice or some subtle change in the intensity of his eyes, that he was backing down. In another moment, Welcome lowered the gun. The confrontation was over. For now.

Welcome brushed by him and strode stiff-legged to the center of the car. Ryder waited until he took up his position overlooking the passengers, then looked out at the tunnel. Nothing moved. He turned away and sat down beside Steever.

"You're certain there was just a single shot?"

Steever nodded.

"No answer after you fired? Or after Welcome fired?"

"Just the one shot, that's all."

"Somebody got nervous or foolish," Ryder said. "I don't think there'll be any more trouble. Can you handle the gun?"

"I handled it, didn't I? It hurts a little, not much."

"It was just some individual stupidity," Ryder said, "but we can't let it pass."

"I'm not mad anymore," Steever said.

"It isn't a question of being mad. We have to keep our promise. Everything depends on their believing we mean what we say."

"Knock off a passenger?" Steever said.

"Yes. You want to pick one out?"

Steever shrugged. "They're all the same to me."

Ryder bent toward the wound. Blood was seeping slowly through the torn cloth of the raincoat. "As soon as it's done, I'll take a look at your shoulder. Okay with you?"

"Sure."

"I'll send one back. Can you handle it?"

"I'm fine," Steever said. "Send him back."

Ryder got up and walked to the center of the car. Which one? The old lady wino was probably the least loss to the world. . . . No. It wasn't his business to make moral judgments, just to designate a casualty.

"You." He pointed at random. "Come here, please."

"Me?" A wavering finger touched a chest.

"Yes," Ryder said, "you."

DENNY DOYLE

Denny Doyle was daydreaming. He was driving a sub-way train, but on a very strange line. It was under-ground, all right, but it had scenery—trees and lakes and hills, all of it bathed in bright sunlight as it flashed by. There were stations, with people standing on them—these were underground, only the track between sta-tions was out-of-doors—but he wasn't required to make any stops. It was a perfect ride, the controller up against the post, all signals green, so that he never once had to touch the brake.

The pleasant daydream dissolved with the first shatter-ing shot from the roadbed, and when the machine gun fired, Denny hunched his shoulders and pulled his head into their shelter. When he saw the wetness on the blue cloth of the heavy man's raincoat, he almost became sick. He couldn't stand the sight of blood, or, for that matter, of any kind of violence, except for the football games on TV, where you couldn't hear the ugly impact of flesh on flesh. If the truth had to be told, he was a physical coward, an unnatural sin for an Irishman.

At first, when the leader of the hijackers pointed, he was going to refuse to get up, but he was afraid to disobey. He stood up on trembling legs, aware that all the passengers were looking at him. His legs were rubbery, and that gave him the idea of purposely collapsing, so that the leader, seeing how helpless he was, would tell him to sit down again. But he was afraid the leader would see through it and get angry. So he moved toward the center of the car with the help of the straps. When the straps ended, he reached for one of the center poles and held onto it with both hands, looking upward into the gray eyes that showed through the leader's mask.

"Motorman, we have something for you to do."

Denny's mouth and throat were filled with wetness, and he had to swallow twice before he could speak. "Please don't do anything to me."

"Come along with me," the leader said.

Denny clung to the pole. "It isn't just me. I have a wife and five kids. My wife is sick, she's in and out of the hospital—"

"Stop worrying." The leader nudged Denny away from the pole. "They want you to move those nine cars back there when the power comes on."

He took Denny's arm and walked him to the rear of the car. The heavy man stood up to meet them. Denny averted his eyes from the bloody sleeve.

"Walk back to the cab of the first car," the leader said, "and wait for instructions from Command Center. I'll help you down to the track."

Denny stared into the leader's eyes. They were expressionless, as he was sure the man's face would be, too, if it was visible. He watched the leader slide back the storm door with its shattered window.

Denny hung back. "The controls," he said. "How can I work the train without the keys and the brake handle?"

"They're sending a full set of tools."

"I hate to use somebody else's brake handle. You know, every motorman has his own brake handle—"

"You'll have to make do." For the first time there was a note of impatience in the leader's voice. "Let's go, please."

Denny stepped closer to the door, then stopped. "I can't do it. I'll have to go past the trainmaster's body. I can't look at it. . . ."

"Just shut your eyes," the leader said. He changed his position and edged Denny onto the threshold plate.

Out of nowhere, Denny suddenly remembered the joke he had made when they first started doing the mass in English: "If that's all the whole thing is about, I never would have started in the first place." Was he to be punished for that harmless joke? God, dear God, I didn't mean it. Get me out of this and I'll be Your most devout and worshipful servant. Never another joke—though I didn't mean any disrespect by it. Never a sin, never a lie, never an impious thought. Oh, dear God, nothing but goodness, faith, belief. . . .

"Swing down," the leader said.

ANITA LEMOYNE

In the instant before the hijack leader lifted his finger to point, Anita Lemoyne experienced an intimation of her own mortality—a phrase she had picked up from the TV putz, who used it a lot *after* he got his rocks off. She lost her concentration on the Latin lover, and her eyes began a kind of nervous shuttling from the square broad cuddling her two boys to the old wino with her encrustation of filth and scabs, with the milky eyes and slack lips opening and closing over her gummy mouth. Jesus!

Intimations of mortality. Not meaning death, exactly, but the knowledge that one of these days her body would thicken, her boobs would droop, her skin would go slack, and that would be the end of high-priced tricking. She had turned out at the age of fourteen, and she was almost thirty now, and it was time she thought of the future. The square mama and the lady wino. They were two forks up ahead in the road she was traveling. The wino was a living death, anybody could see that. But what about the fat little mama, snug as a bug in a cramped spick-and-span apartment, buying her clothes at the cut-rate stores, doing motionless fucking now and then with the same man, cleaning, cooking, wiping the snot off of her kids' faces? Two fates worse than death. Maybe it was high time she started saving up her bread so she could open up a little shop, a boutique that would cater to the girls in the life. The way whores spent their money it could be a real good thing. The way *they* spent. The way *she* spent! Between her apartment and her clothes and her bar bills and the crazy way she tipped. . . . The leader's eyes came to rest on the motorman, poor bastard, and his finger pointed.

Intimations of mortality!

Frightened, her eyes sought out the Latin creep. He was laughing at the way the motorman was walking, supporting himself with the help of the straps. Never mind him, she thought, look at me, *look at me*. As if he had heard, he turned toward her. She held his eyes and gave him a big smile, then dropped her eyes and stared boldly at his middle. Almost at once his raincoat began to make a tent. Thank God, Anita thought. If I can get that kind of a re-action out of a man just by looking at him, I don't have too much to worry about yet.

Intimations of mortality, my big white ass!

SERGEANT MISKOWSKY

"What are we supposed to do," Miskowsky said, "start walking like nothing happened?" Behind the money bag, his cheek was pressed to the filthy roadbed.

"Goddamn if I know," the TPF cop said. "Whoever fired that first shot is going to have his ass in a sling, I'll bet on that."

"So what do we do?" Miskowsky said.

"I'm just a patrolman. You're the sergeant. So what do we do?"

"I ain't *your* sergeant. Anyway, what's a sergeant with all this brass around? I want orders before I move."

The TPF cop was up on his elbows, looking over the top of the canvas bag. "There's somebody at the door there. See? Two guys. No, three."

The sergeant peered around the edge of the bag. "They just opened the storm door, and they're talking or some-thing." He stiffened. "Look—one of them just jumped out on the roadbed."

Miskowsky watched the shadowy figure straighten up, look back at the car, face about again, and then slowly, almost in a shuffle, start walking.

"He's heading this way." Miskowsky's whisper was

hoarse. "Better get your gun ready. He's heading straight for *us*."

Miskowsky, focused on the walking figure, never saw the looming shape in the open doorway. There was a flashing stab of brightness, and the walking figure reached upward and then crumpled. The tunnel repeated the shots in a series of echoes.

"My God," Miskowsky said. "It's war."

TOM BERRY

When the motorman started walking toward the rear of the car Tom Berry shut his eyes and flagged down a taxi—what else, for God's sake, a subway train?—and whipped downtown to Deedee's slope-floor Caligari pad.

"There was nothing I could do about it, absolutely nothing," he said as she opened the door.

Deedee pulled him inside and threw her arms around him in a frenzy of relief and passion.

"All I could think of was: I'm glad it's the motorman and not me."

She was kissing his face wildly, her lips taking inventory of his eyes, cheeks, nose, and then she was dragging him to the bed, tearing at his clothes, at her own.

Later, when they lay exhausted, their limbs entwined like an indecipherable monogram, he tried again to explain himself. "I threw off the shackles of servitude to a false master and saved myself for the revolution."

Suddenly, her skin surface cooled perceptibly. "You sat there with a loaded revolver in your belt and did nothing?"

She disengaged her arms and legs, dissolving the monogram. "Traitor! You were sworn to uphold the rights of the people, and you betrayed them."

"But, Deedee, they outnumbered me four to one; they had submachine guns."

"During the Long March, the Eighth Route Army faced the Kuomintang's machine guns with knives, stones, even clenched fists."

"I'm not the Eighth Route Army, Deedee. I'm just one lone pig. The reactionary bandits would have shot me dead if I had twitched a muscle."

He reached out for her, and she leaped off the bed in a spasm of revulsion. Pointing a quivering finger, she said, "You are a coward."

"No, Deedee. Dialectically, I declined to lay my life down to protect the money and property of the ruling interests."

"The people's rights were being trampled on. You violated your solemn oath as a police officer to protect those rights!"

"The police are the repressive tentacle of the capitalist octopus," he shouted. "They pull the chestnuts of the ruling class out of the fire of contradiction over the prostrate body of the workers and peasants. Off the pigs!"

"You failed your duty. It's people like you who have given the pigs a bad name!"

"Deedee! What has happened to your *Weltanshauung*?" He held his arms out pleadingly. She withdrew to the farthest corner of the room, where she took her stand ankle-deep in record albums. "Deedee! Comrade! Brother!"

"The Provisional People's Court has weighed your case, Comrade Ratfink." She whirled suddenly, picked up his gun, and pointed it at him. "The verdict is death!"

She fired, and the room disintegrated. The motorman was dead.

BOROUGH COMMANDER

A Special Operations Division sniper in the tunnel reported the shooting. The borough commander's first reaction was bewilderment, even before anger.

"I don't get it," he said to the commissioner. "We're still under the delivery deadline."

The commissioner was pale. "They've gone ape. I thought we could trust them at least to stick to their own rules."

The borough commander remembered the rest of the sniper's message. "Somebody threw a shot at them. That's it. Reprisal. They're sticking to their rules, all right, the fucking cold-blooded monsters."

"Who fired the shot?"

"I doubt we'll ever know. A SOD sniper in the tunnel said it sounded like a pistol shot."

The commissioner said, "They don't fool around. They're merciless."

"That's what they're telling us. The message of this killing is that they're men of their word, and we'd better act accordingly."

"Where are the two men with the money?"

"The sniper says they're about fifteen feet away from him. They hit the deck when the machine gun went off, and they're still there."

The commissioner nodded. "What's your next move?"

My next move, the borough commander thought, but knew that he wouldn't have liked it any better—in fact, liked it less—if the commissioner had given him an order. "There are sixteen hostages left, that's still the prime consideration."

"Yes," the commissioner said.

The borough commander excused himself, and, taking the walkie-talkie, spoke to DCI Daniels on Pelham One Two Eight, instructing him to contact the hijackers through Command Center and inform them that the ransom money would be on its way again, but that more time was needed because of the delay owing to the recent incident.

"You hear all that?" the borough commander said. "You ever hear a cop kowtow to murderers like that before?"

"Easy," the commissioner said.

"Easy. They call a tune, and we dance to it. An army of cops, with guns and grenade launchers and computers, and we suck their ass. Two citizens killed, and we still suck ass—"

"Cool it!" the commissioner said sharply.

The borough commander looked at him and read a mirror reflection of his own anger and misery. "Sorry, sir."

"All right. Maybe we'll have a shot at them later on."

"Maybe," the borough commander said. "But I'll tell you something, sir—after this I'll never be the same man again. I'll never be as good a cop."

"Cool it," the commissioner said.

ARTIS JAMES

The man who gunned down the motorman was the one Artis James had hit or thought he had hit. He didn't connect the two events; at least, not yet. He had been hugging his pillar ever since the machine-gun fire responded to his shot, and it was coincidence that he took his first peek just as the motorman—he could make out the pinstripe overalls—was climbing down to the roadbed. When the man in the doorway fired, Artis ducked again. By the time he thought it was safe to take another look the motorman was a motionless hulk lying three or four feet away from the other motionless hulk that used to be the trainmaster.

Artis turned carefully, putting his back against the pillar. He switched on his radio, and, holding the transmitter so close that his lips touched the metal, signaled headquarters. He had to repeat three times before headquarters came in.

"I can barely make you. Speak up, please."

Whispering, Artis said, "I can't do no better. I'm too close, and they might hear me."

"Speak louder."

"No louder, or they'll hear me." Artis spaced his words and spoke with exaggerated distinctness. "This is Patrolman Artis James. In the tunnel. Near the hijacked car."

"All right, that's a little better. Go ahead."

"They just shot the motorman. They put him out on the tracks, and they shot him."

"Christ! When did that happen?"

"Maybe a minute or two after the first shot."

"*What* first? Nobody was supposed to . . . Did somebody shoot?"

It struck Artis all at once and left him numb. Oh, God, he thought, I never should have fired. Oh, God, if it had something to do with killing the motorman . . .

"Come in, James," the radio voice said impatiently. "Somebody shot at the train."

"I told you," Artis James said. You did it, baby, he thought, oh, God, you did it. "Somebody shot at the train."

"Who, chrisesake, *who*?"

"Don't know. Came from behind me someplace. Maybe scored a hit. I can't say for sure. Shot came right out of the tunnel behind me."

"Oh, Jesus. The motorman. Dead?"

"Not moving. Don't mean he's dead, but not moving. What do I do?"

"Nothing. For God's sake, don't do *anything*."

"Right," Artis said. "*Continue* not to do anything."

RYDER

By the time Ryder picked up the first-aid kit from his valise in the motorman's cab Steever had almost finished stripping down. His raincoat and jacket were neatly folded on the seat, and after Ryder helped him with the money jacket, he removed his shirt, peeling the bloody right sleeve down over his heavy upper arm. Ryder looked out through the shattered storm door window. The motorman lay face up, a few paces nearer the car than the train-master. Dark splotches on his pinstripes showed where Steever's shots had exited.

Ryder sat down beside Steever, who was now stripped to the waist, his torso massive, dark-skinned, matted with whorls of thick hair. Ryder examined the entry wound, a neat round hole oozing blood. The underside of the arm, where the bullet had emerged, was somewhat mangled. Blood had trickled down Steever's arm in a series of rivulets that played out in the hairy thickets of his fore-arm.

"Looks clean," Ryder said. "Painful?"

Steever tucked his chin in to look at the wound. "Nah. I never feel pain too much."

Ryder rummaged in the metal first-aid box for the antiseptic solution. "I'll use this and then bandage it. It's the best we can do now."

Steever shrugged. "It don't bother me."

Ryder doused a square gauze pad and dabbed it on the wound, then scrubbed the bloodstains. He wet two more pads and covered the wound front and rear. Steever held the pads in place while he bound them firmly with surgical tape. When he was finished, Steever started dressing.

"It might get stiff after a while," Ryder said.

"No problem," Steever said. "I can't hardly feel it."

When Steever was fully dressed, Ryder picked up the first-aid kit and left. He noted the interplay between Welcome and the girl in the Anzac hat, and beneath the mask his jaw hardened. But he didn't stop. At the front of the car Longman stepped toward him.

"The motorman?" Longman said.

"The motorman is dead." He went inside the cab and shut the door. A voice on the radio was calling frantically. He stepped on the foot pedal, activating the transmitter.

"Pelham One Two Three to Command Center. Come in."

"Prescott here, you bastard. Why did you kill the motorman?"

"You shot at one of my people. I warned you what the penalty would be."

"Someone disobeyed orders and fired. It was a mistake. If you had checked in with me first, you wouldn't have had to kill him."

"Where is the money?" Ryder said.

"About a hundred yards down the track, you cold-blooded bastard."

"I'll give you three minutes to deliver it. Same procedure as before. Acknowledge."

"You bastard, you shit! I'd like to meet you some time. I'd really like that."

"Three minutes," Ryder said. "Over and out."

SERGEANT MISKOWSKY

A voice came out of the darkness. "Hey, you two guys."

Miskowsky, gun in hand, said hoarsely, "What?"

"I'm over here behind a pillar. I'm not going to show myself. I got orders for you from the borough commander. Resume delivery of the money, according to instructions."

"They know we're coming? I mean, I don't want them to start shooting again."

"They got the welcome mat out for you. Why not, with a million in cash?"

The TPF cop got to his feet and picked up the canvas sack. "Here we go again, Sarge."

The voice from the shadows said, "The order is, move it, and move it fast."

Miskowsky got to his feet slowly. "I wish to hell I was someplace else."

"Good luck," the voice said.

Miskowsky turned on his flashlight and fell in beside the TPF cop, who was already moving.

"Into the valley of death," the TPF cop said.

"Don't say that," Miskowsky said.

"I'll never get this shit off my uniform," the TPF cop said. "Somebody ought to clean up this subway one of these days."

THE CITY: STREET SCENE

A human torso rolled along parallel to the curb, mounted on a dolly covered with a remnant of Oriental rug. Its legs and thighs had been severed in a straight cut a few inches below the hips. It sat squarely on the dolly, broad-shouldered, with a strong lined face and long black curls, punting itself forward with its knuckles, which dipped effortlessly into the asphalt. It said nothing, but held up a large tin cup. The cops looked at it helplessly as it rowed along the curb. The crowd rained coins into the cup.

"My God, I wouldn't believe it if I didn't see it with my own eyes," a tall man with a Midwest accent said to his neighbor as he dug into his pocket for a handful of coins.

The neighbor gave him a knowing, almost pitying, smile. "It's a phony."

"A phony? But it's impossible to fake—"

"You're from out of town, right? If you knew this town the way I did . . . *How* he does it, I don't exactly know, but take my word for it, it's a fake. Save your money, Mac."

The crowd remained intact by some magic numerical process of slough and renewal. People departed, and others arrived to take their place, and the shape of the great animal hardly changed. As the sun lowered behind the surrounding buildings, the air grew chill and a wind sprang up. Faces became pink or pinched, people danced in place, but few were daunted.

In some unaccountable way, the crowd learned of the killing of the motorman before most of the policemen guarding them. It became a signal for blanket condemnation of the police, the mayor, the transit system, the governor, the transit unions, a well-known minority group, and, above all, the city, that vast monolith which they hated and from which they would have divorced themselves except that, as in an old, stormy, but durable marriage, they needed each other for survival.

The police reacted to the motorman's death by taking out their frustrations on the crowd. Their good humor disappeared, and they became surly and stone-faced. When they acted to contain a bulge or rupture in the crowd, they snarled and pushed against the surge of bodies with hardhanded force. Individuals and groups in the crowd struck back vocally, citing irrelevant charges of police corruption, bringing to the cops' attention exactly whose taxes were paying whose swollen salaries, condemning them for living in Ozone Park and Hollis, and even, in the safe reaches of the back rows, hurled the challenging epithet "Pig!"

But, finally, nothing changed. Greater than its individual parts, rising above provocation, never losing sight of its purpose, the crowd maintained its character inviolate.

SIXTEEN

TOM BERRY

Tom Berry watched the leader wedge the rear door open and then take his place beside the heavyset man on the isolated double seat. Both of them trained their guns on the open door. Then Berry saw the fitful flash of a light on the tracks and knew what it signified. The city was paying off. A million dollars, cash on the table. He wondered idly why the hijackers had set the ransom money at a million. Were their acquisitive horizons limited to that talismanic figure? Or—he remembered the old man's comment—had they determined, either cynically or actuarially, that the lives of their hostages were worth sixty thousand apiece?

The light on the track was moving closer at a slow, almost liturgical pace, which, Berry thought, was the way he would walk himself if he had been advancing toward a couple of machine-gun muzzles. He made out two figures, wavering in the half-light leaking out of the car. He couldn't see whether or not they were cops, but what else could they be? Certainly not bank tellers. He felt a sense of agonized empathy with what those two out there must be thinking, and then, for no good reason, the image of his late uncle obtruded on his thoughts.

What would Uncle Al have said about a pair of cops meekly delivering a million bucks to a gang of hijackers (or crooks, as he would have called them; all lawbreakers were crooks in Uncle Al's simplistic vocabulary)? Well, Uncle Al wouldn't even have believed it, for starters. Uncle Al, if he had had his way—and he, or his superiors, certainly would have, in that era—would have barreled in shooting. Fifty, a hundred cops, attacking the car with guns blazing, and in the end the crooks would have been dead, and a half dozen or so cops, and most of the hostages. In Uncle Al's lexicon—and in his day—people might pay kidnap ransom, but not cops. Cops were crook catchers, not crook payers.

In Uncle Al's time everything was different. People might not have been wild about cops, but they feared them. Try a word like "pig" and you would wind up in the basement of a precinct house getting beaten to a pulp by a succession of joyful sadists. And in Uncle Al's *father's* time, police work was even simpler; most problems were solved by a beer-belly Irish cop hauling off and kicking some harmless kid in the ass. Well, the policeman's lot had undergone quite a change in his family's third generation of cops. People called cops pigs and nobody laid a hand on them. A lieutenant would chew your ass if you booted a kid's behind (and, if it happened to be a black behind, you could start a riot and maybe get stomped to death before a ten-thirteen brought help).

His recent dopey daydream to one side, he could well imagine how horrified Deedee would have been by his Uncle Al, not to mention Al's fat-bellied, corrupt old man. On the other hand, she would probably take satisfaction in the idea of cops serving as messenger boys to thieves, viewing it as some kind of new dispensation in which cops properly became the servants of the people. Oh, well, Deedee. There were quite a few things Deedee had ass backwards. Not that he had such a clear idea himself of exactly what ass *frontwards* was. But he could hope that the two of them, confused and in love, might eventually produce a viable baby, a philosophy with the requisite number of arms and legs.

Two faces appeared at the rear door. One belonged to a blue-helmeted TPF cop, the other to a transit cop, the badge on his peaked cap a dull gold. The TA cop shone his light into the car, and the TPF man unslung a canvas sack from his shoulder and flipped it onto the floor of the car. It landed with a soft thud. Toilet paper would make no less distinguished a sound. The officers, their faces red but unemotional, turned around and walked away.

LONGMAN

Longman watched the money dump out onto the floor as Ryder opened the neck of the sack and held it upside down—dozens of green slabs, neatly tied up with rubber bands. A million dollars, everybody's dream, tumbling out

onto the filthy composition floor of a subway car. Steever
stripped, placing his coat and jacket neatly on the seat, and
Ryder checked the ties on the money belt. Four of them
had cost Ryder a pretty penny to have made up. They were
on the order of a life jacket, fitting over the head and tying
at the sides. Each one contained forty pockets, distributed
front and back in two tiers, evenly spaced. Altogether,
there were a hundred and fifty packets of bills, which figured to thirty-seven and a half packets to a man. Not that
they were going to split it that finely. Two of them would
have thirty-seven; two would have thirty-eight.

Steever stood like a manikin, hands at his sides, as
Ryder inserted a package in each pocket of the money
jacket: When he was finished, Steever dressed, and then
went to the center of the car, where he changed places with
Welcome. Welcome kept gassing while Ryder filled his
jacket, but Ryder was silent, working methodically but
swiftly. When Ryder signaled to him the length of the car,
Longman's heart began to thump, and he felt almost jubi-
lant as he hurried to the rear. But Ryder started shucking
his own coat and jacket, and Longman felt a pang of re-
sentment. It wasn't fair that he was to be last. After all,
whose idea was it in the first place? But his feeling of pique
vanished at the touch of the money. Some of these packets
he was pressing down firmly into the slots of Ryder's jacket
were worth ten thousand each, and others were worth
twenty thousand!

"All this money," he whispered. "I can hardly believe
it."

Ryder was silent, turning so that Longman could get at
the rear pockets of the jacket.

"I just wish it was all over already," Longman said. "All the rest of it."

Ryder lifted his right arm, and his voice was icy. "The rest of it will be fun."

"Fun!" Longman said. "It's risky. If anything goes wrong—"

"Get your stuff off," Ryder said.

When Ryder was finished with him, they all returned to their places. Walking to the front of the car, Longman felt weighted down, although he knew that his thirty-seven packages didn't add up to more than five or six pounds. It amused him to see that some of the passengers were looking at him with envy and maybe wishing that *they* had had the guts and brains to pull off something like this. Nothing like money, hot naked money, to change the thinking of a lifetime. He smiled broadly, stretching the mask. But when Ryder went back inside the cab, he stopped being amused. The getaway was still to come, and it was the trickiest and hairiest part of all.

Suddenly, he was convinced that it wouldn't work.

RYDER

Ryder said into the mike, "Pelham One Two Three calling Prescott at Command Center."

"Come in. This is Prescott."

"Have you got your pencil, Prescott?"

"Yes. How's the money, leader? All in order? The right amount and color and all that?"

"Before I issue instructions, I'm reminding you that

they must be obeyed to the letter. The hostages' lives remain in jeopardy. I want to impress that on you. Acknowledge."

"You fucking bastard!"

"If you understand, just say yes."

"Yes, you bastard."

"I'm going to give you five items. Write each one down and acknowledge without comment. Point One: At the end of this conversation you will restore power to the entire sector. Acknowledge."

"I read you."

"Point Two: After the power is restored, you will clear the local track from here to South Ferry station. By that I mean switches properly set, all trains between here and South Ferry cleared out, and all signals green. I emphasize the signals. They will be green. We are not to be held up or tripped by a red signal. Repeat, please."

"Local track cleared from here to South Ferry. All signals green."

"If we see a red signal, we'll kill a hostage. *Any* infraction and we'll kill a hostage. Point Three: All trains—local and express—all trains behind us are to lay dead. And nothing is to move northbound between South Ferry and here. Check me."

"The trains running behind you can't get too close. They'll be tripped if they try to jump a block."

"Nevertheless, they are to lie dead. Acknowledge."

"Okay, I've got it."

"Point Four: You will contact me as soon as the track is clear to South Ferry and the signals are all green. Acknowledge."

"Contact you when track is clear, signals green."

"Point Five: All police personnel in the tunnel are to be removed. If this is not done, we will shoot a hostage. Absolutely no police personnel are to be on the South Ferry station. If this is not done, we will shoot a hostage."

"I check you. Can I ask a question?"

"About your instructions?"

"About you. Are you aware that you're insane?"

Ryder looked out at the empty track, peopled with shadows. "That isn't relevant," he said. "I'll answer questions on my instructions only. Do you have any?"

"No questions."

"You will have ten minutes from this moment to comply. You will then contact me again for final instructions. Confirm."

"You've got to give me more time."

"No," Ryder said. "Over and out."

CLIVE PRESCOTT

Prescott was relieved when the NYPD high command agreed to comply with the hijackers' instructions. Not that they had an alternative, but he knew cops, being one himself, and he knew how the pressures of frustration could warp judgment. Cops were, after all, human beings. Of a sort.

He jumped up from his seat at the console and ran across the room. Frank Correll, occupying one of his dispatchers' desks, was shouting into his microphone. In other parts of the huge loft, the Command Center was running smoothly; after all, there were no problems in the other divisions.

Prescott tapped Correll on the shoulder. Correll, without turning or looking up, continued his tirade into his mike. Prescott squeezed the shoulder, and Correll whirled around, glaring.

"Don't say a word," Prescott said. "Just listen to me. I have new instructions—"

"I don't give a shit about your instructions," Correll said. He shook Prescott's hand off his shoulder and turned back to the console.

Prescott folded back the flap of his sharkskin jacket with his left hand and with his right drew his service revolver. He cupped Correll's chin, pulled his head back, and placed the muzzle of the revolver in Correll's eye.

SEVENTEEN

BOROUGH COMMANDER

The borough commander issued orders for compliance with the hijackers' new instructions, but also arranged for a dozen plainclothes detectives to mingle with the crowd on the South Ferry station platform and for a saturation of police in the area aboveground. Then, in his bafflement, he consulted with TA Police Chief Costello.

"What have they got in mind, Chief?"

"Use all sixteen hostages as a shield? Could they possibly swing anything as awkward as that?" He shook his head. "It beats the hell out of me. Myself, I wouldn't have picked a tunnel to have to make a getaway from."

"But they picked it," the borough commander said, "which presumes they have some well-organized plan for getting away. They want the power back on and the track cleared. What does that suggest to you?"

"That they're going to run their car, obviously."

"Why did they specify South Ferry?"

The chief shook his head. "Damned if I know. The Lex local doesn't even run there at this time of day; they'll have to be switched at Brooklyn Bridge. The water? Could they have a boat there in the harbor? A seaplane? I just can't imagine what they're up to."

"South Ferry comes after Bowling Green. What happens *after* South Ferry?"

"The track loops around, and heads northward and comes back to Bowling Green. I don't see how that would help them, there are trains standing in Bowling Green station, they'd simply be blocked."

The borough commander thanked him and glanced at the commissioner, who looked worried, but profoundly neutral. He's giving me my head, the borough commander thought; he's displaying implicit trust in his subordinates. And why not, since there damn well won't be any glory at the end of all this?

"We can tail them in another train," the TA chief said. "I know we promised not to—"

"Don't the signals turn red after their passage, and won't our train be stopped by trippers?"

"On the local track, yes, but not on the express track," the chief said. "Maybe they won't think of that."

"They'll think about it," the borough commander said. "They know too much about subways not to. Okay, maybe we can tail them on the express track. But if they make us, they might kill a passenger."

"We can also follow their progress on the Model Board at the Grand Central Tower—as far as Brooklyn Bridge

Station. After that, Nevins Street Tower takes over south-ward into Brooklyn."

"That tells us exactly when they move?"

"Yes. And exactly where they are every moment they're on the tracks. Of course we'll have TA cops on all the platforms, too."

"Okay," the borough commander said briskly. "Let's set it up. Your Tower to track their movements. An express train to follow behind. Is it possible to turn off all its lights, inside and out?"

"Yes."

"Okay." The borough commander shook his head. "Hell of a thing to stalk somebody with—a subway train. I'll put DCI Daniels in charge of the express train. Patrol cars will follow on the surface. The big problem is communication. Tower to here to Central to patrol cars? It stinks. Better place two men at the Tower on separate phones, one to me and one to Central, so a dispatcher can pass it on directly to the cars. I want every car we've got on this. Every cop. NYPD and TA, both. Cover all stations, all exits, all emergency exits. How many emergency exits are there, Chief?"

"About two to a station."

"Just one thing." The commissioner broke his silence. "Every care must be taken. The hostages. We don't want any of them dead."

"Yeah," the borough commander said. "We've got to remember they're still calling the shots."

Deflated, he suddenly felt the cold. Shadows had closed in, and the crowd seemed to be congealed; his cops looked like frozen sticks of blue. He recalled what he had told the commissioner earlier—that he wouldn't be the same man after this was over. It was true. It had taken the mickey out of him.

TOM BERRY

The sudden return of full lighting in the car caught the passengers unawares, and they blinked in confusion. The bright neons showed up stresses the emergency lights had softened: tight, trembling mouths, lines of strain, eyes dulled by fear. Tom Berry observed that the girl in the Anzac hat showed mileage; the dimness had been kind to her. The younger of the two boys looked cranky, as though he had waked prematurely from an afternoon nap. The handkerchief the militant spade held to his face was no longer fresh, and its stains were shockingly red. Only the old wino lady was unchanged. She slept noisily, her lips blowing small iridescent bubbles. The hijackers seemed bulkier and more menacing. Well, Berry thought, they *were* a little bulkier; they were each a quarter of a million dollars larger.

The cab door opened, and the leader stepped out. His appearance produced an undertone of babble from the passengers, and the old man, who seemed to have appointed himself spokesman, said, "Ah, here's our friend, now we'll find out what's next."

"Your attention, please." The leader waited, poised and patient, and Berry thought: There's something almost professional about it, he's used to handling groups of people. "All right. In about five minutes we're going to move the car. You will all remain seated and quiet. You will continue to do exactly as you're told."

An idiosyncratic emphasis on *will* snatched at Tom Berry's memory. Where had he heard it? The army. Of course. That particular usage was standard in the orders of instructors, officers, noncoms. "You *will* wear Class A uniforms. . . . You *will* fall out at oh eight hundred hours. . . . You *will* police the area." Okay, small mystery solved—the leader had been in the army and had given orders. So what?

"We expect to release you unharmed in a short while. But until then you are still hostages. Conduct yourselves accordingly."

The old man said, "Since you're moving the train, if it's not too much trouble, can you drop me off at Fulton Street?"

The leader disregarded him. Without another word he went back to the cab. Most of the passengers were glaring at the old man, disapproving of his levity. The old man smiled sheepishly.

And so, Berry thought, the ordeal was almost over. Before long the passengers would be taking deep drafts of the polluted air of the surface and plying the police with inaccurate and widely divergent eyewitness details. All except for Patrolman Tom Berry, who would offer a disciplined version, despite the contempt his fellow officers would make no effort to conceal. When he walked in on Deedee, after the interrogation was finished, he would all but officially be unpigged, and that would not be long in coming. What would he do after he was fired from the force? Marry

Deedee and settle down to a life of revolutionary bliss, hand in hand chanting antiwar slogans, side by side cussing out the CIA? Two hearts as one protesting welfare cutbacks by throwing ashcans through plate-glass windows?

The smaller of the two boys began to whimper. Berry watched his mother try to shake him into silence. "No, Brandon, you have to keep quiet."

The boy squirmed and said, loudly, "I'm tired, I want to go out."

"I said quiet." The woman's whisper was fierce. "You heard what the man said? Quiet, he said!"

She slapped the boy's behind.

GRAND CENTRAL TOWER

When the trains south of Pelham One Two Three began to move and the red slashes twinkled on the Model Board in Grand Central Tower, a cheer rose from the dispatchers. Marino frowned and glanced over his shoulder, knowing that Caz Dolowicz liked quiet in the Tower Room. But of course, there was no Caz there; Caz was dead. Which, it occurred to Marino, made him senior man. Well, *he* liked it quiet, too.

"Let's keep it down," he said, and realized he was using Caz's favorite phrase. "Let's keep it down in the Tower Room."

Marino was holding a telephone pressed tensely to his ear, connected to a dispatcher in the Communications

Room at Police Headquarters on Centre Street. Next to him, her brown face impassive, Mrs. Jenkins was connected to Operations at Transit Police Headquarters.

"Nothing yet," Marino said into the phone. "They have begun to clear the track to South Ferry."

"Okay," the police dispatcher's voice said, "nothing yet."

Marino gestured to Mrs. Jenkins. "Tell him nothing yet, Pelham One Two Three is still laying dead."

Mrs. Jenkins said into her phone, "Nothing yet."

"I want everybody to keep it down," Marino said. "Right now it's us who's carrying the ball. So keep it down."

His eyes returned to the Model Board and focused on the red slashes that represented the position of Pelham One Two Three. It was very still in the Tower Room.

"Keep it down," Marino said sternly. "Just as if Caz was still with us."

DCI DANIELS

DCI Daniels led a picked squad of thirty men along the roadbed to Woodlawn One Four One, laying dead on the express track 500 feet north of the Twenty-eighth Street station. His force was composed of twenty Special Operations Division specialists and ten blue-helmeted TPF men. The motorman saw them coming and hung his head out of his cab window.

"Unlock your door," the DCI said, "we're coming aboard."

"I don't know," the motorman said. He was a coffee-colored man with a downcurving moustache and a small chin whisker. "I got no orders to let nobody aboard."

"You just got orders," the DCI said. "What do we look like, the Russian Red Army?"

"I guess you cops all right," the motorman said. He left his cab and appeared at the storm door with his key. The door slid open. "I guess you got the authority."

"You're a good guesser," the DCI said. "Give me a hand up."

He clambered into the car, grunting. Half of the thirty or so passengers crowded forward. He held up his hand. "Back up, folks. You're all going to move back into the other cars." He crooked his finger at four TPF cops who were already aboard. "Move them."

A single voice, outraged, rose above the general protest. "You know how long I been in this goddamn train? Hours! I'm gonna sue the city for one hundred thousand dollars! And I'll collect, too!"

The TPF men, experienced at crowd handling, charged forward. The passengers gave ground grudgingly. The DCI breasted the crush of police piling into the train and took a grip on the motorman's arm.

"We're going to chase a train," he said. "I want you to turn off all your lights, then separate this car from the rest of the train."

"Man, I am not allowed to do any of that."

The DCI tightened his hold. "All lights out, including your headlights, those colored marker lights, destination lights, everything. I want this car dark inside and out, and then I want it separated from the rest of the train."

The motorman might have been disposed to argue further, but the increasing pressure on his arm convinced him otherwise. With the DCI half pushing him he went into the cab and gathered up his brake handle and reverse and cutting keys.

The DCI assigned a man to accompany the motorman, and they hurried to the rear of the car, where the last of the passengers were being herded through the door by the straining TPF cops like animals through a chute. He told off an additional three blue helmets to help keep order, then instructed the main body of his force to take seats. Carrying rifles, shotguns, tear-gas guns, the men shuffled about awkwardly before settling down. The DCI went into the cab. Through the front window the tunnel was brighter than before, but it was still a gloomy place of occasional lights and an endless procession of pillars like a forest of precisely spaced denuded trees.

RYDER

Ryder opened the cab door, motioned, and Longman joined him. He stepped back and Longman squared off in front of the panel. "Go ahead," Ryder said.

Longman edged the controller forward to switching position. The car began to move.

"It's scary." Longman spoke nervously but without turning, his eyes fixed on the track ahead, on the signals, green as far as the eye could see. "Knowing there are cops hidden out there."

"Nothing to worry about," Ryder said. "They won't try anything."

What he meant, of course, was that there was nothing to worry about as long as the other side had to accept the terms of the strange warfare whose rules he himself had formulated. But Longman seemed reassured. His hands were steady on the controls. This was his element, Ryder thought; this was his strength. And everything else was his weakness.

"You know exactly where we're stopping?"

"Exactly," Longman said. "On the dime."

GRAND CENTRAL TOWER

When the little red blips denoting the position of Pelham One Two Three began to flicker on the Model Board in the Grand Central Tower Room, Marino gave a hoarse shout into the phone.

"What's the matter there?" the police dispatcher on Marino's line said.

"She's moving!" Marino waved excitedly at Mrs. Jenkins, but she was already speaking over her connection to TA Police Headquarters. Her voice was level and carefully modulated. "Pelham One Two Three has begun to move southward."

"All right," the police dispatcher said to Marino. "Continue to report as she moves, but calm down."

"Still moving," Marino said. "Moving pretty slow, but not stopping."

"Keep talking. But keep it cool. Okay?"

240 CENTRE STREET

In the Communications Room at NYPD Headquarters, a lieutenant signaled the borough commander. "Sir, the train is moving. Patrol cars are pursuing according to plan."

"It's too soon," the borough commander said. "They're supposed to wait until the track is cleared to South Ferry. What the hell's going on?"

"Sir?"

The borough commander, sounding agitated, said, "Stay with it," and rang off.

"Still moving?" the lieutenant asked the dispatcher connected to Grand Central Tower.

"Still moving."

NERVE CENTER

At Transit Police Headquarters, Operations Lieutenant Garber held the phone to his ear and listened to Mrs. Jenkins' calm voice.

"Okay," he said. "Hold it for a minute." He turned to a dispatcher. "They're moving. Every available man to be alerted. Patrol cars, too. NYPD is tracking them, but so are we. Make sure patrolmen on the Twenty-third Street station get the word fast." He looked at his watch. "Damn it, they jumped the gun. They're up to something."

The Operations Room was bustling. Lieutenant Garber observed it with dour satisfaction. Christ, he thought, wouldn't it be beautiful if we got them? I mean *us*, and not the NYPD.

"I want every ass in this place moving," he shouted.

"Yes," Mrs. Jenkins' voice said. "They are moving, Lieutenant."

COMMAND CENTER

At Command Center there was a flurry of excitement when a dispatcher at an IND desk casually remarked that he had figured out how the hijackers planned to make their getaway.

"They're gonna use Beach's old tunnel."

His announcement drew the immediate attention of his fellow dispatchers. For the benefit of those among them who wanted to know what the hell Beach's old tunnel was, he shifted his cigar to speaking position in a corner of his mouth and expounded. In 1867, one Alfred Ely Beach, unencumbered by a railroad franchise or other legal inconvenience, rented a basement in a building at Broadway and Murray Street and proceeded to construct New York's first subway, a tunnel that ran a distance of 312 feet to Warren Street. He brought in a single railroad car and blew it back and forth through his private tunnel by means of compressed air. The public was invited for a ride but showed scant interest, and the project died.

"The Lex local goes right by where that old tunnel is," the dispatcher said. "These fellas go into that tunnel and hide—"

The IND desk trainmaster, who had been listening, put his own cigar in speaking position and said, "That old tunnel has been gone for at least seventy years. They destroyed it when they started to dig the first real subway back in 1900, thereabouts. Don't it figger?"

"I admit it figgers," the dispatcher said. "But just because it figgers don't mean it *is*. You got proof?"

"Proof," the desk trainmaster said. "Some of the original bricks of Beach's old tunnel are built right into the regular IRT tunnel wall. Next time you ride down there, look out the window, just past City Hall, and you'll see the old bricks."

"I never looked out a subway window in my life," the dispatcher said. "What's to see?"

"The bricks of old Beach's old tunnel."

"Well, it was an idea," the dispatcher said, and shifted his cigar to the center of his mouth.

"Better go back to work," the desk trainmaster said.

EIGHTEEN

RYDER

Longman said, "Can I push it up a notch?"

"No," Ryder said, "Steady as it goes."

"Are we past where the cops were hidden by now?"

"Probably," Ryder said. He watched Longman's left hand polishing the handle of the controller. "Keep it steady."

"Calling Pelham One Two Three. Prescott here. Pelham One Two Three, come in."

Ahead, Ryder saw the long spread of brightness that was the Twenty-third Street station. He picked up the microphone. "Come in, Prescott."

"How come you're moving? The track isn't clear to South Ferry yet, and we've still got five minutes. Why are you moving?"

"A slight change of plan. We decided we wanted to remove ourselves from all those cops you had hidden in the tunnel back there."

"Hell," Prescott said. "There weren't any cops there. Look, if you keep on as you are, you'll begin to run into red signals. I don't want you to blame us for it."

"We'll stop soon and wait for you to clear the track. You still have five minutes."

"How are the passengers?"

"The passengers are fine, so far. But don't play any tricks."

"*You* crossed *us* by moving."

"You have my apology. Instructions remain the same. Get back to me as soon as the track is clear. Over and out."

Longman said, "You think they know anything? I mean—all those questions?"

"The questions are natural ones," Ryder said. "They're thinking as we want them to."

"Jesus," Longman said. "Look at them hanging over the edge of that platform. When I was a motorman, I had nightmares about a dozen of them tumbling in front of my train."

As the car entered the north end of the Twenty-third Street station, they could hear shouting from the platform. Fists were shaking, and at least a dozen people spat at them. Ryder spotted a number of blue uniforms mingled with the crowd. Just before they passed beyond the platform, he saw a man double up his fist and swing at the car.

BOROUGH COMMANDER

The commissioner's limousine jolted over the curb and swung downtown onto Park Avenue South. The commissioner and the borough commander sat side by side on the rear seat. At Twenty-fourth Street, a cop was frantically trying to clear cross-traffic out of their path.

"We might make better time by subway," the commissioner said.

The borough commander looked at him in open astonishment. In all the years he had known him, he had never heard the commissioner make a joke.

The driver turned on his siren and shot through the intersection. The cop at the corner saluted as they went by.

The borough commander spoke into the mike. "Still moving?"

"Yes, sir. Moving slowly, in low gear, what they call switching position."

"Where are they?"

"Almost to Twenty-third Street."

"Thank you."

The commissioner was peering through the rear window. "We're being followed. A television truck. Maybe a second one behind, too."

"Shit," the borough commander said. "I should have given orders to impede them. They're a pain in the ass."

"Freedom of the press," the commissioner said. "We don't want *them* on our back. We're going to need all the friends we can get after this is over."

The radio crackled. "They're entering the Twenty-third Street station, sir, speed still about five miles per hour."

"Some sort of traffic jam up ahead," the commissioner said.

The radio voice said, "Not stopping. Going right through Twenty-third Street station."

"Open it up," the borough commander said to the driver. "Make that siren sing."

DCI DANIELS

In the cab of the darkened front car of Woodlawn One Four One, the DCI watched impatiently as the motorman replaced his instruments on the panel.

"Now," he said, "you understand what I want you to do?"

"Follow that train. Right?"

The DCI, suspecting mockery, looked at the motorman sharply. "Get moving," he said roughly. "Don't go too fast, and don't get too close."

The motorman pushed his controller forward, and the car started abruptly.

"A little more speed," the DCI said. "But not too much. I don't want them to see or hear us."

The motorman nudged the controller into series. "See is one thing. Hear is another. No such thing as a quiet subway train."

They sailed past the Twenty-eighth Street station, empty except for a handful of patrolmen. When the lights of the Twenty-third Street platform became visible in the distance, the DCI said, "Slow it down now. Crawl. Keep your eye peeled for their lights. Crawl. And don't make so much noise."

"This a subway train, Cap'n. No such thing as no noise."

The DCI, peering through the window, felt his eyes begin to water with the strain.

"Red signal there on the local track," the motorman said. "Means they went by here not too long ago."

"Slow," the DCI said. "Very slow. Crawl. And quiet. Don't make a sound."

"You sure asking a lot out of one little old subway car, Cap'n," the motorman said.

THE CITY: STREET SCENE

The crowd's antenna, an organ tuned to a permanent wavelength of suspicion, evaluated the departure of the commissioner's limousine as a prelude to breaking camp. The subsequent dispersal of police cars and personnel merely confirmed its judgment. A few of its members struck off southward, in hope of catching up with the action, but these were viewed with disdain; the mountain might *come* to Mahomet, but it didn't *chase* him.

In a matter of minute's the crowd ceased to exist as an effective entity. Shuffling, then pushing, it fought its way free, and, once clear, picked up its pace briskly, because its time was valuable and must not be wasted in meaningless standing around. A few hundred remained, idlers or romantics, clinging to the forlorn hope of a shootout taking place in front of their eyes. Philosophers and theorists held seminars in small clusters. Individuals aired their opinions.

"What about that mayor! They needed him down here like they needed a second hole in their ass."

"They should of gone in with guns blazing. You start coddling crooks and they take advantage. A good crook knows his psychology."

"Basically, they're small-timers. If it had of been me, I would of asked for *ten* million. And of got it."

"Black guys? Never! Black guys are the quick knockover artists for ten dollars and like that. These were white guys, and I got to give them credit for thinking big."

"The police commissioner? He don't even *look* like a cop. How can you respect somebody who don't look like a cop?"

"What about that mayor! You think a rich guy can really care about a poor guy? Never the twain will meet!"

"Tell me one way, just one little way the hijackers are different from big business. I'll tell you the only way—big business is protected by the law. As usual, the little man gets it in the neck."

"You know how they're gonna get away? I figgered it out. They're gonna fly that train to Cuba!"

"What's up, Mac?"

NINETEEN

RYDER

The emergency exit was located north of the Fourteenth Street station, an opening in the tunnel wall providing access to a ladder that led to a grate in the sidewalk on the east side of Union Square Park near Sixteenth Street. Ryder watched Longman work the brake handle and bring the car to a stop a hundred feet short of the white light marking the position of the exit.

"Right?" Longman said.

"Fine," Ryder said.

Longman was sweating, and Ryder became aware for the first time of how badly the tiny cab smelled. Well, he thought, we can't pick our working conditions on hygienic principles, and since when did a battlefield smell like a field of daisies? He put his hand into the brown valise cautiously and took out two grenades. He inspected the pins and then placed the grenades in the deep pocket of his raincoat. He opened the first-aid box and brought out the spool of adhesive tape. He handed the spool to Longman, who fumbled it momentarily.

"Just hold it steady," Ryder said.

He tore two strips of about sixteen inches each from the spool and wound them loosely around the grenades.

"Those things make me nervous," Longman said.

"Everything makes you nervous," Ryder said factually. "They're safe as tennis balls as long as the pin remains in and the lever is not released."

"Do you *have* to?" Longman said. "I mean—suppose they *aren't* following us on the express track?"

"In that case we took an unnecessary precaution."

"But if they *aren't* following us, then eventually an innocent express train will come along—"

"Don't argue," Ryder said. "I want you to start working as soon as I leave. You *must* be finished by the time I get back, so we can move the train immediately."

"Command Center calling Pelham One Two Three. Command Center to Pelham One Two Three."

Ryder pressed the transmitter button. "Pelham One Two Three. Track clear yet?"

"Not quite clear yet. About two to three minutes more."

"Be quick about it. And no police on the track, anywhere, or we'll react. You understand the meaning of react, Lieutenant Prescott?"

"Yes. We're complying with your instructions, there's no need to hurt anybody. Acknowledge, Pelham One Two Three."

Ryder hung the microphone back on its hook. "Don't

answer," he said to Longman. "He'll get tired and quit after a while. All right. Get started."

He turned the latch and went out of the cab. Welcome was lounging against the center pole, the submachine gun dangling from his right hand. Ryder suppressed a twinge of anger and continued by without comment. Steever stood up as he approached and slid the rear storm door open.

"Cover me," Ryder said.

Steever nodded.

Ryder stepped onto the threshold plates, crouched, and dropped lightly to the roadbed. He straightened up and began to trot northward between the gleaming rails.

TOM BERRY

As the leader came out of the cab, Tom Berry caught a glimpse of the smallest of the hijackers straining to lift some kind of heavy metal construction out of what looked like a Valpac. The door snapped shut, and the leader went through the car. He said a brief word to the heavy man at the rear door, then jumped down to the track. And now, Deedee, Berry thought, will I take advantage of his absence to storm the Winter Palace? No, Deedee, I will not twitch my ass off this seat by so much as a millimeter.

Ah, Deedee, he thought, by what right do I mock you? At least, right or wrong, you believe in something, you have a place to stand. But who am I? Half a cop, half a surly doubter. If I believed in being a cop, I would probably be dead by now, but honorably dead by those lights, and if I didn't believe in being a cop, I wouldn't be gnawed by

guilt. But, Deedee, why in hell should I feel guilty for
having rejected suicide?

And as long as I'm being selfish, Berry thought, I hope
the hijackers make a nice unmessy getaway so that I don't
die accidentally in a crossfire between trigger-happy hoods
and trigger-happy cops. Not that a getaway seemed easy
or even possible, given that the hijackers were bottled up
in a tunnel with all exits plugged by cops. Still, it was reasonable to suppose that the hijackers were resourceful and
had figured out a happy ending for themselves, wasn't it?
Well, that's their problem. Not mine. Tom Berry passes.

DCI DANIELS

"Shshsh," the DCI said. "Keep it quiet."

"No way," the motorman said. "Train don't move on
no tippy*toe*."

"Shshsh." The DCI was peering out of the front window, his forehead almost touching the glass. The motorman applied his brake suddenly, and the DCI's nose
bumped the window. "Jesus!"

"There she is," the motorman said. "If you strain, you
can see her up ahead."

"That little bit of light?" the DCI said doubtfully.

"That's her," the motorman said. "She's laying dead."

The radio crackled, and the DCI listened intently to
Command Center's end of a conversation with Pelham
One Two Three.

"She's lying there, like you said," the DCI said to the
motorman. He listened to Command Center trying to

continue the conversation with Pelham One Two Three, but the car was obviously not responding. "They won't answer. Arrogant murdering bastards."

"What we do?" the motorman said. "Stay like we are?"

"We can't get any closer or they'll spot us. My God, I never felt so helpless in my entire life."

"You see something out there on the bed?" the motorman said.

"Where?" The DCI stared through the window. "I don't see a thing."

"Looked like a man," the motorman said. "But I don't see nothing now. Might be I could been mistaken."

"You don't see anything now?"

"Sure. See the train."

"That's all I see, too. Keep looking. Let me know if you see any movement."

"Just the train, and it's not making no movement." The motorman took his eyes off the track and looked at his watch. "Except what happened, I'd be home right now. Got me working on overtime, way it stands. Time and a half, but I rather be home."

"Keep watching."

"Time and a half don't mean that much to me. Taxes get it, anyhow."

"Just keep watching."

LONGMAN

The parts of the Gimmick were neatly arranged in the Valpac—Longman had packed it himself—and except for the weight of the shaped iron piece that fitted over the controller, it was all as easy as it had been in rehearsal. Yet he could remember when the crucial problem that the Gimmick had eventually solved had seemed hopeless, and their entire plan had appeared doomed. At least, that was how *he* had felt about it. Ryder had been calm.

"A few years ago," he had complained to Ryder, "the deadman's feature was a nipple in the head of the controller. All we would have had to do was tape it down and then find some way of pushing it into drive. But with the feature built into the mechanism itself, like it is now, it's impossible. If you taped the whole controller down to the panel, you would deactivate the deadman's feature, but then you couldn't move it into drive. If it was only still a nipple—"

"It isn't a nipple now," Ryder said, "so there's no point dwelling on it. Concentrate on the present problem."

The present problem was that you couldn't possibly drive a train without a motorman. Yet, when they found the solution, it made his earlier despair seem ridiculous. The heart of the Gimmick was a heavy iron mold cast roughly in the shape of the controller. Set in place over the controller, its weight substituted for the pressure of the motorman's hand. It deactivated the deadman's feature, permitted the controller to be moved into driving position, and, most important, by its weight *kept* the deadman's feature deactivated.

Simple and beautiful, Longman thought, and grunted as he hefted the Gimmick out of the Valpac and fitted it over the controller. The rest of it was equally simple. Three joining lengths of pipe—the first less than six inches in length and fitting into a receptacle at the front of the iron weight; the second about three feet in length, angled downward toward the tracks; the third three feet long and angled toward the tunnel wall.

The lengths of pipe had been tooled to fit into each other with different degrees of firmness. The short piece joined tightly with the receptacle in the Gimmick, the second piece loosely at its inner end with the first piece, and securely at its outer end with the third piece. But before he could join the pipes together, Longman had to break out the front window. Irrationally, it bugged him, made him feel like a vandal. He hesitated for a long moment with the butt of his machine gun poised, then slammed it against the window, opening up a great splintered hole. He struck several times more, until nothing remained of the glass but a few tiny shards clinging to the edges of the frame. He was willing to let it go at that, but Ryder had been emphatic about it. "No glass. Absolutely none or it could wreck the illusion."

Scraping with the barrel of his gun, Longman cleared all the small pieces out of the frame.

RYDER

Northward from the rear of the car, Ryder paced off about 300 feet. He stopped, and in the same motion went to his knees beside the inside express rail. He took one of the grenades from his pocket, removed the adhesive tape, and ripped it across in two unequal lengths of six and ten inches. He paused and peered intently along the roadbed. In the distance, he saw the dark hulking shadow of a train. He nodded, as if in acknowledgment of a judgment confirmed, and then put it out of mind.

Holding the grenade in the palm of his left hand, he covered the lever from end to end, leaving the tape extending a few inches beyond the casing at each end. Dipping his head almost to the level of the track, he placed the grenade beneath the lip of the rail and carefully smoothed out the loose ends of the tape so that they held the grenade in place against the rail. He tore the smaller length of tape in half and plastered the pieces across the two ends to guard against accidental dislodgment. When he was satisfied the grenade was firmly in place, he reached in and pulled the pin. Then he moved to the outside rail and repeated the entire procedure with the second grenade.

He stood up and, without a backward glance, began to trot back to Pelham One Two Three. With the pulling of the pins, the grenades were fully armed. When the wheel of a train struck, the lightly taped grenades would be dislodged, automatically releasing the levers. The grenades would explode in five seconds.

Steever was standing guard at the rear door. Ryder nodded to him, then rounded the dirty red sides of the car to the front. Longman looked out at him through the glassless window. The middle length of pipe protruded. He held out his hand and Longman passed him the third length of pipe. He screwed it tightly into the second length, with the end angled in toward the tunnel wall.

When the pipe construction was pushed inward toward the train, it would shove the controller clockwise through switching into series position, where the bulk of the cast iron weight would serve to prevent it from moving further into multiple position. A sharp pull backward would then disengage the two long pieces of pipe, leaving only the short first piece, which would not be visible from outside the train.

For the rest, Ryder was banking on "illusion," on the power of assumption to triumph over actuality. People didn't really *see* glass, and so, with no shards to pick up a stray beam of light, they would *assume* it. The police would know that a train could not move without a motorman (the more knowledgeable they were, the more strongly they would accept the fact), and so they would *assume* the presence of a motorman in the darkened cab. He acknowledged that some observer, hurdling the psychological barrier, might perceive the truth, but even then it would be met with official skepticism long enough for them to make their escape.

When he had checked the arrangement of pipes to his satisfaction, Ryder hauled himself up into the car and entered the cab. Edging Longman to one side, he inspected the placement of the weight over the controller.

"It's all set," Longman said impatiently. "I wish we were getting started."

"We'll start when Command Center tells us the track is clear."

"I know," Longman said. "It's just that I'm getting itchy."

Ryder was silent. He estimated that Longman had about ten minutes more of courage—such as it was—before he went to pieces. Well, ten minutes should be enough; in ten minutes they should be home free.

WELCOME

Ever since the lights came back on, Joey Welcome had been feeling pissed off. For one thing, he had cooled on the chick. The bright light took something away from her. Still a hot chick, sure, but the mileage was showing. Not that he didn't dig older broads, too—he dug broads, period—but this one was beginning to look too professional, and he wasn't all that wild about a thousand or so guys being up the same road ahead of him.

She was still giving him the eye, but he wasn't all that horny anymore. Instead, he was beginning to get uptight about the operation. It was too long drawn out, and there wasn't enough action. Though he had almost had a little unscheduled action with General Ryder a while ago. To be continued—right? The best part had been back at the beginning, when he had unloaded on that fat guy on the tracks. That was how he liked it—fast and tough. Ryder was a brain, Longman was a brain, but they were too fancy. Himself, he would have done it the simple way. You want to get out of someplace? Come out fast, and come out zapping. Sure, there was lots of cops around, but they had four fast shooters, didn't they? Some big attack soldier Ryder was!

And the smg's—that was another one of his beefs. It

surprised the hell out of him when Ryder said they would have to ditch them, and he didn't agree with it one little bit. The whole strength of the thing was in the firepower, in the tommy guns, that was why everybody was scared of you and the cops were kissing your ass. So why weaken yourself where you're strongest? Ryder's way, ditching the fast shooters, if something screwed up, all you could count on was four handguns. Handguns to shoot a hundred cops? But give him a tommy gun, and he would face up to a *thousand* cops.

The girl was giving him one of those fuck-me-faster looks, mouth open—she knew the tricks of the trade, all right—and he began to feel a little horny again, but just then Ryder climbed in through the front door. Too bad, sister, it's just about getaway time.

ANITA LEMOYNE

Somewhere along the line, Anita Lemoyne realized, the creep had gotten away from her. Okay, so she lost the creep. What was she supposed to do—blow her brains out? Now that it was beginning to look as if they would all be getting out of this with a whole skin, there were more important things to think about—for instance, what line to take with the television crumb, assuming he didn't just hang up on her when she phoned him. The one thing she knew for sure was that he wouldn't think she had a reasonable excuse for standing him up. Knowing him, she could practically write the whole conversation.

"Of course I believe you were involved in the subway

rip-off, but that's irrelevant to the main point, which is that you *wanted* to be."

"Yeah, sure. I woke up this morning and said, 'Anita, doll, go see if you can't get your ass shot off.' "

"Exactly. Though not consciously. Have you heard of accident-prone people? Well, there are people who are danger-prone, who court disaster without being aware—"

"You're full of shit, buster."

"Look, that kind of talk is perfectly acceptable in bed, but not otherwise."

"I'm sorry, honey. But that talk about prone. Maybe I'm prone-prone, if you know what I mean."

"Don't try to be funny."

"All I did was take a goddamn *subway* train, honey."

"Perfect. Tell me—when was the last time you rode the subway?"

"I just happened to be feeling cheap today. Is that so criminal?"

"With all the money you make peddling your ass, and in view of the well-known profligacy of whores, do you expect me to buy that?"

"Okay. Fine. You got me cornered. I took the subway train because I knew it was going to get ripped off. Not only that, but I knew the exact subway line, and the exact time—all because I'm prone, right?"

"An ignorant whore shouldn't challenge well-established psychiatric assumptions. Any number of variables governed your actions before you left the house this morning—having to return for a handkerchief, dawdling five minutes longer than usual in your bath—"

"All for you, sweetheart, so my cunt would smell pretty."

"—deciding to stop at the liquor store to place an order when you could just as well have done it in the evening, taking a different route than usual to the subway—"

"It happens I went shopping today, and took the subway at Thirty-third."

"You ruined my sammawich, you bitch."

"I know, and I feel rotten. Because I get the sweetest fucking of my life out of you, every time. You're the best, honey."

"You spoiled my sammawich."

"That dirty subway, I'll never ride the sonofabitch again in my whole life."

"You ruined my sammawich."

That was the way it would go, Anita thought, and she would end up losing him. Clients like him didn't grow on trees. If she was going to open up that boutique, every John counted. Well, maybe she could crawl on her knees, lick his ass, kiss his goddamn feet. . . . Shit, that was what she did anyway, in the sammawiches.

Gloomily, she watched the leader climb back into the train.

BOROUGH COMMANDER

"They're sitting right there," the borough commander said, pointing to the carpeting of the limousine. "If the street collapsed we would probably land right on top of them." The commissioner nodded.

Union Square Park, deceptively attractive in the lowering light, lay to their right. A block to the south, and on the left, was S. Klein, the ramshackle department store that had been a discount house long before the term became current. The crowds that normally thronged the sidewalks were beginning to coagulate, attracted by the swarm of police cars that had spilled into the area. Traffic was piling up, and policemen at intersections were attempting to siphon it off into the side streets.

The driver turned around. "Sir, we got an opening. Want me to move on?"

"Stick here," the borough commander said. "It's the closest I've been to those bastards since the whole thing began."

The commissioner, watching through his window, saw a cop getting bowled over by a sudden surge of the crowd on the sidewalks. He picked himself up and hit a woman a backhanded blow in the chest.

"If the street collapsed," the commissioner said, "it wouldn't be such a bad idea. The whole city, sinking down and disappearing. It's not such a bad idea."

The commissioner's pessimism came as still another surprise to the borough commander. But he said nothing, instead directing his gaze to the park and coddling an old memory that it evoked and that he found comforting.

"The people," the commissioner said. "Subtract the people from the scene and it would be easy to catch crooks."

The borough commander wrenched his eyes away from the park, whose stone retaining walls were beginning to be obscured by the gathering crowd. "You know what I'd like to do, Mr. Commissioner? I'd like to slip down one of those emergency grates and shoot the hell out of those bastards."

"Haven't we been over that before?" the commissioner said wearily.

"I'm just talking. It makes me feel better."

The borough commander glanced upward at the bare scraggy branches of the trees in the park, and his old memory came to the surface. "One of the first assignments I ever had when I joined the force was right here. Nineteen thirty-three. Or four? Three or four. I was a horse cop, and I was detailed to keep order at a May Day parade. Remember when those parades were a big thing?"

"I never knew you were a horse cop," the commissioner said.

"A real Cossack. My horse was called Daisy. A beauty, with a white blaze on the forehead. Cossack. They really called us that in those days."

"They call us worse now, don't they?"

"Once every hour or so there would be a clash, and we'd hit a few heads, Daisy would step on a few feet. But those were different times. Nobody tried to kill anybody. And if you split a few Commie heads, there was no outcry except from the Commies themselves. Anyway, radicals were a lot softer in those days."

"How about their heads?"

"Their heads?" The borough commander paused. "I see what you mean. Yeah, we used the nightstick more freely in those days. Police brutality. I guess there was some of that. Cossacks. Maybe there was something to it."

"Maybe." The commissioner's voice was flat and gave no clue to his emotions.

"Daisy," the borough commander said. "The Commies used to hate the horses almost as much as they hated the cops. In their cell meetings, they used to hype themselves up: 'Hamstring the Cossacks' horses!' And they would discuss how to duck under the horses' belly with a knife and cut the hamstrings. But I never heard of a horse actually being hamstrung."

"What the hell is going on?" the commissioner said. "They're sitting down there, and we're sitting up here, and it's like a holiday truce."

"Right there," the borough commander said, "on the Seventeenth Street side, from that balcony, that's where the Commies did their speechmaking. But the action could be anywhere around the square or in the park. Forty years ago. How many of those Commies do you think are still Commies? Not one. They all became businessmen, exploiters of the masses, and they live in the suburbs, and they wouldn't hamstring a horse if you turned it upside down and held its head."

"Their kids are the radicals now," the commissioner said.

"And much tougher. They *would* hamstring a horse. Or tie a bomb to its tail."

The radio crackled. "Central to PC. Come in, sir."

The borough commander answered. "Come in, come in."

"Sir, the hijackers are being informed that the track has been cleared."

"Okay, thanks. Flash through as soon as they start

moving." The borough commander signed off and looked at the commissioner. "Wait, or get started?"

"Get started," the commissioner said. "For once we'll be a step ahead of them instead of behind."

TWENTY

RYDER

"Command Center to Pelham One Two Three."

Ryder pressed the transmitter button. "Pelham One Two Three here. Report."

"The track is cleared. Repeat, the track is cleared."

Longman was pressed against him, his breathing a succession of deep sighs that sucked his mask into his mouth. Ryder glanced at him and thought: He'll come to grief. Whatever happens, however well it comes out, in the long run Longman will fail.

He spoke into the mike. "Is the track cleared all the way to South Ferry? Confirm."

"Yes."

"You know the penalty if you're lying?"

"I want to tell you something. You're not going to live

to spend that money. I have a strong hunch about it. Do you read me?"

"We're starting the train now," Ryder said. "Over and out."

"Mark my words—"

Ryder switched the radio off. "Let's go," he said to Longman. "I want the train to be moving in thirty seconds."

He opened the latch and gave Longman a nudge. Longman half stumbled through the door. Ryder took a final look at the Gimmick, then followed Longman out of the cab. The door clicked, locking behind him.

TOM BERRY

The emergency brake cord hung out of a metal-lined hole in the ceiling of the car just behind the motorman's cab. It looked like a skipping rope, with a red wooden handle dangling to a point about six inches below the ceiling. Tom Berry watched the small hijacker reach up with a long thin scissors, insert the scissors an inch or two into the hole and cut the cord. The wooden handle clattered and rolled as it hit the floor. From the tail of his eye Berry saw the heavy man at the other end of the car cutting the second cord. He caught it as it fell and put it in his pocket.

The small man made a hand signal, and Berry saw the heavy man acknowledge it with a nod before he opened the rear door, crouched, and dropped out of sight to the track. The small man, moving with awkward speed, slid by the leader, who was covering the passengers with his tommy gun, and pulled the front door open. He sat down before dropping to the track. The leader nodded crisply to the man in the center of the car, who started to turn, paused, and blew a kiss to the girl in the Anzac hat. Then he trotted jauntily to the rear. He opened the door and, barely bending his knees, jumped down.

The leader was looking at the passengers, and Berry thought, He's going to make a farewell speech, tell us what a great bunch of hostages we've been. . . .

"You will remain in your seats," the leader said. "Don't try to get up. Remain seated."

He felt behind him for the handle and slid the front door open. He moved out onto the steel plate, and Berry thought: Now is the time, his back is turned, whip out your gun and plug him. . . . The leader dropped from view. Just before the door slid shut, Berry caught an oblique view of the small man on the tracks. He was holding what seemed to be a length of pipe, and Berry, with a sudden flash of insight, knew what was going to happen to the train and made a wild guess at how they proposed to throw off pursuit and, as the press would surely refer to it, make their brilliant and daring escape.

He didn't believe what he was doing. He was really still sitting in his seat, not running in a crouch with his drawn gun in his hand. The train started with a shattering jerk, and the momentum carried him past the center poles and almost to the end of the car. His hand struck the yellow metal of the door handle. He found a grip on it and slid the door back. He stared at the tracks fleeing backward beneath him and thought: You were a parachutist, you know how to make a landing, and then he thought: There's still time to go back and sit down.

He jumped, sailed, and felt an agonizingly prolonged moment of sickening pain before he blacked out.

GRAND CENTRAL TOWER

When the red blips on the Model Board at Grand Central Tower indicated that Pelham One Two Three was moving, Marino was passably cool. "They're on their way," he said.

In a matter of seconds the information was broadcast from Police Headquarters to all cars.

Simultaneously with Marino, Mrs. Jenkins, in her quiet voice, was saying to Lieutenant Garber, "Pelham One Two Three has begun to move and is presently about a hundred feet south of its former position."

All foot patrolmen and cars were alerted to the new development.

The entire pursuit, aboveground and below, surged southward as if attached by invisible strings to Pelham One Two Three.

RYDER

Longman had been overanxious and had stumbled after pushing the pipe. But he had kept his grip on it as he recoiled when the train started, and it came away in his hand. Ryder pulled him off the track into the shelter of the tunnel wall and braced an arm across his trembling chest as the car rumbled by, a towering, terrifying bulk.

Ryder took the pipe from Longman's unresisting hand and tossed it across the track. It struck a pillar and skittered away to the northbound track. Steever and Welcome were waiting for them, close to the tunnel wall, a car's length back.

"Let's move along," Ryder said.

Without waiting to see if they were following, he trotted southward and stopped in the white glare of the light marking the emergency exit. The others straggled up to join him.

"Let's keep it lively," Ryder said sharply. "You know the drill."

"I thought I saw something fall out of the end," Steever said. "The end of the car."

Ryder looked down the track. The light from the moving car was fading. "What did it look like?"

Steever shrugged. "Big. A shadow, like. Could be a person. But I'm not even sure I saw it."

Welcome said, "If anybody fell out of the end of that car, he's ready for the embalmer." He hefted his machine gun. "You want me to take a look? If anybody's there and still alive, I'll finish him off."

Ryder looked down the track again. There was nothing, no one, visible. He glanced, at Steever. Battle nerves? He had seen tension conjure up ghosts before, and in men equally as self-contained and unimaginative as Steever. Troops on night patrol screaming a warning where no threat existed. Guards blazing away at shadows. Yes, it could even

happen to a Steever, taking into account some pain from his
wound, the lightheadedness of loss of blood. . . .

"Forget it," he said.

"I only wasted one all afternoon," Welcome said. "I
wouldn't mind another notch on the gun."

"No," Ryder said.

"No," Welcome said in mimicry. "Suppose I decide
that's what I want to do?"

"We're wasting time," Ryder said. "Let's get started."

"By the numbers, right?" Welcome said.

Longman said, "You're sure it's clear up there?" He
tilted his chin upward. "The cops will take off?"

"Yes," Ryder said. "They'll follow the train." He heard
the rasp of impatience in his voice, and paused. "Ready?
I'm going to give the commands."

"Commands," Welcome said. "Real chickenshit."

Ryder ignored him. The precision drill had been a matter of necessity, not choice. In rehearsal, with each man
on his own, one or another of them kept slipping up on
details, and so he had devised a simple by-the-numbers
routine. He had also decided against entering the emergency exit chamber at this point, against the possibility
that some passerby looking through the grate above the
escape ladder might see or hear them.

"Submachine guns," Ryder said crisply. He put his gun
down on the roadbed. Steever and Longman followed,
but Welcome still held his, fondling it possessively.

Steever said, "Come on, Joey, you need two hands to
work."

Welcome said, "What are you, the assistant captain?"
But, reluctantly, he put his gun down.

"Hats and masks," Ryder said.

The reappearance of their faces came as a shock, and Ryder thought: These seem less real than the masks. It surprised him, when Welcome spoke, to hear his own sentiments echoed.

"Tell you something," Welcome said, "you all looked better with your masks on."

"Disguise," Ryder said.

He had removed the wads from his face before putting his mask on, and Longman had removed his eyeglasses at the same time. So it remained only for Steever to take off his white-haired wig, and Welcome to strip off the moustache and elaborately curving sideburns.

"Coats," Ryder said. "Remove, turn, put back on."

Each of the navy raincoats was lined with a reversible material. Welcome's was a light beige poplin waterproof, Steever's a medium gray with a black fur collar, Longman's a tan herringbone tweed, his own a pepper-and-salt Donegal tweed. He watched closely as they reversed the coats and buttoned them up over the bulging money jackets.

"Hats."

They took their hats from their pockets. Welcome's was a powder-blue low-crowned golfing hat with a narrow red-and-navy-blue band, Steever's a gray with a short upturned brim, Longman's a gray Astrakhan Russian hat, his own a sporty brown cap with a short brim.

"Gloves."

They peeled their gloves and dropped them.

"Handgun in coat pocket? Check." He waited. "Okay. Wallets. Show the ID card and shield."

He hoped they would have no reason to use them, but

it was conceivable that a cop or two, remaining on the scene, might question them. If so, they were to say they were part of the force stationed in the tunnel and present their police credentials, which had been even more expensive to obtain than the submachine guns.

"Can't you go a little faster?" Longman said.

"This character is scared of the sound of his own farts," Welcome said.

"Almost finished," Ryder said. "Pick up smg's, detach magazine, put in pocket. Put smg down again." It was a simple precaution; he just didn't want to leave armed weapons behind.

All four bent for their guns, but only three began to remove the magazines.

"Not me," Welcome said, smiling. "I'm taking my little fast shooter along with me."

GRAND CENTRAL TOWER

Marino, his voice ringing in the stillness of the Tower Room, said, "Pelham One Two Three just passed Fourteenth Street station and is proceeding toward Astor Place station."

"Any idea of the speed?"

"Well," Marino said, "it's moving along. I would guess it's in series."

"What does that mean?"

"Say about thirty miles an hour. Can the police cars keep up with them through the traffic?"

"We don't have to do that. We've got cars in position

all along the route. They pick up as the train hits their area."

"They're now about halfway between Fourteenth and Astor Place."

"Okay. Keep talking to me."

NERVE CENTER

At the Nerve Center a radio man handed Lieutenant Garber a message. He read it as he listened to Mrs. Jenkins. A TA patrolman on the Fourteenth Street station had reported that Pelham One Two Three had gone by without stopping.

". . . Pelham One Two Three is now about fifteen hundred feet south of Fourteenth Street station."

From the soft, modulated quality of her voice, Lieutenant Garber visualized Mrs. Jenkins as a slender, willowy blonde in her early thirties.

"Keep feeding me, honey," he said.

CLIVE PRESCOTT

At the desk trainmaster's console at Command Center, Prescott gave up trying to contact Pelham One Two Three by radio. He listened to Mrs. Jenkins' voice coming over the squawk box and speculated on its owner. About thirty-five, cafe-au-lait, divorced, cool, loving and experienced. He considered being soothed by her in expert ways, and immediately reproached himself for faithlessness to his wife.

". . . continuing to proceed downtown, estimated to be in series position speed."

It made no sense, Prescott thought. Inch by inch their position was monitored, so how could they hope to evade pursuit? It was dumb. But who ever said criminals were smart? And yet, thus far, they had not made a single mistake.

He turned to the console. "Pelham One Two Three. Command Center calling Pelham One Two Three. . . ."

ANITA LEMOYNE

In exactly one minute, Anita Lemoyne thought, I'm going to get hysterical. *Can't the stupid bastards count?* Everyone was babbling about the hippie who had jumped out, even the old dude, who she judged to be the sharpest of the passengers.

"Momentum," the old man was saying. "From all that momentum he couldn't be alive."

Someone else said, "What made him do it?" and then answered himself. "Bombed out. They get high and then do crazy things like that and get killed."

"Where are they taking us?" the boys' mother said. "You think they'll let us go soon, like they said?"

"So far," the old man said, "they have been as good as their word."

Anita jumped to her feet, screaming, "Don't you dumb

bastards know how to count? All four of them got off. There's nobody *driving* the fucking train!"

The old man seemed startled for a moment, then shook his head and smiled. "My dear young lady, if they all got off, we would be standing still. One of them has to be on to drive it."

Anita's eyes went wildly from one uncertain face to another and rested on the mother's. She must have been doing some simple arithmetic, Anita thought, because she looked like she was getting the message.

The mother screamed on a sustained ululant note, and Anita thought: If that doesn't make believers out of the rest of them, nothing will.

TWENTY-ONE

TOM BERRY

Young Tom Berry's father was bawling him out for some crime he hadn't committed, scourging him with that cold voice that could draw blood. His mother was pleading for him, but her voice was strange. It sounded like a man's. He opened his eyes, and pain drove his dream away, though the voices continued.

He was lying against a pillar, off the roadbed, and he knew that he was hurt. His head, his shoulders, his chest . . . He put his hand to his mouth; it felt pulpy and wet. His fingers traced upward to his nose, which was seeping slowly, down into the delta over his upper lip. He probed his head and found a huge lump. The voices worried him. He lifted his head an inch or two and found their source.

He could not judge the distance in the dimness of the

tunnel, but he could see them clearly enough, all four of them. They were ranged against the wall and they were undressing. They no longer wore their nylon masks, and their faces under the naked bulb marking the emergency exit were erratically lit: brightly on the prominence of nose and ears, hollowed by deep shadows on the flatter planes. The leader was doing most of the talking. Gradually, Berry began to realize what they were up to. Their hats and coats were different, they were disguising themselves. In their new clothing and with the police in wild pursuit of the train, they would come up through the emergency exit and simply mingle with the crowd.

His gun. He had been holding it in his hand when he jumped. At some point it had been jarred loose. He raised himself on his elbow to look for it, then, in a sudden panic, huddled behind the pillar. They might see him, the whiteness of his face might give him away. But he couldn't look for the gun if he kept his face pressed into the tunnel floor. Screw the gun. He could always get another gun, but not another face. He groaned, then hastily muffled the sound. Why was he here? Why had he jumped from the frying pan? Where was his head?

The four hijackers were arguing. No, two of them. He placed the angry voice as belonging to the stud. The cold, uninflected voice was the leader's. The other two were silent, looking on. Thieves falling out? Would they now proceed to slaughter each other with the machine guns? If they did, he wouldn't hesitate to crawl over there and collar them.

"You men—dead though you may be—are under arrest. You are entitled to one phone call each, and I hereby notify you of your rights according to Supreme Court decision . . ."

Where was the gun? It could be anywhere in the tunnel between Fourteenth Street and Twenty-third. *Where is my gun?* He began to scrabble with his hand on the grimy tunnel floor.

DCI DANIELS

Through the window of Woodlawn One Four One, the faint rectangle of light that marked Pelham One Two Three wavered, liquefied. DCI Daniels rubbed his eyes.

"They just begun to move," the motorman said.

"Well, what the hell are you waiting for!" the DCI shouted.

"For your signal, like you said. You're killing my arm, Cap'n, I can't drive no train that way."

The DCI loosened his grip. "Get going. Not too fast."

"*They* sure as hell ain't dawdling," the motorman said. He pushed his controller, and the train began to crawl forward. "Look like they take off like a bullet. See how fast those green signals turned red? You sure you want me to go all this slow?"

"I don't want them to see us."

"This speed they sure won't see us. Nor us see them."

"Then go faster, dammit, if that's your judgment."

"Faster," the motorman said. "That's my judgment."

He nudged the controller to series position, and the train shot ahead, but only for a moment. The forward wheels made a faint metallic sound, and then the entire tunnel seemed to explode. The rear of the car lifted from the tracks, and hung suspended for a split second before crashing back heavily. The huge wheels glanced off the rails, and ground down on the roadbed. The car swayed and bounced crazily, and, as the motorman applied his brakes, sideswiped a half dozen pillars before it came to a stop in a haze of dust and overheated metal.

"Sonofabitch," the motorman said. Beside him, the DCI was holding his hand to his head. His eyes were crossed, and a thin stream of blood trickled out of his hairline and wound its way slowly down his forehead.

The DCI pushed by the motorman and went out of the cab. There, leaning against the door to steady himself, he surveyed the car. Everyone seemed to be shouting. A half dozen cops were on the floor. Weapons were strewn about. A light, acrid dusting of smoke drifted lazily through the car.

The DCI watched the men get off the floor, feeling curiously detached from the scene. One man was rolling from side to side, crying in oddly controlled gasps, clutching at his kneecap.

"Help that man," the DCI said. He was going to say something else, but lost the thread. He felt the bloody place on his head. It didn't hurt. In fact, he couldn't quite seem to make contact with it through his fingertips.

"Are you hurt, sir?" It was a burly sergeant, speaking very calmly. "What happened, sir?"

"Booby-trapped," the DCI said. "Tell your men to sit down, sergeant. The Jap bastards booby-trapped us off the track."

He was amused by the curious look the sergeant was giving him. A young fella, the sergeant, too young for the big war, he didn't understand about booby traps or recognize the stink of a grenade.

"What I mean, sir," the sergeant said, "what do we do? What orders, sir?"

"We're off the track," the DCI said. His mind drifted. "I'll reconnoiter. Just stay put."

He went into the cab. The motorman had let his metal stool down. He was sitting on it, shaking his head from side to side.

"Report the incident, Sergeant," the DCI said. "Find out how soon the corps of engineers can get us back on the track, or secure other transportation."

"Take a crew of car knockers couple or more hours to get us back," the motorman said. "What you mean, *sergeant*? You a little shook up, Cap'n?"

"Don't argue, Sergeant. Get on that radio and report."

He went out into the car, and slid the front door open. As he was crouching for the jump to the roadbed, the sergeant who had spoken to him before said, "Can we give you any help, sir?"

The DCI smiled, and shook his head. Funny new breed of cops, spoiled by cars and partners and computers. They didn't realize that the old-timer walked his beat alone and unafraid, and beware the miscreant who trifled with him. He dropped to the tracks and was somewhat jarred by the impact, but he straightened up quickly. Then, hands behind his back, eyes moving slowly and watchfully from side to side, he began to walk his beat.

RYDER

Facing Welcome in the first silence since they had left the train, Ryder heard the inexplicable sounds of the tunnel—rustlings, creakings, echoes, the faint sigh of the tainted wind. Steever and Longman were looking at him questioningly.

"As before," he said. "Detach magazine."

Almost in precise unison with Steever and Longman he removed the magazine and slid it into his left coat pocket. Welcome, smiling, shook his head from side to side.

Ryder said mildly, "Disarm your gun, Joe, so we can get out of here."

"I'm ready right now," Welcome said. "Me and the gun is going out together."

"You can't take it," Ryder said, still mildly.

"My friend goes with me. The old firepower, you know, if the fuzz turns up."

"The whole point of the escape plan is to walk away unnoticed. You can't do that if you're carrying a submachine gun." The argument—the very words he was using—was a replay. It had come up several times in the past weeks, but Welcome had eventually conceded—or so it seemed.

"Not *carry* it." Welcome looked at Steever and Longman as if for confirmation that he was scoring a major point. "I slip it under my coat."

The old record played on, Ryder thought. "A submachine gun can't be hidden under a coat."

Longman said shrilly, "This is crazy. We have to get going."

Steever's face was impassive, showing neither annoyance nor partisanship. Longman had begun to sweat again. Welcome, still smiling, was watching Ryder with hard, narrowed eyes.

Ryder said, "Will you leave your gun?"

"Shit, no, General."

He was still smiling when Ryder, firing through his pocket, shot him in the throat. The shot was soundless, overwhelmed by a shattering explosion northward in the tunnel. Welcome collapsed. Longman sagged against the tunnel wall. Welcome lay on his side. His legs were twitching, his left hand clawed at his throat, and his fingers were stained red. His hat had rolled away, and his long black hair had broken down over his forehead. He was still holding the submachine gun in his right hand. Ryder kicked it loose. He bent down, removed the magazine, and put it in his pocket. Longman was leaning against the wall, vomiting rackingly.

Ryder crouched for a close look at Welcome. His eyes were shut, his skin was the color of old paper, and his breathing was shallow. Ryder took out his automatic and placed it against Welcome's head. He looked up at Steever.

"He might last long enough to talk," he said, and pulled the trigger. Welcome's head jerked with the impact of the slug, and a bit of bloody bone flew away. He looked up again into Steever's expressionless face. "Get Longman straightened out."

He unbuttoned Welcome's coat and untied the money jacket. The edges of one of the packets of money was bloodstained. To free the jacket, Ryder held one end of it and flipped Welcome over on his face. He stood up with the jacket. Northward in the tunnel a moiling cloud of smoke and dust was suspended between the roadbed and the roof.

Steever was supporting Longman with a hand around his waist and was wiping off the front of his coat with a handkerchief. Longman looked ill. His face was drained of color, and his eyes were red-rimmed and weeping.

"Open his coat," Ryder said.

Longman stood limp and helpless as Steever tugged at the buttons of his coat. When Ryder moved toward him with the jacket, Longman looked terrified.

"Me?" Longman said. "Why me?" and Ryder realized that his fear had passed beyond being rational and that he was afraid of everything.

"You're the thinnest of us. Two jackets under your coat won't show. Hold your hands away from your sides."

Slipping the belt around Longman and tying it, Ryder was almost overpowered by the stink of vomit and terror. But he worked methodically, feeling Longman's sweat-soaked body trembling under his touch. When the jacket was secure, he buttoned up Longman's coat.

Steever said conversationally, "The train blew good."

"Yes," Ryder said. He looked Longman over. "All right. I think we're ready to go upstairs."

BOROUGH COMMANDER

"That short move they made to Union Square," the borough commander said. "It wasn't in the script. It's got me worried."

They were speeding downtown, the siren wide open, traffic scurrying out of their way toward the curb.

The commissioner was pursuing a path of his own. "They know we can follow every move the train makes. They know we're covering them every inch of the way on the surface. But it doesn't seem to bother them. They can't possibly be that stupid, so they may be very clever."

"Yes," the borough commander said. "That's what I've got in mind. The move to Union Square. They said they did it to get away from the police staked out in the tunnel. How come?"

"They don't like policemen."

"They knew we were in the tunnel before, and didn't seem to mind. Why now?"

The borough commander paused for so long an interval that the commissioner said impatiently, "Well, why?"

"This time they didn't want us to see what they were doing."

"What were they doing?"

"They don't care that we're following them—right? In fact, stretching the point, you could say they want us to follow them all the way downtown—right?"

"Stop dragging it out," the commissioner said. "If you have a theory, spit it out."

"My theory," the borough commander said, "is that they aren't on the train."

"That's what I thought your theory was. But how can the train move if they're not on it?"

"That's the catch. Except for that, it makes sense. The

whole pursuit flows south, but they stay near Union Square and pop up through an emergency exit. How about this—three get off and one stays on to drive the train?"

"A selfless criminal, sacrificing himself for the others? Did you ever meet a criminal like that, Charlie?"

"No," the borough commander said. "A more logical tack—suppose they figured out some way to make the train go with nobody in the cab?"

"If they did that," the commissioner said, "they're dead ducks. Daniels is following on the express track. He would spot them."

"Maybe not. They might be able to conceal themselves until he went by." He shook his head. "That short move. That unexpected move."

"Well?" the commissioner said. "You want to play your hunch?"

"Yes sir," the borough commander said. "With your permission." The commissioner nodded. The borough commander leaned forward to the driver. "Next corner," he said. "Turn off and head back to Union Square."

The radio broke in. "Sir. The motorman of DCI Daniels' train has reported that they were blown off the track. By an explosive placed on the track."

The commissioner asked about casualties and was told that one policeman was hurt, not seriously. "That was the purpose of the short move," he said to the borough commander. "They didn't want anybody around when they mined the track."

"Never mind the turn," the borough commander said to the driver. "Go on as you were."

OLD MAN

The old man, calling on ancient memory, activating dis-used impulses, held up his hand (that famous hand that once was a scepter, demanding obedience at home, sub-servience in the shop) and said, "Quiet down. Everybody quiet down a minute."

He paused to savor the thrill of the faces turned to him, to the Authority. But before he could speak again, he had lost them. The big man, the theater critic, had lumbered forward and was trying to turn the recessed handle of the cab door. Then he began to pound on the door with his fist. The door rattled but remained firmly shut. The big man stopped, turned abruptly, and went back to his seat. They were entering a station. Bleecker Street? Maybe Spring Street by now, he couldn't read the signs. Several passengers had their windows down, and they were screaming for help at the crowd on the plat-form. The crowd shouted back angrily. Someone threw a folded newspaper that hit the window, spread open, and bounced back onto the platform in a shower of pages.

"My friends. . . ." The old man stood up and reached for a metal strap. "My friends, the situation is not so bad as it looks."

The black man gave a snorting laugh into his bloody handkerchief (*my* handkerchief, the old man thought), but the rest became attentive.

"In the first place, we don't have to worry about those bastards no more." Three, four faces turned apprehen-sively toward the cab door. The old man smiled. "As the young lady pointed out, the bastards are off the train. Good-bye and good luck."

"Then who's driving it?"

"Nobody. Some way, they got it started."

"We'll all be killed!" An agonized scream from the mother of the boys.

"Not so," the old man said. "I admit that right now we are on a runaway train, but only temporary. Purely temporary."

The car entered a curve and careened wildly, the wheel flanges grinding, bumping, as they resisted the pull of the car to follow the curve off the tracks. The passengers swayed, fell against one another. The old man, clinging desperately to the strap, was half lifted from the floor. The black man reached out a bloody hand and steadied him. The train straightened out.

"Thank you," the old man said.

The black man ignored him. Leaning across the aisle, he pointed his finger at the two black errand boys. Their faces were ashy. "Brothers, you have got one last chance to be men."

The boys looked at each other in bewilderment, and one of them said, "Man, what you talking about?"

"Be black men, brothers. Show these honkies you are a *man*. The worst that can happen to you is death."

Softly, his voice barely rising over the noises of the train, the boy said, "That's worst enough."

The girl in the Anzac hat came halfway out of her seat. "Stop all this bullshit, ferchrisesake, and bust down that door, somebody."

"Ladies and gentlemen." The old man held up his

hand. "If you'll only listen to me. I happen to know some-thing about the subway, and I tell *you* it's not too much to worry about."

He smiled confidently as the passengers turned to him again, anxious but hopeful—the way his sons would look when they asked him for a new ball glove, the way his employees sued for assurance that, depression or no de-pression, nobody would be fired.

"Trippers," he said. "The safest railroad in the world, like they call it. They got these things on the track, trip-pers. Whenever a train goes through a red light, the trip-pers come up, automatically, and stop the train!" He looked around him in triumph. "So. Soon we will run into a red light, the trippers will come up, and presto! the train will stop."

GRAND CENTRAL TOWER

"Pelham One Two Three is now passing Canal Street sta-tion. Still proceeding at the same speed."

In the reverberant stillness of the Tower Room, hushed except for Mrs. Jenkins' voice, Marino savored the unhur-ried, professional steadiness of his tone.

"I read you," the NYPD dispatcher said. "Keep talk-ing."

"Roger," Marino said crisply. "Four more stations, and then they're at South Ferry."

TWENTY-TWO

TOM BERRY

With the first impact of the explosion, Tom Berry curled into the fetal position and sustained another minor injury in the process. His knee struck against a heavy object and went numb. Nursing his knee, he raised his head an inch or two and saw one of the hijackers lying on the roadbed. It was the lover boy, and Berry concluded that the explosion had felled him. Then he saw the leader slapping at his coat and realized that the explosion had been something separate, that the leader had shot the lover through the pocket of his coat.

Suddenly, with wild hope, Berry remembered the object his knee had struck. He patted the grimy floor frantically, and found his gun.

He rolled over on his stomach, still in the shelter of the pillar, and propped the short barrel of the .38 on his left wrist. He looked for the leader through the sight, but he had disappeared. Then he picked him up. He was bending over the figure of the lover. Berry heard him fire and saw the lover's head jerk. The leader unbuttoned the lover's jacket and removed something from the body. It was the money belt. Berry watched him slip it onto the small man's shoulders and tie it in place.

He was having trouble with his vision. He shut his eyes for a moment, squeezing them hard to rupture the film that obscured them. When he opened his eyes, the little man was disappearing through the break in the tunnel wall, and the heavy man was right behind him. Berry put his sight on the broad back of the heavy man and squeezed off. He saw the heavy man convulse and then topple backward in a crushing fall. He shifted the revolver quickly to find the leader, but the leader was gone.

ANITA LEMOYNE

Anita Lemoyne swayed to the front of the car. Behind her, the old man, the self-made prophet, was still holding forth. Anita braced herself against the sway of the car and looked through the window. The tracks, the tunnel, the posts, were swept up in the rush of the train as if by some powerful vacuum cleaner. A station whipped by, an oasis of light, crowds of people. Two names. Brooklyn Bridge-Worth Street? Three or four more to South Ferry, the last stop. And then what?

"I never knew these things went so fast."

The theater critic was standing behind her, a towering

man, rumpled, wheezing, as if supporting his weight was an effort. His face was tinted with a booze flush, his eyes were blue, combining innocence and knowingness. Which meant, Anita thought, that the innocence was for show, the knowingness couldn't quite be concealed.

"Are you afraid?" he said.

"You heard the old guy. He knows the subway. He says."

"I just wondered . . ." His eyes more innocent than ever, he brushed up against her lightly. "Did you ever work in the theater?"

Men. Well, it helped pass the time. "Two years."

"I thought so." The wheezing stopped. "I see so much, but I knew I had seen you in a theater. I wonder where."

"You ever been in Cleveland, Ohio?"

"Sure. You worked there?"

"The little Gem Theater? I worked in that theater. Usher and sell popcorn."

"You're joking."

He laughed and used the sway of the train to give her a solid bump in the ass. Out of habit, automatically, she returned a little grind, and it started him wheezing again.

"Who would joke at a time like this? We could all be dead in five minutes' time."

He backed off. "You don't believe the old man? About the red signal stopping us?"

"Sure I believe him." She pointed a finger at the window. "I'm looking for the red signals. But all I see is green."

She backed her butt into him and gave it some pressure. Why not? It might be the last time ever. She arched her back and felt him rise to the occasion. Letting him have a joggle or two to keep him interested, she continued to watch the dismal flying landscape. They sailed past Fulton Street and back into the tunnel. Ahead, as far as she could see, the signals were all bright green.

TA PATROLMAN ROTH

Patrolman Harry Roth phoned headquarters as soon as the train flashed by the Fulton Street station.

"She just whizzed by."

"Okay. Thank you."

"Listen. You want to know something funny?"

"Some other time."

"No. I mean it. You know what? I didn't see anybody driving the train."

"What the hell are you talking about?"

"I didn't see anybody in the cab. The front window is busted out, I think, and nobody is in the cab. I was right at the edge of the platform, and I still didn't see anybody. I'm sorry, that's what I saw."

"Don't you know trains can't drive all by themselves, because of the deadman's feature?"

"Okay. I'm sorry."

"You really thought there was nobody in the cab?"

"Maybe he was bending down."

"Oh, bending down. Over and out."

"I know what I saw," Patrolman Roth said to himself. "If he don't believe me, fuck him. I'm sorry."

RYDER

The pillar was a defensible position, but defense was not one of Ryder's options. The man who fired the shot had to be killed, quickly, if he was to make it back to the emergency exit.

He had acted instinctively when the shot was fired, sensing that he couldn't get by Steever's body and into the emergency exit without drawing a second shot, and so had taken off on a crouching run across the tracks to the shelter of the pillar. The shot had come from the south, and since he had seen no one on the roadbed, the assumption was that the enemy, too, was hidden behind a pillar. He wasted no effort speculating on the enemy's identity or in self-recrimination. Both were irrelevant. Whether he was a cop or the passenger Steever thought might have jumped from the train did not affect the problem, which was to dispose of him.

He glanced at the exit. Longman was framed in the opening, staring at him. He pointed at him urgently, then pantomimed climbing, a series of rising handover-hand gestures. Longman still stared. He repeated the gestures decisively. Longman hesitated for another moment, then turned toward the ladder. Steever lay where he had fallen. He had crashed onto his back with a shattering force that might have cracked his spine even if the bullet had not done so. His eyes were open, moving in his expressionless face, and Ryder was certain that he was paralyzed.

He put both men out of his mind and returned to his problem. The enemy knew precisely where he was, and he knew only in a rough way where the enemy was. The solution was to flush out the enemy's position, and there was no way of doing it except by taking what would otherwise be an imprudent risk. He checked his automatic, then, deliberately, stepped out from the shelter of the pillar. The shot rang out at once, and Ryder fired at the muzzle flash. He fired twice more before drawing back into the shelter of the post. He strained for some sound, but heard nothing.

He had no way of knowing if he had scored a hit, and now he must pile risk upon risk. The enemy would not be fooled by the same trick again, and there was no time for maneuver. He stepped out from behind his pillar and ran forward to the next one. No shot. Either he had hit the enemy, or the enemy was waiting for an unmissable shot. He ran forward to the next pillar. No shot. He had closed the distance by a third. And now he could see the enemy. He was sprawled on the track, only his legs still in the shelter of a pillar, and Ryder knew he was hurt. He didn't know how badly—he was conscious, at least, trying to raise his head—but you didn't expect gifts, you were satisfied with an advantage. That was what he had now, and it remained only to exploit it.

He stepped out from behind his pillar, and walked down the center of the track toward the enemy. The enemy stretched out his right hand, and Ryder saw his gun, lying on the roadbed a few inches beyond the extended fingers. The enemy saw or heard him, and tried to crawl toward the gun but collapsed.

It was safely beyond his reach.

OLD MAN

As Pelham One Two Three ran by the Wall Street station, the passengers became agitated again and crowded around the old man.

"Where are the red lights?"

"We're not stopping! We'll all be killed!"

The young mother sent up a shrill keening sound that struck the old man to the heart. It was such a cry, sixty, sixty-five years ago, that his mother had made when his brother, her eldest child, had been struck by a trolley car.

"It will be a red light," he shouted. "It *must* be a red light!"

He turned toward the girl at the front of the car. She shook her head.

"The train will stop," the old man said falteringly, and knew that his life was over. The others would die in an accident; he was already dead of failure.

TOM BERRY

The first slug had hit under Tom Berry's upraised right arm, and his revolver flew away. The second had seemed to strike in front of him and then skid into his body, below the chest. The impact threw him to his left, onto the roadbed, where he came to rest in a wetness his mind refused to identify as his own blood.

Losing his revolver was getting to be repetitious. Freudian? He lost it because he wanted to lose it? This time it wasn't really lost. It lay on the roadbed in plain sight about two arm lengths away, but it might just as well be lost. He couldn't reach it.

He watched the leader approach—calm, unhurried, his pistol hanging down at his side. What's his rate of speed? That's exactly how much more time I have to live. The leader could have stopped, taken careful aim, and finished him off (after all, he was two for three from a greater distance), but, Berry thought, he was a compulsive perfectionist. He would administer the *coup de grâce* in the traditional way, gun to temple, as he had done with his late colleague, the lover. He could count on it being done expertly, no fuss and no muss. Just a single instant of monstrous red explosion, and after that peace. What was so good about peace? What was so fucking good about that kind of peace?

He was sobbing when the leader paused above him, and he had a view of sensible unstylish black shoes. The leader was starting to bend. Berry shut his eyes. *Will she weep for me?*

Somewhere in the tunnel, someone was shouting.

PATROLMAN SEVERINO

At Bowling Green station, Transit Patrolman Severino was so close to the edge of the platform that Pelham One Two Three actually brushed him back, leaving an imprint of dust and grime on his uniform. He looked directly into the cab, and his report, when he radioed headquarters, was so concise and disinterested that it left no doubt of its plausibility.

"Nobody in the cab. Repeat, nobody in the cab. Window busted out and nobody in the cab."

DCI DANIELS

The scene kept shifting in DCI Daniels' head, the way it did when you were catnapping. One moment he was back on Ie Shima with his old division—good old Statue of Liberty, good old 77th—and the Jap navy were bombarding the hell out of them, and his buddies were screaming as they were hit. Next moment he was in a subway tunnel, feeling the rank wind touching his face.

But mostly he was walking his old beat. Third Avenue, in the Thirties, it was. Still plenty of Irish around, but the Armenians predominated. Doc Bajian, in the drugstore. Menjes, the grocer. Maradian in the Near East Food Store—couldn't eat that stuff, too spicy, too many powders. No, Menjes was a Greek. . . . There were the rows of crosses, a few familiar names, in the white sunlight of Ie Shima. No again. That was a picture he had seen in a magazine once, graves of the brave GI's of the 77th who had died on Ie Shima. . . . He was bleeding from a wound on his forehead. Nothing serious, didn't even hurt. Jap gun butt had grazed him?

A man was walking along the street in front of him. He frowned and quickened his pace. He was on the track, in the tunnel, and ahead of him a man walked slowly southward on the roadbed between the local tracks. He knew every last soul on the beat by sight. Didn't recognize this man. Didn't like the way he walked. What was he doing here late at night? Not doing anything suspicious, but the old instinct was at work, the old cop's instinct that smelled out the troublemaker. Catch up and check him out.

Man on the tracks. Holding something. A gun? Could be a gun. Nobody could be allowed to have a gun on *his* beat, beat of a bright, ambitious cop who was going to climb all the way up to rank of DCI. He slipped his own gun out of the holster. Saw the man stop. Look down. Start to bend over somebody. . . .

"Hey! Freeze right there! Drop that gun!"

The man whirled, in a crouch, and the DCI saw muzzle flash. He returned fire, and the thunder of the gun through the silent midnight streets cleared his head and oriented him. He was shooting it out with a gunman who had broken into Paulie Ryan's saloon. . . .

RYDER

Ryder had no last thoughts. He died instantaneously, with a metallic taste on his tongue, from a .38 caliber round that entered just below his chin, smashed his teeth and palate, and curved upward through the roof of his mouth into his brain.

DCI DANIELS

Some shooting, DCI Daniels thought, good as thirty-five years ago, when he killed the armed man who tried knocking over Paulie Ryan's saloon. His first commendation for it, not to mention Paulie sending him a full case of whiskey every Christmas for over fifteen years until he passed away and his educated son took over with his high-hat ideas and no sense of carrying on his father's obligations.

Funny that he had just done it all over again. And what was he doing in a subway tunnel?

He moved up on the fallen gunman, who lay face up, his eyes open and staring at the tunnel roof. Tunnel? The DCI bent over the gunman, not that there was much to see—a dead, neatly dressed man with a ruined bloody face. Well, this one would do no more felonies, nor try shooting it out with a police officer.

He turned to the victim, poor thing. Bloody, too, but alive. Lustrous blond hair down to the shoulders, bare toes in open sandals a bit grimy, but that was the city pavement for you. He knelt and said in a gentle, comforting voice, "We'll have an ambulance along in a jiffy, miss."

The face screwed up, the eyes narrowing, the lips parting, and the DCI bent closer to catch a whisper. But instead of words there was laughter, surprisingly booming and hearty to come from such a young girl.

TWENTY-THREE

CLIVE PRESCOTT

Prescott didn't understand how a train could be driven without a motorman's hand on the deadman's feature, but he did understand the urgency in Lieutenant Garber's voice. He dropped the phone and, already shouting, ran across the floor to Correll.

"Nobody driving the train!" He was screaming into Correll's face. "Have to stop it!"

Correll said, "A train can't drive all by itself."

"It *is* driving itself. They doped the controller somehow; it *is* driving itself. Don't argue. It's nearly to South Ferry, and it'll loop back to Bowling Green and smash into the rear of the train that's standing in the station. Can you turn a signal red and trip it? Hurry, for God's sake!"

"Christamighty," Correll said, and Prescott saw that he had become a believer. "Tower can trip it if there's time." He whirled toward the console, and just then Nevins Street Tower came in on the squawk box.

"Pelham One Two Three just cleared South Ferry Station, going strong at about thirty, headed toward loop. . . ."

Prescott groaned. But Correll, unaccountably, was suddenly grinning. "Don't worry. I'll stop the son of a bitch." His grin broadened as he rolled up his sleeves in dumb show, waved his hands in the air and said, "Presto! Pelham One Two Three, the desk trainmaster commands you to stop!"

Prescott threw himself at Correll and began to choke him.

It required all four of Correll's dispatchers to pry his fingers from Correll's neck, and reinforcements to bring him down and pin him to the floor. Then, with three men sitting on him and two more holding his threshing arms, they told him about the time signal.

"There's a timer in the loop," a white-haired dispatcher with a dead cigar in his mouth said calmly. "If a train hits the curve too fast, like this one will do, already has, the signal turns red and activates the trippers and the train brakes and stops."

Lying back in his chair, the center of another small group, Correll, clutching his throat, was croaking hoarsely.

"He knew it," the white-haired man said, nodding toward Correll. "He was just making a little joke."

Prescott's rage was damped down, but not quite extinguished. "That's why I tried to choke him," he said. "I can't stand his little jokes."

BOROUGH COMMANDER

"Controls doctored, nobody in the cab?" The borough commander yelled back at the radio voice, repeating its message.

"Yes, sir. That's correct, sir."

The borough commander leaned toward the driver. "Back to Union Square. Open it up, break the speed laws."

As the car turned right, cornering on two wheels, he said to the commissioner, "Should have known better than to deny a hunch. They're back there."

"Were," the commissioner said. "They took us in, Charlie."

"Speed. More speed," the borough commander yelled.

"There'll be a dozen cars there ahead of us," the commissioner said. "They'll be too late, too."

The borough commander smashed his fists together, spraining his left wrist and shattering two knuckles.

ANITA LEMOYNE

Somebody was cursing the old man, and by the time Anita Lemoyne glanced over her shoulder to see what was happening, at least a dozen of the passengers had broken for the rear of the car. The theater critic was still jammed up against her, but all of a sudden he was at half-mast, and then he was no mast at all. He muttered something and was gone. She watched him walk to the rear of the car.

The old man was sitting with his head bowed, his lips

trembling. What the hell was he crying about, him and his no-show red lights—didn't he have a long enough life? Next to him, the militant spade was sitting very straight, his chin up, his long legs crossed and one foot casually swinging. Okay. At least he would go in style. Him and me, a proud doomed black stud and a piece of aging white ass. Oh, yes, and the old wino, still asleep, still drooling, sitting in filth and stink and dreaming of her next bottle. Some trio.

The car rattled into South Ferry station and the by now familiar scene of fist-shaking people on the platform. They swept by into the dimness of the tunnel. Now what? Ahead, she saw the tunnel wall curve, and she *knew* what. They were going too fast to make it. The wheels would leap off the track, the train would smash into the wall, the pillars . . . She braced her feet wide apart, and directly ahead was a red signal, with a white light underneath it. Well, the old man was right, after all. But it was too late, they were hitting the curve. . . .

She felt a terrific drag under her feet and she was thrown forward against the window. There was a hissing sound, and screams from the rear of the car. But through the window everything was running down, tracks, pillars, walls . . . The car lurched to a full stop.

From stunned silence the rear of the train exploded into a hysterical chorus of joy, and Anita thought: Well, folks, we'll all live to fuck another day. She turned and sagged against the door. The old man was looking at her, trying to smile.

"Well, young lady, didn't I say we would stop?"

The militant spade took the bloodstained handkerchief

from his face and put it into the old man's hand. "Better burn this, dude, it's got nigger blood on it."

The wino lady belched and opened her eyes. "'s Forty Secon'?"

Punch line, Anita thought, the old bum came up with the punch line. She opened her purse and dropped a ten-dollar bill in the spread lap with its ragged layers of wildly mismatched clothing.

LONGMAN

Through the emergency exit grating, Longman heard the sounds of the city. As he started to push upward a foot came down directly over his hand, and he recoiled. The foot moved on. He edged up further on the ladder and pushed at the grate with both hands. The grate squealed on rusty hinges, and a cloud of gritty particles showered down on him. But he held fast to the grate and walked up with its weight. When his head reached the level of the sidewalk, he heard shots behind and below him. He froze for an instant, then continued upward. He stepped out to the street level.

Facing the park wall, his back to the sidewalk, he lowered the grate slowly and didn't release it until it was an inch off the ground. It settled in place with a clang and a rising of dust. Several passersby glanced at him, but none stopped or even looked back. The famous New York indifference, he thought exultantly, and crossed to the east side of the street and into the stream of pedestrians flowing past Klein's. Ahead, near Seventeenth Street, he saw a police car. It was doubleparked, and a man was leaning on the window, talking to one of the cops. Keeping his eyes straight ahead, he quickened his pace and turned the corner into Sixteenth Street. He forced himself to slow down as he walked eastward. At Irving Place he turned left, crossed the street, and walked past the weathered colorless brick pile of Washington Irving High School. A small group of kids was hanging around the entrance—a heavily lipsticked Chinese girl in a very short miniskirt, a black girl, and two black boys in leather coats.

As he went by, one of the boys fell in beside him. "Man, can you unload two bits on a deserving student?"

Longman brushed by the outstretched palm. The boy muttered something and dropped back. Longman walked on. Ahead was the grillwork fence and stripped trees of Gramercy Park. He thought of Ryder, and remembered the shots he had heard as he climbed the emergency ladder. Ryder would be okay, he told himself, and, with an odd reluctance to dwell on the matter, put it out of mind. He turned eastward on Eighteenth Street.

He crossed Third Avenue, then Second, with the massive pink buildings of Stuyvesant Town dominating the view. Then he was at his own building, the drab stone tenement with the grayed-down façade and scarred entry, and, at the windows, people and dogs gazing out, identically wistful and bored. He climbed the stairs, past blind impermeable doors, to the second floor. He fumbled for his keys, opened the three locks in order from bottom to top, went inside and locked the door, top to bottom.

He edged through the narrow hallway to the kitchen and turned on the water tap. While he was waiting for the water to run cold, a glass in his hand, he suddenly let out a shout of wild and abandoned triumph.

ANITA LEMOYNE

About five minutes after the car had stopped, Anita Lemoyne watched two men climb in through the front door. The first, wearing motorman's stripes, opened the cab door with a key and went inside. The second was a city cop.

The cop held up his hands to ward off the passengers who crowded around him and kept saying, "I don't know nothing about it. We'll have you off the train in just a few minutes. I don't know nothing about it. . . ."

The train started, and in a matter of moments pulled into the lighted area of the Bowling Green station and came to a stop. Anita looked out the window.

There was a line of cops on the platform, arms linked, holding back a pressing crowd. A man in a conductor's uniform was bending down at the side of the car with some kind of key in his hand. The doors clattered open. The cops on the platform were overwhelmed. They were tossed aside, borne back, crushed by an irresistible mob of passengers storming their way into the car.

TWENTY-FOUR

CLIVE PRESCOTT

Prescott left at six thirty. It was dark, with that washed-down air the city sometimes wore in crisp cold weather, a dark sheen that masked its ugliness. He had doused his head in water, toweled until his skin tingled, but it was no relief for his exhaustion. He looked up at the great dignified buildings the borough had inherited from its past, deserted, glowing palely with night-lights. The lawyers and lawmakers and judges and politicians had fled. There was no more than a sprinkling of people on the streets, and soon these too would disappear, leaving only drunks and muggers and the homeless, prey and hunter.

On Fulton Street, the stores were closed or closing, and soon the whole shopping area—which the disinherited, people of his own race and the parvenu Puerto Ricans, had inherited from those who preferred losing it to sharing it—would be deserted, too. The department stores were barricaded, their watchmen alert, their burglar alarms set for intruders. A newspaper vendor was closing up her stand, a weathered woman of some fantastic age and durability. He averted his eyes from the giant newspaper headlines.

A black boy, grand in a cowboy hat and red buckskin coat, thrust something in his face. "Panther paper, Brother."

He shook his head and moved on. The boy fell in step. During the day, the streets were lined with young blacks selling the Panther paper. He had rarely seen anybody buy one. Maybe they sold to each other. No, he said to himself sharply, don't knock it. You got anything better to believe in?

"Come on, man, get to know what it's all about. You want to go on being Charley's field hand?"

He pushed the paper away roughly. The boy glared at him. Prescott walked on, then stopped.

"I'll take one."

"Right on."

He tucked the paper under his arm. Across the street, a record store, its gate closed, its lights dimmed, blared hard rock through a speaker in the transom. Had the owner forgotten to turn it off? Would that hammering bass and those rubbery voices go on all night and pollute even the stillness of dawn?

I am sick, Prescott thought, sick of cops and criminals and victims and bystanders. Sick of anger and of blood. Sick of what happened today and will happen tomorrow. Sick of white and of black, of my job and my friends and my family, of love and of hatred. Above all, I am sick of myself, sick of being sick at the imperfections of the world that nobody would try to fix up even if they knew how.

If only he had grown three inches taller. If only he had had a good outside shot. If only he were white. Or truly black.

The one thing nobody could ever take away from him was the way he had been able to drive. He was fearless coming down the middle with the ball, contemptuous of the big men who lay in wait to clobber him when he was in the air, suspended, with the ball already arching toward the basket. BOOM! But he came in every time, long, stretching steps, loping into the wall of waiting big boys. . . .

He crumpled the Panther paper into a crude ball, crouched, wheeled, drove, and released a graceful hook shot at a storefront sign. Two points. A derelict, leering, clapped his hands, then shoved out a grimy palm. Prescott pushed by.

Tomorrow he would feel better. But the day after tomorrow and the next day? Never mind. Tomorrow he would feel better because there was no way he could feel worse. Good enough.

DETECTIVE HASKINS

Detective Second Grade Bert Haskins, who, his Englishy name to one side, was one hundred proof Irish, had once regarded detective work as the most glamorous available to man. For about a week. Then, disabused of every notion he had ever entertained about brilliant deductive reasoning, *mano a mano* confrontations with vicious criminals, and matching wits with masterminds, he buckled down to the real job of criminal detection: plodding and patience. Detective work was legwork, was interrogating a hundred blind leads in the hope of coming up with a live one, was climbing stairs, ringing doorbells, dealing with frightened, belligerent, closemouthed or dunderheaded citizens. Detective work was based on the law of averages. True, now and then you picked up a useful tidbit from a stoolie, but mostly you plugged. And plugged. And plugged.

The Transit Authority files had already yielded over a hundred names of employees who had been discharged for cause, and the delving would continue into the night. Most often the cause had nothing even remotely to do with criminal activity. Nevertheless, it had to be assumed that every discharged employee had reason to be disgruntled. Disgruntled enough to hijack a subway train? That was another matter. But how could you find out if you didn't plug?

Three of the hijackers had been shot to death. A quarter of a million dollars each had been recovered from money jackets worn by two of them. That left one hijacker and half a million dollars missing. No official identification had yet been made of any of the dead hijackers, so although it was conceivable that one of them might turn out to be a disgruntled former TA employee, that didn't eliminate the missing fourth man.

Haskins, his partner, and eight other teams of detectives had been assigned to this aspect of the case, and unless somebody got lucky, it would take days to check out the complete list. They had whacked up the list of names and set forth on their mission, after a passionate exhortation from their chief. These men are vicious killers, safety of the citizens of this city, slaughter of two innocent victims . . . Translation: The brass is on my tail, so I'm on yours, and you guys better slap shoe leather. And shoe leather they had slapped, for more than four hours now.

Shoe leather, bus, subway, and, above all, climbing muscles. It was an axiom of the trade that nine out of ten people you had to track down lived in walkups. It figured. Poor people committed more crimes than rich ones. Or, more accurately, more crimes that violated the criminal code.

Haskins, you're a Communist.

A half hour ago he had told Slott, his partner, who had an ulcer and whose bitching was getting on his nerves anyway, to go home. He could handle the three remaining names on their list himself before calling it a night. When Slott left, Haskins went into a small dry-cleaning store owned and operated by an ex-TA employee who had been fired six years before for spitting. On passengers. He had been a platform guard at the Times Square station who became so fed up with his job that he would spit surreptitiously on passengers' backs as he pushed them into rush-hour trains. Eventually, after surveillance, he was caught, charged, given a hearing, and fired. As the verdict was delivered, he spat on the referee's lapel.

In response to Haskins' questions he said first that he no longer had any animus against the Transit Authority, second that he hoped the whole fucking subway system would burn down to the ground one day, and third that he had spent half of the afternoon in a dentist's chair, having his gum sliced to ribbons and a couple of roots dug out by brute force. Dr. Schwartz was the name of the butcher, and his phone number was . . .

Detective Haskins made a note to call Dr. Schwartz in the morning, yawned, looked at his watch—quarter of nine—and then checked his list. He was equidistant from Fitzherbert, Paul, residing on Sixteenth Street West of Fifth Avenue, and Longman, Walter, Eighteenth Street East of Second. Which one? No difference—whichever he took first, it was an equally long walk to the other. So, which one? Such was the difficult nature of the decisions a detective had to make. Too tough to handle without coffee, but luckily there was a joint right at the corner. He would go in there, drink his coffee, maybe eat a piece of apple pie, and then, the inner man fortified, the brain stoked up, he could make the big decision a detective (second grade) was so well equipped to handle.

LONGMAN

Longman couldn't bring himself to turn on the radio. He had seen criminals in the movies too often give themselves away by buying all the papers or clipping out stories. Of course, he was being silly, nobody would even hear his radio if he turned it down low, but still, irrational as it was, he wouldn't do it. So he wandered around his apartment aimlessly, still wearing his coat, averting his head each time he passed the clock-radio near his bed. If Ryder had been killed, what was his hurry to find out?

But at six o'clock, without thinking about it consciously,

he had turned on his television set to a news program. The hijacking was the top story of the day, and the coverage was remarkable. The cameras had even got into the tunnel, and they showed shots of the derailed express train, close-ups of the scarred tunnel walls and twisted tracks. Then they showed "the sector of the tunnel where the shootout took place." When the camera swung around to the spot where Steever had fallen, he winced, not wanting to see any bodies or, for that matter, any bloodstains. There were dark areas that could have been bloodstains, but there were no bodies. Later, though, the cameras were on hand when three bodies on stretchers, covered by canvas sheets, were brought out by cops. He felt no emotion, not even for Ryder.

Next, there were interviews with police brass, including the commissioner. None of them said very much, except that each one referred to it as a "heinous" crime. Questioned by the reporters about the missing hijacker—Longman felt a hot flush sweep through his body—the commissioner said that they knew only that he had escaped through the emergency exit. As he spoke, the screen split to show the exit both from the street and from the foot of the ladder. The commissioner added that the department had not yet identified any of the three slain hijackers, two of whom had died instantaneously. The third, shot in the spine, had died a few minutes after the police found him. He had been questioned but had been unable to respond, his speech centers, among other things, apparently paralyzed.

What leads did the police have to the missing hijacker? The chief of detectives took over and said that a very large number of detectives had been assigned to the case and would work long shifts until the criminal was apprehended.

The TV reporter pressed: Did that mean there were no solid leads? The chief of detectives said sharply that it meant the division was following well-established lines of police procedure and that he hoped to be able to report progress before long. Longman felt the hot flush again, but relaxed a bit when the camera showed the reporter with a sardonically lifted brow.

There was no mention of checking the files of ex-TA employees. He remembered when Ryder had brought that matter up. At the time, he had been less thankful for Ryder's foresight in anticipating all eventualities than alarmed at the idea.

"They don't have to find me," he had said to Ryder. "I can stay at your place."

"I *want* you to be at home. They'll be immediately suspicious of anything out of the ordinary."

"I'll have to work out an alibi."

Ryder shook his head. "They'll check more carefully into details on the people who have alibis than on those who don't. *Most* of the people they see won't have an alibi, you'll be lost in the crowd. Simply say you spent part of the afternoon taking a walk, part of it reading a book or taking a nap, and don't be the least bit precise about what time you did one or another."

"I'll give it some thought—what I'm going to say."

"No. I don't want you to rehearse it or even think about it."

"I can say that I heard about it on the radio and that I'm horrified—"

"No. It's not necessary to make a case for your righteousness. They're not interested in your opinions, anyway. They'll be checking out hundreds of people as a matter of routine. Keep in mind that you'll just be one in a very long list of names."

"You make it sound easy."

"It is easy," Ryder said. "You'll see."

"Still, I'd like to give it a little thought."

"No thought," Ryder said firmly. "Not now, or after it's over, either."

He had followed Ryder's advice, and actually, this was the first time he had thought about it in weeks. It was strictly routine for the cops, and he was just another ex-TA employee in a long line of hundreds of others. He could handle it.

He listened to the chief of detectives admit under questioning that descriptions of the missing man were sketchy, that there were too many conflicting versions to help in the formulation of an Identikit face, but that a number of passengers were going through the picture files at headquarters. Longman almost smiled. He had no record; there would be no pictures of him.

Several of the passengers were interviewed: the girl in the Anzac hat, photographing a little heavier than he would have expected; the big fellow, the theater critic, who used a lot of big words to say very little; a couple of the black boys; the militant black, who refused to answer questions on the grounds that they were irrelevant to the race issue, but instead raised his clenched fist and shouted something that was blipped out. Suddenly, the passengers made Longman uncomfortable. They faced head-on to the cameras, in tight close-up, giving the appearance of looking straight at him. He switched off the set.

He went into the kitchen and boiled water for tea. Sitting at the linoleum-covered kitchen table, still wearing his coat, he ate graham crackers that he dipped into the tea. He smoked a cigarette—it amazed him that he hadn't even wanted one before this, though he was normally a heavy smoker—then went into the bedroom. He switched on the radio, but turned it off before it had warmed up. He started to lie down and felt a dull pain in his chest. It took him a long moment to realize that he wasn't having a heart attack, that it was the weight and pressure of the money jackets. He got off the bed and went to the front door. He checked all three locks and returned to the bedroom. After pulling the dark-green window shades down as far as they would go, below the sill, he took off his topcoat and jacket and then the money jackets. He placed them carefully on the bed, side by side, in precise alignment.

Walter Longman, he said to himself, you are worth half a million dollars. He repeated it in an audible whisper, and then another uncontrollable scream raced up his throat. He clapped his hand over his mouth to muffle it.

ANITA LEMOYNE

Anita Lemoyne had known some rotten days in her life, but this one was hands down the rottenest. As if being hijacked wasn't enough of a bummer, she had had to suffer through two hours of boredom looking at mug shots, a parade of cruel or scruffy faces that were a composite reminder of every John she had ever met who felt that his few lousy dollars entitled him to feel loved or to hurt her.

It was after eight when the cops finally let them all go. They straggled out of the old Police Headquarters building and stood in a daze on the sidewalk. A couple of blocks to the south a steady flow of traffic was moving on Canal Street, but Centre Street was chilly, bleak and deserted. They stood silently in a ragged group. Then the old wino lady gathered her rags around her and shuffled off unsteadily into the darkness. A moment later the militant black man settled his cape on his shoulders and walked briskly and erectly toward Canal. That one and the old wino, Anita thought, were the only ones who would not be affected by what had happened; it was unconnected to—like the title of the book the TV jerk kept talking about—the main currents of their thought.

And what about *her* main currents? Well, her main currents were: Anita, move ass out of this forsaken place and find a taxi to take you home. A hot bath with a lot of those salts from Paris in it and then, maybe, she just might check in with her telephone answering service.

"I don't even know where we are." A teary voice—the mother of the two boys, who stood beside her yawning, out on their feet. "Can somebody please tell me how to get to Brooklyn from here?"

"Certainly," the old man said. "You take the subway. It's the quickest and the safest."

He whooped, but beyond a few pained smiles he had no takers for his wit. Again no one moved until, abruptly, the two young black boys, still carrying the packages they had set out to deliver half a day ago, mumbled something and moved off.

The old man called after them. "Good-bye, boys, good luck."

The boys turned and waved, then went on.

"Quite an extraordinary experience, to say the least."

The drama critic. She didn't even look at him. He was going to invite her to share a cab and then ask her up for a drink. No dice. She turned from him, and the change of direction brought her into the wind. A cold gust whipped up her skirt and between her legs. She turned away. Mustn't let it catch a cold, or I'm out of business.

"I got an idea." The old man—his scrubbed face no longer rosy, his borsalino hat dented. "After all we have been through together, it seems a shame we should just all say good-bye and . . ."

Lonely old man, Anita thought, he's afraid he'll die without a cheering section at his bedside. She looked at the faces around her and thought: I won't remember a single one of them by morning.

". . . reunion, say a year, even every six months. . . ."

She started walking toward Canal Street. At the corner, the drama critic caught up with her. He bent his ruddy face toward her, smiling.

"Get lost," Anita said. Her heels clacking in the stillness of the street, she walked on toward Canal.

FRANK CORRELL

Frank Correll refused to give way to his relief. Back in his own chair—he had wiped it ostentatiously after Prescott had left, to "get the nigger dust off"—he worked the console like (as *Transit*, the employee paper, had put it once in a feature article) "a man possessed, a dervish, body and soul dedicated to making the railroad run as smooth as ice cream." He screamed a great deal, whirled in his chair to shout instructions to his dispatchers, swept coffee off his desk in a wide flail of his arm when somebody in misguided kindness brought him some. In constant, sometimes simultaneous, consultation with the Yard, with Operations, with Maintenance, with Tower Rooms, with motormen, he organized new flexes, discarded old ones, worked miracles of manipulation until, at 8:21 P.M., A Division was back on schedule, all trains running on time.

"Okay," Correll said to his relief, "I'm giving you back your railroad."

He stood up, put his jacket on over his sweat-soaked shirt, pushed the knot of his tie up to his bruised throat, and slipped into his topcoat.

His relief, taking his place at the console, said, "Good job, Frank."

"I have only one regret," Correll said. "That I was not able to get the road straightened out before rush hour."

"No human being could have done that, in the circumstances," the relief trainmaster said.

"In that case, I wish I wasn't human." Turning abruptly, his hands plunged deep into his pockets, Correll strode off.

The relief man said, "He makes a nice exit."

At the Communications Desk, Correll paused and listened. ". . . and full service restored at eight twenty-one."

It would be picked up by the radio stations on the hourly news, and tomorrow, buried somewhere in a tailpiece to the story of the hijacking, it would appear in the daily newspapers. One line, he thought. Service restored at 8:21. So much for blood, sweat, and tears.

"Beautiful job," one of the men at the Communications Desk said.

Correll shrugged. "All in a day's work," he said, and went out into the quiet corridor. Except for bringing charges against that nigger cop, tomorrow would be pretty dull. Well, you couldn't expect to make railroad history *every* day.

TOM BERRY

The senior resident in surgery accompanied Tom Berry's stretcher down from the recovery room and remained after a nurse and an orderly transferred him to the bed.

"Where am I?" Berry said.

"In a hospital. Beth Israel. You've just had two bullets removed."

He hadn't meant to say where but how. He said it now. "I mean *how* am I?"

"Okay," the resident said. "We issued a bulletin saying that your condition was fair."

"I rate a bulletin? I must be dying."

"The media wanted to know. You're in good shape." The resident looked out the window. "Nice view. Looking right down into Stuyvesant Park."

Berry explored himself. His arm was bandaged from the shoulder to the elbow, and there was a fat dressing in the approximate center of his torso. "How come no pain?"

"Sedation. You'll feel some, don't fret." The resident said enviously, "My room—it's about a quarter of the size of this one, and it faces a brick wall. Not even *nice* bricks."

Tenderly, Berry touched the dressing on his body. "Was I shot in the gut?"

"You weren't shot any place in particular. Missed the important things by a millimeter here, a hair there. Luck of a hero. I'll drop by later on. Terrific view."

The resident left. Berry wondered if he was lying, if his condition was critical. They never told you, the mysterious bastards; they didn't trust you to understand something as complicated as whether you were going to live or die. He tried to generate indignation, but he felt much too relaxed. He shut his eyes and dozed.

Voices woke him. Three faces were looking down at him. One was the resident. The other two he recognized from pictures—His Honor, the mayor, and the PC. He guessed at the reason for their presence and warned himself to portray surprise and modesty. He was a hero, as the resident had suggested.

"I believe he's awake now," the resident said.

The mayor smiled. He was wrapped in a huge coat, a voluminous muffler, and an Astrakhan hat with earmuffs. His nose was red, and his lips looked parched. The commissioner was smiling, too, but not very well. He just wasn't a smiling man.

"Congratulations, Patrolman, ah . . ." The mayor paused.

"Barry," the commissioner said.

"Congratulations, Patrolman Barry," the mayor said. "You performed an act of extraordinary valor. The people of the city are in your debt."

He put out his hand, and with some effort, Berry shook it. It was icy cold. Then he shook the commissioner's hand.

"Splendid work, Barry," the commissioner said. "The department is proud of you."

They were both looking at him expectantly. Of course. The modesty bit. "Thank you. I was lucky. I only did what any man in the department would have done."

The mayor said, "Get well soon, Patrolman Barry."

The commissioner tried to twinkle and botched it. He wasn't a twinkling man, either. But Berry knew what was coming. "We're looking forward to your rapid return to duty, *Detective* Barry."

Surprise and modesty, Berry reminded himself, and lowering his eyes, said, "Thank you, sir, thank you very much. But I only did what any man in the department—"

But the mayor and the commissioner were already leaving. As they went through the door, the mayor said, "He looks better than I do. I bet he feels better, too."

Berry shut his eyes and dozed again. When he woke, it was because the resident was pinching his nose.

"There's a girl outside," the resident said. Deedee was standing in the doorway. Berry nodded. "About ten minutes," the resident said.

The resident left, and Deedee came in. She was solemn and on the verge of tears.

"That doctor said you weren't badly hurt. Tell me the truth."

"Mere flesh wounds."

A few tears spilled out of her eyes. She took her glasses off and kissed him on the lips.

"I'm all right," Berry said. "I'm glad you came, Deedee."

"Why *wouldn't* I come?" She frowned.

"How did you know where I was?"

"How *wouldn't* I! You're all over the radio and telly. Is there much pain, Tom?"

"Heroes never feel pain."

She kissed him and left tears on his face. "I can't stand the idea of your hurting."

"I don't feel a thing. They're taking terrific care of me. Look out the window. Some view!"

She picked up his hand and put her cheek against it. She kissed his fingers and then released his hand. She looked out the window.

"Terrific view," Berry said.

She seemed indecisive for about a fifth of a second, then said, "I must say this. You risked your life in an unworthy cause."

I'm not up to it, he thought, and tried to divert her. "A little while ago the mayor and the police commissioner were here to see me. I'm promoted to detective. Third grade, I guess."

"You could have been killed!"

"It's my job. I'm a cop."

"Killed to save the city a million dollars!"

"There were people involved, too, Deedee," he said gently.

"I won't argue with you now. I can't fight with you when you're hurt."

"But?"

"But when you get better, I'm going to make you promise to quit the pigs."

"And when I get better, I'm going to make you promise you'll quit the Movement."

"If you don't know the difference between being a fascist epigone and the struggle for freedom and the people's rightful—"

"Deedee. Don't make a speech. I know you've got beliefs, but so do I."

"Pigs? Is that what you believe in? You've said yourself you had a million doubts."

"Maybe not a million, but doubts, yes. But not quite enough to discourage me." He reached for her hand. She drew back, then surrendered it to him. "I like the work. Not all of it. Some parts of police work are shitty. I haven't figured out the proportions yet."

"They took you in." Her eyes darkened, but she didn't relinquish his hand. "They sold you the whole bundle, and you bought it."

He shook his head. "I'm going to stay with it until I know how I feel. Then I'll either buy the whole bundle or get out."

The resident appeared in the doorway. "Time's up. Sorry."

"I guess we better stop seeing each other," Deedee said. She walked quickly to the door, then stopped and looked back at him.

He thought of some temporizing things, even winning things, he might say to her, but he didn't say them. The game was over, the exasperating, amusing, but, finally, childish game they had been playing for so many months. The issue was real and maybe irreconcilable. It had to be faced.

"It's up to you, Deedee," he said. "Just one thing—think it over first."

He didn't quite see her leave because the resident was in front of her, blocking his view. "In about ten or fifteen minutes you might start to hurt a little," the resident said.

Berry looked at him suspiciously, then got it straight. What the resident was talking about was physical pain.

LONGMAN

Longman finally turned on the radio at nine o'clock. The news was a rehash. No fresh developments, and only one reference to the missing hijacker—the police were bending every effort toward his apprehension. He switched off the radio and went into the kitchen, for no particular reason except that he was restless and had been doing a lot of moving from room to room. He was wearing the money jackets again—the bed didn't quite seem the place for half a million dollars—and had put his topcoat on, partially to conceal the jackets, partially because it was chilly in the apartment; as usual, they were chintzy with the heat.

He looked at the linoleum on the kitchen table and for the first time appreciated how ugly it was, how badly worn, how marred with slices and cuts. Well, he could well afford

a new linoleum now. He could well afford to live somewhere else, too—any part of the country he chose, any
part of the world, for that matter. It would be Florida, as
he had planned. All year sunshine, not too many clothes,
fishing, maybe even a shack-up with some widow looking
for a little action. . . .

Half a million. It was too rich for his blood. So was a
quarter of a million. Still, it beat a boot in the ass, didn't
it? He smiled, for what must have been the first time in a
week. But the smile disappeared when he suddenly remembered the three bodies being brought out of the tunnel, three mounds, covered with canvas, and maybe—though
the camera didn't pick this up—maybe even leaking a little blood. Three dead, and one survivor—Wally Longman, of all people.

He thought of them laid out on a morgue slab, and except for Ryder, he had no reaction. Welcome was an animal, and Steever. . . . well, he didn't dislike Steever, but he
was an animal, too, a kind of obedient dog, a Doberman
pinscher, say, trained to respond to a command. He hadn't
given much thought to Ryder. Yet, in Ryder's death, he
had lost—what? Not a friend, he and Ryder were never really friends. Colleagues, maybe that was the word. He had
a great deal of respect for Ryder: his reserve, his courage,
his coolness. Above all, Ryder had been kind to him, and
not too many people had been that.

What would Ryder be doing if he had been the sole
survivor? Well, he would certainly be calm, relaxed, probably just sitting and reading in his apartment, that large
impersonal room furnished as sparsely as an army bar-
racks. He wouldn't be sweating out the police—what with

no record, no fingerprints, no adequate description of him, no live confederates to give him away even by accident, he would feel very secure. Well, Longman thought, even though he was nervous where Ryder would be glacially cool, he was sitting pretty, too.

He experienced a rush of pleasure at the thought and jumped to his feet. He felt so full of energy that he began walking around the table to work it off before he started letting out whoops that would bring the neighbors on the run.

He was still loping around the table when someone knocked at the door. He froze, terrified, and the hot flush surged through his body.

There was a second knock at the door and then a voice: "Hello, Mr. Longman? Police Department. I'd like to talk to you."

Longman looked at the door, at the scarred, thickly painted surface half covered by a garage calendar featuring a pretty girl in hot pants and no top, looking down cross-eyed at her own boobs. Three locks. Three strong locks that no cop could manage to open. What would Ryder do? Ryder would do exactly what he had instructed *him* to do. Open the door and answer the cop's questions. But Ryder had not anticipated his own death and the fact that the money was *here* instead of cached away in Ryder's apartment, as planned. Why hadn't he thought about the damn money before? He was *wearing* it, for God'ssake. Still, it was well concealed under the topcoat, and he could easily justify the coat because it was so cold in the apartment. But how could he justify ignoring the first two knocks? If he opened now, the cop couldn't help being suspicious and might even reason that he had delayed in order to stash the money away. Not answering was a giveaway. He had blown it.

"It's just a minor matter, Mr. Longman. Would you mind opening up?"

He was standing next to the window. The window. The three locks. Without moving his feet, he reached over to the table, picked up the gray Russian hat, and put it on. It was quiet on the other side of the door, but he was sure the cop was still there, that he would knock again. He turned silently to the window, gripped the sill, and slowly raised it. Fresh night air entered, soft and cooling. He ducked through the window onto the fire escape.

DETECTIVE HASKINS

You were supposed to stand clear of a closed door, so that somebody shooting through it would miss you. But the heavy silence inside and the indifferent fit of the door with the jamb were too inviting. So Detective Bert Haskins pressed his ear to the uneven vertical line and heard the distinctive squeal of wood against wood. A little soap, he thought, as he turned away and started down the stairs, a little soap rubbed on the runners and he might have got away with it. On the other hand, if Slott hadn't taken his ulcer home, he would have been a dead duck anyhow, because one of them would have covered the back way out.

He made practically no sound going down the stairs. You never learned how to use a magnifying glass in the detective dodge, but you did manage to pick up a few useful aptitudes—the gumshoe bit, for instance. You also learned to case a joint on arrival, so that you knew there was a door under the stairwell that led outside to the rear of the building.

The door was equipped with a spring lock. Haskins turned the latch, opened just enough of the door to accommodate his body, slipped through, and eased the door back quietly. He was in a small courtyard. Its darkness was broken up in an uneven pattern by spills of light from the apartments above. He took note of a few fruit rinds, a magazine, some newspaper pages and a broken toy. Not too bad. They probably cleaned it up once a week or so. He eased into a shadow and looked upward.

The man—Walter Longman—was almost directly above him, fiddling with the bracket that hooked the ladder to the guard rail of the fire escape. Forget it, Longman, Haskins said to himself, those things are always rusty and immovable. You're better off if you just let it be and drop down a few feet from the bottom rung.

Longman made a last effort to release the bracket, then gave up. Haskins watched him lift his leg awkwardly over the guard rail and probe with his foot for the ladder rung. Very good, Haskins thought, now the other foot . . . excellent. Longman was no acrobat, in fact he moved like an old man. Well, hadn't he once put the collar on an eighty-year-old armed robber?

Longman was dangling, his hands clenched tightly around the rusty metal of the bottom rung, his body swaying. But he seemed reluctant to let go. Shame on you, Haskins thought, a vicious hijacker afraid of a little four-foot drop? Longman's legs were swinging now, and his knuckles looked dead white. He let go of the ladder rung with one hand, but still he dangled.

Haskins watched the clenched right hand. As soon as the fingers opened, he took a single step out of his shadow. He was perfectly placed. Longman dropped, and Haskins caught him neatly against his own body. Longman's head whipped around, presenting a pale, crumpled face and startled eyes.

"Surprise," Haskins said.

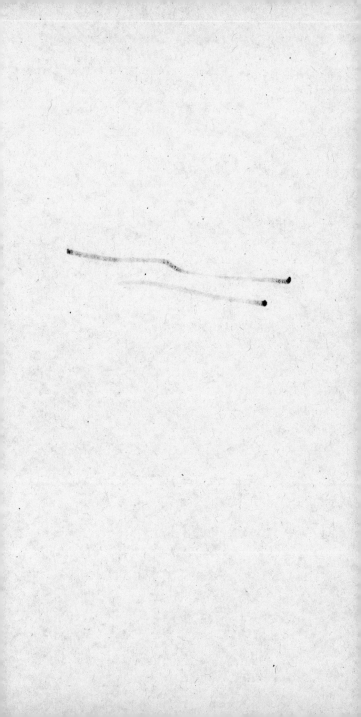